Where Shadows Breathe And Truth Sleeps

A.Gavazzoni

Book 4-Hidden Motives Series

DEDICATION

Thank you, God, for making my path Your will and not mine.

Elderslie Lane

CT 2016

"The stillness of her body told him she was dead. He would've loved to play with her before granting her mercy, but today he just needed a female body—any woman´s corpse would do. She was just a message. He released his grip on her neck and supported her weight as he removed her clothes.

Minutes later, he carried her to the end of the dark alley. She was a large woman, but he moved her with ease, placing her in the passenger seat of the cab he was driving He climbed behind the wheel, started the engine, and eased out onto the main road. Beside him, the dead body slumped toward the door, her head resting against the window, her long, brown hair hiding her face. He averted his gaze and focused on the road.

The radio was set to a classical station. He scowled and pressed a button on the steering wheel to scan for something a little more upbeat. A song he recognized blared through the speakers, and he pushed the button again to stop the scan.

Avicii's "Wake Me Up". He knew all the words, and began to sing at the top of his lungs.

The lyrics resonated deeply with him; each word struck a chord that echoed his own feelings. The music fueled a surge of adrenaline, heightening his senses. By the time he pulled up in front of the recipient's address, an euphoric excitement and energy had taken hold of him.

It was dark, wore a black coat with the hood up, hiding his hair and face. The day before, he had conducted a brief but thorough surveillance of the area. The house had no security system, and the neighbors were conveniently out of town. He ´d noted that the outdated cameras were angled just wrong, missing his movements. Everything was falling into place.

What a bitch. So full of herself. Thinks she's untouchable! I'd love to hear her screams when she finds my gift...

He stepped out, scanning both sides of the street. Empty. He circled around the car, opened the passenger door, adjusted his hood so it covered his eyes, and pulled the body out.

Bitch! You should´ve been on a diet!

He hated fat women. Actually, he hated most women, but he *specially* despised the fat ones. He carried the body to the wide front stoop and placed it on the pavement, arranging her for maximum impact—arms out, legs spread. Then he took the small glass bottle from his jacket pocket, opened it, and poured the contents over her body.

Beautiful! Even if this one hadn't done anything to deserve her death, she had a purpose; she was a message.

The recipient was going to be so confused! *Why me?* He could almost hear her voice tremble when she asked the question.

He smiled, thrilled by his power to disrupt someone's life. Returning to the cab, he climbed in, took out his phone, and redialed the last number.

"It is done," he said.

He ended the call, started his truck, and sped off into the night."

The man closed his notebook, leaving the pencil inside it. He knew his memories would make a great book.

CHAPTER ONE

SIMONE – 2018

Simone and Carl sat at the breakfast table in the kitchen of their home in New Haven. It was early November, and a fresh layer of snow had fallen the night before, piling up along the shore of the Long Island Sound and transforming the landscape outside the big bay window into a winter wonderland.

They had married the year before and bought a house near Yale, where Simone worked as a professor. Carl kept his apartment in New York, where he worked, and they split their time between the two cities.

Simone's previous house had been the scene of too many unpleasant events. Peter Hay, a serial killer, had murdered a woman and left her body on Simone's front steps. He had invaded her house many times when she wasn't there and rifled through all her belongings. Later, he'd kidnapped and tortured her, claiming he'd learned about her by studying her life.

Simone had survived, but the horror continued, and she found herself surrounded by a sea of death. Her secretary and several of her dearest psychiatric patients were murdered. Then Edward—her best friend, business partner, and boyfriend—had been arrested, convicted, and sentenced to life for being an accomplice in the murders.

In the wake of it all, Simone closed her practice and retreated to academia, hoping to regain her courage and perspective before treating patients again. She had known Edward for half her life—they had attended medical school together, shared countless experiences, and yet, she hadn't recognized the pathological issues that had been right under her nose all along. How could she continue to treat patients and trust her judgment as a psychiatrist when she had missed something so significant?

The Woodbridge house had been her home for almost twenty years. But after everything, it felt tainted. Selling it had been part of her attempt to move forward and feel safe again.

Carl insisted on paying for half of their new home, and they were both thrilled with their choice—a peaceful, waterfront property where they could enjoy beautiful sunsets and quiet mornings together.

"I love this weather; I think we made a great choice, Mrs. Lourenzzo." Carl gestured toward the snowy scene outside.

"I don't think I'll ever get used to being called Mrs. Lourenzzo." Simone smiled. Although they were married, she still used her maiden name in her professional life. After a lifetime of being called Doctor Bennet, she'd struggled with the idea of changing something so critical to her identity. She and Carl had agreed she would use his name only in their private life.

"I know, but I love the sound of it. More coffee, my love?" He got up and went to the kitchen island to make another expresso.

"Thanks, but no…not right now," Simone replied, her gaze drifting back to the water. It was almost Christmas, and the season brought with it a dull ache she couldn't quite shake. She hadn't bought a tree, and her daughter, Tammy, wouldn't be home this year. Tammy had been living in

France for a while, and the distance was a constant, quiet pain in Simone's chest. But it wasn't just missing Tammy that weighed on her, nor was it the typical end-of-year melancholy that always seemed to settle in.

Lately, several things had been bothering her, gnawing at the edges of her thoughts. If she was honest with herself—and she tried to stay grounded in reality, even when it hurt—she missed her patients...and she missed Edward.

Carl made her happy; she loved him and she enjoyed teaching, but something was missing. Sooner or later, she would have to face the fact she needed more out of life and decide what to do about it.

I can't become a miserable woman because I've made wrong decisions.

"You're missing your old life." Carl set his cup on the table and moved to stand behind her, to massage her shoulders.

He must read minds...

"No...well..." She sighed. "It's not that I miss my old life. I just..." She glanced over her shoulder to look up at him. "I love my students, but to be honest, I really miss my patients."

"I love teaching too, Carl said, "but I wouldn't give up being a lawyer. Teaching can´t replace the excitement of litigation, and if your job doesn't excite you or fuel your passion, what's the point?"

"Exactly! I think I miss the adrenaline rush I used to get when I met new patients and heard their stories."

"I'm sure that's a part of it, but do you know what I think you're missing the most?"

Simone shook her head. Carl came around to face her.

"Helping people. It's what you do best! Go back to treating patients. Open a new office or go back to your old one. You haven't sold it yet, right?" He lifted his eyebrows.

"No, not yet, but I think I'll have to. Half of it belongs to Edward, and his share of the money we get from the sale probably must go to paying his child support."

"Buy it from him. Go back to the excitement." Carl placed both hands on the table and leaned down, holding her gaze.

"And what about my lack of judgment? My partner took part in horrible crimes, and all the while, I believed he was the most wonderful person on the planet."

"Because he was important to you." He paused and grinned. "If he was the most wonderful man on the planet, then I hope you think I'm the most perfect man in the galaxy." He chuckled and kissed the top of her head.

"You are." Simone put her hand on his.

"Visit him in jail..." Carl whispered.

Simone looked up, searching his expression.

Could he be serious?

"Try to understand why you didn't see what was beyond the façade," he continued gently. "Unravel the riddle! Surgeons don't operate on themselves, and that's essentially what you're blaming yourself for not having done. I'm not a shrink, but I think the answer is simple. You were emotionally involved, and when we care about someone, we tend to see only what we want to see."

Simone knew he was talking from experience. Years ago, during a sex game, he'd accidentally killed his girlfriend—and Simone's half-sister— Lara. Simone was sure of Carl´s love, but Lara's ghost brought the occasional irrational pang of jealousy, along with feelings of sadness and regret for having never met her.

I could have helped her overcome her traumas.

The thought surprised Simone, and she knew Carl was right; she missed helping people. She nodded at her intuitive husband and made herself a promise—she would visit the prison and make an appointment to see her psychiatrist soon...

CHAPTER TWO

The MacDougall-Walker -Walker Correctional Institution

The metallic sound of the electric gate sliding open at the MacDougall prison snapped Simone out of her thoughts. She had butterflies in her stomach as she tried to imagine how Peter would react to seeing her. After all, she'd been responsible for sending him and Edward to prison.

Simone's deposition and her ability to maneuver Peter into a confession had caused him to incriminate Edward. If she hadn't gotten under Peter's skin, Ed might still be walking free. The thought gave her chills...

She had decided to visit Peter first. She needed to understand his motives, to peel back the layers of his twisted mind, and maybe-just maybe- gain some insight into Edward's actions through Peter's words, before facing her ex-lover again."

Coward, you're just afraid to visit him.

Ahead of her, the correctional officer opened another gray iron door. Holding her breath, Simone followed him inside. An empty room. Thank goodness. She relaxed, and her heart slowed.

"Please wait here, Doctor. I'm going to bring the prisoner in. If you need anything, there's a buzzer right there." He pointed to a small black button on the wall. "Press that and we'll come running."

Simone nodded.

As the door closed, she sat on the cold metal chair behind a simple wood desk. She had never studied an admitted serial killer, and she hoped to analyze his thoughts and emotions. She still didn't know what she would do with the information, but she'd find some way to make use of it—even if she only managed to resolve her own feelings.

Nearly a quarter of an hour passed, and Simone began to shiver. The place was cold, and her suit wasn't warm enough.

Or my nerves are making me freeze.

The sound of the electronic door opening startled her, and her heart started racing again. A vein in her neck throbbed, and her throat tightened.

Peter stepped into the room, and for a moment, Simone was transported back in time. He strolled around the desk to face her and smiled. The same mischievous smile she remembered, the one that made her tremble and twisted her insides. Simone inhaled slowly and exhaled to regain control of her emotions.

He can't do anything to you. Stop being silly. He's wearing a prison uniform and handcuffs, for God's sake!

Simone held his gaze for a moment, but she didn't return his smile. Instead, she glanced at the handcuffs around his wrists. A long, thick chain hung from one of them. He took a seat in the chair across the table from her, and the officer attached the chain to a metal ring on the table then went to stand in the corner closest to the door.

"Could you leave us alone, Officer?"

"Are you sure?" He looked from Simone to Peter.

"I don't think he'll hurt me. Besides, he's chained up." She nodded toward the handcuffs. "Don't worry; I'll ring the buzzer if he gives me any trouble."

"I'll be right on the other side of the door," the officer said, addressing Peter.

A moment later, the door closed again, and Simone and Peter were alone.

“Hello, Peter.” The words came out as a whisper, and then Simone fell silent.

His powerful presence intimidated her. He was a tall man, and prison had done nothing to dull his good looks and masculine allure. His brown hair was shorter than she remembered, and he had lost his tan, his bright green eyes pierced hers.

Like a cat facing a mouse.

“Dear Doctor, so sorry I can’t offer you a drink. What brings you here? I mean, since you were the one who put me in here, I thought you wanted to keep some distance.”

“I need to understand…” Simone found her voice but struggled for the words to explain.

“Me? Do you want to psychoanalyze me?” He chuckled and tried to point at his chest, but the chains prevented him from completing the movement.

Good to know how far that chain allows him to go.

She cleared her throat and gathered her courage. “I want to understand you, your story, your reasons.”

“And what’s in that for me?”

Simone hadn’t prepared an answer for that question, but she came up with one quickly.

“I intend to write a book about you. Of course, we can share the profits… I imagine I could find a publisher who’d offer quite a lucrative contract.” Simone forced a smile.

“I don’t think that’s legal, and, you know, I don’t want to commit any crimes…” He laughed at his own joke, but as Simone remained silent, he continued, “But I do like the idea of a book about me. And what will we call this book?”

His green eyes sparkled.

One can always count on the vanity of a psycho...

"I haven't thought about the title yet." Simone shook her head.

"How about *Peter*?" He smiled.

"We can think about that later, but *Peter* is a possibility. So, you agree to talk to me?" If he was already choosing a title, he must have decided to cooperate.

"If you write exactly what I tell you—and only after you check its legality with your husband and he drafts a contract that suits us both. Congratulations on your marriage. I never imagined Carl would be attracted to someone like you... But yes, after we sign a contract, I'll talk. I want people to know me...but not today. Today, I want to know how the world looks, now I'm not in it to make it shine."

Simone rolled her eyes but remained silent, and with a smile that reminded her of a naughty teenager, Peter started to question her about everything, from books to the weather.

*****

During the one-hour drive home, Simone's thoughts remained in the prison. It was a cold place where, according to Peter, each inmate was assigned to a housing unit. Simone hadn't asked about Edward, but Peter was smart, and at the end of their conversation, as she got up to leave, he'd raised the subject himself.

"I will say hello to your friend for you."

Almost to the door, Simone had paused and turned to look at him, raising an inquisitive brow.

"We don't reside in the same unit, but sometimes, we cross paths in the infirmary. He works there, you know...smart cookie... I work in the vegetable garden, but who am I? Just a simple merchant man while he's a brilliant Doctor..."

Without responding or saying goodbye, Simone had turned and left, but Peter's smile told her he knew he had achieved his goal. He had entered Simone's mind with the information about Edward, disrupting her life, at least, for a little while.

Strangely, knowing Edward was working in an infirmary gave her a sense of peace. He was a Doctor, and at least, he was being useful.

Should I see him?

Even though Simone was annoyed she hadn't gotten Peter to talk about anything consequential, she was proud of herself for facing her fears. To spend almost forty minutes talking to Peter after he'd kidnapped and tortured her meant she had healed, and if she could understand why he'd done all those evil things... Well, maybe understanding him would be another step in her career.

She could become a profiler, work for the FBI, or simply write a book as she had promised Peter. Simone needed a new direction for her life.

CHAPTER THREE

2016 – Like Gods

There were three people in the room, two dressed in firefighter coveralls, hoods covering their heads and gas masks hiding their faces. One was slightly shorter than the other.

The third person, a naked woman, lay trembling on a makeshift litter, her hands and feet bound to its four corners.

The crackling logs in the fireplace muffed her soft cries. Outside, the night was cold, and the old, wooden plank house didn't have a heating system. The three occupants had only the fire to keep them warm.

"Why are you doing this to me?" she asked between short sobs. "What did I do to you?" She sucked in a trembling breath. "Do I know you?"

"No, honey, you don't know us," one of the tormentors said, his voice sounding mechanical behind the mask. He reached out and caressed her black hair.

"So, why me?"

They both stared at her. Tears ran down her face, but she no longer struggled. Surely, she must have understood that escape was impossible, and by now, the drug would be making her dizzy.

"Why me, why me, why me! Always the same question. I'm

sick and tired of the lack of creativity."

"Please let me go. I won't tell anyone. I haven't seen your faces. Let me go!" Her pleas were weak, the ketamine injected in her arm ten minutes before was taking effect.

"I love when they beg; the sound is like music to my ears," the taller of the two said, moving to the fireplace and rubbing his hands in front of the flames.

"Bring the pan. It is time," the shorter one said.

"How do you know? She is still crying," the taller figure replied, turning from the fire and pointing at the woman.

"But she no longer feels pain. Right sweetie?" He glanced down at the young woman's pale face as he pinched and twisted her nipple. "No reaction. See?"

The one by the fire nodded and turned away, retrieving a pan off a table next to the wall, while the other person inserted a dental mouth prop between the woman's open lips.

The taller one finished the adjustments, secured the device, and ensured the woman's mouth was completely open, then asked, "Is it melted?"

The shorter one glanced into the pan they'd placed on a hot log in the fire. "Bubbling."

The pair exchanged glances, sharing a moment of pure pleasure and excitement. The shorter one retrieved the pan and handed it to the taller one.

"Be careful, it's super-hot. Pour the butter before it gets cold."

"Yes, but before I give her the pleasure of greeting death, she must recognize who granted her mercy and released her from her miserable life."

The shorter one removed the mask, revealing a face that would be the last vision the woman would ever have. A moment later, melted butter filled her mouth. She couldn't feel anything anymore, her tears had stopped. A few minutes later, she was dead, suffocated by the butter, her eyes still wide open.

The man and his companion locked gazes as she drew her last breath. The shorter one laughed, a metallic-sounding chuckle but full of delight.

They stood near the body, admiring their handiwork, caressing her as rigor mortis began to set in. There was nothing sexual in their actions. They took no carnal pleasure. Instead, both felt an overwhelming sense of power. Like gods, they believed they could grant life or take it away."

Should I try to publish this book myself? Or give it to the Doctor and trust her handle it for me? The questions kept humming in Peter's mind.

CHAPTER FOUR

New Haven

Simone's hands trembled as she tried to put the key into the lock. After several attempts, she finally managed to open the front door of her office. She entered, turned off the alarm, and walked farther into the house. Dust covered every surface, and seeing the place so neglected made her heart hurt. She set her purse on the secretary's desk, marched down the hallway to her office, and opened the door. The curtains were all closed, and she could barely see inside. Rather than enter, she turned around, closing the door behind her.

Why did I abandon my dreams like this? Pain tightened her chest. *Is this* really *your dream?*

She went down the hall to the next door and looked inside. Again, the blinds were closed, so she turned on the lights.

Amazing how we managed to design two completely different offices in the same house.

Edward's was a modern display of glass and granite, while she'd put together a classic French beauty.

More amazing that a necrophiliac and murder's accomplice lived nearby and was my partner and lover, and I- the super shrink- couldn't see who he really was.

But nobody ever really knows anybody, not even themselves—

or so she told herself repeatedly in an effort to calm down.

But you're supposed to know the human mind.

She shook her head, dismissing the disturbing thoughts as she crossed the room to Edward's glass and chrome desk. Picking up a remote control, she opened all the blinds then blinked against the bright sunlight. She closed her eyes for a moment then opened them again, trying to adjust her vision to the sudden change.

Simone turned and gazed around the office. Apart from the rare, brief visits she'd made to this room to discuss business with Edward, she'd spent no time there. She´d certainly never noticed his décor. As she did so now, she shivered. The place had all the warmth of a walk-in freezer. She walked to the walls for a closer look at the pictures, black and white photos of random places, totally impersonal.

It seems as if his heart wasn't here...or maybe this is what his heart really looked like...

Edward's desk had been reorganized after the police had finished their search for evidence, but Simone still had the image of opened drawers and cabinets and papers spread everywhere. They hadn't found anything relevant.

Ed is much smarter than that.

Other than the sperm he'd given to Peter, left on the bodies to throw off the police, the detectives had never found any other evidence to implicate Edward in the crimes. But they hadn't needed anything else, and he'd spend the rest of his life in prison for being an accessory to murder.

Simone finished her tour of the house, set the alarms, and left.

As she walked toward her car, she glanced back over her shoulder.

God, I miss this so much!

Strangely, as she unlocked her vehicle and opened the

door, she didn't tense like she used to, always expecting to find a body inside. But over a year had passed since she'd discovered her dead secretary sprawled inside the poor woman's car. Simone had obtained some bit of peace, even if her heart longed for the office and her patients.

That was your choice...you can always change your mind...

On her way home, she made a split-second decision and switched directions, turning right when she should have turned left.

*****

Simone parked in the lot of the New Haven Police Department.

What in the hell am I doing here? Before she lost her nerve, she grabbed her bag and got out of the car.

The brown building didn't bring back good memories. The last time she'd been there, she'd reported the body she'd found on her doorstep. Squaring her shoulders, Simone went directly to the reception desk.

A Black woman in a dark blue uniform sat behind a computer at the reception desk. She looked up and smiles to Simone.

"Doctor Bennet!" Her tired expression lifted.

"Sorry, have we met?" Simone smiled back, but she couldn't place the woman's face.

"No, no, sorry. I saw you on the news back when we had all those cyanide crimes, and I feel as if I know you. I'm Corella. How can I help you today?"

She smiled again, and Simone smiled back, but she wasn't comfortable with the idea of people recognizing her because they'd seen her at the scenes of her patients' crime murders...

"Nice to meet you, Corella. About a year or so ago, I met an officer named Carlo... He used to work with a friend of mine, Doctor Reynolds, I'm sorry, but I don't know which division he's in, and I can't recall his last name. I do know he and Doctor Reynolds used to work on psychiatric profiles together. Do you happen to know if he's still around?"

How little I knew about Ed's life.

"Criminal Intelligence Unit. Hold on I'll find him for you."Corella seemed like the kind of long-term employee who knew everyone on the police department—from fresh recruits to seasoned veterans. She probably knew their names, their departments, and nearly all their life stories.

Nothing escapes her sharp ears and observant eyes.

The woman picked up the telephone receiver and punched in a few numbers.

The officer turned her back to Simone and spoke in a low voice that didn't allow Simone to hear the words.

Why so secretive?

Simone forced a smile as the woman turned back and hung up the phone.

"Doctor Bennet, Officer DiMario—that's Carlo—will be with you in a few minutes. If you would please wait? We have a coffee machine at the end of this hall." She pointed to the right. "Or you can wait here."

Corella pointed at a nearby wooden bench, but Simone, too restless to sit, headed down the corridor to check out the coffee machine.

She added some coins, chose a regular coffee, and waited for the machine to do its work. Simone had just lifted the coffee to her lips when someone touched her shoulder. She jumped and turned, her heart racing, holding out the cup to keep the hot liquid from sloshing onto her clothes.

"Doctor Bennet? I'm sorry. I didn't mean to startle you." Carlo gave her a lopsided grin.

"Carlo... I mean, Officer DiMario, how've you been?"

She reached out, and he greeted her with a firm handshake.

"Call me Carlo, please. Did you want to see me, Doctor?"

"Yes, Carlo. Please call me Simone. I'm sorry to drop in unannounced, but I was hoping you could give me a few minutes." She turned to watch a group of people pass by. "Do you have some time now? And is there a place where we can speak in private?"

Carlo glanced at his watch. "Sure. I don't have anything pressing now. Come with me."

He spun around, and Simone hurried to follow his quick steps down the long, cold corridor, almost running to keep up with him. Her high heels echoed like staccato gunshots on the floor. Finally, he stopped, at a gray door, opened it, and gestured for her to step inside.

"Please take a seat," he told her.

There were two armchairs, and Simone chose the one that looked the least uncomfortable. She sat and hung her purse on the arm.

"Carlo..." She paused. Now that she was here, sitting across from him, her ideas seemed a little bit foolish. "I don't know exactly what I'm doing here, but you worked with Edward for a long time, before everything with Peter Hay happened..."

"We worked together for almost five years. I still can't believe how things turned out. Edward was the best. He really helped us solve a few major cases, and he knew his work." He shook his head.

"That's why I'm here. I still can't wrap my mind it. Ed was a wonderful friend, he was a real professional, and then, before I could blink, he's a convicted criminal, sentenced to life ..."

"My thoughts exactly. None of it made much sense to me..." Carlo scratched his head.

“I was wondering if you could help- me or know someone else who could help me to...”

To do what? What do I want to do?

She took a deep breath then answered her unspoken question. “To understand the case.”

“Edward wasn’t just a colleague; we were good friends... But honestly, I don’t think I know much more than you do. How do you think I could help you?”

“Well...could we start with something he was working on? Did he have a place to store his things? Documents? Unfinished projects?”

“There were a lot of things to deal with when he was convicted. We had to clean out his office—you know, to make room for someone else.” He lowered his head, paused for a moment, then looked up and continued. "The FBI agents went through everything, but they didn’t find any incriminating evidence, so they just left it all. I ended up boxing his stuff myself and taking it down to storage. There are three or four boxes down there."

“The FBI agents went through everything, but they didn’t find incriminating evidence, So they just left it all there. I ended up packing his things, including some medical books he used, and took everything down to storage. There are three or four boxes down there.”

He sighed and looked away, clearly uncomfortable.

“I didn’t examine anything; it wasn’t my job, and it was painful. I just put all his paperwork and belongings inside the boxes. Nobody seemed to care or have any use for any of it.”

“Can I have them?” Simone blurted out. Carlo shook his head. “Unfortunately, only an immediate family member—or someone who has power of attorney—can sign for them. Procedure ...” He frowned.

“I understand, Carlo I’ll find someone who qualifies.

Thanks for your help!" Simone said, standing.

She gave him her hand, and once more, her fingers disappeared inside his enormous grip.

"If there's anything else you need, Simone, please call me. I owe the Doctor for everything he did for us. If I can be of any help, just let me know."

"If there's anything else you need, Simone, please call me. I owe the Doctor a for everything he did for us, especially for me, he treated my teenage son without charging anything."

"I didn´t know that."

"He used to help people at the police station once a week for three hours, in addition to his other volunteer work as a profiler. Everyone loves him. If I can be of any help, just let me know."

It's no surprise. I don't know much about Edward, but his behavior doesn't seem criminal at all

They said goodbye, and she returned to her car. Simone pulled out of the parking lot with an address in mind, determined to complete her next task. She didn't bother phoning Carl to let him know she'd be late. He'd gone to New York City that morning, so she was on her own for the night.

CHAPTER FIVE

Why not her?

Simone rang the doorbell and waited. Lights glowed inside the house, signaling that someone was home. As she waited, she looked around, taking in the surroundings. Ed's former wife had gotten the house in the divorce—a beautiful, spacious home, surrounded by a lush garden filled with flowers and trees.

"Hold on, I'm just getting out of the shower!" Beth's voiced echoed from somewhere inside the house.

Simone cringed.

How had a man like Ed ever gotten into a relationship with a woman like Beth?

She was the sort of impolite, uncouth person Simone preferred to keep at a distance. When Ed had gotten Beth pregnant, he'd married her, and she'd had every opportunity to go back to school or learn a new skill and change her life, but she'd decided to settle for being a frustrated housewife. She'd driven Ed crazy until he finally filed for divorce.

After several long minutes, the door opened, and Beth appeared wearing a faded-pink bathrobe and a towel wrapped around her hair. Her normally marble-white skin had red blotches, no doubt from the hot water in the shower. *She's aged.*

"*You.*" Beth pointed at Simone and tried to close the door.

"Beth, wait. I need your help!" Simone held the door with her hand.

"To do what? Send my son's dad to the electric chair?" Considering they were in front of each other, Beth didn't need to shout, but it seemed it was the only way she knew how to communicate.

"Connecticut doesn't have the electric chair," Simone answered without thinking. At Beth's furious scowl, Simone rushed to explain the reason for her visit. "Beth, listen... I want to understand what Edward did and why... Maybe I can help him."

"Isn't it too late for that?" Beth tried once more to close the door.

"Christ, Beth, be rational. Peter Hay was the one who sent Ed to prison, and that never would have happened if Ed hadn't helped him! I had nothing to do with any of that. I was a victim, but here I am, trying to figure out if there's any way I can help. Now, do you want to help Ed, or do you want to let him stay behind bars forever?" Simone paused then added, "Besides, we need to talk about the clinic. Ed and I were partners, remember?"

Beth remained silent for a moment, no doubt considering how she might benefit if she decided to talk. "Come in." She opened the door and let Simone in. "Let's talk before Noah gets home."

Simone nodded. Noah was Beth and Edward's only child, and from what Simone had observed over the last several years, he was Beth's reason for living. Simone followed the other woman into the living room, and Beth pointed to a sofa without saying a word.

"I'm trying to find out what Ed was up to before he went to jail," Simone said, her voice steady. "Who knows? Maybe we can find something that could help overturn his conviction or at least reduce the penalty. Maybe, if we're lucky, he could even get out on parole."

Simone paused and gathered her thoughts. If Ed was as guilty as he seemed, he could stay right where he was, but she needed to understand what had happened.

"I need access to his police work product. There are some boxes in storage down at the station—they contain the materials he kept in the office he occupied there, but they'll only turn them over to a relative. Can you go with me?"

"I'm not a relative," Beth snarled. "I`m his *ex*-wife. You do remember he dumped me because he was in love with you, right?"

How easy it is to blame someone else for your own faults.

Simone rarely encountered a person who assumed responsibility for his or her mistakes. Usually, people found a scapegoat for the stupid things they did. She sighed and shook her head.

"You're not being fair. You and Ed were divorced years before I dated him."

"But he left me because he loved you. You were always there between us. Glorious, perfect, clever Simone. Who am I compared to you? I'm a housewife, I'm not as pretty, I haven't gone to college, I'm not a professor..." Her voice rose steadily, escalating until she was shouting once again, spitting out each word.

Exasperated, Simone sat forward on the sofa and glared at Ed's ex-wife.

"We're wasting time here. Will you help me or not? I don't need to sit and listen to you blame me for all your problems." Simone spoke firmly, using the same tone of voice she used with her patients when she needed to get them back on track.

Beth lowered her head.

"I'll help you. I can't raise Noah alone. He's being rebellious and needs a strong hand...and I don't know what to do..." Her eyes filled with tears.

Simone's heart went out to the woman. Beth was lost without Ed's guidance. He'd always been the one to solve all her problems.

"How are you financially?"

"Ed had some properties that are rented, so we're managing. If we need more money, I can work." She shrugged.

About time... Did she ever work?

Simone didn't have that information. Noah was a teenager, and Beth could no longer use him as an excuse for not working. Considering her completely biased opinion when it came to women who didn't work outside the home, Simone thanked God Beth wasn't a mind reader.

"Well, Ed is half owner of the house where he and I set up our practice. I'd like to reopen the office under just my name. I can't afford to buy it from you now, but I can pay rent until I can get the funds to buy you out."

The minute she finished saying the words, Simone realized her subconscious mind had just made the decision for her, and she would go back to working with her patients.

"That's fine with me." Beth shrugged. "I don't want to sell Ed's stuff. My son will need those assets someday. He wants to be a Doctor. I'm so proud of him, but med school is expensive."

"We'll handle those things in due time, if he has good grades, I can help him get a scholarship, but right now, I need you to agree to go with me to the police station."

"Not today. It's almost six, and Noah will be home soon. I need to make dinner." Beth paused then looked Simone in the eyes. "I'll help you, but I need something in return..."

*****

Balancing several bags of groceries and her purse, Simone struggled to enter her code into the digital lock panel beside the door between her garage and kitchen. The phone in her handbag started ringing, but she ignored it and pushed her way inside.

Breathing heavily, Simone kicked the door close and put the groceries on the island. By that time, the phone had gone silent. A quick glance told her it had died. She shrugged. If it was important, they'd leave a message. Simone found a charger, plugged up the phone, then rummaged through the shopping bags to find the frozen lasagna she had just bought for a quick dinner. After such a long day, she lacked the energy to cook.

That's the kind of energy I'll always be lacking.

Simone studied the back of the lasagna box, wrinkling her nose at the list of preservatives and off-the-charts calories per serving. She sighed and ripped open the end to remove the aluminum container.

Just once won't kill me...I hope.

After popping the lasagna into the oven and setting the timer, she put the rest of the food in the fridge then took off her shoes. Her phone was back on, so she checked her list of missed calls. She frowned, and her heart started racing. Carl had phoned her twelve times throughout the day. It had to be urgent; He never called her that much. Simone called him back, putting her cell on speaker so she could set a place for herself at the kitchen island while they talked. He answered immediately.

"What happened? Where are you? Are you okay?" His questions came out in a rush.

"I'm fine, nothing is wrong." She answered his last question first.

His heavy sigh came through the speaker. "I was worried. I tried to reach you all day, but I kept getting your voicemail."

"I was in places where I couldn't use my phone."

"Like where? Church?"

Simone chuckled at his obvious joke. Even though she believed in a major force ruling the universe—what they call agnostic—Carl knew she wasn't religious.

"Funny... No, more like prison and the police department." She grabbed a plate from an upper cupboard and a knife and fork from the drawer.

"What happened? Is everything okay, or did you decide...?"

"Yes, I went to visit Peter." She set the utensils down on the island gently, as if making any noise might conjure up the man's presence.

"Peter? Why him? When we talked about this the other day, I thought you would go see Edward."

"I want to understand things, and besides, I had to face my fears. I don't want to go through life having a panic attack every time I think of Hay." She climbed up on a barstool, prepared to make her case to her lawyer husband.

"And did you?"

"Yes. In the beginning, I was trembling inside, but then my fear faded, and I realized he can't hurt me now. What happened with Peter Hay is part of my past."

"So, why are you bringing it into the present?" Carl sounded tired.

"Because those memories will be part of my life forever, and as a shrink, I need to understand his mind—how a criminal´s mind works—and what made him do what he did. I decided to go back to the office and start seeing patients again, and I can't be fooled by mentally disturbed people like I was by Hay and Edward." She picked up her fork and twirled it between her fingers.

"So, you will go back... I'm so happy for you. If I was there, I'd pull you into my arms, spin your around, and dance you across the room. You, my love, are the best psychiatrist I've ever met, and the world of psychiatry lost an amazing talent with you away!" He sounded excited.

"I love you, Carl. Thank you so much for your support." Simone set down the fork and sighed. She'd been prepared to argue her point of view and further explain why she needed to do this, but things with Carl were easy. He was always there for her, no matter what she decided to do.

"I love you, Doctor Bennet, and we are a team. No need to thank me," he said in a sultry voice.

The same voice he sometimes used when they were intimate. Simone shivered and rubbed the goosebumps that had risen on her arms.

"No fair! Don't you dare get me started, or I'll burn my frozen lasagna."

"Frozen lasagna?" Now he sounded outraged. "You poor thing. You really do suffer when I'm gone, don't you?"

"Like you'll never know." Simone realized she'd spoken the truth. "And we're not talking just food and sex. You're my biggest fan, and I don't know what I'd do without you in my corner."

"I feel the same way. Why do you think I was so panicked when I could reach you today?" Carl chuckled. "I better let you go so you can eat."

The buzzer on the oven sounded, and Simone slid to her feet.

"Perfect timing. Will you call me later?"

"Of course, my love..." Carl said. "Have a wonderful meal."

After pulling the lasagna from the oven and cutting herself

a serving, Simone sat on the stool at the island, feeling a deep sense of gratitude for her current relationship. No drama, no jealousy, no disputes.

What more could I ask for in life?

An image flashed through her mind—her sitting in her office, listening to a patient. The thought brought a pang of uncertainty. Would anyone trust a psychiatrist who had been involved in so many bad situations?

The question lingered, casting a shadow over her sense of peace.

The sun was setting on the frozen water, Simone pushed away the last half of her lasagna. Appetite gone, she decided to go for a run and try to clear her head. She went to her room, carrying her shoes, which she placed on the floor inside her large walk-in closet. After putting on a pair of warm navy-blue sweatpants and a matching hoodie, she slipped on her sneakers then left the house.

Despite her intentions to de-stress, her thoughts kept racing. Not even the icy cold air on her face could distract her from thinking about recent events—her decisions to try to help Edward and to return to practicing psychiatry, and her visit with Peter. Had she made the right choices? For the last year, her life had been peaceful and balanced, and now, in the space of an afternoon, she had decided to change everything, a return to uncertainty. She took a deep breath and smiled. This was exactly what she needed, something to shake her stable life.

CHAPTER SIX

Keep Your Voice Down

The next morning, excitement filled Simone as she anticipated returning to the office and her patients. She woke up eager to face the day and even sang as she showered and dressed. She couldn't carry a tune to save her life, but she felt like a little songbird that morning.

While she cooked breakfast, she set a place at the island with linen placemat, porcelain dishes, a cloth napkin, and her best silverware.

A little bit pompous for scrambled eggs, but I deserve it. In Simone´s opinion the best things at home should be for the residents—*we are the most important people, after all.* She prepared a latte using Carl's coffee machine, placed her eggs on the plate, picked up her fork, and dug into her food with an appetite she hadn't had in a long time.

After she ate, Simone started to organize her schedule. The blank pages annoyed her, and she'd feel much better after she filled them with appointments.

A little after 10:00 a.m., Simone got her phone and dialed Patricia's number.

Patricia Bravesh had been Simone and Edward's last secretary. Elegant and highly efficient, Patricia had most likely found another position, but maybe she would know someone who could work with Simone.

"Hello, Doctor Bennet. How've you been?" Patricia answered.

"I'm doing fine." Simone had to smile. She'd missed hearing Patricia's raspy, ex-smoker voice—she sounded like Janis Joplin. "How about you? I haven't talked to you in ages."

"I`m well, thank you. How can I help you today, Doctor?"

Typical Patricia...

She didn't waste time on chitchat but went straight to the point, always eager to be of service.

"Well...I decided to go back to the office and..."

"Yes, I would love to go back to work for you!" Patricia answered in a rush, unusually enthusiastic for someone who always kept her composure. "I'm working with the lawyers again, and they're lunatics. I need the peace of our office. Working for these people feels like a constant cardio workout —my heart is always pushed to its limits.

Simone smiled.

Our office. Excellent.

When a person thought of a business as partially theirs, chances were good they'd put their heart and soul into making it a success.

"That's wonderful, Patricia. I had no hope you would be free, and to be honest, I'm not sure how things will turn out because I've been away for a while. By now, my patients should have other psychiatrists... I don't know... Your salary would be the same, but things are a little bit uncertain right now. It's possible I've been away too long."

"Your patients love you! Let me make some calls... When do you intend to start?"

"Well, that's another thing. Can you quit your current job without giving much notice? I'd love to have you start on Monday. I need to hire someone to clean a little bit and freshen up the place…"

"I can, and don't worry about cleaning or the patients. I'm in charge now. Can I drop by your house and get the keys from you today?"

"You certainly may, but I moved."

"Please text your new address to me. I apologize for cutting this short, but II need to handle something else right now," she said quickly.

"Bye, Patricia. I'm so happy you decided to join me." Simone smiled.

"So am I. See you soon, Doctor."

Simone ended the call still smiling. She could imagine what was happening at the law office where Patricia worked. She was tough and didn't take any guff.

Later, Patricia told Simone that after hanging up, she had stormed into her boss's office with folders in her arms. He looked at her, surprised, as she had never entered without announcing herself. Before he could say anything, she threw the folders on his desk and said,

"Go fuck yourself, you son of a bitch. I'm out of here."

She then turned and left, later sharing the immense satisfaction she felt from being spontaneous for once.

*****

At about noon, Carl phoned Simone. The moment she answered his call she began telling him all about her plans for going back to work. By the time she paused to catch her breath, Carl was laughing.

"What's so funny?" she asked.

"You sound like a little girl who just received a pile of presents from Santa." He chuckled then added, "I'm so happy to hear you like this, but I have bad news. Something happened at the office, and I can't make it home this weekend, so I was thinking... How about you come here Friday, and we can do something together before I dive into a pile of paperwork? I can't promise you company the whole weekend, but I can make sure your nights are filled with fun!" The suggestive tone he used told her exactly what kind of fun he had planned.

Simone grinned. Would she still get this excited by thoughts of being with him when they'd been married for twenty years? She hoped so. "I think I'll accept your kind invitation, sir. A weekend in the city will be great before I dive into an ocean of lunatics." Or a small stream of them, at least.

*****

That Thursday morning, Simone returned to the MacDougall Walker Correctional Institution. Thanks to Patricia and her contacts, Simone had managed to secure special permission in less than twenty-four hours to treat Peter as a pro bono psychiatrist. According to the person Patricia knew, this was a welcomed service in prisons, where mental health care was often in high demand.

As a psychiatrist, she would have more liberty to ask questions unsupervised. A Doctor-patient conference wouldn't be recorded the way an inmate-visitor meeting would.

Before Simone was admitted to the facility, the warden's secretary had some legal paperwork for her to complete. After signing her name and the date on half a dozen standard forms, she waited for a prison officer to come and escort her. He took her to a room nearby where he instructed her to leave all her belongings in one of several lockers along the wall.

"May I take this inside with me?" she asked, holding up her portable, voice-activated recorder. "I record my sessions so I can review them later and make certain I didn't miss anything important."

The correctional officer nodded. "We'll have to run it through a metal detector first, but yes, you can take it in with you."

Once she'd stowed her belongings and the officer scanned her recorder, Simone followed a second officer along the maze of corridors and past dozens of closed doors until they reached a small infirmary. The officer gestured toward a table and chairs.

"Take a seat. Someone will bring your patient in to see you soon."

"Thank you." Simone sat in the chair farthest from the door, putting her back to the outside wall. While she waited, she took a quick inventory of her surroundings. The drab gray walls and bar-covered windows gave her the creeps.

I can't imagine being locked up in a place like this for the rest of my life. Did the prison's surroundings cause them to become more depressed—or even violent?

When Peter finally arrived, escorted by yet another correctional officer, he looked directly into her eyes, just as he always had, but his body language remained neutral—no surprise, no emotion, nothing that indicated any kind of reaction.

"Good morning," Simone said, addressing both men. She then turned to the man who'd escorted Peter. "Officer, can you remove his handcuffs please?"

"Good morning, Doctor." The officer shook his head. "I can't take off the cuffs. I'm sorry. Unfortunately, you will be unsupervised in here, so we can't take any risks." He touched Peter's shoulder then indicated a steel armchair in front of Simone.

Peter sat, and the officer hooked one of the cuffs on one of the arms of the chair.

"This should hold him. It's screwed to the ground." The

officer pointed to the four screws in each of the chair legs.

Simone shrugged. Strangely, she wasn't worried about Peter attacking her.

"I'm going to leave, but there's always an officer in the corridor. Just shout and someone will come running. When you're ready to leave, you just leave him here"—he pointed at Peter as if he was talking about an object—"and tell the officer to come and get him. Did you understand?"

He must think I'm an idiot.

"Understood. Thank you. Have a nice day."

Simone smiled at the officer, but he didn't smile back. He gave a quick nod and left.

"Good morning, Doctor Bennet," Peter said, his voice measured. "May I ask to what I owe the pleasure of receiving two visits in such a short space of time?"

Ignoring Peter's flowery sarcasm, Simone smiled.

"I'm not a visitor; I'm your Doctor now. *Pro-bono.*" Simone sat back and waited for his reaction.

"Am I ill? I didn't know that. What is my problem? I thought we had a deal.

"To answer your question, it is not for me to define your problem. At least, not yet. We will discover it together."

"And if I don't want to discover it? And if I'm happy being just the way I am? Have you ever thought about it? That a criminal, as they label us here"—he lowered his voice and leaned toward her as if he was telling her a secret— "*likes* being a criminal?"

"I've never treated a criminal before. You're my first, so it's going to be interesting to learn about how you feel regarding everything that happened and about what's going on now, here in this place..." Simone spread her arms, indicating the prison. She wouldn't let him know her true feelings about criminals.

Peter raised an eyebrow, and Simone experienced a bit of relief.

The show goes on. I still have the ability to put on my poker face.

"How about my contract, the one you promised me? The book you were supposed to write about me?" Peter asked, his tone slightly demanding. I already have a few small things to give you...I´m writing you know..."

"That´s great news. Regarding the contract, I can't give you one yet," Simone replied evenly. "I'm here as a Doctor. I'm allowed to record our conversations, and if you agree, at some point, I will write a book with all the material I gather, including your stories. That decision is entirely up to you. Or we can simply sit and talk—it's your choice."

Simone smiled and leaned toward Peter.

"Why don't you tell me... How do you feel about, as you said, being a criminal?" she asked, her gaze locked on his, probing for any reaction.

Peter laughed, but it sounded forced. Simone waited for him to get serious and answer her. She didn't believe patient-Doctor relationships were about analyzing reactions, but about letting the patient try to explain themselves if they chose to, and guiding them in the process of understanding their feelings. Peter was a talker. She felt certain he would enjoy telling his stories, maybe even bragging about the things he'd done, as most psychopaths tended to do.

"Since I don't have any other interesting appointments until your next visit, I suppose I'll talk to you," Peter said, a hint of sarcasm in his voice. "I've seen many shrinks throughout my life. First, my parents sent me, and later, I went on my own. But I could never talk about the feelings I have while committing a crime—it's something I never trusted them with."

Suddenly, Peter darted his gaze around the room, scanning all four corners of the walls, as if checking for something unseen.

"They told me no microphones or cameras are allowed in here...don't worry," Simone reassured him, her voice calm. "Just my small recorder. Whatever we say will stay between the two of us, until you give me written permission to disclose anything."

"And the judge and jurors if you decide I represent a risk to society... I know all about so-called Doctor-patient confidentiality."

Simone had to smile. "Peter...you're here serving a life sentence without parole. Even if I could reveal what you tell me, which I can do only if you intend to commit new crimes, what harm would that do to your sentence? Next life punishment?"

Peter laughed, short and hard. It sounded more like a bark.

"And I thought you were dull," he said and pointed at her. "There's a naughty girl under your good-girl façade. Tell me everything you hide from the world, Simone. Maybe there's a fascinating person under the prude."

"Fascinating you is not a part of my job description, and lest you forget, I'm not the patient here; you are." Simone kept her tone firm.

"I'm not!" Peter shouted. He altered his voice, switching to the feminine tone he used when he wanted to be funny. "But if you ask me nicely, maybe..."

Talk about an unbalanced personality.

"Well, I would like to treat you," she told him. "Maybe a I can help you feel better. Even if I can manage to make you a little happier, isn't it worth giving it a try?"

"You know what would make me happy? Putting my hands

around your wrinkled neck and crushing it until your throat feels like mashed potatoes." Peter grimaced.

Wrinkled neck?

Simone started to lift a hand to touch her neck but quickly dropped her arm and clenched her hand into a fist.

Don't let him into your head, Simone! Don't lose your focus.

She remained outwardly calm and forced herself to lean forward a bit to indicate her interest.

"Tell me more about this desire..."

I'm on the right track. He's getting angry.

Peter shook his head.

"I don't think so... *Guard, come quick!* This woman is molesting me! She said she wants my body! Hurry!" Peter shouted at the top of his lungs, using his feminine voice again.

An instant later, the door flew open, and a correctional officer rushed inside.

Damn officer...

He had to have had one ear pressed against the door so he could eavesdrop on their conversation, or he'd have never reacted so quickly. Simone made a mental note to keep her voice down so the entire prison wouldn't learn what Peter and she were talking about... Assuming they ever talked again.

"What's the problem in here? I told you a hundred times I ´m no guard, I ´m a correctional officer!"

The officer stood with one hand on his hip and the other resting on the butt of his holstered gun, his legs spread wide.

Peter turned to him with an innocent, wide-eyed expression and shook his head.

"Nothing's wrong! The good Doctor here told me to express my feelings, so I thought about something that really frightens me—the idea of a woman touching me—and the only way I could express my revolt was to shout. After all, I'm chained up here." He lifted his hands to show off the cuffs that had been attached to the chair. "So sorry to disturb you. I didn't know these walls were so paper thin." Peter put on the most angelic face, his expression a picture of innocence, as if the outburst had never happened.

The man pointed at Peter.

"Don't bother me again, you piece of—" He glanced over at Simone and snapped his mouth shut, perhaps realizing he was mistreating an inmate in front of a Doctor. He grumbled beneath his breath and shook his head. "Just don't bother me!" The door slammed shut behind him as he hastened from the room.

Peter turned to Simone.

"See? They can hear everything. Even if you *don*'t snitch on me, they'll know everything we talk about in here."

"Of course, they did—you screamed at the top of your lungs. My secretary could probably hear you from my office. Let's keep our voices down for today, and then the next time we meet, I'll try to get us more privacy," Simone said, talking quietly.

"Oh... How juicy! Just you and I in our own, private, little space." Peter chuckled, but then his mood changed once again, his expression turned dark. "Let me ask you, Doctor, who's paying for this? My stupid sister?"

"No... This one's on the house. Call it a case to benefit scientific interest. Now, let's get back to you, shall we?" Simone nodded toward the recorder. "May I?"

Peter nodded, and she pressed the power button. The device would only record when it detected sound.

She rose and went around to stand behind Peter's chair.

"I'll stand right here next to you. You can speak as quietly as you want, and I'll listen. Why don't you tell me about your childhood?"

Simone put a hand on his shoulder in a show of support, but he recoiled as if her touch had burned him.

He turned his head to look up at her.

"That's a totally *lame* idea. I've already done that. Why don't I tell you how I killed your fat secretary?"

CHAPTER SEVEN

Hidden Motives, Dark Pasts, and Disturbed Presents

Without waiting for Simone to respond, Peter started his story, turning his head back and facing the wall. Simone didn't want to know how Mona died—not then and not now—but she let him speak.

"That was a beautiful day when I saw your precious secretary leaving the clinic. She headed to the park on the corner, the same one where I met you. She even chose to sit on the same bench, and I thought, this must be fate, or the stars had perfectly aligned, or something. I followed her there, and the fatty was eating a sandwich the size of her ass!"

Peter tried to motion with his hands to indicate the size, but the cuffs wouldn't allow him. He shrugged and went on.

"I introduced myself, and she seemed pleased to know I was a friend of Carl's. She told me she'd never met him, but she knew about the work you were doing for him, so when I invited her to join me for tea and pastries, she didn't hesitate to get into my car. You know, fat people never refuse free food," he said, a sly grin spreading across his face.

He paused, clearly waiting for Simone's reaction, but she bit her tongue and forced herself to remain silent. After a moment, he shrugged again and continued with his story.

"Do you know why people die? Because they're stupid!

Don't you think?"

"I think people should die when they are old or ill and not because they made a mistake, but please proceed."

"Once I got her into my car, I gave her a dose of chloroform, and she slept so hard, she didn't wake up until I got her into my playground."

This time, Simone couldn't resist asking a question.

"Your playground? You mean that place you set up to torture your victims?" She kept her voice neutral, as if she wasn't really all that interested but merely wanted to clarify a detail of his story.

"Yes, the same one where you and I had so much fun together," he said, referring to the time he kidnapped and brutalized her.

"Lots of fun..." she said, crossing her arms to stop her hands from shaking. Bits of memories flashed through her mind... Being naked, wet, and burned... The terror... She pushed those thoughts away and redirected his attention back to Mona. "Nobody saw you and asked questions about you carrying around an unconscious woman?"

"We pretended like she was drunk and carried her between us."

"We?" Simone went to stand in front of Peter and looked into his eyes, but he lowered his head before answering.

"Me, myself, and I..."

My ass, you have an accomplice... Edward? Did he do more than just hand over some of his sperm? I can´t believe that...

Simone had to calm herself to let him continue. She drew in a deep breath.

"Okay, so you carried her, pretending she was drunk... Surely she was heavy."

"Oh, yes...she needed to go on a diet. By now, she must

be very skinny. See? I helped her to get rid of all those extra pounds!" He'd softened his voice again.

When he wanted to be funny, he was more effeminate, the stereotypical gay man, but when he wanted to make an impact, he reverted to a hard voice...rough and edgy.

Schizophrenia? Too soon to know.

"Super funny. I need to think about it deeply before I can laugh. But go on," she said without looking away. He was not going to get a reaction from her. Once again, she prompted him to continue with his story. "So, you tortured Mona?"

"Nope, I didn't have time for that... The drive from that hole-in-the-wall you call your office into the city and back takes time..."

Simone closed her eyes and breathed a sigh of relief, thankful to know Mona hadn't been tortured. How many times had Simone been haunted by thoughts of what Mona might have gone through during her final hours?

"Well, then, why take her into the city? Why not just kill her quickly right there in the park?" Simone resumed her seat across from Peter and leaned toward him, speaking as softly as possible.

Before Peter could answer, the door opened again.

"Your time is up, Doctor." The officer entered the room, unchained Peter from the chair, re-cuffed his hands behind his back, then tugged him to his feet. The man then nodded at Simone. "As soon as I leave with him, another officer will come to show you out."

"Thank you."

Peter allowed the officer to herd him to the door, but then he paused and turned to look at Simone. "We needed to talk..."

"Talk?" Simone frowned. *Who? Mona?* "You could have talked to her in the park."

But Peter had left the room.

*****

The officer who came to show Simone out was nicer than the previous one. He entered the room with a smile and pointed at the engraved badge on his chest.

"I'm Liam, Doctor. How are you today? Would you care to follow me? I'm going to guide you out."

"Nice to meet you, Liam. I'm fine, how about you?" Simone rose, put her recorder into her purse, and followed the guard. "Have you worked here for a long time?"

"Long enough," Liam seemed inclined to talk. "About a year."

He continued walking, Simone on his heels.

"Tough job?"

"No…most of the time, it's just sad. I pity these guys…" He moved his hands around.

"Why? Aren't they all convicted criminals?"

"Yes, they are…but can you imagine being locked up here for years, in some cases forever? This is just a job for me. At the end of the day, I can leave, breathe, drink a beer with my wife… But these guys have thrown their lives away. It's such a shame. Life is so short, and nobody knows the hidden motives for their crimes. I always ask myself: What happened to them to drive them to commit their crimes?"

"It's always about hidden motives, dark pasts, and disturbed presents. It's really sad, you're right… Where exactly do you work?" Simone asked. Might Liam know Edward?

"The infirmary section, four days a week, and two in the therapy program."

"Therapy program? What's that all about?"

"It's a pilot program. We have about fifty inmates doing

group and individual therapy sessions, and they're taught how to deal with anger, fear, and frustration."

"Is it working?"

"Yes, the participants are a lot less depressed, not nearly as hostile, and they're learning how to analyze what went wrong with their lives that brought them to this point. It's a beautiful thing. I'm in charge of keeping order during the sessions, but the cooperation is incredible, and mostly, I just stand there and listen. The work they're doing is so good I think my own life improves after every session."

"Are the Doctors volunteers?"

"Nope. One of our inmates is a psychiatrist—he proposed and developed the program himself."

"Doctor Edward Reynolds?" Simone asked. What were the chances of another inmate having a background in psychiatry?

"Exactly. Great guy! A waste of a great mind to the world but a blessing for this place. Life has its mysterious ways of putting things in the right places, even if it uses crooked paths to get there."

CHAPTER EIGHT

New York

On Friday, Simone took the 4:00 p.m. train from Union Station in New Haven. Although she was tired, she decided to read. She pulled the book out of her purse. One of her students had recommended it. It was written by a South African author, Angela Shearer, and Simone admired the cover, running her fingertip across the large white letters of the title, *Relevant*.

Intrigued by the book blurb, she opened to the first page and dove into its easy and funny narrative. She barely noticed the time, and when the train stopped, two hours had passed, and she had arrived at Penn Station in New York. She saved her page with a bookmark, closed the book, and reluctantly put it back inside her purse.

That is one writer I would like to have coffee with and share some ideas.

Taking the subway to Canal Street seemed more reasonable than trying to find a cab at this time of the night. Simone would have to walk the five minutes to Carl's place on Laight Street, but at least she didn't have a bag to carry. Instead of lugging clothing back and forth, she'd acquired an entire second wardrobe to keep at Carl's apartment.

It was a great excuse for new clothes.

Simone almost regretted her decision to take the subway

when she boarded the crowded train at six o'clock, but she'd just have to suffer through. After twenty minutes spent traveling compressed like a can of sardines, Simone left the subway. As she opened the door of the station, the New York November wind smacked her in the face. She shivered and hurried down the sidewalk. As she reached Laight Street, the wind grew worse, blowing directly in from the Hudson River. The steady gusts reminded Simone of an old movie where people were carried by the wind.

If I lived here full time, I'd probably believe something like that is possible.

Simone arrived at Carl's apartment frozen solid. She saluted the doorman, and as she climbed inside the gold elevator, the sound of Tommy barking came from above her. She grinned, and warmth filled her heart. She missed that dog.

Dogs change people.

Simone had never owned a dog, before Tommy. Her parents wouldn't allow her to have one, and then when she'd become an adult and moved out, her life had been too busy to have a pet, Tommy came with her marriage, and now she couldn't imagine life without him.

Tommy's barks grew louder and more frantic as Simone approached, and when she punched her code into the lock and opened the door, the dog leaped onto her, embracing her with his paws.

"Hi, big boy, I missed you, too!" Simone caressed the dog's head.

I may be going crazy, but I swear he's smiling at me.

"Okay, Tommy, now be a good boy and sit."

The dog immediately got down, sat, and when she moved, began to follow her through the apartment. He was the nicest dog ever—sociable with everyone—but she doubted he'd make a great watchdog if the need arose. He was just too friendly to attack anyone.

Simone pulled her phone from her purse and sent a message to Carl, telling him she was home. He answered with an emoji face sending a kiss.

Sometimes, he is so juvenile...

Simone sent back a heart in response. Maybe it was the lack of children in his life that made him act like a boy sometimes. Carl was a serious lawyer and professor; those who didn't know him well would never imagine he was funny and sweet in his personal life.

Thinking about him made Simone's heart warm, feeling emotions she hadn't experienced in a long time, emotions she'd nearly forgotten she could feel. Love, kindness, and desire.

I've never cared so deeply for a man...

They had an amazing relationship—great companionship, respect for each other's space, passion, great sex... What else could a woman want from life?

An answer flashed into her mind.

From a man, nothing more, but how about a successful practice and the confidence I'll be able to heal my patients again?

She'd had a long day. She'd gone to New Haven to teach in the early hours of the morning, intending to travel from there to New York. But her cleaning lady had called her and said a pipe was leaking water all over the kitchen, so Simone had to drive back home to call a plumber and have it fixed. She'd eaten a salad for lunch, talked to Patricia about her schedule for Monday—not very promising...only two clients, but she'd known her old patients wouldn't be sitting at home waiting for her. They needed permanent care, so it would be a challenge to have a full schedule again. Then again, did she want a full schedule? She could choose this time, so maybe she'd take on less responsibility.

Maybe I'm getting old.

*****

After a quick shower, Simone curled up on the couch to read a few chapters of *Relevant* and wait for Carl, but Tommy kept poking at her hand with his nose, so she finally gave up and closed the book.

"If you were a man, you could get anything you wanted in the world with that doe-eyed look of yours," she told him as she petted his head. "Just like your owner. Let's go for a walk."

Simone got up, went to the kitchen to find the dog's collar, fastened it around Tommy's neck, and together they stepped out of the cozy apartment.

Despite the biting cold that even made the dog shiver, they bundled up and stepped out for a brisk stroll. After a short while, they returned to the warmth of their apartment.

Simone carefully washed the dog's paws. Once Tommy was clean, she sank into the sofa, nestling into the comforting embrace of the pillows, and closed her eyes.

*****

Simone woke up to the sound of someone entering the code into the lock and a welcoming bark from Tommy. She looked at her watch—seven o'clock—and got to her feet.

Carl entered the condo, giving Simone a bright smile. He had a few wrinkles around his mouth and eyes.

He's been working too much.

"Hello, beautiful, so good to see you here when I come home." He opened his arms.

Simone smiled back and walked into his warm embrace.

"Missed you, love. You seem tired. Why don't you take a shower, and then we can think about something to eat. I'll order in. I don't think you have the energy to go out."

"Nope. After a quick shower, I'll be good as new, and we can go out for a nice dinner. I've ordered stuff all week. Besides, I want to show my beautiful wife around. I'm going to walk Tommy, then I'll be ready in a few minutes."

"I already took him. Go ahead and take your shower—no worries."

"Love you!" He kissed her neck then headed for the shower.

Simone followed him, and Tommy followed her.

No one is ever alone with a dog.

"I'm going to doll up a little bit," she said.

"You don't need much for that, honey, just a beautiful dress."

Carl entered the bathroom, and she went to the closet to dig around for a dress. She ran her fingers through the hangers and found a red dress she didn't remember she had. She pulled it out to examine it more closely, certain she'd never seen it. The skirt was long, much longer than anything she would buy. The dress had to belong to someone taller. Immediately, the beginning of Carl's diary came to her mind.

I was sipping whisky when a woman started to walk toward me. A knockout, I thought. She was sensual, blonde, and tall, almost as tall as I was, and she had eyes the color of the Caribbean.

Simone lifted the dress to her nose, sniffed it, and cringed at the odor of powerful parfum. *Lara.* Simone was positive the dress belonged to the dead woman, and a pang of jealousy made her stomach churn.

Why did he keep her dress? Will he ever forget her? Does he really love me? Should I confront him about this?

She turned, her mind racing, and nearly ran into Carl. He was right behind her, wrapped in his ancient bathrobe, rifling through his side of the closet in search of clothes.

"Nice dress! I rarely see you in red," he said, barely glancing at her before he went back to looking for a suit.

"It is not mine," Simone said.

Finally, he turned to her. "What?"

"It is *not mine.*" She handed him the dress.

He took it, but he didn't seem to recognize it.

"I think it's Lara's." Simone could barely get the words past the tightness in her throat.

"I don't think so." He gave an adamant shake of his head. "When she died, I gathered up everything I had that belonged to her and gave the stuff to her siblings. I didn't keep anything, and don't you look at me like that. We'll have to talk to Marisa. I'll bet she'll know how that dress ended up in our closet."

Simone closed her eyes and drew in a deep breath. Marisa was his cleaning lady, a nice woman who treated Simone like a beloved niece.

"Sorry," she said. "It just shocked me to find it here...and you're right, after we got married, I emptied your closet and reorganized everything, and that dress wasn't here. I'm sorry. I was being stupid. Maybe she found it somewhere inside a box you forgot to give them and decided to hang it up."

Carl pulled her into his arms.

"Please never doubt how much I love you, Simone."

He kissed the top of her head, and tears came to her eyes, but she hid her face against his shoulder.

How stupid love has made me! I was never the jealous type. Take care my dear, jealousy is not love, it is passion.

"I know..." She nodded. "It just caught me off guard. Sorry..."

"Your reaction was pretty normal. I'd be jealous as hell if I found Doctor Frankenstein's clothes in our closet."

Simone laughed and pulled away so they could get dressed.

*****

Twenty minutes later, they were ready to leave. Tommy followed them to the front door, and Simone patted his head.

"Be a good boy. We'll be back soon," she told him.

His sad look said, *I will never forgive you for leaving me alone while you go have fun*, but Simone knew better. Tommy wasn't the sort to hold a grudge, and he'd be all over her when they walked into the condo a few hours later.

CHAPTER NINE

Chivon and Nuisances

Simone's stomach had butterflies, her palms were sweaty, and her heart raced when the intercom on her desk buzzed.

"Doctor, your first patient of the day is here," Patricia said.

Simone took a deep breath and forced herself to remain calm.

"Let her in."

A lovely, curvaceous woman entered Simone's office. Although she couldn't be more than five feet tall, her tight green dress showed a muscular physique and curves in all the right places. She looked like she was in her thirties, but according to her file, she was fifty.

How did she ever manage to reach middle age and still have such a flawless body and face?

The woman smiled at Simone, a confident smile. Apparently, psychiatrists didn't intimidate her.

"Good morning, Doctor, how've you been? I'm Chivon." She held out her hand to Simone.

"God is gracious," Simone said.

"Amen."

Simone swallowed back a laugh. "No, I was talking about the meaning of your name. Good morning, please take a seat."

Simone pointed to the green velvet sofa across from her leather armchair, but the woman chose the burgundy armchair next to Simone.

Not afraid of human contact I see.

"Yes, it's Irish for Siobhan. My father is Irish." She pointed at her red hair, the color of which could never be found in a bottle.

"Nice to meet you, Chivon! What brings you to my office?" Simone asked with a smile.

"Well, I'm a lawyer. I work in the office where your secretary used to work before you stole her from us, and she and I are friends. I happened to mention I needed therapy, and she always spoke so highly of you and your work, but you were on a year-long sabbatical, so I postponed my time on the couch"—she made quotation marks in the air— "until you came back. That was almost a year ago, but I decided if I needed to see a shrink, I would wait for the best."

Patricia had been telling people Simone was vacationing and would be back? That was news to Simone... She'd have to ask Patricia about that later.

Hell, I *didn't even know I would be back; how did Patricia know?*

"And why do you need therapy?"

Simone rested her elbows on the arms of the chair, assuming an open posture that would send a subconscious signal to her patient that she was willing to listen.

"I`m getting old...and I need to change my life, but I don't think I can change without help." She rested her hands in her lap and relaxed on the couch.

"What do you need to change? And why, exactly? You don't seem old to me. You come across as a confident, pretty, young woman."

"Tons of cosmetic treatments, lots of working out...this body and face are almost a second job for me, but time is cruel, and I don't know how long I can keep it in shape. I think it's time to settle down, find a good man to spend my so-called golden years with, and stop with all the fuss..."

"And by 'fuss,' you mean...?"

"Stop sleeping with men here and there, fucking around, you know?" She twirled her index finger in the air.

Simone raised a brow but kept silent.

"I have a different partner every night. Last night, for example, I had two guys in my bed." Chivon rolled her eyes and smiled, obviously pleased by the memory.

"You don't seem unhappy about that," Simone remarked.

"Well, no, I'm not! I really love sex, and when I can have two gorgeous guys to make me come, one in each hole, that's glorious... One sucking my clit while the other fucks me." She sighed. "That's my idea of perfection." Again, she rolled her eyes toward the ceiling, as if she was mentally reliving her orgasms.

Simone's vivid imagination conjured up the hot scene, and she decided to change the subject and try to lead the patient.

"Do you feel it's necessary to have someone special in your life?"

"It's worse than that! I don't! I like my life, but one must plan for the future and my future is not going to be defined by playing around." Chivon shook her hands in front of her, as if to dismiss such a horrid idea. "I need to settle down!"

"Well...let's define a few things. Do you want a man in your future because you need support? Company? Money? Maybe raise a family?"

Hard to do at her age, but not impossible.

Simone looked to the ceiling, trying to think of other

reasons a woman might want to get married and settle down.

"I've been a lawyer for almost twenty years. I'm a partner with the firm I work at, and I'm a good one. I have my own apartment, I have money, I've traveled the world, so no, I don't need someone to support me. And Jesus, a family? Never! I hate kids!" She turned a little bit, her back toward Simone. Her body language couldn't speak louder.

"So, we've established you don't *need* a man, and you don't want a family. You need to help me here… Why settle down if you're happy with the way things are now?"

"Who's going to fuck me when I'm an old lady? I mean, a husband is legally obligated to do that, aren't they?" She shrugged.

Chivon turned abruptly back to Simone and leaned toward her, throwing her arms in the air.

Simone struggled to keep a straight face.

She looks so clever, but she's emotionally an idiot.

"Well, correct me if I'm wrong, but I'm guessing you've never been married, right?" Asked Simone.

"Thank God, I escaped that fate until now." She lifted her arms toward the ceiling as if to praise the Lord.

Talk about dramatic… She should try the stage.

"Well, Chivon, I have some bad news. Usually, married couples have sex less and less often because as time goes by, their desire for intimacy decreases." Simone frowned.

Is that what's happening to me and Carl?

But no… She wanted him…badly. Yet, they hadn't had sex once throughout the entire weekend.

He's been really busy with work… He was tired…

"That's what my married friends say, but I think it's their fault. Every one of them decided to slack off after they got married."

"Slack off?"

"Yeah, you know…they stopped taking care of themselves. Let themselves go… They stopped dressing sexy and bought sweatpants to wear while they lounge around the house. Who'd want to fuck someone with tangled hair and dressed in old sweatpants?"

"Not all women do that."

I don't.

But then again, she had stopped bothering to put on makeup on her days off…

"I've seen plenty… A woman is the most beautiful girl in town, but then she finds a man, gets married, has kids, and decides beauty is a thing of her past. And the men? They immediately grow a belly, start wearing long shorts and shirts that are so tight, the buttons look like they're ready to explode off at any moment, and they hold barbecues as if life revolves around eating!"

Immediately, Simone thought of Carl wearing his old robe around the house.

At least he still goes to the gym.

"You have a very pessimistic view of marriage, and yet, you still want to join the lifestyle. What's to guarantee you won't find yourself in the same kind of trap you just described? There are no guarantees in love." Simone shook her head.

Chivon smiled and gave Simone a look of superiority, as if the woman knew something the rest of the human population was too stupid to comprehend.

"I have the solution for that. I won't fall in love. I'm going to find a man who loves me, who's mad about me, and then I'm going to marry him and make him my permanent slave." She reclined back in her armchair, looking as pleased with herself as if she had just invented the wheel.

"Do you really think that's such a good idea? Have you ever talked with women who married for reasons other than love?" Simone had to fight the urge to make a harsh response. She wanted to shout at the woman...tell her how dumb and pretentious she was if she thought married life could ever be as sweet as pie, especially if a couple weren't in love. But she couldn't do anything so unprofessional. Instead, she would work to try to make the woman see reality for herself.

"Nobody will confess they married for reasons other than love..."

Chevon glanced away, but not before Simone spotted the doubt flickering in the woman's eyes, which were now slightly narrowed. The know-it-all smile that had been on her face moments earlier had vanished, as well.

"Yes, they will. Well, maybe not directly, but you're a lawyer. You know when people are using metalanguage. So, this is your homework for next week. I want you to ask your married friends why they tied the knot, and then find out how the marriage is going. I think you're going to be surprised by what you discover." Simone glanced at her watch then smiled with relief. "Our time is over for today."

As Chivon left Simone's office, she checked her schedule. Just Chivon for the whole morning, and then a woman named Elizabeth in the afternoon.

Good times! I remember when I didn't have time to take a lunch.

A year ago, Simone wouldn't have kept a client like Chivon because she couldn't dredge up the required sympathy to treat a woman whose selfish, self-centered attitude had created her present struggles. But after giving up her practice —or, as Patricia called it, taking a year-long sabbatical— Simone couldn't afford to be picky about her patients. She found herself back where she started, taking on any patient who walked through her door and dealing with a lot of uncertainty.

Despite the challenges, Simone was grateful for her job at the university, which provided stability and allowed her to avoid the true hardships of starting over. It wasn't like being back in the dark ages or having to count pennies, It was a humbling experience that reminded her why she started this journey in the first place. She truly believed she could help people achieve balance in their lives, and she didn't mind if the person was someone she despised; every patient deserved professional treatment.

*****

Instead of sitting around the office until her afternoon appointment, Simone decided to head home and take care of a few house maintenance tasks that had piled up recently. After she had done everything, she could, she decided to go for a short run. She needed to get back into shape; for the past few months, she had been lazy, and she could really stand to lose about five pounds.

Simone had lunch on her porch. It was cold and cloudy, but the view of the ocean compensated for the bad weather. Looking out on the water always calmed her mind and helped her think more clearly.

Fifteen minutes before three, she was back in her office, ready to greet one more client. Beth sat in a chair in front of Patricia's desk, and the two women were chatting and laughing. Several boxes sat near Beth's feet. Simone sighed. What a time for Beth to bring Ed's stuff.

"Hello, Beth. How've you been? Are these Ed's belongings? Sorry, but I don't have time to check them now. Can you leave them with Patricia? I have a client in few minutes."

"I'm your new patient." Beth smiled, seeming to enjoy the surprised look Simone gave the woman. "Do you remember I told you I needed a favor in return for gathering up all Ed's stuff?"

CHAPTER TEN

Something Admirable About You

The audacity of this woman is truly unbelievable. I dislike Beth so much—how can I treat her?

"Well...yes, you said so, but I can't treat you. It wouldn't be ethical. Your ex-husband was my partner..." Simone searched her mind for the words to explain.

Beth didn't allow Simone to finish.

"And you slept with him, I know, but I also know you are the best shrink in town. I need therapy, and you promised me, so I think—" Beth looked on her phone. "Our session begins in five minutes!" She smiled and sat down again.

Simone stared at the woman for a moment before walking down the hallway to her office.

How do I get rid of that pain in the ass without her making a scene?

Beth had a bad habit of throwing a tantrum when she didn't get her way or things didn't go as planned. Simone didn't have an easy answer. Resigned, she put her handbag on her desk, buzzed Patricia to let her know the patient could come in, and then went to her leather armchair, picking up her notepad and pen from her desk as she passed by. She had barely settled when Beth entered.

"So, you have guts after all..." Beth remarked, a skewed

smile playing at the corner of her mouth.

Simone sighed. She'd have to establish the pecking order here, or she and her new client would have problems. She pointed to the green velvet sofa. "Doctor Bennet or just Doctor."

"What?" Beth widened her big brown eyes.

"If you want me to treat you, from now on, you'll address me as Doctor Bennet or just Doctor, and if you call me by my first name again or 'shrink,' I'm done."

"That's ridiculous." Beth's face turned red.

"No, that's professional. Do you want a professional, or do you need someone to listen to your complaints? If you're only looking for a shoulder to cry on, I won't be able to help you. We aren't friends. In fact, I've never liked you, but as a professional, I will treat you the best I can and will try my best to ignore the things I know about you and listen to your version. So, what will it be?"

Beth sat quietly for a few seconds, looking at the floor, and then said, "Doctor Bennet it is."

Simone had learned throughout her career that maintaining distance between herself and her patients was essential for preserving perspective and objectivity. But the woman had always managed to get under Simone's skin. Preoccupied with her own struggles and a messy divorce at the time, she didn't remember the exact timing or details of how Beth had come into Edward's life. When she realized that Beth—an eighteen-year-old high school cheerleader, who seemed to have no more than two neurons in her head—had crossed Ed's path, it was too late: the girl was pregnant."

From the moment Beth had a baby in her belly, she'd turned Simone's friend's life into a living hell.

That's what he told you, and you believed him. You also thought he was a good person, but he ended up helping a criminal.

Simone closed her eyes and regrouped, pushing back the past. She took a deep breath then looked at Beth.

"Elizabeth, what brings you to my office?" Simone started with the first question she asked all her new patients.

Beth leaned forward, joined her hands, and looked deeply into Simone's eyes.

"I don't want to live anymore. I only keep going for my son, and he'll be leaving home soon. I don't know if I'll have the strength to continue living, but he only has me. My husband is in jail for life, and I'm alone, lost and done, I'm an old rag!" A stream of tears accompanied the angry tirade.

"Elizabeth, how old are you?" Simone lowered her gaze to the notepad.

"I'll be thirty-nine next month. An old lady!"

"Hardly. Only if you want to think about yourself that way. Have you ever worked? Had a job?"

"Yes, I'm a full-time mom!" Anger filled her tone once again.

"No, that's not a career, that's a choice. I'm not saying it's not important, but what I'm trying to establish is if you have any skills to survive outside your home."

"I don't, and I don't intend to work, and that's not the point here. The point is to make my life easier, not to add more problems."

Simone kept her gaze on her notepad to hide her annoyed expression. Beth sounded like a spoiled child.

"That's exactly what I'm trying to do. Your first complaint is that your responsibilities involved with raising your son are almost over, and you feel empty. So, let's look at your choice of being a full-time mom as if it was a career, and let's compare it to that of a secretary trained to use an old-fashioned typewriter. What did those professionals do when the computer came along? They had two choices; learn new skills or stop growing and expanding their abilities and lose their jobs. You are about to lose your lifetime job as a mom, so, what can you do to give a new meaning to your life?"

"Have another child?" Beth waved a hand in a way that seemed to indicate she hadn't taken the question seriously. As if she'd given up seeking an answer before she'd even begun to give the question any thought.

What a perfect drama queen.... Two patients in one day, and both are candidates for an Oscar. God, give me patience, lots of it. I must at least try.

"That's a possibility," she said, playing along as if Beth's suggestion had any merit. "But do you think it would be wise? You'll need to be in some kind of an intimate relationship—is there a man in your life now?"

Or will you just trap another idiot who trusts you enough to have unprotected sex?

Simone bit her lip to keep from uttering the statement aloud.

Beth answered with a shake of her head.

"Okay, well, even if you could find a man and form another relationship quickly, you'd have to face a few more challenges. Carrying a baby when you're in your forties can be dangerous. You'd probably need to get your son's approval, or he may feel betrayed, and you'd be juggling another relationship with a new baby in your arms—that means tons of problems, endless sleepless nights, and overwhelming exhaustion for at least a year... Are you up to handling all that?"

"I...I don't think I can." Beth lowered her head. "See? I don't know what to do!" Her shoulders drooped in an overly exaggerated show of helplessness.

“You don’t have financial problems as far as I know. You are your son’s legal guardian, and Ed had some properties that give you some income, right?”

“Right...And I have some that are mine, which I received in the divorce. I’ll have to pay my son’s tuition and his expenses while he’s in college, but there’s plenty left for me.” She lifted her nose.

It’s important to her not to be confused with someone who is poor. What issues did she face in her past? Simone could only guess.

“Let’s do something different here. I need to understand you better to help you, Elizabeth. So, I need to know about your childhood.”

“And if I don’t want to go there?” Beth’s inquisitive eyes were on Simone.

“Then I won’t be able to help you.” Simone placed her notepad and pen on the coffee table next to her.

Hold your ground, Beth. Tell me thanks but no thanks and leave...

Simone kept her fingers crossed. Maybe she wouldn’t have to treat this annoying woman after all.

“Pick up your tablet again please. I’ll tell you.” Beth pointed to the abandoned notepad.

“So, tell me...” Simone said, paper and pen in hand.

“I’m the only daughter of an older couple. I don’t know anything about my birth; I don’t think I ever heard them talk about it. My mother was always working until late, and my father was distant. When they used to come home from work, I was already sleeping, and when I was ten years old, they both died in a stupid accident.” She paused, looked at her perfectly manicured red nails, and then continued.

“I only had an auntie on my mother’s side left, and she took me in. Aunt Lisa was a widow, and she worked even harder than my parents to make ends meet. I had a cousin who was three years older than me, and I had to wear all her old clothes—clothes Aunt Lisa had purchased at the second-hand store, and believe me, by the time I got them, they were practically rags! Food was scarce, bathroom outside, no heating… I'm sure you can imagine how fun all that was for a little girl."

"Yes, I can."

"But my aunt believed education was the key to escape that life, so my cousin Priscilla and I attended the public school in our neighborhood... Can I trust you, Simone? Are you supposed to keep anything I tell you confidential? You wouldn't disclose any information about your patients, right?" Beth's eyebrows rose as she asked the question.

"I wouldn't do it, even if I could—unless your behavior put your life or someone else's in danger. Simone spoke in a serious, authoritative tone, looking directly into Beth's eyes. This seemed to put her at ease, as the woman nodded and continued with her tale."

"That´s not the case. It is shameful, but not dangerous." She shook her head and continued: "Well, when I was about sixteen years old, my cousin started to buy new clothes, and suddenly, she had some money. She started to help her mom, and for the first time we had heat during the winter. She wouldn't tell us where the money came from, and I don't think my aunt wanted to know, but I did. So, one day I followed my cousin, and I discovered she was going out with a man who looked like he was in his seventies! I quickly understood what was happening, but I couldn't say she was wrong. She'd come up with a ticket out of that miserable life! Only people who have lived a life like we did know the feeling and the importance of getting out of it!"

"Was she a prostitute?"

"In a way, yes, but she only had that old bat, her sugar

daddy…" Beth rolled her eyes. "Even if she was selling her body and soul, she wasn't standing on a dark corner like a hooker. And I thought she was clever, because her only asset was her beauty, which wouldn't last forever without proper care, and we couldn't afford to take proper care of anything—not even our health!"

"Did you try the same path?" Simone looked directly into Beth's eyes.

The woman answered without averting her gaze.

"I have to confess I considered doing the same thing, but I came up with a better idea." Beth put a finger to the side of her head and tapped her temple. "I would find myself a good husband, not just a lover, so I started looking, and two years later I met Edward. But from the beginning, he only had eyes for you, even if he denied it. I fell in love with him. He was so polite, so considerate, and so charming."

That's the Edward I knew my whole life.

Simone sucked in a deep breath at the sharp pain in her chest.

I need to know the truth about him, and I need to try to help him.

"I needed to have him for myself—it became my only goal. He was responsible… He would support me… The only problem? He didn't want me, and I tried everything to seduce him. Finally, I decided I would drag him to my bed and get pregnant." She lowered her head and continued without looking at Simone. She was ashamed.

"One day, he got drunk because of you and your lack of interest, and I took advantage of the opportunity. When he woke up the next morning and found me in his bed, he was miserable. I told him he had taken my virginity, which was true, and he didn't know what to do. A month later, I told him I had conceived. Of course, he did the right thing and married me, so yes, I trapped him, and I paid for my actions throughout all the years of our marriage."

She paid? She was always yelling, embarrassing Ed, making his life miserable!

Simone blinked and cleared her mind of the thoughts.

"The more I loved him, the more I knew he would never love me. I could see he felt trapped in a marriage he didn't want. He considered me more of an embarrassment than a woman, and besides, he had always loved you, always praised your talents, your beauty... I had to listen your name... a thousand. times a day!" Beth banged one hand against the arm of her chair, emphasizing each word.

"I tried my best to make him fall in love with me, but he couldn't. You were like a disease in his life, and only death could break the bond he had with you! And then one day, when I confronted him about his feelings for you, he didn't deny it. In fact, he confessed to everything I always suspected —you were the love of his life. I told him to leave, and he marched out the door. Just like that, he had the courage to get out. He left me!

When Beth finished, she had tears in her eyes, and Simone pitied her and Edward, both trapped in a marriage without love.

But she's to blame her. Ed was just being the perfect gentleman all the time, and— Before she could finish her thought, she gave herself a mental shake. *That's so biased!*

"Congratulations, Elizabeth, you were able to summarize an entire life in a few sentences. Not many patients can do that! Let's establish some points here. You were poor, you decided to leave a difficult life behind you, and you had the courage to pay the price. You know a lot about choices and consequences. Now you're approaching middle age—"

"Middle age?" Beth shouted.

"How long do you think you can live? Have you ever thought about that? A hundred years? Eighty? The life expectancy statistics say women in America live to age seventy-eight, seventy-nine years old. So, if we consider the statistics, you're going to be middle aged in one or two years."

"I want to die now. I came here for help, and you make me feel like an old bat!" Beth shouted again.

My God, I'll need ears tampons to get through sessions with this woman. How did Ed ever put up with her?

"No, you're not an old bat; you're a pretty woman, and what you must do is establish new goals for your future. When you wanted to escape poverty, you had a goal, and not even Edward's lack of love for you made you give up. You're a fighter. However, you're not really living right now."

As Beth lifted her head and stared, Simone explained.

"You started off today by telling me—" Simone looked down and read from her notepad. 'I don't want to live anymore,' am I correct?"

"Yes, that's what I said." She pointed to Simone's notepad.

"So, in my opinion, you're not living; you're just existing, which is no life at all. You might not be poor anymore, but at least back then, you had a goal. Now, you don't have that. You have nothing to work for and nothing to look forward to. You need to establish a goal for the rest of your life, or at least for the next few years, or your life will become even emptier and more meaningless."

Usually, Simone wouldn't tell a patient what to do, but this was not a regular patient. This was Beth, and Simone needed the woman back on track quickly to get rid of her.

Petty feelings, Doctor Bennet...

"I would like a man to fall in love with me and make me happy again!" Beth said.

"That's not possible! Nobody can make you happy. That's

fairy tale stuff. Real life doesn't work that way. You must make yourself happy before you can expect someone else to be happy with you. You don't need a rescuer anymore. Edward was the man who saved you—he took you out of poverty, gave you a comfortable life, but as you said, he never loved you. Do you want someone to love you? Do you know what true love is? How love works?"

Do I?

Simone asked herself, waiting for the woman to answer.

"Love is when your legs shake, and you feel butterflies in your stomach." Beth spoke with a dreamy expression.

That was exactly how Simone felt about her husband, but that wasn't true love...

"No, that's adrenaline, passion. Love is companionship, the pleasure of being with someone, even if you do nothing but hold hands and watch a movie. Love is creating and pursuing common dreams, planning a future together, and knowing someone will be there for you when you're feeling blue or to help you celebrate when you accomplish something important. Have you ever had that?" Simone smiled.

I have that with my husband...and the butterflies...

"No. I haven't. I just had Edward in my life and then a couple morons. Nothing even close to what you just described."

"That's because you need to revise the way you think. You're not Cinderella... There is no charming prince coming your way to rescue you. A man falls in love with a woman he admires, but how do you expect someone else to respect and adore you when you don't love yourself? You don't want to live anymore... What admirable qualities do you have?"

"I'm a good mom, and I'm still pretty..." Beth grimaced.

"Most men don't need another mother, and if you find one who does, I recommend you run to other way. Besides, even if you found yourself attracted to a grown man who needed mothering"—Simone paused to make a derisive sound and shake her head— "you don't want to be a mother anymore. And if someone loves you just because of your figure or your pretty face, that won't last. Homework for next session—find something admirable about you, a positive quality—and we can work to enhance that and think about ways to give significance to your life from now on. Our session is over."

CHAPTER ELEVEN

Some Bears and Some Delusions

Thursday morning, Simone had an empty schedule. Instead of sitting around worrying about how she was going to pay the office bills and how to increase the number of patients she treated each month if she wanted to keep the clinic running, she decided to go to MacDougall again.

Inmates couldn't receive visitors whenever they pleased—they were only allowed to see friends or family on weekends, federal holidays, and on specific days of the week. But she was his psychiatrist, so her visits could be less rigid.

As Simone drove to prison, she asked herself why she was making these visits.

Maybe I'm trying to face my demons, or maybe I really do want to understand what happened and why. I really don't know what I'm doing...and not just about those visits...

Sooner or later, I'll figure it out...

She arrived at the prison, parked her car, and went directly to the visitors' center. Despite having special clearance, she still had to pass the inspection process to be admitted.

After stowing her belongings in a metal locker, Simone stood still while a tall, female officer patted her down. Ugh, she hated this part.

Another correctional officer, Mathew Wilson, with the

personality of a rock, who didn't bother to speak to her after greeting her and giving her his name, showed Simone to the visitors' room. People sat lined up along a bank of bulletproof glass and half-walled booths, where they talked on a telephone with the prisoners on the other side.

Simone paused. Why had the officer brought her here? Although this wasn't an authorized visitation day, she had come to see Peter in her capacity as a Doctor of psychiatry. She couldn't very well treat a patient in such a public area.

"Officer Wilson, please, can't we go to the infirmary? Perhaps you're not aware, I'm a psychiatrist, and Peter Hay is my patient." Simone did her best to maintain a pleasant tone and expression. Some of these guards were on a power trip and hated being questioned.

"Yes, Doctor, I know, but no, we can't go to the infirmary today." He gave her no explanation as he opened the door for her to enter the visitation area.

Simone sighed.

"After I meet with my patient, may I see Liam?"

"You mean Officer Sanderson? Here, we address people by their last names," he said, his nose in the air.

"Sorry, I don't know his last name."

"It is Sanderson."

Wilson's lips twisted in a scowl, but he said nothing more. He turned and left the room.

Simone chose an empty seat and watched through the glass partition as a guard led Peter to a small desk opposite of where she sat. He took a seat but didn't face her, his body turned to the phone on his left. He lifted the receiver and gestured for her to pick up the handset on her side to talk to him. Simone had seen this kind of communication set-up in movies, so she lifted the receiver and put it to her ear.

"I don't want visitors!"

Peter shouted so loudly, Simone's eardrum rattled, and she jerked the phone away from her head. An officer rushed over, and Simone put the phone back to her ear, listening as the man ordered Peter to behave unless he wanted his visit cancelled.

"Good morning, Peter, how've you been?" Simone spoke in a low, soothing voice, hoping to calm her patient enough for him to have a conversation with her.

"Great, I need to go to China… I must see the little bears. I *must* see the bears, or they are going to die! I don't think the caretakers are doing a good job, and we need more bears."

"I understand. You are not in the mood to talk today, but I would like to go back and pick up where we left off talking about Mona's death if you don't mind."

Peter finally turned to look at Simone through the smudged glass.

"Who is Mona? How about my little bears?" He lifted his cuffed hand to scratch his head, and the hand holding the phone rose, as well.

Simone waited until he put the receiver back to his ear, and then said, "Chinese bears? Do you mean pandas? Do you have one back in China? Do they allow people to own pandas?"

"Allowed? What does that mean? Do you think I need permission to do anything? I take what I want!" His voice rose, vibrating with anger.

Immediately, the officer returned to Peter's side and put a hand on his shoulder. Clearly, the man was positioned nearby, listening to their conversation.

"You need *my* permission to be here, and this is the last time I'm going to tell you to lower your voice!" the man yelled and shook Peter's shoulder.

Peter seemed unaffected. Instead of responding to the officer, he turned to Simone again.

"The bears are going to be dead if they don't behave! We need to replace them. I need to go to China," Peter rambled, his eyes darting rapidly back and forth, unfocused.

Simone studied him closely. He appeared disconnected from reality, as if something had triggered a complete psychotic break.

I must engage with his delirium and try to figure out what he's talking about. She prepared herself to carefully navigate the conversation.

"I think there's a nature reserve for them in China, isn't there?" she asked.

"Yes, that's what I'm talking about. But someone needs to go there to get them." Peter scratched his head again. "All my hard work is going down the drain!"

His voice rose again, and Simone cringed and steeled herself for the guard's angry response.

An instant later, the big man appeared on the other side of the glass, grabbed Peter by his elbow, and yanked him to his feet. Giving him a small shove, the officer forced Peter from the room. Simone craned her neck and watched as her patient shuffled out the door, looking more like someone who'd lost his marbles than an intelligent, cunning killer.

Bears? China? We need to replace them? What does all that mean?

How had Peter gotten into such a state? What had made him lose touch with reality? Simone hung up the receiver, and a few minutes later, someone put a light hand on her shoulder. Simone spun around in her seat, heart racing, and then let out her breath and relaxed.

Liam!

"Doctor, good morning! How've you been? My colleague told me you wanted to see me. Let me take you out of here."

"Good morning, Liam, yes, please. Can we go somewhere

private? I'd like to talk to you for a minute."

"Absolutely. How was your meeting with Hay today?"

"Not good…" She shook her head. "He seemed to be on the moon. Do you know if something happened? Did he have any other visitors recently? Peter wouldn't be acting that way for no reason. Something must have triggered him."

"I don't know, but I can check for you if you think it's important. What was he doing when you tried to talk to him?" Liam asked.

"He is having a sort of psychotic crisis today, and he only gets that way if something happens to cause it," she explained as she walked by his side down the dismal gray corridor.

"I don't know anything about triggers, but more and more lately, he seems to be off his rocker. He talks about things nobody can understand. Seems to me he's clearly losing control, as if his dark side is taking over. It's a pity, really, because he seems to be a smart man when he pulls himself together." He shook his head.

"He is smart. Smart and dangerous, and probably he'll never get any better because he doesn´t want to be treated. I don't trust him, so I advise you to be cautious. Maybe he's faking these supposed breakdowns." She shrugged. "Or maybe they're real. It's hard to say with Hay."

They arrived at a set of sliding doors made up of iron bars. Liam put his finger into a security scanner, and a second later, a loud buzz indicated the door was unlocked. They crossed through, and Liam closed the doors behind them. A second set of security doors opened, and Liam led the way through them and down a hall to a room Simone recognized. This was where they registered visitors. Liam approached a computer, typed in a password, and booted the system.

"Hay had a visitor on Sunday, a man called Wang Zhang Li.

Says here he has special permission to visit Hay." He pointed to the screen.

"Special permission? Is he a relative?" Simone asked.

"It doesn't say." Liam shrugged. "Sometimes, people get permission for various reasons. I'm sorry I can't be more helpful." Liam clicked the mouse, and another page opened on the computer monitor. He glanced at it for a moment then turned to her. "He's been here several times. I have a suspicion—since Peter identifies as gay—he must be a boyfriend or something like that." He smiled. "Is there anything else I can do for you, Doctor?"

"Would you tell Doctor Reynolds I would like to see him? He doesn't want to talk to me. We used to be friends…but I think he's hurt because I didn't support him when he went to trial…" She averted her gaze and lowered her voice, her throat growing tight. "But you know… The evidence was so solid…"

She looked back at him.

"I understand…I can try…" He nodded.

"Or better yet, would you find a way for me to be a volunteer in the program you told me about the other day?"

"I can check. I'll have to ask to the coordinator."

"Is Doctor Reynolds the coordinator?" If that was the case, she'd have a better chance at winning the lottery.

"No, he was the creator of the program, but the coordinator must be a correctional officer. I'll ask him. I think he'll be happy to grant you permission to help. We can always use more volunteers around here."

Simone smiled and reached out to shake Liam's hand. "Thanks a lot, Liam, that will mean a lot to me."

"You're welcome, Doctor. Please leave me a phone number, and I'll contact you with an answer."

Simone gave him her cellphone number, and they said goodbye.

*****

On the drive home, Simone's head spun with the information about Peter's visitor.

Can he be the accomplice? The we *Peter mentioned while telling me about Mona? Who is this guy, and how did he get permission to visit Peter?*

The moment Simone arrived home, she parked in the garage, jumped from the car, opened the door, locked it behind her, and then turned on the alarm system.

Old habits die hard...

After everything that had happened—the deaths of her secretary and patients, her housekeeper, the kidnapping of both her and her daughter- personal security had become an obsession she wished she could leave behind, just to feel safe again. Simone entered the kitchen, put her purse on the island countertop, and hurried into the in-home office she and Carl shared. She turned on her computer, dropped into the office chair, and opened a browser. "Wang Zhang Li," she said as she typed the name into Google.

The search returned with thousands of results; apparently, the last name came first in Chinese. She tried typing in Wang, only to learn it was the most common surname in China.

Not helpful. But at least I know he is Chinese.

How can I find out who this guy is? Is he important or just some distant cousin or friend, or maybe a boyfriend as Lian suggested?

If she could uncover his identity, she might find a clue related to the murders that resulted in Peter's life sentence.

The sound of her phone ringing drew her from her thoughts. She hurried back to the kitchen and pulled her cellphone from her purse, but the ringing had stopped. A missed call from Carl... She dialed him back.

"Hello, love, busy?" Carl said in his husky voice.

"Hello, honey not at all. I'm home," she replied.

"The complicated case I was working on is over. I know it ruined our weekend last time, but I was thinking... If your schedule is not too hectic, how about coming here tomorrow? We could be together, have a nice meal, I could have you in my arms and in my bed..."

"Honey...you said the same thing last weekend, and you ended up working the entire time I was there. Can I trust you this time? Because, besides walking Tommy, I don't have much to do in the city."

"Yes, I promise. I was hoping to finish the case by the time you got here last weekend, but as I read through it, I found so much relevant information that I had to keep going, I needed more research. But I'm almost finished, I swear. I might have another two hours of work to do tomorrow then I'll be done. So, will you spend the weekend with me again? *Pleaseeeee*."

"Okay. I suppose I can give you one more chance. Besides, it's not like I have a dozen handsome men calling and begging me to spend the weekend with them. And my schedule is almost empty—not so great when I think about how I'm going to pay the office bills next month, but since I don't have a long line of clients waiting to see me this weekend, it's great news for you. I'll be happy to join you in the city."

"Excellent! How has your day been so far?"

Carl always asked that question, and unlike most people, he had an honest interest in her answer—in who she saw, what she did, how difficult or easy things were going for her. He loved telling her about his day, but she didn't enjoy sharing those kinds of details about her own. To her, it felt like reliving the entire day, and she found it exhausting—like working all over again. But Carl seemed to need to hear every detail.

"I went to MacDougall..."

"Really? Again? Can you go in and out of there any time you want?"

"I have special permission—a Doctor's pass—now. Patricia got it for me."

"I think I'm going to hire Patricia. I could use someone with her kind of connections. But you know I could have fixed that for you, honey. I'm a lawyer, remember?"

"For me, you are my love... I didn't want to disturb you. You have plenty of responsibilities already. Carl, changing the subject, do you recognize the name Wang Zhang Li?"

"Nope, should I?" he answered quickly.

"I saw Peter today, and he was completely out of it...talking about bears and China, total nonsense. One of the guards said he's been like that since Sunday, so I thought he might have had a visitor who upset him or made him... I don't know, disconnect? The same guard who told me Peter had been acting oddly since Sunday checked the visitor log for me. Peter had a visitor by the name of Wang Zhang Li. It seems this guy has been visiting him for some time now."

"It's hard to get permission to visit someone in jail if you're not a family member or a Doctor." Carl sounded intrigued.

"Can you find out how this guy got permission? I'd appreciate your services, Counselor."

"Before you can visit MacDougall, you need to be placed on the inmate's approved visiting list. I don't think it will be too hard to find that information, and if it's important to you, I'll find a way to get it.

"There's a very nice officer there who could confirm that the guy is on the list, but he couldn't figure out the reason why."

"That shouldn't be too hard—it's usually public information. Maybe they classified it for some reason... but

I'll find a way to get it."

"How?"

"I have an idea..."

CHAPTER TWELVE

The Perfect Woman and a Bear

After her Friday morning run and a good breakfast, Simone prepared for the day. She was going to the city in the afternoon.

After a quick shower, she sat at her vanity and applied a tiny bit of makeup. Her skin looked better than usual—no dark circles under her brown eyes—so she opted for just a little powder, some mascara, and an almost transparent lipstick. Then she vigorously brushed her hair.

Simone went to her closet to find something to wear and chose the purple sheath dress she loved. Sleeveless and made of a cotton-rayon blend with just a little spandex, the dress caressed her skin. She pulled a matching suit jacket off its hanger and grabbed a pair of black patent leather high heels.

Once dressed, she took a last look in the full-length mirror.

Perfect... and ready to face the world. Not that she had many things to face that day...

Damn it, I really need to fill my schedule!

Simone forced herself to stop stressing. Worrying caused too much anxiety, and she was trying to practice meditation and mindfulness again.

It's time to regain control of my life.

If she didn't, her fears were going to rule her, and her life would be hell.

The purse she'd carried yesterday was still on the kitchen island countertop.

I'm getting disorganized!

Promising herself she'd do better, she headed out, closing the door and engaging the security alarm behind her.

*****

When Simone arrived at her office, she pulled in and parked beside a beautiful black Lamborghini. Another black car with two men inside was on the other side.

Someone wealthy is in my office!

She'd never had a patient with a Lambo before.

Simone entered her office, ready to greet her mysterious visitor, but only Patricia was in the reception area. She welcomed Simone with a huge smile. "Good morning, Doctor! Your first patient is in the waiting room."

Waiting room? I don't have one of those...

She opened her mouth to ask Patricia what she meant, but the mischievous look in her eyes made Simone pause. Apparently, there was more going on here than met the eye.

Oh, what the hell. Might as well play along.

She cleared her throat.

"Sorry, Patricia, I didn't check my schedule for the day. Who is my first patient?"

"Mr. Benjamin Taylor-Miller, Doctor."

Patricia handed a file to Simone. She shook her head. The name didn't ring a bell, but Simone could tell by the excitement in her secretary's voice, their new patient was a huge deal. Simone leaned close and whispered near Patricia's ear.

"And where is our waiting room?"

"The room between your office and Doctor Reynolds' that you set up as a place to get some rest," she whispered back. "Last night when I heard about the new patient, I came back, found the keys to the connecting door, and organized a bit in there. Now you can receive your patients through the connecting door, and when they finish, they can leave through the door that leads from your office into the hallway. Famous people don't want to be seen going to a shrink, and they believe they deserve special treatment, such as private exits and entrances so they aren't seen by other patients who are being treated before and after them."

How clever is this woman?

"And who is this famous man?" Simone whispered again.

"The king of insurance in America. Filthy rich. Billionaire. You get him, and you'll need more lines in your schedule and more hours in your days!"

"Now, *that* sounds like a problem I'd love to have! I'm going to take a moment to look over his file. I'll ask him in myself in just a moment." Simone went into her office, grateful for Patricia's ideas. Whoever this guy was, he'd be an important start for her to rebuild her career.

Simone entered her office, put her purse on the desk, and looked at the connecting door. She saw it every day—had looked at it in passing for years. So how had she forgotten about it until Patricia mentioned it? The room that separated Edward's office from her own was supposed to be used as a place for either of them to get a little rest in between clients, but Simone had never used it. Back then, her schedule had been so tight, she'd never had a spare minute to take a quick break.

Simone stood before the decorative mirror in the corner, inspecting her outfit for any signs of disorder, but everything was perfectly in place. She took the brush from inside her purse, ran it through her hair again, and then reapplied her lip-gloss.

Dress for success and it will come!

She put her hand on the brushed gold doorknob but then stopped. Her stomach lurched a little, and she grew queasy. Nerves? At this late stage of her career? Ridiculous. Get yourself together, Simone!

Riding a wave of adrenaline over the idea of taking on a new client—a *wealthy* new client—she took a deep breath and opened the door.

Benjamin looked nothing at all like a billionaire, except for the suit. Made of very fine wool, the suit looked as if it had been handcrafted and screamed, *"You could never afford me!"*

The man was sitting on the blue velvet couch, his legs hanging over the front and his feet dangling inches above the floor. When he saw her, he leaped from the couch, took her hand, and kissed her knuckles.

My God, he's less than five feet tall!

Simone forced herself to keep a straight face and cleared her throat.

"Good morning, Mr. Taylor-Miller, nice to meet you. Please come into my office." Simone pulled her hand from his grip and stepped back, indicating the open door behind her.

"After you, Doctor, and please call me Ben. All my friends do!" He gave her a broad smile, showing off a set of porcelain capped teeth.

Too white...no way they're real...not at his age! *Money don't buy good taste.*

He waved his arm, gesturing for her to pass in front of him.

"Mr. Taylor-Miller..." Purposely, Simone used his complete last name. "Please have a seat. I'm going to sit on the green couch, and you can choose whatever looks most comfortable to you—" She waved toward the chairs and sofa. "But please stay where we can see each other."

In Simone's experience, rich men needed discipline, and she was going to start early with this one.

"As I said before, no need for formalit—"

"Yes, there is all the need for formalities here." Simone gave an emphatic nod. "If I'm supposed to be your Doctor, we need to set some boundaries, or we can't work together."

His smile disappeared, but he sat on the couch directly across from her.

Not worried about a bit of combat. Brave, little man.

"I must insist on you using my full first name at least. Call me Benjamin. Mr. Taylor-Miller is my old man—not a very good person—and I don't want to be confused with him." He waved his little hands in a negative gesture and shook his head.

Little people often went overboard when trying to make a point...

"Fine, Benjamin it is...but don't even think about calling me Simone. Please use Doctor Bennet."

He issued a military salute and said, "Yes, General."

She had to restrain a smile. She kind of liked the little guy...

"Who recommended you, and what brings you to see me, Benjamin?"

When it came to patients who seemed to have trouble getting to the point, she almost always started a session with the same set of questions. They seemed to help stop the inane chatter and helped the patient focus.

"Well...an acquaintance told me some time ago you were a great Doctor. I took your contact information and thought many times about calling you. Obviously, I didn't, though your name never left my mind. Now, I've forgotten who the friend was."

He smiled, and Simone could tell he was lying—a horrible way to begin and a sign of future trouble—but she didn't have the luxury of rejecting patients these days.

"I can't be your Doctor if your friend is still my patient."

"I don't think so... I've heard you only recently restarted your practice and don't have many patients." This time, his smile said, *I know you need me.*

"And what about my second question? What brought you here?" She tried to regain control of the situation, refusing to comment on the fullness of her schedule—or lack thereof.

"So many things..." The man rolled his eyes.

"Let me ask this another way... What is the most urgent thing that brings you here?" Simone took her notepad from the coffee table.

"I'm in love, she is all that I hate and that I love at the same time, and she is precisely what I don't need in my life!" He stopped and waited for Simone's reaction.

"Are you single? Divorced? Married?"

"Oh, sorry...divorced twice," he said, holding up two fingers. "And I told myself I'd never get married again. But now, all I can think about is going to the nearest Tiffany's, buying the most ridiculously large diamond to put on her finger, saying some vows—and doing my best to believe in them for once—and then locking her in my room and fucking her the whole day!"

Aha...and here comes sex...

Simone drew a deep breath.

"Well, let's break this down a little bit. There are two particular things in what you just described that I'd like to understand a little better, and then we can go through the rest, okay?"

"Yes, yes, go ahead, Doc!"

He moved his little arms and legs at the same time, and Simone had to work hard not to laugh. He had to be in his mid-forties, and his tiny body didn't match his age. It had a childlike quality; a charming advantage small people have.

"You just said you would like to say some vows and try to believe in them for once. What did you mean by that?"

"It means my previous marriages were not based on sweet promises of love and fidelity; they were based on the practical reasons most men marry—the woman would be the perfect housewife, the perfect companion, and the perfect person to help me make more connections for my business... and of course, beautiful."

He used his fingers to create quotation marks each time he listed a previous motive for getting married.

"But some men marry for love, don't they?" Simone asked.

"Maybe the poor ones, or the richest ones, old money, the ones without goals and ambitions. I've always wanted to be somebody."

"Were you poor?"

"I was not exactly poor, but middle class is poor in my opinion, so I needed to think outside the box." He used his hands a lot, waving them around as he explained his reasoning.

Simone tipped her head.

"What does that mean, exactly?"

"Planning the way strategically." He used two fingers to move, like little legs climbing imaginary steps.

"So, you had to marry the so-called right woman, but what about now? You're wealthy, so you don't need the perfect woman anymore. What's wrong with marrying someone you're in love?"

"Rich men always need the perfect woman. What would

our investors and friends think? That we can't afford a proper woman?"

Afford? Did the little man believe women were objects? Some kind of merchandise?

Simone grew annoyed. "And this woman you're in love with...she's not perfect? Is she ugly? Poor?"

"She is beautiful! A beautiful face and the most delicious body!" He rolled his eyes. "But she is old!"

Theodora, one of Simone's previous patients, popped into her mind.

Is this guy in love with someone old enough to be his mother?

An older woman who'd been in a relationship with a man half her age, Theodora had been one of Simone's patients who had been murdered.

"How old is she?"

Benjamin lowered his voice and said, "About fifty."

Simone remained silent for a moment. A few years from fifty, she'd just been told a millionaire had no use for a fifty-year-old woman.

How nice...I will be an useless old bat.

"I don't see the problem here. Let's see...you're what? A millionaire?" She knew the answer, but she didn't want him to know she'd been informed of his background.

"Billionaire!" He corrected her and inflated his chest like a peacock.

This guy is outrageous... And yet, for some strange reason, she found herself appreciating his ways, at times, he felt like a living caricature.

"On the other hand, you could look at it this way; you're a billionaire, so you can *afford* any relationship that pleases you. Another man might need to parade around with a trophy wife on his arm, but you can have the one you love and make them jealous over your happiness. Because you are so sure of yourself, you don't need to prove anything to anybody."

"Yeah...good point, Doc, but...there are other things I hate about her, and since I know you're going to ask me what those are, here it goes: she is too independent, she won't give up her career, and..." He hesitated for a minute, looked around the room as if someone might be spying on them, and then added, "She fucked the whole town, and I have no faith she'll stop just because we get married!"

And they were back on the topic of sex... Simone gave him a small smile. *It always comes down to sex.*

"You're smiling, Doctor..."

She nodded. He seemed very observant.

"Sorry, I'm not smiling about your list of her flaws, but I do think you're contradicting yourself. A little bit ago, you said —" Simone looked down to read from her notepad. "And I'm paraphrasing here: 'I would like to lock her in my room and fuck her the whole day'. Apparently, the woman likes sex, am I wrong?"

"Likes isn't a strong enough word. She craves it like an addict. She wants to do it everywhere, every moment we're together, and in all kinds of strange and unusual ways... She learned quickly what I like!"

"I must ask...do you think she learned all that locked inside her house? What you've just described comes from experience."

"I know! I know! But it bothers me a lot to know she can compare me to other men."

"Did she do that?"

"No, but she complains when I don't deliver what she considers a good round of sex."

"She likes sex, and she's confident. She wants to receive

as much pleasure as she gives. Women who don't complain sometimes are not worried about satisfying themselves; they're worried about pleasing their man. That's not good in a relationship because they'll end up unsatisfied and unhappy."

"You're talking about all the women who've been a part of my life! They never complained!" His eyes were wide open as if he was having an epiphany.

"And tell me, did your sex life become less satisfactory after your marriages?"

"Yes! Totally!"

"My point is this; apparently, your previous wives didn't like sex. Rather, they wanted to please you to lure you into marriage. On the other hand, this woman seems to truly desire you."

"You're probably right, but there are other things that bother me. She does things in bed with me I shouldn't like, but I do, and that scares me..." He glanced away. "But I don't think I'm prepared to discuss that part with you. We'd have to sign a confidentiality agreement..."

"Ah...so, you want me to sign a paper guaranteeing something I'm already obligated to do? If I disclosed anything you told me during our sessions, I'd lose my license. There's no point in having me sign anything—check with your lawyers if you like." She closed her notepad and set on the table. "And I expect you at the same time next week. Your time is up for now."

He opened his mouth as if to answer and then smiled.

"I *like* you. You're tough!" He jumped from his seat and held his hand out to her. "I'll be here! But what if I need to talk to you before that? Like, if I have an emergency?"

"An emergency is something like attempting suicide—or thinking about doing it—or feeling a desire to murder or molest someone. If any of those things happen, please call my personal number. My secretary will provide it to you. But I warn you, if you call me for anything less than a real emergency, I'll bill you double my normal rate for the time!"

*****

After Benjamin left, Simone had two hours before her next patient, so she decided to use the time to check the boxes Beth had dropped off. Simone sat behind her desk and called Patricia on her cellphone. Their old intercom had gotten damaged, and they'd decided to forego the additional expense to have it fixed or buy a new one until business picked up again.

"Patricia, where did you put the boxes Beth brought the other day?"

"In Doctor Reynolds office, Doctor Bennet. I hope that's okay? I didn't think you'd want all that mess cluttering up your office while you were seeing patients."

"It's perfect. Thank you!"

Simone disconnected the call. Taking her cellphone with her in case Patricia needed anything, she walked across the hall to Ed's old office. The room was bathed in sunlight, and the shiny, modern furniture seemed to glow. She closed the door behind her and crossed the room, reaching for the boxes which Patricia had stacked in a corner. Simone kneeled on the floor beside the first box, took off her shoes and crossed her legs beneath her.

A memory hit her—the image of her and Edward, chatting there in his office, laughing about something—and her heart shrank.

I miss my friend.

She missed their close friendship, the companionship. Her thoughts flew to MacDougall and her throat grew tight. How was he coping, locked up in a place like that with no hope of getting out?

He helped a murderer—he should have snitched on him. He's not some innocent angel.

She shook her head. She could argue with herself all week, and still never resolve her conflicting emotions where Edward was concerned. She lifted the lid off the box in front of her and reached inside.

The first thing she pulled out was a picture of herself. She didn't remember where it was taken, but it showed her smiling at some happy point in her life.

As Simone sifted through the contents of the box, she came across a stack of papers and...pictures of dead bodies. The photos made her pause, her breath catching in her throat. She picked up one, her hand trembling slightly, and stared at the lifeless face.

Were these images part of a criminal profile Edward had been working on, or were they something far more sinister—a reflection of his illness? The unsettling thought crept into her mind.

She dug deeper and pulled out a manila file full of papers and more photos. She took a minute to scan the pages and then set the file aside. The photographs and paperwork belonged together; they were part of a report and psychological profile Ed had been working on. The information didn't fully reassure her.

Did he enjoy his work so much because he was great at it or because of the dead bodies he could admire?

Had Edward masturbated over the pictures? Thought about them when he and Simone were in bed?

When did this paraphilia start? How could I have never noticed it?

Simone closed her eyes and focused on her breathing for several seconds. The technique worked, banishing the uncomfortable thoughts—at least for now—so she could continue her search.

Books about criminal profiles, reports from other Doctors, and brochures on techniques on how to compile a profile filled the second box.

Nothing outside of the ordinary.

Simone took the books, blew off the imaginary dust, and rose to put them on the shelves. She needed to stretch; her knees ached from staying in the same position for so long. She flexed her legs a little until she felt a little less stiff. As she started to arrange the books on the shelf, a picture slipped from between the pages and landed on the floor.

Simone bent to pick it up. The photo had landed upside down, and on the back, there was a note in Edward's handwriting. *What is PH doing with these girls? Where did they come from?*

What the hell? PH? *Peter Hay*?

Curious, Simone turned the photo over to see the picture, steeling herself for the sight of another dead body. She'd never been fond of viewing dead bodies even when she'd had to study them back in college, and she'd never understood how Ed could deal with such grizzly subject matter all the time. Surprisingly, the woman in the photograph was not dead. She was a young Eastern girl, dressed like a sort of sexy cheerleader in a short, pleated red skirt, garter belt, and fishnet stockings. She wore her hair in ponytails, heavy makeup on her eyes, and her lips had been painted a deep red.

A juvenile prostitute. Pedophilia?

Simone was about to put the picture inside the first box she had opened when something caught her attention. The girl's white T-shirt had some kind of symbol just above the right breast. It looked like a logo or emblem representing a school of some kind, but without her reading glasses, she couldn't be certain.

"Damn aging! Having to wear glasses at this point really sucks," she murmured. Simone went to Edward's desk where he kept a magnifying glass he'd received as a gift from the local police. She held the magnifying glass over the photo and studied the symbol. What she saw gave her chills.

CHAPTER THIRTEEN

Enigmas from the East

A round logo on the girl's T-shirt displayed a panda, bold and unmistakable.

I have to see the bears. I must see the bears!

Peter's words came crashing through Simone's mind.

What the hell?

Had Peter been referring to this girl? Was it possible Peter had a girlfriend or some kind of long-term relationship? Simone's thoughts spun with all the possibilities.

Was Edward trying to investigate Peter, hoping to find some evidence to use against him in order to scape his blackmail? I need to talk to Ed!

Simone left the picture on Edward's desk and dug through the contents of the boxes, like a miner searching for gold.". She emptied two more, her sense of organization offended by the haphazard way the people who'd gathered Edward's stuff had just tossed everything inside each box with no rhyme or reason.

Simone examined every piece of paper and file but didn't find anything interesting. When she had finished going through the contents of the last box, she went back through everything, this time with the intention of sorting and organizing the contents in a way that made sense. Then she closed the cardboard flaps and used a marker to note the contents on the top of each box. She would ask Patricia to tape them up and put them in their archive storage area.

Hands on her hips, Simone looked down at the stack of boxes.

Damn it. One lousy picture.

All that work, and she'd only found a single clue, and even that had only given her more questions to answer. Still, she'd gotten lucky when that photo had slipped from the book...

The book! She spun around, hurried back to the shelf, and snatched the book out of the stack. As she flipped through each page, her heart began to race. Another picture had been stuck between the pages. This one depicted another Eastern girl wearing the same white T-shirt with the symbol above the right breast, but this girl was dead. Blue lips, naked from the waist down, her body lay in an impossibly awkward position. Her legs were contorted, and bruises covered every exposed area of skin. A hypodermic needle hung from her arm.

Simone took the picture to the desk and compared the girls in both photographs. Not the same girl, for sure. She turned the picture over, but Ed hadn't left a note on this one.

need to go to MacDougall!

When Peter had talked about bears, he hadn't been referring to cute pandas. In this case, the word had an entirely different meaning.

After digging around in Ed's desk drawers, Simone found an envelope, put the pictures inside, and took it with her. On her way to her office, she made a quick detour to tell Patricia what to do with the boxes.

"Patricia, please. I arranged Doctor Reynolds' belongings as best as I could, but there are still boxes on the floor. If you can, please organize his office."

"Sure, Doctor Bennet! I'm on my way!"

The woman jumped from her chair and quickly headed to Edward's office, completely ignoring Simone, who stood in front of her desk.

Efficiency should have been her first name—lack of politeness, her last.

Back in her office, Simone chose a book from her collection, so she'd have something to read on the train to NYC in the afternoon. She placed the envelope inside the front cover and put the book inside her purse. She would show the pictures to Carl. Maybe he would have some ideas.

*****

Simone called Carl as soon as the train stopped at Penn Station.

"Hello, love. I just arrived. I haven't gotten off the train yet, but I imagine the wind must be freezing today. I checked the forecast in my phone earlier, and it's cold out there, so I guess I'll take the subway."

"Absolutely not! You're not taking the subway. I just finished up an appointment near the station, so just wait for my text and then leave by the main entrance. I'll pick you up out front. The wind is worse than ever, and besides, I miss you."

Excitement filled his voice, and Simone smiled, warmed by his show of love and consideration.

"Really? What a fantastic coincidence. You always did have great timing. I'm on my way. As soon as I reach the escalators to Seventh Avenue, I'll let you know."

"Do that please. It's impossible to stop on the street for very long this time of day, and there are traffic guards out front."

"Okay. See you soon!"

Simone ended the call, put her phone back inside her

purse, and strode in the direction of the main entrance. She texted Carl when she reached the escalators, and five minutes later, she was sliding into the front passenger seat of his warm car. She sighed and brushed her hair back out of her face, relieved to be out of the wind and cold.

They kissed briefly, and then Carl took off, merging with the traffic.

"I'm really happy to see you. It feels like a holiday!" He glanced over at her and smiled before refocusing his attention on the road.

"I agree, and how wonderful it is to arrive and have my husband pick me up at the station. I was prepared to face a crowded subway."

"Not today. My life is relatively back on track. I finished that job, and I'm feeling almost lazy, dealing with normal office stress and not a tsunami of crises."

"Was it that crazy? You were busy and worried last weekend, and we didn't make love..." The moment she said the words she regretted them.

Don't play the needy wife.

"I know, honey, and I'll make it up to you; I promise, but whenever I'm that worried about a huge case it's hard for me to concentrate on anything else."

"Don't tell me you're just a regular guy. And all this time I thought you had a cape hidden somewhere." Simone released a dramatic sigh. "I'm so disappointed."

He laughed.

"Hey, what do you want to do tonight? How about I make reservations somewhere, and we have a cozy dinner?"

"How about us on our bed, having some great sex beforehand?" she asked mischievously.

"Hey, woman, that's a really good idea." He smiled again.

"I'm sorry to change the subject, but were you able to find out anything about Peter's visitor?"

"I've done a little research, but I didn't get any results yet. The only thing I know is he is registered as Peter's boyfriend, mate, something like that."

"Have you ever met the man? Did you know Peter had a boyfriend?"

"Never met him, and as far as I knew, Peter's last boyfriend was a man named Charles, but they had called it quits long before the trial."

Carl turned right on North Moore Street, and Simone admired his profile. What a beautiful man she had married. She loved the way his eyes sparkled and seemed to glow whenever he smiled.

He's so different from Ed. Ed would dedicate his life to me. Carl has his own life and doesn't need to live mine. Ed always made me feel as if I owed him as much dedication and time as he gave me, but with Carl, I always feel at ease. So easy I just coerced him into sex.

"Don't worry, I'll contact a few more people and try to find out more about this mysterious visitor. I know how important it is to you."

"Thanks, Carl!" She thought about talking to him about the pictures she'd found but decided to leave it for later.

*****

When they reached the apartment building, they parked in the underground garage.

As they walked hand-in-hand to the elevator, Carl gave her a sideways look and then cleared his throat. Simone studied his profile and frowned. Nervous? Had something happened this past week?

"I saw Sean a couple days ago... He moved back to the city," Carl said and looked at her again.

Sean was one of Lara's siblings and Simone's half-brother, a fact she had discovered in the worst possible way. During his sentencing, Peter had disclosed the information in front of the packed courtroom, telling Simone she had been born an illegitimate child, and the woman who'd raised her was no blood relation.

Her biological mother, Sabine, who was Lara's mother, as well, had become pregnant by her gynecologist, a much older man, when she was a young woman. She had given baby Simone to her father, the Doctor, who, along with his wife, had raised her. They had died without ever telling Simone the truth.

"Humm..." Simone made a noncommittal sound. What did he expect her to say?

"He would like to meet with you, he and his sister—well, *your* sister, Deborah."

They entered the elevator, and Carl's expression told her he was waiting for her to answer.

"I've been thinking about them lately...since the judgment...but I didn't want to intrude. I don't know how they reacted to the news that they have a half-sister, and it seems to me those kids have been through a lot in their lives."

"They're not kids anymore, and yes, their lives have been marked by losses, but they are wonderful people. You wouldn't be a loss—you'd be an addition to their lives and meeting you would be a meaningful experience for them."

Carl unlocked the door and opened it, then stepped aside for her to enter, but Tommy blocked the entrance. He'd never let her pass if she didn't greet him properly first.

"Tommy, my boy, missed you!" She caressed behind his ears, and he showed his deep appreciation by closing his eyes.

I'm sure he's smiling at me.

Simone caressed the dog a little more and talked to him

till he was satisfied and headed for the kitchen, probably to get a drink since that was where they kept his water bowl.

Simone turned to Carl.

"I'll try to schedule something with Debbie and Shawn. Maybe you should give me their numbers, and I can call them. If they're sure they're ready, we can meet."

Simone put her purse on the coffee table near the sofa, approached Carl, and kissed him on the lips. He wrapped his arms around her, and they deepened the kiss, needing the contact, to bond again. Living in separate houses and not seeing each other all the time caused them to behave like young newlyweds, always seducing each other. The heat of their desire for each other never seemed to grow cold.

"I missed you, wife," Carl whispered near her ear.

"And I missed *you*, husband."

Simone lowered her hand to his pants, rubbing him over the fabric. Carl caressed her arms then lowered his hands to her buttocks, squeezing her cheeks.

"Let's take this to the bedroom," she said, already breathing hard.

They shed their clothes on their way down the hall, and by the time they reached the bed, they were fully nude. Carl pulled her in for a warm hug, and although she was anxious to have him and relished the feel of his flesh against hers, she also longed for a nice, hot bath.

"Let me take a bath first?" Simone tried to escape his embrace but failed.

"No way. Just lie down and let me touch you."

Carl helped her to lie back on the bed and settled in by her side. He covered her lips with his in another hungry, deep kiss, then he began to make his way down her body, kissing her neck, her shoulders, until he reached her breasts. He cupped them and gently pinched her nipples, then continued his journey south to her belly and then to her center of pleasure, caressing her clit with his tongue.

Suddenly, he pulled back.

"Hold on. I bought us something." He jumped from the bed, went to the closet, and came back carrying something that looked like a massager.

"What's that?" Simone asked, supporting herself on her elbows as she watched him.

"Just wait, my curious woman, and close your eyes."

Simone closed her eyes, and a moment later, a sound that reminded her of a swarm of bees came from beside her. The bed dipped, and then heaven descended on her as he touched her clit with the massager while putting a finger inside her. The sensation was like ten tongues licking her, and she came hard on his hand, gasping at the intensity.

"Oh, my God, that was..." She shook her head, unable to find the words.

Simone opened her eyes. Carl smiled down at her, his expression one of total satisfaction.

"I was using this thing to massage my sorry lawyer's neck the other day, and it occurred to me that this would work great for other things, too..."

"Come here, creative man of mine, and let me return the favor!"

Simone pulled him down onto the bed. He laid by her side, and she took his dick between her palms. He was already hard from watching her pleasure. She massaged the shaft with both hands, starting from his testicles and working upward. Carl watched her for a few minutes, until he moaned and closed his eyes. Simone replaced her hands with her mouth and took one of his balls between her lips, then the other, while continuing to massage his shaft. She then took the head of his cock inside her mouth and did a back-and-forth movement until he pushed her away.

"Stop that or I'm not going to make it until the main event."

Simone stopped, kneeled over him, his body between her thighs, and then guided his shaft to her entrance, slowly lowering herself until he filled her completely. She controlled her internal muscles, squeezing him as she moved up and down, lazily at first, until she needed to accelerate her movements and ride him with all speed, seeking another orgasm.

They came nearly simultaneously. Simone's leg muscles were trembling from effort and from pleasure, and she fell forward, plopping down to lie on his chest, listening to his racing heart, until their breathing grew less strained.

CHAPTER FOURTEEN

NYC

After a long bath, Simone and Carl decided to order Italian and stay in. The wind howled outside, and they were in no mood to get dressed and brave the weather. Wearing only their robes, they cuddled on the couch in front of a black TV screen, wineglasses in hand, chatting about everything and nothing. Times like these, when they could be alone together without one or both of their businesses keeping them miles apart were rare, and they never took them for granted.

"How is Peter?" Carl asked. Peter and Carl had been brothers-in-law years ago, and when Carl's marriage to Peter's sister Deena ended, the two men became good friends. Even now, Carl had a hard time believing the man he'd once considered his best and funniest friend was a criminal.

"I told you the other day, he was completely off his rocker. All that talk about pandas missing him, a lot of total nonsense, and then this morning... Wait. Let me get something so you can see..." Simone left the sofa and went to her purse, which she'd left on the table near the front door. She pulled the envelope from inside the large, zippered compartment and returned to the sofa. She curled up again at Carl's side, sitting with her legs tucked under her.

Simone opened the envelope and gave the first picture to

Carl.

"I was going through the stuff Edward's ex-wife got from the police station—all his work product—and this picture slipped out of a book. The notations on the back caught my attention."

Carl turned the picture over and squinted at the writing before looking up at her.

"Do you think PH is Peter?"

"Yes, I think so, because after I saw those notes, I studied the picture more closely, and I noticed something." She turned the photograph and pointed at the girl's T-shirt. "That logo includes a figure of a panda."

"I can't see it. Sorry, my reading glasses are at the office."

"Don't worry, they wouldn't be much help. I had to use a magnifying glass to see the image. There must be a connection. Peter was worried about bears. What if he wasn't talking about those cute, little black-and-white bears? What if he meant something completely different?"

"It sort of looks like a logo." Carl pointed to the image, squinting again, which caused dozens of tiny wrinkles to form around his eyes.

"Yes, maybe. And maybe he refers to girls as bears... Maybe there's a connection that Edward was investigating. Look at this picture." She handed him the one that depicted the dead girl and pointed to the young woman's face. "She's Asian..." She pointed at the symbol on her T-shirt. "Panda. A bear. But what does Peter have to do with this, and what does it all mean?"

"Hey, my sweet Hercule Poirot, I think you need to visit your precious Edward. He can probably explain some of this for you. After all, these belong to him and Peter talking about bears could be a coincidence. As you mentioned before, he did seem a little unhinged." Carl gave the pictures back to her.

Simone shook her head and patted him on the leg.

“He is not my precious anything, but you’re right. However, there’s just one tiny problem....” Simone held her hand up, index finger and thumb nearly touching. “He doesn’t want to see me.”

“I wouldn’t want to ever see you again, either, if you traded me in for another much more handsome guy and then married him a few months later...” Carl poked her chest lightly and smiled.

“Ha-ha-ha, funny boy! It wasn’t like that, and you know it.”

Carl wrapped his arms around her and pulled her close.

“I do, but you made me suffer a lot because you didn’t want to hurt him, and then there was all that bullshit about Doctor-patient relationships being taboo.”

“Do you know I love you, and I think you’re adorable when you’re jealous?” Simone kissed Carl’s lips.

“Woman, I’m not jealous. I’m simply recalling that I do have grounds to claim injuries...”

“So says the lawyer...”

“Well, maybe I’m a little bit jealous. Okay, okay, I hate the guy, and I’m happy he’s locked up.” He gave her a mischievous smile.

“You are not petty like that.”

“I am when it concerns the woman I love.”

Thank God Carl doesn’t give me the third degree every time I talk to another man.

Confident in his relationship, Carl could make jokes about his occasional bout of jealousy. Edward, on the other hand, had become aggressive.

Carl knows you love him; Edward sensed you didn’t have a clue about your real feelings for him.

*****

While Carl went down to walk Tommy, Simone got ready for bed. She went to the closet in her dressing room, took off her robe, tossed it on the ottoman in the middle of the room, and opened a drawer to find a nightgown She had the lavender silk one in mind—she loved the smoothness of the fabric against her skin. But as she started to dig through the drawer, she discovered a photograph beneath a pile of underwear. Simone held the picture of the smiling blonde woman toward the light. She wore a super-sexy black leather skirt paired with a silver metallic tank top, high-heeled black boots, and at least a dozen chain-like metal necklaces draped around her neck. Heavy, dark makeup gave her a fiercely beautiful look. All curves and a mischievous smile.

Lara. She was sexy like the devil! How could a man fall in love with a woman like that and then with me?

There was a mirror on the wall, and Simone looked at the reflection of her naked body. She was slender, not curvaceous like the girl in the picture. Her breasts were still firm—she'd had silicone implants many years ago after breastfeeding—but they were just okay. Her skin was tight. She touched her face, placing a hand on cheek, and stretched.

I could do with a neck lift; there's a little excess here.

She lowered her chin toward her neck to see if a bulge formed.

Stop that, Simone. The man loves you for the person you are, not for your body or face.

She comforted herself, but then another thought crossed her mind.

Would he love me if Lara was still alive?

Overwhelmed by the sobering thought, Simone paused and stared off into space. The slam of the front door shook her from her frozen state. Carl had returned from walking the dog. She'd get dressed and go ask him about the picture instead of allowing her mind to drive her crazy with unanswered questions.

Simone stepped out of the closet and made her way to the bedroom, holding the picture tightly in her hand. Carl was already lying in bed, wearing a pair of old pajamas he loved even though they were ready for the rag bin.

"My lady looks amazing in that nightgown... Unfortunately, I don't have the strength for a second round today."

Would he dress like that if Lara were joining him tonight? Stop it, stop it, you are not a teenager!

Simone forced a smile and went around to climb in on her side of the bed.

"I found this inside my nightgown drawer. Is that Lara?" Simone handed him the picture. She knew the answer, but she wanted to hear it from Carl.

He took the picture, squinted as he had when he'd examined the other photographs earlier, then handed the picture back to her.

"I've never seen that photograph," he said, his voice calm and even. "It looks like her, but I'd need my glasses to be sure." He paused and frowned. "The real question is how did that end up in your drawer if I've never seen it before? I think you need to talk to the cleaning lady. That's the second time you've found something of Lara's mixed in with your stuff. Maybe I missed a box of Lara's things, and Marisa found it and decided to put the stuff away thinking they belong to you. But I'm positive I gave everything to her siblings and all I found were a few items of cosmetics she'd left in the bathroom. No clothes or pictures."

"I'm going to talk to Marisa." Simone snatched the picture from his hand and threw it in her nightstand drawer.

And tomorrow, I'm getting rid of that photo.

"Hon, I'm going to sleep." Carl leaned up and gave her a light kiss then settled under the covers. He pulled one of the pillows from beneath his head and tossed it into the corner, fluffed the other pillow, then lay back, his eyes closed.

Simone scowled. He had the annoying ability to fall asleep in minutes. She tried to do the same, but her mind was not her friend when she had a puzzle to solve, and she had a hard time calming her thoughts enough to sleep. She wondered about Lara, comparing the two of them again, and made a mental list of things she must do. She needed to know more about her half-sister, so she would start by contacting her half-siblings. She could give them the picture and ask them to tell her more about the sister she'd never known existed. And Simone would talk to Marisa, too, and ask if there were more objects in the house that had belonged to Lara.

And I'll try to be sexier for my husband... But I'll never wear a short leather skirt. I just don't have it in me.

The sky had begun to grow lighter by the time Simone fell into an exhausted sleep, and when Carl woke her by caressing her hair, she opened one eye and sighed. Obviously, he'd been up for quite a while. Long enough to shower and get dressed for the day. He stood there by the side of the bed, patiently waiting for her to respond, and she struggled to form a coherent thought. Surely, she'd slept only minutes... She felt crushed.

"Good morning, my love! So good to have you here, to wake up with you!"

Simone gave Carl a tired smile. "I love being here with you." Her voice sounded husky from lack of sleep. "Let's do something special tonight."

"Hmmm, special? What do you want to do?" He sat on the bed, leaned toward her, and kissed her neck.

"Does Behind the Door still exists?"

CHAPTER FIFTEEN

Behind the Door

"Behind the Door? Are you talking about the place for people who are into swinging?"

The surprised, questioning look he gave her had her swallowing back a laugh.

"Yes. That's the place!" Simone rolled over onto her back and nodded.

"Don't you remember when you were working for me, and we visited a swing club? I told you that Behind the Door was decadent, so we decided to go to Silk Lips instead. Why? Do you want to go to a swing club?"

"Well, the thought has crossed my mind... The last time we went to a place like that, I thought it was sexy as hell, but we had that Doctor-patient issue between us... Do you think Silk Lips is still open?" She teased him.

"I don't have any idea if it's still open." He paused and grinned. "I do remember attacking my Doctor while we were there! Um, I guess I can check for you if you really want to go..." His expression turned from one of sexy mischief to that of a man who felt uncertain in the blink of an eye.

"I just thought it could be sexy, something different for us to do."

"It's that ridiculous picture you found last night, isn't it?

Do you think I miss Lara and her lifestyle?" he asked, looking directly into her eyes.

Yes, I do.

She kept that thought to herself and used her years of practice at keeping a poker face to hold his gaze and answer with a smile.

"No way. I just remember being there with you, and you were so forbidden to me, and I was attracted to you." She rolled her eyes, recalling the scene.

"Do you know we shared our first kiss that night, too?" he asked.

"Indeed! Our first kiss and the first time we ever messed around," Simone rose from the bed and hugged Carl from behind.

"I was so embarrassed after I touched you, but here's something I've never told you…a secret I've kept all this time. Since the day I first saw you on that stage, all confident and sure of what you were saying, I was seduced by you."

Simone had given a presentation at the Society Sex Therapy and Research Conference at the New York Academy of Sciences, and Carl and she had met there that evening. He'd been a mess, trying to understand his life, and she'd been a somewhat famous psychiatrist who specialized in paraphilias. It seemed like centuries ago, not less than two years.

"You weren't!" Simone couldn't believe his words.

"I was, and I am! Now, get out of bed, and let's make some breakfast. I'm starving!" He rose and started for the door.

"What about my suggestion that we go to a swinger's club?

At her question, he stopped and turned to her.

"I don't know if I want to go down that path again…"

"Oh, c'mon! We don't have to join the swingers; we can just

watch. I want to find out what we would have done that day if we hadn't had a professional relationship."

"We would have fucked in the middle of that place, Simone, and it wasn't our professional relationship that stopped us; it was the people trying to get out the door we were leaning against. I'll do a search and see what I can find, but woman, just one word of warning." He pointed at her. "My days of sharing a woman are long gone. You're mine, and mine alone." He turned and left the room.

Simone smiled, pleased to know he didn't want to share her.

*****

Around ten a.m., Simone heard noises coming from the kitchen. She remembered that Marisa, the cleaning lady, was supposed to be there—it was her scheduled day. Curious, Simone made her way to the kitchen to talk to her about the photo she had found in the drawer.

"Good morning, Marisa. How have you been?" Simone asked the woman who was washing dishes at the sink.

Startled, Marisa turned.

"Oh, Simone! You scared me—I was lost in my thoughts. I'm fine, thanks, how about you?" She smiled..."Fine, thanks." Simone handled her Lara's photography. "Do you recognize this?"

"I've never seen that picture before." She shook her head.

"It was inside my nightgown drawer..."

"I organized that drawer last Monday, and it was not in there."

"How about a red dress? It's not mine; I found it inside my wardrobe. Did you hang it there?"

"I have no idea which red dress you're talking about. The one in lace is the only one I know. It's inside your wardrobe."

"No, that one is mine. The other one..."

Marisa shook her head.

Frustrated, Simone thanked the woman for her time. As far as she could tell—and she considered herself great at spotting a lie—neither Carl nor Marisa had a clue about where the picture or the dress had come from.

What is going on here?

Simone went to the bedroom and sat on the bed, holding the photograph...

I'm going to call Sean.

But was she prepared to do that? To have siblings after being an only child all her life?

Oh, c'mon, Simone, she mocked herself. *It's not as if you're going to have to share Mommy and Daddy.*

Simone looked at the cellphone in her hand, tapped the screen a few times, and found the contact Carl had shared with her, which she still hadn't added to her own. She took a deep breath to calm the strange sensation of having her legs trembling.

What is going on with me?

She looked at her arms. White spots dotted her flesh. The title of a book by a Brazilian author came to mind. According to the book, *Body Language,* white spots on arms were a symptom of internal conflicts, feeling threatened about your siblings.

Does the idea of approaching them make me feel threatened?

Simone put the phone on the nightstand.

Are you a rat or a woman? You've been through everything in this life, and you're afraid of meeting a couple new relatives?

After drawing another deep breath, she picked up the phone and dialed Sean's number.

A man with a deep voice answered after just a few rings.

"Hello?"

"Hello, I would like to speak with Sean Parker please."

"This is Sean. Can I help you?" The man replied.

"This is Simone Bennet."

An absolute silence greeted her statement, then a long sigh filled her ear.

He's as nervous as I am.

The idea made Simone grow more relaxed. The situation was tough for them both.

"Hello, Simone, I've been waiting for this call."

"I know. Can we meet? I'm ready if you are."

And if he says he's not? Simone closed her eyes. *Think positive...*

"I am, and so is my—*our* sister... Can I invite her to join us?"

Two at once?

Might as well get it over with...

"Okay." Simone looked at her watch. "Do you have time for lunch today?"

"I'll make time. Let me talk to Debbie, and then I'll text you and let you know where we can meet. Are you a vegan?"

"I'm not; are you?"

"I lived in Texas. You can't be a vegan there, or you'll die. Besides, I'm addicted to brisket."

Simone laughed, her imagination conjuring up a cowboy eating a salad.

*****

Sean had made reservations and arranged for them to meet at Colbeh, a kosher restaurant he claimed had the best kebabs in town. He said it was one of those wonderful, hidden places in the Diamond District.

As Simone sat at a four-top table against the wall, sipping a sparkling water and waiting for the rest of her party to arrive, she took in the restaurant's unusual décor. Crystal chandeliers hung from the ceiling, a contrast to the forests of tree branches covering the walls, but somehow it worked, comprising an understated yet elegant atmosphere.

If the food is good, I'll have to remember to bring Carl here someday soon.

Carl loved lamb kebabs, and he would enjoy adding a new venue to his long list of favorite places.

As she lifted her glass to take a sip, someone touched her shoulder, and she turned. A gorgeous couple stood smiling down at her. She leaped to her feet and extended her hand to greet Deborah, but the other woman wrapped her in a warm hug, instead.

"So happy to have a sister again! I'm Debbie."

Simone had never done well with affectionate greetings, but she tried her best to return the embrace.

"Nice to meet you, Debbie."

When her sister released her, Simone extended her hand to Sean. Thankfully, he accepted the gesture rather than trying to hug her. He gazed at her for several seconds, his expression speculative. Maybe he noticed how embarrassed she was, or maybe he had trouble showing affection, too.

They were simply beautiful.

I think I got my dad's genes. I'm not at all like these people.

Sean and Debbie were both tall and fair and blond. While Debbie had sparkling blue eyes, Sean's were an indefinite greenish color.

They belong on a runway somewhere.

They sat at the table, and at first, the conversation was a little stilted and awkward—natural enough between total strangers -Debbie was the one to break the weird atmosphere.

"Simone, I'm so curious about you," she said, grabbing Simone's hand. "Tell me everything about your life. What kind of childhood did you have? What were your parents like?" The woman had naïve sparks of curiosity in her eyes.

She seems to have retained the innocence of a child.

Debbie asked Simone question after question. Sean seemed to be more cautious and kept a reserved attitude.

Either he's normally this way, as Lara had described her father's personality, or he's feeling uncomfortable. Or maybe he thinks he must protect his secret.

As Simone answered all of Debbie's questions, a female couple walked into the restaurant., holding hands. Sean glanced at them and then quickly looked back at Simone.

Was he afraid she might be prejudiced?

Poor guy.

She had to find a way to let him know everything was okay. Luckily for Simone, one of the women approached their table.

"Doctor Bennet!" The young woman glanced at Debbie and Sean and smiled. "I'm sorry to interrupt." She returned her attention to Simone. "What a nice surprise! How have you been? I must introduce you to my wife, Camille."

Simone's mind spun for a moment, and then she remembered.

Emmanuelle...

She'd been a patient years ago, back when she had been a teenager trying to come to terms with her sexuality.

"Emmanuelle, how've you been? Nice to meet you, Camille!" Simone rose and kissed Emmanuelle on the cheek. She shook hands with Camille then turned to the table.

"These are my half-sister and half-brother, Debbie and Sean."

After a round of hellos, Emmanuelle paused then said,

"Camille, Doctor Bennet helped me come out of the closet. She's the best shrink in the world." Emmanuelle turned back to Simone. "Don't tell me you're living in the city now. I would love to go back to seeing you again. A girl can always use a good psychiatrist."

"Not exactly, but I'm here at least once a week, so call my office, and we can figure out something convenient for both of us."

I can use all the clients I can get at this point.

"Same phone number?"

"Same."

They said goodbye, and Simone sat down again.

"I'm so sorry. I don't like when that happens, but she used to be my patient years ago, and when a patient runs into me outside of the office, they normally react in one of two ways. Either they pretend they never met me, or they are just like that." Simone smiled; happy Emmanuelle had decided to approach their table. Plus, Simone appreciated knowing that her work had helped someone find their way in life.

"You seem to be the kind of Doctor patients love," Sean said, curiosity in his eyes for the first time.

"Well...some hate me, too... We psychiatrists have the worst job in the world." Simone scowled. "We need to help people face the truth about themselves, and sometimes, that's not pleasant."

"I know... I've been there...having to face the realization I'm attracted to men." He locked his greenish-eyed gaze on her.

Simone nodded.

"I read your sister's diaries... I'm sorry your father couldn't understand. Parents usually have a child and hope the kid will grow up to follow in Mom or Dad's footsteps, to be a miniature of themselves, so when it goes another way, they can't control, they tend to react badly because they don't understand."

She usually didn't give her professional opinion like this, but for once, she didn't overthink the situation. Counseling Sean seemed like the right thing to do in the moment.

"Exactly. My dad, he never accepted me." Sean gave a sad smile.

"I don't think he could understand you because you're so different from him, and Dad was an engineer, all square thoughts. We talked about you a few times, and he always said the same thing. 'I want Sean to be happy, and I don't think his choices are leading him in that direction,'" Debbie said.

Sean's eyes filled with tears, and he didn't bother to hide them.

"I always felt he died thinking I was a disappointment." He pressed his lips together in a thin line.

"In some ways, we're all disappointments to our parents. We're unique human beings, not appliances with instruction manuals or little robots they can program to become just like them only better."

They laughed.

"I wish my kids had come with a manual..." Debbie said, still chuckling.

"So do I... One beautiful day, my daughter said she didn't belong in America, that her soul was French, and she moved away, just like that. For a while, I tried to figure out what mistakes I must have made while raising her to send her to another continent, and then I felt cheated—after all the diapers, sleepless nights, and worries, she just up and moved to France." Simone paused, her jaw clenching as she mulled over the thought.

By the time their lunch came, the three of them were talking like old acquaintances, discussing all sorts of things. When the meal was over and they said goodbye, promising to get in touch soon, Simone had a warm sensation in her chest.

*****

Simone decided to go on a little shopping expedition. She wandered through several stores before finally making her way to Saks, where she picked out a sexy new dress. After tiring herself out from all the walking, she stopped for a coffee to recharge before heading home.

When Simone's Uber dropped her off in front of Carl's building, she glanced up at the corner of the four-story brick structure. There were a couple of cameras—one on each outside corner—facing the street.

How come I never noticed those before?

"Good afternoon," she said to the doorman as she entered the building.

"Good afternoon, Mrs. Lourenzo," he replied.

As she crossed the hall, she realized there were more cameras facing the elevators. Inside the elevator, there was another one on the ceiling.

Well, I'm certainly not very observant.

All those cameras, and she'd never noticed a single one.

Had they really been there this whole time? I should ask the doorman for the past two days of footage.

But first, She ' d check with Carl—no point asking if it's not even legal.

Stepping off the elevator onto their floor, she glanced around, searching for more cameras. There weren't any.

Simone unlocked the front door, and as she closed it, she

changed the code on the lock. She went directly to the closet, where she found Carl getting dressed to go out.

"Good evening, husband. Where are you going?"

Simone leaned in for a quick kiss. As she moved to step back, Carl dragged her close and kissed her again—a deep, passionate, breath-stealing kiss. When he finally released her, she put a hand against the wall to steady herself.

"Whoa!" She was breathless. "What was that all about?"

Carl's mischievous grin sent pleasurable tingles racing along her arms. "I missed you, that's all," he said. "And *we* are going to Asha Club."

Simone lifted an eyebrow.

"Asha Club?"

"I called Neno, and he told me Asha is the best swing club in New York right now. You remember him, don't you? He's a gay man who was a friend of Lara's, and he has a lot of experience in that area. In fact, he's the one who—"

"Who introduced Lara to swing clubs. Yes, my love, I remember from her diaries..."

"Okay, then go get ready, woman!"

He gave her a teasing swat on the butt, making Simone laugh as she ran off toward the bathroom. She'd fill him in on the meeting with her siblings later.

*****

After a long shower, Simone used a scented lotion, spreading it carefully over her entire body. When she did her makeup, she mixed several shades of metallic gold on her eyelids. She put on a pair of silky black lace stockings and then slipped into her new dress—a low-cut black sheath that hung just to her knees. Black sequins and metallic black bugle beads covered the entire dress, and they twinkled like black diamonds every time she moved. Simone picked up a brush and ran it through her hair until it was shiny, and let it fall loose around her shoulders.

"You sexy thing, you," she said to her reflection and laughed. "And the finishing touch…a luscious red lipstick."

"Hello, gorgeous."

Simone straightened and spun around.

"Hello, yourself."

Carl stood just inside her dressing room door, and as usual, her heart did a little flip at the sight of him.

He looks so hot.

His white shirt under a navy blazer was sexy as hell, his hair was still wet, and his powerful cologne tickled her senses. He came to her, pulled her into his arms, and kissed her lightly on the lips.

"My sexy man. Eyes just for me tonight," she whispered against his lips.

"I've only had eyes for you since the day we met." He kissed her again.

"Liar… If I remember correctly, you were testing the waters…"

He gave her a little squeeze.

"So were you! Are you sure you want to go out? We could enjoy ourselves here." He nodded toward the floor.

"Here, as in, right here on my dressing room floor?" She laughed and then shook her head. "Oh, come on, Carl. Let's do something different. I promise you'll have a good time." She pulled from his embrace to get her stilettos and put them on.

"If you say so, boss. Let's hit the street."

Carl left the room, and she grabbed her purse and followed him. He pulled his cellphone from an inside jacket pocket, called the doorman, and asked for his car.

As they reached the front door, Simone glanced down and then paused. The saddest dog in the world gazed up at her, and she sighed.

"Mommy and Daddy won't be long, promise." She caressed the dog's head, but his eyes remained sad. "This guy knows how to make someone feel guilty."

"That's because you're new to the world of dogs. All dogs know that trick with the eyes. They can get anything with that."

"I think we should find a companion for him," Simone said.

"I've thought about that, but then we'd have two manipulative dogs at the door every time we went out," Carl replied with a grin.

"At least they wouldn't be alone," Simone countered, smiling.

They went down the hall to the elevators, talking about adopting another dog.

"So, what do you think? Should we start looking?" Simone stepped into the elevator car.

"I'll give it some serious thought," Carl said, pushing the button to the garage.

*****

Carl and Simone arrived at the club, and Carl pulled into a private parking lot beside a tall, thin gray building.

They walked quickly from the parking lot to the club entrance, heads down against the harsh, buffeting wind.

They buzzed the intercom, and Carl said the word "hope." A moment later, the door opened. Holding hands, they walked down a deserted, narrow corridor until they reached a set of elevators. Another couple entered behind them, and Carl held the elevator door for them. He pressed the penthouse button, and the couple gave a knowing look, as if silently acknowledging they were all headed to the same forbidden place. They exchanged an awkward "good evening," but no one said a word as the elevator ascended, before stopping at the fifteenth floor.

CHAPTER SIXTEEN

What Happens on the Other Floors

The Asha Club occupied the top three floors of the building. The elevator stopped, and the door slid open. A bar was directly in front of them, and round tables were situated around the room, far enough away from each other to allow guests to walk around and mingle. Through a doorway on the opposite wall, a barman had set up shop and was mixing drinks, and a billiards table stood off in one corner. Simone eyed the empty pool table.

Who comes here to play? She smiled as the answer popped into her head. *Everybody, but not that kind of game.*

Unlike the first—and only—swing club Simone had been to, this one didn't have a dance floor, but loud music blared from overhead speakers, and people paraded around with their drinks in hand. Carl talked to a tall man with a tag on his chest, and then she and Carl followed the man to a table in a corner.

Simone pointed at the little cardboard reserved sign propped up against a candle on the table.

"Did you make a reservation?" She didn't know you could do that at a place like this.

"I did. We're too old to stand all night, my lady." He smiled and held the chair for her. "What do you wish to drink?" he asked, standing behind her.

"A dry martini, please."

As there were no servers, Carl headed back over to the bar. He had no sooner stepped away than a gorgeous man, who couldn't be older than thirty-five, approached her.

"Good evening. Are you and your husband here just for drinks, or are you going to the next floor?"

He stared into Simone's eyes, and his expression made her smile, reminding her of how Tommy had gazed at her earlier.

"We don't know yet." She shook her head.

"Patrick." He gave her his hand. "Consider me if you decide to climb the stairs." He pointed to the ceiling.

"Lea. And thanks for the offer." She answered without thinking, and to give a false name seemed natural.

Carl came with the drinks. Still holding them, he stepped up to Patrick.

"We're not sharing. Leave now. Please."

Simone's mouth fell open, and she stared at Carl. Had she ever seen him behave so rudely?

"I'm sorry…" Patrick turned away as he mumbled, "Selfish bastard."

"Did he molest you?" Carl still wore a hostile expression as he pulled up the chair next to hers.

"I was handling the situation. He just offered to be my plus one on the next floor." Simone felt good about someone so young thinking she was sexy enough to be a partner in a swing club.

"Oh, is *that* all?" Carl's voice dripped with sarcasm. "Can't leave my girl alone for what…?" He looked at his watch. "Three minutes without the vultures swooping in!"

His tone was light, but Simone could sense he wasn't pleased.

"Can I have one?"

Simone reached for the drink Carl seemed to have forgotten to give her, and they sat there, sipping their cocktails, and watching the crowd coming and going from the stairs in the corner.

After two martinis, and with the mood lighter, Simone wanted to see what was happening on the other floors. She rose and took Carl's hand, and they moved to the stairs.

The second floor of the club was totally different from the first one. At the door, young women waited to show the guests around and explain the rules.

"You may touch whomever you want, wherever you want. If someone touches you, don't touch them back if you don't want further advances. Respect other people's boundaries, and if you're into BDSM, go to the third floor." Their guide stopped, looked at them, and smiled. "Any questions?"

"I would like to see that." Simone pointed toward the ceiling.

Before the young woman could answer, Carl spoke up, "BDSM? Trust me, I've been to this kind of shit before, and it's not pretty to see people humiliating themselves or others. It's the kind of nonsense that makes me feel sick." He looked like he'd just bitten into a fresh piece of lemon.

Simone could understand his feelings. Lara had forced him into a position of playing the Dom and inflicting pain when they were together. Without being a sadist, without having knowledge of the subject, naturally, Carl had hated the entire experience. But according to some of Simone's patients, the people who practiced BDSM didn't see themselves that way. The participants were in search of sexual gratification the only way they knew—through pain—and they didn't see anything humiliating about it.

The roots of that kind of sexual choice run much deeper and, according to traditional psychology, could result from multiple traumas. However, some of Simone's case studies involving practitioners showed they were less depressed and anxious than others who didn't practice it. Some considered it a way of life and couldn't trace it to any trauma, so she didn't condemn it; she simply observed, as she had not yet formed a medical opinion.

"Okay, let's walk around here and see what's going on." Simone nodded her thanks to their guide, and then with more courage than she'd believed herself capable of in a place like that, she started toward a nearby hallway.

Rows of doors—some open and some closed—lined both sides of the wide corridor. As Carl took her hand, Simone passed the first to closed rooms then paused and looked inside the next. Two men sat on a long couch, surrounded by a small group of onlookers. Each man held the waist of a woman who straddled them. As the ladies rode their partners like experienced cowgirls, the one on the left leaned down to kiss the man on the right while some of the spectators fondled her breasts.

The scene was crazy but sexy, and Simone's excitement grew. They moved to the next room, where a round bed in a corner provided a stage for a beautiful brunette. She lay on her back, supporting her upper torso with her elbows, while three men lined up to wait for their turn with her.

They penetrated her, one after the other, and she made them all come. When the men were finished, she shouted to Carl.

"You, come here. I still need to come. I need more." She tapped the bed.

"No, thanks." Carl spoke politely and turned to leave. "She is voracious."

"Maybe she has anorgasmia. She could have all the men here and still wouldn't be satisfied. That's why she needs a lot, always trying to reach an orgasm," Simone said, unable to stop her clinical mind from analyzing the behaviors of the people they encountered.

Carl stopped, turned to Simone, and caressed her neck.

"How about you? Will just one man be enough for you?"

He leaned in and kissed her neck, causing goosebumps to pop up all over her skin.

"If the man is a charming yet serious lawyer, he will be more than enough..." Simone bit his neck lightly. "Can we go to a more private spot? I don't need to put on a show, but I'm really dying to fuck you, mister." All the erotic sights and sounds had excited her, and she needed to be filled. That was exactly what she needed...a hard dick inside her.

"Private? I don't think that's possible here, but I saw one room that looked like it might be for people who aren't full blown exhibitionists."

Carl pulled her by the hand and led her to a room a few yards back in the direction from which they'd come. Someone had created holes in the wall on each side of the door, ostensibly so others could observe. A small table holding a basket of condoms sat off to one side, but there was no other furniture. No seating of any kind. Carl closed the door behind them, thrusting them into semi-darkness.

"Come here," he said. "I think fewer people can see us if we stay in the corner."

Carl kissed Simone's lips and touched her pussy over her lacy thong panties, and she opened her legs, allowing him more contact. Her belly contracted in pleasure, the need to feel him inside her more intense.

"You are so wet...so good..."

Carl ran his tongue down her neck, giving her chills with his day-old beard. Simone touched his hard shaft over his pants.

"Wet and ready for you," she whispered back.

Carl didn't wait for more of an invitation. He opened his zipper and dropped his pants to his knees while Simone removed her panties. She leaned against the wall and propped her foot on the low table, knocking over the condom basket. Carl took his hard cock in his hand and positioned the head at Simone's entrance.

The touch of his shaft made Simone even wetter, ready for him. With one thrust, Carl sank deep inside her, making her come immediately with a low moan.

As they continued their dance, the sound of people whispering made its way through to her lust-addled brain. She couldn't see anyone, but she could sense their presence on the other side of the wall. Intoxicated by the idea of being watched, she lost herself in her pleasure. After helping her reach several more orgasms, Carl came, filling her, making her come again with the sensation of his liquid pleasure. They stay there, holding each other until their breathing returned to normal. Then, Carl adjusted his boxers and pants while Simone slipped her panties back on.

The dampness inside her and between her legs didn't bother her a bit. When they opened the door, five people were walking away, but one man remained. His shaft in his fist he stroked himself, and as they walked past him, he came all over his hand.

"Let's get out of here… Any more of this and I'll set up a desk in the corner somewhere and start asking people to tell me their stories." Simone teased Carl, but she really wanted to leave.

A nice, intoxicating experience, but now I need to return to my real life.

I've never had so many multiple orgasms before. It's easy to get addicted to that kind of experience.

"With pleasure!"

Hand in hand, they left the club—Simone glowing from the thrilling experience, though Carl's silence left her slightly unsettled.

Hand in hand, they left the club—Simone felt marvelous after the thrilling experience, though Carl's silence left her slightly unsettled.

He is upset about something, but I won't ask now.

CHAPTER SEVENTEEN

Pandas in the Park

Simone had intended to leave on Sunday evening so she could have time to rest for the beginning of the week, but Carl had other plans.

"You could leave in the morning. I can take you to the station early, and you'll be in New Haven by nine. What do you think? And best of all, you can have this man"—he pointed at himself-"all to yourself for a few more hours, and we can cuddle." He smiled and gave her that pleading puppy-dog look that always reminded her of when they first met.

"How can I say no? But I'll need to leave super early. If I'm going to get to work on time, I'll have to be on that seven-a.m. train. Will you be up that early to take me?" She raised an eyebrow.

"I will sacrifice a few hours of sleep if you stay. Or you can get an Uber."

He shrugged and cracked a mischievous smile, and she poked him. She couldn't say no to an opportunity to spend more time with him instead of returning to her empty home.

*****

By six o'clock Monday morning, they were already in Carl's

car, heading to Penn Station. Both Simone and Carl were still half asleep, so they weren't talking much. Simone had just rested her head back and closed her eyes to relax a few minutes when the morning show radio host interrupted the music to deliver breaking news.

"The Central Park Precinct police just discovered the body of a young girl lying on the rocks near the Pool. Officers describe the girl as being of Asian descent and in her mid-teens. She is dressed in wool pants, a black coat, and a T-shirt, and police suspect she is the victim of an overdose."

Another victim of an overdose wouldn't draw much attention on a New York City morning, but the reporter continued.

"The police are asking for your help in identifying the body, as they found no identification. However, the outfit she wore might provide a clue, as her gray sweatpants and T-shirt appear to be some kind of school uniform, and a panda logo covered the left breast of the shirt. If you have any information regarding a missing person who matches this description, please call The Central Park Precinct."

Their eyes met, and Simone was wide awake now, alert and present. "I need to go to the precinct!" Simone said. "That girl must be connected to the others, but I'll have to see the T-shirt to be sure."

"I don't think you should get into it, honey. We should keep other people's mess far away from us. We've had plenty of problems, and now that we're finally in a moment of peace, just let it go," he said, keeping his eyes on the road as he continued driving.

"I can't turn a blind eye to this," she replied. "The pictures I found might help the police. Please—just take me to the Central Park Precinct."

"Do you have the pictures with you?" Carl asked.

"I do." Simone tapped her purse and then took out her phone to send a message to Patricia. and ask her to reorganize the schedule for the day.

Carl changed direction and drove to the Central Park Precinct. He dropped Simone off in front of the glass entrance and went to find a place to park. Simone entered the lobby where, for so early in the morning, there were quite a few uniformed policemen and other people gathered.

Simone approached the front desk, and an officer behind the gray counter immediately addressed her.

"Good morning. Can I help you, madam?"

"Good morning, Officer. Yes, please, I think I may have some information about the dead girl found this morning, the one wearing the panda T-shirt."

"Your name, please?"

"Simone Bennet." She reached into her purse, pulled out her driver's license, and handed it to him.

"Hold on a second, and I'll find the detective in charge and ask him to come talk to you. Just wait here, and I'll be back soon."

As there were no chairs in the lobby, Simone stood waiting near the desk. Carl called to tell her he found a spot in one of the pay parking garages nearby.

After another ten minutes, the officer who had greeted her returned, accompanied by a man wearing an ill-fitting, dark suit and tie.

"Miss Bennet, good morning. I'm Detective Bradley Thompson. Please follow me. We can talk in my office."

He turned and strode quickly back down the hall, and Simone followed him, rushing to keep up.

Detective Thompson opened the door for her, went to his desk, and pulled out a black leather chair for her to sit. While she settled into the seat, he addressed her.

"Sorry for being rude," he said, as if he'd read her mind, "but the day started off crazy, and sometimes, I just forget my manners." He gave her a tired smile, causing his already wrinkled pink face to crease further. He was one of those typical blonds, the kind of person whose skin aged easily and turned red as the years go by.

"No worries, Detective." Simone sat with her purse on her lap.

"So, did you know the deceased girl?" The detective didn't beat around the bush.

"Maybe...can I see a picture of her and the panda T-shirt?" She adopted a nonchalant, professional tone. "The girl's death might be linked to a case my former partner was working on. And I'm not here out of curiosity or to stick my nose in police business. I'm a Doctor." Simone pulled her Doctor's license from her purse and showed it to him.

"Normally, I wouldn't share evidence with a member of the public—Doctor or not—but we need help to identify the girl." Thompson picked up an envelope from a pile of documents lying on his desk, removed two pictures, took a magnifying glass from a drawer, and handed the photos and magnifying glass to Simone.

She examined the first photograph, which showed an Asian girl, her eyes open and glazed, her lips blue, lying on a rock with her jacket partially open and a syringe in one hand. The other one showed her on a gurney. Someone had removed her jacket, and as Simone had suspected, the young girl wore the same T-shirt as the two girls in Edward's pictures.

"I'm a psychiatrist, I'm not a police expert but I think we have a pattern here, Detective. I don't know the deceased girl, but recently I came across these pictures," Simone said. She dug in her purse, pulled the pictures from the middle of her book, and handed them to the man. "The image on both T-shirts depicts a panda, exactly like the one on your dead girl's shirt."

"Doctor Bennet, can you lend me that magnifying glass please?" he asked and held out his hand.

"Sure, I'm sorry."

Simone handed over the magnifying glass. He analyzed the pictures in silence for several minutes. Simone gripped the edge of her chair seat with both hands to keep from squirming. For God's sake, how long before he admitted she was right and that there was a connection? Finally, he lifted his head and looked at her.

"It seems you're right. I suppose this girl is dead, too?" He put the picture of the girl in fishnet stockings in front of Simone and pointed at it.

"I really don't know." She shook her head. "I found them in the middle of a book that belonged to my former associate."

"And why did he have these pictures?"

The detective's piercing gaze indicated he was analyzing the situation, trying to determine if he had a suspect.

"I haven´t had an opportunity to ask him about them. He is...was a psychiatrist, as well, and he used to do criminal profiles for the police in New Haven."

"Well, where is he now? How can I get in touch with him?" His voice sounded tight, as if he was impatient or perhaps just highly stressed.

"Unfortunately, he is in MacDougall-Walker Correctional Institution.

Simone drew a deep breath, and then, for the next several minutes, she ran through the entire story. The detective listened intently, his posture shifting as she spoke, and the gravity of the situation began to sink in.

*****

After leaving the police precinct, Simone called Carl.

"I'm finished," she told him. "Where are you?"

"Too far away for you to walk. The parking around here is insane. Just wait there, and I'll pick you up in a few minutes."

Ten minutes later, Carl pulled up in front of the glass entrance, and Simone got into the car.

"Guess what I discovered?" she asked him.

"Another of your pandas?" he asked, merging with the heavy traffic.

"Yes, another one... There's something going on here—some kind of connection—and I think Peter is in the middle of it."

Carl shook his head.

"Peter is locked up for life, and this crime seems recent. How can he be connected?" He sighed. "If there is a connection, I should have my brain analyzed because I really don't know anything about my supposed best friend."

"Nobody does...don't worry...he was your best friend. It's normal to think the best about our friends. Mine was my boyfriend, and I had no idea he had a thing for cold, dead bodies—or that he would take part in homicides just to avoid getting caught masturbating over a cadaver! And to make matters worse, I'm a psychiatrist; I'm supposed to recognize abhorrent behavior when it's right in front of my face."

Simone tried to make light of the subject, but Carl remained serious.

"Honestly, honey, I'm just so disappointed... I used to trust that guy. You can't imagine how fun he was and what a good friend he was."

"Yes, I can... I felt the same way about Edward. We were partners, friends, confidants—"

"Lovers!"

"Yeah, jealous guy, lovers, too."

"Not jealous...just...okay...jealous. I hate the idea of ever sharing you!" His tone of voice remained the same, but she could sense the subtle emphasis, revealing the underlying intensity in his words.

"I have no intention of sharing you, either. No belly dancers are in your future, my dear husband," Simone told him, referencing a part of his old diary where he'd written about Lara hiring a belly dancer for him and encouraging them to fuck. "So, don't worry about any of that. I just wanted to know how far we would have gone if we had let our first experience in a place like that play out..." Simone touched his hand.

"I don't need belly dancers or any other woman..." He paused then changed the subject. "Honey, we're closing the office for Christmas on December fifth. What do you think about spending the holidays at home? We'll have a nice, quiet, peaceful few days, looking out at the water... Or do you have other plans?"

Simone breathed a quiet sigh of relief. She hated to discuss jealousy or other complicated emotions unless she was working with a client, so she happily talked about their plans for Christmas throughout the rest of their trip to the station.

*****

Simone took the next available train to New Haven. She'd done her duty, and now, the matter was in the hands of the police. But as she pulled her book from her purse to continue reading, she couldn't stop thinking about the dead girls and the connection that must exist between them and the bears Peter had mentioned.

Was Ed trying to figure that out, too?

Her mind didn't rest the whole trip, revolving around the

subject.

CHAPTER EIGTHEEN

Marriage Sucks

From the station in New Heaven, Simone took an Uber to the clinic, and when she arrived, Patricia was busy on the phone. Simone waited until her secretary finished the call.

"Good morning, Patricia. How've you been?" Simone smiled a greeting. "Do you have my schedule for today?"

"I'm fantastic, Doctor Bennet. This afternoon, you've got an appointment with Elizabeth, followed by a two o'clock with Chivon." Patricia looked at the schedule and back at Simone.

"That's good, but I can't pay the bills around here with two clients a day."

"You'll be okay. Don't worry. You've been back one week, and you already have five patients. How many other psychiatrists can grow their business that quickly? And I've been in touch with many of your former patients, and some are thinking about coming back." Patricia smiled.

My biggest cheerleader...

Simone held up her hands, fingers crossed. "I hope so."

"Don't hope, think positively. You're an amazing Doctor."

Patricia was showing an optimistic side Simone hadn't

ever seen. In the past, the secretary had been composed and efficient, but now she seemed happier and more relaxed.

Maybe I'm different, too, and that's reflecting on the people around me.

"Can you get something for my lunch, please?" Simone headed down the short hallway to her office to prepare for her first patient, but she still had to eat lunch. Her growling stomach told her she'd regret it if she didn't feed it something soon.

"Anything special?" asked Patricia called out.

Simone paused, turned back, then shrugged.

"Surprise me."

*****

Despite needing every patient she could get right now, Simone dreaded the time she spent with Elizabeth. Even though she recognized she was being petty, Simone couldn't help herself and had privately labeled her *Boring Betty,* and the woman's weekly timeslots had become.

The Boring Betty Bitch Sessions.

For half an hour, the woman rambled about her life, her misery, her concerns, while Simone struggled to stay awake. Betty's appointment was right after lunch, and the combination of tedious conversation and the blood flow toward the stomach and intestines process turned Simone's brains into a foggy gray mass.

Simone shifted in her chair, sat forward, and blinked several times.

I need to change the course of this conversation before I begin snoring!

"Betty, let's back up a little and talk about your marriage. I think it's the root of many of your problems."

"Oh, it was. The trauma that man put me through..."

Here comes more complaining.

"Trauma? What kind of trauma?" Simone raised an eyebrow.

"You know... Edward turned my self-esteem into powder. All his comments about my background, my lack of education... He wanted me to go back to school when I had a small child at home so he would be proud of me, always comparing my lack of knowledge to your super-exclusive education..."

And here comes the pinprick...

"But in the end, you remained faithful to your choice of being a mom?"

"That I did; I thought it was better to raise a good son than to lose myself in a stack of tedious textbooks. Besides, I have no idea what I would study. I never liked school, never wanted to go to college, and I would be a failure, anyway, so he would blame me for being a failure. If I never tried, he would just suspect I'd fail, right?" She blinked at Simone.

Yeah, clever. Give people reasons to believe you're stupid, but don't let them be sure about it...

"Were you afraid people would think you're a failure? Do you still have these feelings? Do you live in constant fear that you will be found out?" Simone kept her face expressionless.

"I was like that during my marriage...all the time... Sometimes, I still feel that way. I'm terrified people will see the poor girl in me, that they'll realize I have no class, no education, and I don't belong in their world."

Well, she wasn't wrong in her diagnosis. This fear indicates low self-esteem, but what are the causes?

Finally, Betty had managed to raise Simone's professional curiosity.

"Did you do your homework? Remember, I asked you to find something admirable about yourself?"

"My ability to adapt! I thought about it, and I'm able to adapt to the worst circumstances." Betty smiled, clearly proud of herself.

"That's good! Most people don't have that kind of ability, and it's a survival skill. How did you come to that conclusion?"

"Looking through the rearview mirror, I thought about where I came from and where I am now, and I can see I was able to shape myself to every situation that was presented in my life. A temptress to get a husband, a mother, a chic, rich Doctor's wife..., I can even play dead if I need to!"

"What was that?"

Did she just tell me she can play dead? Like a dog? Tommy can play dead.

"Yes, it was one of Edward's fantasies. At some point in our marriage, around the fifth year, I think, he wanted me to lose weight. And I'm not talking about losing a few pounds to have a better figure; he wanted me to be skinny, practically nothing but skin and bones. I suffered a lot to lose twenty-two pounds, but I did it. I wanted to save my marriage, and I could see our sex life was almost nonexistent, so if he was a fan of models, I would pretend I was a model for him..."

Simone leaned toward Betty, even more interested in her story.

"And when you lost that much weight, did your sex life become better?"

Betty looked in Simone's eyes.

"Yes, much better than it had been before, for him at least... I think..."

"But not for you..." Simone said.

Betty shook her head.

"No, I was always hungry, and before sex he wanted me

to bathe in cold water, which I hated, and to lie down motionless in our bed like I was dead."

She crossed her hands over her chest like a dead person and closed her eyes. When she opened them again, tears stuck to her long false lashes and trickled down her cheeks.

"It had to do with his fantasies about dead people, didn't it? The one they mentioned in court...necro-something?" Betty asked in a strangled voice.

"Necrophilia. Unfortunately, I think so. Tell me a little bit more about the fantasy. You used to lie in your bed, your body cold from a shower, and you were to remain motionless?"

"Yes, he demanded I not move the entire time we had intercourse, but he worshipped my body, doing things to me that you do to a normal person, so it was pleasurable, and I couldn't just lie there for long... But when I moved, he used to get mad and say I had ruined the moment."

Simone's stomach was in turmoil.

I won't throw up... I am a professional, and I can deal with this, no matter how disgusted I am now.

She shifted on the couch and focused on keeping a serene expression. For the first time, she pitied Betty, as tears ran down the poor woman's cheeks. Simone handed Betty the Kleenex box and waited until she calmed.

"I feel like I could never please him. Did he do that to you?" She stared at Simone.

Not to me, thought Simone, but a memory of waking up and finding Edward watching her attentively came to her mind. Chills raced up her arms.

Was he exciting himself, fantasizing I was dead? No, that's not the Ed I know...

"I'm not in treatment here, and we need to work on your self-esteem. Betty, I'm going to recommend a book for you to read..." As Simone rose to get the book from her shelf, she paused. Betty had just said she hated books. Simone turned. “Do you think you could read it for our next session?”

She nodded. “I will if it will help me. I can do that.”

Simone found the book and returned to the couch. Betty lifted her chin, as if to harden her resolve, accepted the book, and placed it inside her expensive purse. She got up to leave, holding her hand out to Simone.

“Thank you, you’re very good. I’m feeling better already just for spilling the beans.”

Yes, you are, and I´m here feeling I´m an idiot and the worst psychiatrist ever.

*****

When Chivon entered the office for her appointment that afternoon, a wave of perfume invaded Simone’s nostrils. Today, Chivon had draped a fur coat, the real thing—an expensive, cream-colored fur—over her shoulders, beneath which she wore a designer-looking, cream-colored wool dress. She had on a matching wool beret and gloves.

What a diva.

Simone waited while the woman took off the coat, gloves, and beret and threw everything carelessly onto the couch.

Ugh…who enters someone’s office and immediately creates a mess?

Chivon must have hoped to appear wealthy and sophisticated, perhaps to assert her dominance. Why else would she ignore the coat closet they had in the reception area? She’d used it during their last visit, and it certainly wasn’t cold enough in the building to warrant wearing a heavy coat!

“Good morning, Doctor!” Chivon plopped down on the couch in front of Simone.

“Good morning, Chivon!” Simone looked at her notes

about the woman and asked, "Did you do your homework?"

"Yes, I did. I've been interviewing some friends, and I've decided marriage is a hard job...even when you marry for love!" She made a heart by joining her hands, but her contorted mouth was miles away from a romantic expression.

"And why do you say that?" Simone raised an eyebrow.

Is she getting realistic in her expectations after only a week?

"Women who married for love have their hearts torn to shreds, since men tend to be disgusting creatures. My friends' words, not mine." She pointed into the air and then back to herself. "Women who married out of love, for reasons other than money, are all unhappy and thinking their lives are over, but they go on for the sake of the kids, tradition, and every other bullshit reason you can imagine; however, women who married for money are in better shape, as they have money as a solace for their loneliness and sometimes a driver or a gardener. I gave your phone number to some of the women I spoke with. They need a good listener." She touched her ear.

Is that what I am? A good listener? A paid friend? Is this how my patients see me?

Simone reflected on the idea, but didn´t bring it up to Chivon.

"Thank you for the referrals. So, I suppose you concluded you should not be married at all."

"No, I will still tie the knot eventually; I just need to find the right guy—one who agrees with an open marriage."

She didn't elaborate. Instead, she sat there staring, as if waiting for Simone's reaction.

"That's a possibility. Usually, open marriages happen when the marriage bed gets cold, but the couple still have feelings for each other or mutual responsibilities. That type of arrangement usually ends with someone getting their heart broken, but maybe you're right. If you can get someone to agree with this from the beginning, it may work."

"Easy to say, hard to find." Chivon made a funny face and smiled.

"Yes, usually it is."

Simone didn't know what else to say. Her thoughts returned to the woman's previous statement about being a good listener.

Is she just using me as someone to talk to instead of trying to get to the root of her problems?

"Well...while I was researching for my homework, I fucked the husband of one of my friends ...She is not a close friend, you know..."

The unexpected confession made Simone start and focus on Chivon's face.

She's not joking...

"Please explain." Simone kept her expression neutral as she gazed at Chivon.

"I don't have many friends, you know. Women are jealous creatures, and when you're pretty, they tend to hate you."

Pretty and modest.

Simone fought to keep from rolling her eyes.

"I have many more people I think of as acquaintances..." Chivon paused.

"Acquaintances?"

"Yes. You know, the people you associate with but know to watch your back, so you don't walk away with a knife sticking out of your spine?" Chivon didn't wait for an answer. "I decided to interview some of those women. One of them, Holly, is someone I met in college, but she didn't stick around to graduate. Instead, she married a rich guy and decided to be a housewife."

Chivon made a noise with her lips as if she had just sucked on a lemon.

"That idea seems to bother you. What's wrong with Holly's choice?"

"In my opinion, putting yourself in the hands of a man is a stupid idea... But anyway, I called her, and we made plans to get together—in her splendid mansion, of course, since she needed to show me what *she had achieved* in life." Chivon used her fingers to make air quotes as she emphasized the words. "I arrived early, and her husband was at home. She was out shopping or something like that. He is still a charming man, and we chatted like old friends. Before I knew it, we were drinking champagne and laughing, and he got a hungry look in his eyes and kept looking at my body. Then suddenly, he got down on his knees beside me and started caressing my legs."

"Did you try to stop him?"

"Not really. My mind was already foggy from the booze. I'm an easy woman. I like to be touched, so I let him caress my legs, then he lifted my skirt, touched my pussy over my panties, and I was lost, already melting for a dick. He pulled me from the couch and put me against the wall near the fireplace, took his cock out of his pants, and filled me." She rolled her eyes toward the ceiling and closed them, no doubt recalling the sensations she'd experienced that day. "He started to move quickly, like a little rabbit, but fortunately, he allowed me to come, and Doctor, I did. But the problem is, when I came, the whole house must have heard it." Chivon kept her eyes closed, her chin up.

Is she going to come in front of me?

"When I started to come, he pushed me down and finished in my mouth." She opened her eyes and looked at Simone with a startled expression.

"It seems you enjoyed yourself. A lot," Simone said.

"I did. I love experiences with a hint of danger, but just as he came in my mouth, Holly arrived and discovered us in that delicate position… Me on my knees, my mouth full, his shaft in his hand, and his pants to his knees."

"What did you do?" Simone asked, taking notes.

"I swallowed, of course; I'm a polite girl, and I wouldn't try to explain myself with a full mouth."

She must be joking.

Simone glanced up, expecting to see a grin on the woman's face, but Chivon's expression remained serious.

"No, I mean, what about your friend?" Simone asked.

"Well, for obvious reasons, I couldn't interview her, and she kicked me out of her house," Chivon said. "I never imagined someone could scream so loudly. My God, no class at all." She put her hands over her ears and shook her head in a dramatic fashion.

This woman is a joke!

Simone was trying to keep her expression impassive, but the more she talked to the debauched woman, the more she wanted to laugh. She needed to use all her self-control, because if she started to laugh, she might never stop.

Simone drew a deep breath.

Calm down… Remember, you've heard worse.

She looked down at her notes and then back at her patient.

"Chivon, you were doing research about married life, then you ended up having sexual relations with your friend's husband…inside her house."

Chivon nodded at Simone's summarization of the encounter.

Simone read from her notepad.

"You told me, your words, 'I love a dangerous experience,' and you're not upset because your friend caught her husband cheating with you. You're not concerned about what happened after you left; you're just annoyed because she shouted at you. Do you really think you're prepared to get married and settle down?" Simone met Chivon's gaze.

"I want to!" Chivon seemed agitated by Simone's words. "But I don't know if I can. As I said before, marriage sucks, but if I find the right kind of man...one who allows me to have whomever I want and whenever I want, it may work! Why must marriage be traditional?"

That's an answer I don't have.

CHAPTER NINETEEN

Do You Want to Meet Me?

The month passed quickly with Simone adding new patients to her schedule day by day. She hadn't returned to MacDougall, telling herself she was too busy preparing material for her classes or finding other excuses. However, she had finally decided to return there on Thursday.

Thursday morning, Simone woke up late—a rare occurrence, but she and Carl had talked on the phone for a long time the previous night. He seemed to need reassurance and had come across as a bit needy. In her opinion, he still hadn't gotten over their experience at the swingers' club last month. Since then, he had constantly asked if she loved him or tried to gauge how deep her love for him truly was.

When they finally said goodnight and hung up the phone, Simone hadn't been able to fall right to sleep. Instead, she kept thinking about what was happening with Carl and wondering how she should handle the situation.

I'm the psychiatrist here; I need to figure it out.

As a result, she'd spent much of the night tossing and turning while the unstoppable work engine inside her mind tried to solve the puzzle.

Simone took a quick shower, threw on a white blouse

and a grey suit, applied tinted sunscreen and lip gloss for a healthier look, and grabbed her purse. As she hurried past the kitchen on her way to the garage, she scooped up an apple from the basket of fruit she kept on the kitchen island.

Inside the car, holding the apple in her teeth, Simone started the engine then turned on the heat. She shivered in the icy December morning air as she fastened her seatbelt and adjusted the radio to a local news station. She pulled out onto the street and sped off. If she got to MacDougall late, she probably wouldn't get a chance to talk to Peter. The institution had strict rules about visitation hours, even for Doctors.

On the radio, the reporter ended one story about a local homicide then started describing the latest on a war overseas. Such misery... Simone had a strong opinion that the news could affect people's moods, and she'd decided a long time ago not to listen to it every day. Instead, she tuned in once a week or so to get caught up on current events, or more often when there was some kind of crisis. That morning, there didn't seem to be anything new—just rehashing the same old, depressing drama.

Simone connected her phone to the car's Bluetooth system and chose one of her French music folders. As she began thinking about her upcoming conversation with Peter, she decided to shift her thoughts and started singing along with the song blaring from the speakers.

"Balance ton quoi Même si tu parles mal des filles je sais qu'au fond t'as compris..."

*****

After following the usual protocol—leaving her purse and phone in a locker and retaining just her small recorder—Simone turned to find Liam waiting for her. "What a pleasure to see you, Liam!"

She extended her hand to him, and he took it in a strong,

warm handshake.

A strong handshake tells a lot about a person. This one is friendly.

“Same here, Doctor. I knew you would come today, I’ve been checking the system and saw your name, so I wanted to be available. I will take you to the infirmary. Peter Hay is already waiting for you, please follow me.” He waved for her to come with him down a long corridor.

“Thanks a lot Liam”.

They strode side by side down the hallway, pausing three different times so another guard could buzz them through a series of sliding iron doors.

“I talked to Doctor Reynolds, and I’m sorry, but he said he’s not interested in seeing you. On the other hand, the coordinator of our program said he’d like to have your help because that would mean we could have more inmates take part in the course.”

Not what I wanted, but it’s a start.

Simone wanted to take part in the program to spend some time near Edward. Even if he was a convict, she still had deep feelings for him. Human beings couldn’t just push a button and stop caring about a friend they’d had for years.

“Sounds great. When can I talk to him?” she asked. “The coordinator, I mean.”

“I’ll check for you.”

They reached the infirmary door, and Liam unlocked it for Simone and allowed her to enter. Peter was already there, chained to a chair.

“I will come for you when it’s time for you to leave. By then, I should have that information for you.” He glanced at Peter then back at Simone. “I hope this goes well.”

She nodded.

"Thanks, Liam."

Simone waited for the agent to leave. At the sound of the door locking from the outside, she suppressed a shiver and turned to Peter.

She drew a deep breath and crossed the room to stand next to him, looking into his eyes.

"Good morning, Peter." Simone smiled, grabbed the chair next to him, and sat down. She arranged the recorder on her lap, ready to begin.

"Good morning, my annoying frog."

Simone raised an eyebrow at him.

Annoying frog?

Peter began making a series of strange noises.

"Bremmmm bremmmm bremmmm, bremmm, breemmm, bremmm."

She frowned, but then it hit her. er daughter had shown her a short, animated film on YouTube of a frog pretending to ride a motorcycle as it made the sounds of the bike's motor revving. She laughed.

"Someone is in a good mood today...Did you get fucked last night?" Peter asked in his sweetest voice.

Simone remained poised, refusing to rise to his bait.

"Well, Peter, how've you been?" she asked, her tone calm and measured. She waited, bracing herself for the sarcastic answers she knew were likely to follow, prepared to navigate his strange behavior.

"I can see you're making friends around here."

Simone ignored his comment.

"The last time I was here, you were very concerned about bears...pandas, I think. Can you tell me more about those and why you were so worried about them?"

"Ah, the pandas. They're cute Chinese bears. There's a huge park for them in China. Wolong. It's beautiful. Do you know the caretakers must dress like pandas and cover themselves in panda piss so the little ones don't get used to humans and can be returned to live in the wild?" He raised an eyebrow and gave her a proud smile.

Instead of reacting to the irrelevant information, Simone cut right to the point. "I don't think you were talking about bears, Peter. I think you were worried about those Asian girls. You know...the ones who wear white T-shirts with logos of pandas on them." Simone made a circle on her chest and watched Peter's reaction.

He didn't blink an eye, but Simone caught the slight twitch of a muscle in his jaw.

Nervous, honey?

Simone cocked her head and stared at him but remained silent.

"Do you know what I did for my last birthday before I came here to this little Switzerland?"

"Switzerland?"

"Yeah, cold, isolated, and populated by strange people... My birthday is in October—the twenty-first—and I decided to celebrate by having some fun. I turned forty, and you know as well as anyone how difficult it is to face middle age. I mean, I know it's been quite a few years since you had to deal with that, but I'm sure you still remember how depressing it was..."

Peter gazed at her for several seconds, but when she didn't react or indicate he'd gotten under her skin, he sighed and continued.

"So, to celebrate and ease my displeasure, I decided to switch things up and try something new. I killed a man...just for the sake of variety," he whispered, leaning toward her.

That was news. Peter's criminal record didn't include the murder of any men. Simone remained silent and waited for more.

"I was tired of those weeping little girls begging me for mercy. I mean, it was fun to toy with them, but their histrionics really made me angry. I had this boyfriend back then—Brian scatterbrain Gonzales, Latin blood, huge dick, empty space where his mind should be—so I decided it was time to get rid of him. I didn't want any kind of party that year, so we decided to have dinner together, and I told him I had this special location in mind, and I took him to my secret place—the one you know..."

Peter was referring to his secret apartment and a special room he had designed—a place where he brought his victims to torture and kill them. Simone had been a "guest" there for some time and the experience had left her with broken ribs, pneumonia, and trauma that would haunt her for years.

"Did he like it there?" Simone asked as she recalled how creepy it'd been. Chills raced up her spine and along her arms. She put one hand over the other to avoid any movement.

"Such a moron...he loved it! The dolt thought I had taken him there for a little bondage session. He volunteered to be chained to the wall. I attached him in the X position, cuffs on his wrists and ankles...a collar around his neck. The idiot was so happy! I flogged him for a while then took his tool in my hands, caressed it, and he began moaning and pulling against his restraints. I sucked him, licked his balls, and he was so hard he probably would have exploded inside my mouth within minutes. He closed his eyes and he never saw death coming." Peter gave Simone a mischievous smile, happy to brag about his sexual prowess.

"How did you kill him?"

"I had this small remote control. One button released the cuffs from his wrists and ankles, and the other tightened the collar around his neck. He died by hanging. Such a big, strong man...but he didn't even last two minutes." Peter scowled.

"And how did you get rid of the body? There's no mention of any of this in your criminal files. Obviously, you were never convicted for killing this man..."

"I'm here for life... It's not like they can add any more years. Unless, of course, they find a way to extend punishment into the afterlife...as you reminded me the other day."

"I'm here in a professional capacity as your psychiatrist, so you can trust me not divulge anything you say."

"*Trust me*...what a beautiful phrase... So many people I trusted in my life...so many disappointments and regrets..." He looked at the ceiling.

Simone wasn't buying his act. Instead of answering her question, he was getting all philosophical and emotional, yet his voice stayed flat.

"How did you dispose of the body?"

"We buried him. Not a proper funeral, mind you. Sorry!"

We again. Was this *we* his Chinese boyfriend?

"Where did you bury him?"

"In a place I could call home..." He flashed that same stupid smile.

"Where is home?"

"Where the heart is."

Peter sang the phrase in a loud, dissonant voice, drawing the attention of the guard in the corridor. The man looked at them through the glass window. Simone nodded at him to indicate all was well.

"How did you feel about his death?"

"I regret it." He lowered his head.

"Do you regret? Explain that feeling to me." Usually,

psychopaths didn't have any kind of regrets. Simone needed to understand what he meant by the word.

"His dick was marvelous, you know…hard to find a good dick these days, so…I regret having killed his owner." He smiled at her.

Simone wanted to smack the bastard, but she kept her cool.

"I understand… Nice story… Now, why don't we talk a little bit about pandas?"

"Sorry, Doctor, I'm no specialist, just an amateur of nature, and my knowledge is limited to what I already told you." He rose and started to shout, "Guard, guard, we're done here."

Simone watched him closely, noting the tightness around his mouth and eyes.

There is much more than what he is telling me.

*****

As promised, Liam returned to the infirmary to escort Simone back to the main building. He gave her his sweet smile, and he seemed overwhelmed with excitement.

"Doctor Bennet, I have good news!" He rubbed his hands together. "Please, come with me." He waved toward the door and let her go in front of him.

How can a man maintain an aura of innocence and be so polite all the time, especially working in a place like this?

"Am I going to meet with the program director?"

"It's better than that! Doctor Reynolds changed his mind; he wants to see you!" Liam's voice was filled with excitement. "I'm a huge fan of reconciliation between friends and relatives. I know it's hard to forgive the reasons that put someone here," he said, waving to the walls around them. "But having someone who cares is so important for the prisoners. You wouldn't believe how much it means!"

While Liam continued to explain the benefits of forgiveness, Simone's heart sank. A mix of emotions swirled inside her, and she wasn't certain if she was ready to face them.

Am I prepared to face Ed?

Suddenly, her mouth was dry, and her legs weren't so firm.

"To-today?"

"No, unfortunately, visiting hours are almost over, and we won't be able to fill out all the required paperwork in time, but we can schedule everything for next Thursday. What do you think? I'll prepare the papers, and if you give me an email address, I'll send them to you. You can fill everything in and sign it, then send it back so when you come on Thursday, we won't have to deal with any additional red tape."

"Sure." Simone released a relieved breath as she opened her purse to find her card holder. She gave Liam one of her business cards.

"The email address is right here." She pointed to the bottom of the card. "Thanks a lot, Liam." She smiled broadly at him.

"You're welcome, Doctor. Oh, and Doctor Reynolds sent a message for you; he told me to tell you not to get involved in Peter Hay's business because it's too dangerous."

Simone frowned.

How does he know?

"How does he know I'm visiting Peter?" She lifted an eyebrow.

Liam opened his arms. "Everybody knows everything inside these walls. We call it the Hall Radio because news spreads through the corridors at lightning speed, just like a live radio broadcast." He shook his head. "You must understand… The inmates don't have much to do, so gossip is a sort of a favorite hobby."

"It's like living in a small town—a real nightmare when it comes to gossip." Simone held out her hand.

"Thank you again."

After collecting her things from the locker, she rushed through the front lobby and out the door, anxious to leave. Her heartbeat was still a little erratic.

After all this time...

In a few days, she'd see Edward again.

CHAPTER TWENTY

A Doctor Without Borders

Once inside her car, Simone pulled out her cell to call Carl, hoping to speak to him on her way to the office. If he was available, maybe they could exchange some ideas about Peter and Edward. As she turned the ringer back on, she saw she had a missed call from John Mayer. She would return his call and then phone Carl.

John was a brilliant neurosurgeon, but he'd been tormented for years after Lara, the love of his life, had rejected him. After her tragic death, he uncovered the truth. He learned about how her mother had handed her over to be abused, and how his mother had blackmailed Lara to keep them apart. After that, he'd completely fallen apart.

He'd been Simone's patient for a while, until he'd had a breakdown and had tried to seek revenge on a man from Lara's past. After that, he'd decided to do the same thing Simone had done—put the brakes on his life for a while and try to regain some perspective. He'd gone on a year's sabbatical, traveling around the world through various countries, but he'd contacted Simone at least once a month to tell her about his progress.

Except for the last two months. What's he up to?

Simone and John's relationship over the past year had changed from Doctor-patient to one of friendship, a fact that made her smile. In her professional opinion, John was in pain, still grieving Lara and their forever lost love, more in need of licking his wounds than receiving intensive therapy. Simone preferred to offer him friendly encouragement, not psychiatric advice.

"Hello, John! How've you been? Where in this huge world are you now? I thought you had vanished!" She teased him, her tone reflecting her anticipation and excitement to learn about his latest adventure.

"Just got back home from Africa last week! What an unforgettable journey! I have so many things to tell you!! I'm preparing to go back to my professional life!" He answered, his voice charged with enthusiasm.

"That's great news! Are you going back to the hospital?"

"Nope… As I told you the last time we talked, my journey has shown me there's much more to life than operating on brains and making money. I'm joining Doctors Without Borders."

"Wow! Seriously? That's amazing news! I'm so excited for you! Those men and women do wonderful work. When do you plan to leave and where are you going? Can we meet before you go? I need you to tell me everything about the last year and of course, what led you to make this huge decision." Simone wanted to evaluate his mental condition to make certain he'd made such a radical change in his life for the right reasons.

"Sure, I have a month to prepare, get all the necessary shots and handle all the red tape stuff. I'll visit you since I'll need hours to tell you every detail. I don't want you to think I've gone crazy. I know you, Doctor Bennet; you're already trying to figure out if I'm insane or if I've made a wise choice."

John laughed, and she had to join him.

"Well, you do know me. Let's get together this weekend, okay? Carl is going to be home. You can come and stay with us."

Simone had met John through Carl, and even though the two men had both dated Lara —at times even simultaneously —they had become close friends.

Two men grieving for one girl... I've never had anyone compete for me like that.

"Sounds great to me!"

"Come on Friday. That'll give us plenty of time to have a good meal and to get drunk over your news!"

"May I bring someone with me?" he asked softly.

"Sure, any friend of yours is a friend of ours," she replied.

"Perfect! See you on Friday."

After Simone ended the call, still smiling over her conversation with John, she tried to reach Carl, but his secretary told her he was in an offsite meeting, so Simone drove to her office, thinking about Doctors Without Borders. Many newly minted Doctors dreamed of joining them, but few had the courage to face the challenge.

*****

Patricia opened the front door before Simone could reach out and turn the knob. Amazing how that woman recognized the sound of Simone's car.

Patricia wore a broad grin as she helped Simone remove her coat.

"You have a new patient today, Doctor." Patricia's voice bubbled with excitement. She took the coat and handed Simone a manila file. "She was a referral from your other new patient, the very rich Mr. Taylor-Miller. Her name is Keanne Milford. It seems her father is a great friend of the Mr. Taylor." Patricia winked, still smiling like the Cheshire Cat.

What happened to this woman over the last year?

Patricia had gone from staid and always composed, to sassy and mischievous.

"When will she arrive?" Simone glanced at the first page in the file.

"At one o'clock. When I told her you didn't have any space in your schedule this week, she insisted it was urgent and kept pestering me. Finally, I told her you decided to open your schedule for her during your lunch break. Of course, I told her we wouldn't be able to bill her at the regular rate, but she had no problem paying a higher rate."

"Marketing is losing a great agent, Patricia." Simone smiled.

"I told you; in less than six months, your schedule is going to be back the way it was—overflowing."

Patricia turned and went back to her desk, humming some indecipherable tune.

That woman is really a box of surprises!

*****

At exactly one that afternoon, Patricia opened the door to Simone's office to allow Snow White to step inside. The resemblance to the Disney character was so amazing, Simone smiled.

I would love to see her in a Snow-White dress. If she had been my child, I probably would have dressed her like that on Halloween.

But Miss Milford wasn't a child... From the file Patricia had provided, Simone had learned the girl was twenty-five years old, even if she looked much younger.

"So sorry to disturb you during your lunch, Doctor Bennet, and thanks for seeing me today!" The voice was as sweet as her porcelain skin was fair.

I need to control myself, or I'm going to call her Snow in no time.

"Good afternoon, Keanne, nice to meet you. You're welcome. Please take a seat." Simone smiled and pointed at the couch to her right. She preferred to keep some distance, but this girl seemed so fragile, Simone wanted her closer.

"Thank you!" Keanne sat, placed her purse next to her side, closed her knees together like a good girl, and gazed at Simone with the most beautiful black eyes.

"What brought you to see me, Keanne?" Simone picked up her notepad, leaned back on her couch, and prepared to listen.

Grumpy was probably mean to her.

The girl didn't answer. Instead, she rolled up the sleeves of her Chanel suit jacket, revealing dozens of bruises and red marks.

"What happened to you?" Simone asked the question in a normal tone, hiding her unease.

"I was raped!" Keanne's eyes filled with tears.

Simone resisted the urge to hug her. "Have you been to the police?"

"No..."

"Do you feel comfortable enough to tell me how it happened?" Simone asked, allowing the girl to avoid the subject of the police. For now... "Do you know the offender?"

"I do...he is a friend..."

Well, I would call him many things, but certainly not "friend".

"A friend?"

"Yes...we were in my apartment, having drinks, laughing, and then suddenly, he was all over me, kissing me, licking me everywhere, it seemed he wanted to devour me. I started to fight against him, trying to resist, but he was much stronger, very muscular, and he pushed me back on the sofa and held my arms." She paused and stretched out her arms.

So, that is how the bruises happened.

The girl took a deep breath and continued. "He managed to hold me down, and he ripped off my clothes, climbed between my legs, and stuck it in me. He still had a hold of my arms, and he started calling me names…" Another pause.

"What kind of names?"

"Slut, sorcerer…that kind of thing… He told me I was a tease, and that he was obsessed with me. He kept driving into me like a madman. He even bit my nipple…" She made a gesture, as if she was going to lower her blouse beneath the suit.

"You don't need to show me. Please proceed."

"He whispered in my ear that he wanted to try new things with me. And I said no. No! He pulled out of me, turned me, and pressed my face against the couch cushion. I felt as if I was suffocating. He held my arms again, this time at my back, and forced himself inside my anus. I screamed in pain, but he kept going despite my discomfort and protests. When he finished inside my anus, he pulled out and told me I was a hot piece of ass. Then he just left me there crying, feeling dirty." She lowered her head, staring down at her hands.

"And how long have you been having these fantasies of rape? Who is the collaborator, your boyfriend?"

The girl's face turned a deep, dark red as she blushed, then she lifted her head, locking eyes with Simone, her own filled with a startled expression.

"Did you know from the beginning it was a fantasy?"

"No…the first two sentences sounded real, but then your voice gave you away. And the clear pleasure you felt. Is that your only fantasy, or do you have others? Does it disturb you? Why are you here? You tried to mislead me into believing your fantasy was reality… Why?"

"It is my only fantasy, and it disturbs me a lot. I can't come if I don't feel as if I'm being forced and abused." She opened her knees and leaned toward Simone.

She has abandoned her pose; now, the treatment begins.

"Have you ever been really raped?"

The girl shook her head.

"Do you remember being abused when you were a child or a teenager?"

"No! My parents were overprotective of me. I'm an only child." She gave an emphatic shake of her head.

"How did your parents approach the subject of sex with you?"

Let's go back and see if there are any Mommy or Daddy issues.

"We are Baptists, so they never talked about it much. My mom just told me sex is for married people…" Keanne massaged her bare ring finger.

"Are you very religious?"

"I used to go to church every Sunday, but now that I'm living far from my parents, I've been avoiding it."

"Because you don't like to go to church, or because you don't believe in their teachings anymore?" Simone continued to take notes, leaving time for her patient to reflect.

"I do believe in God; it's not that…"

"Maybe you feel ashamed about your sex life?" Simone fixed her gaze on the girl's face.

Keanne lowered her head again.

"Ashamed, definitely."

"Well, Keanne, there are many studies on the subject of fantasies. None are conclusive; however, in your case, one of those studies fits perfectly. People who fantasize about being forced are usually looking for a way to absolve themselves from the guilt. If you were forced to perform certain acts, no one can blame you. You didn't disobey your parents; you were saving yourself for marriage, but you couldn't do anything to avoid what happened to you, and you weren't a willing participant. As I said, it is just one of many theories..."

While Simone talked the girl nodded.

"Is the pain part of the fantasy?" Simone asked.

"Always...and I usually get bruised like this...or worse..." She lowered her head once more.

Shame and guilt.

"Shame and guilt are powerful components of masochism, according to the psychiatrist Michael Samsel..."

"Well, he is wrong! I'm not a masochist!" Keanne shouted, her body growing rigid, her nose suddenly in the air.

"How often do you play being raped? It is a regular fantasy, or is it sporadic?" Simone already knew the answer. Keanne had said she couldn't reach an orgasm without incorporating the fantasy, but it was important to construct the thought and lead the girl to her own conclusions.

"I told you. I can't have an orgasm without that fantasy..."

"How often do you get hurt while pretending to be raped?" Simone asked.

"Always..." Keanne looked as if she was trying to disappear into the sofa.

"Do you feel pleasure in the pain?" Simone locked eyes with Keanne.

"Yes." She answered in a barely audible voice.

"I don't like labels, but it sounds like masochism to me. You feel guilty about sexual relations because you're contradicting your parents' beliefs, so you need to fantasize you're being raped to alleviate your guilt—if you're raped and in pain, you feel complete relief, am I right?"

"Yes, you are." Again, she spoke in a strangled voice, and her eyes filled with tears. "I've never connected the dots like that, but it's exactly how I feel!" A fat tear rolled down her cheek. "Can you treat me? I feel like such a freak!"

"You are not a freak, and if you can admit all that in one session, you are already being treated and on your way to understand yourself and your needs. It's not wrong to have fantasies; it's a good thing, and most people have them. In your case, the problem is that your fantasies are hurting you and have deep roots. We need to understand the guilt, because when we do, you can decide whether you need to get hurt to feel pleasure or not.

"And if I like the pain?"

*****

Simone found a *bouef bourguignon* in the back of the freezer.

How long has this been in here?

She didn't remember the last time she'd eaten *bouef bourguignon*, but the other option was frozen lasagna, so... She put the container into the microwave, then set the machine to defrost.

The telephone she'd left on the kitchen island started to ring. Simone picked it up and answered.

"Hello, my love. I bet you're home defrosting your dinner," Carl said in a husky voice.

Simone smiled.

He knows me well...

"You bet right. I think the dish I'm heating up was on Noah's Ark. I can't even remember the last time we had *boeuf bourguignon*. How are you, love?"

"Tired, missing my girl, and Christmas is still three weeks away!"

"You're coming home on Friday, right? I invited John to come for a visit. He's back and has a million stories to share. I thought we'd enjoy his company for an evening. Is that okay with you?"

"Sure, I've missed John! How is he? Feeling better?"

"I really don't know... I mean, he wants to join Doctors Without Borders..."

Carl let out a low whistle.

"That's a little bit radical, isn't it? Like going from Johns Hopkins to no hope. I don't know much about them, but those guys work in the worst places in the world, don't they?" Carl's voice held a note of concern.

"They do, and to be honest, that's one of the main reasons I invited him for a visit. I want to ask him some questions, watch his reactions, and see if I can figure out whether he's made a well-thought-out, rational decision or..."

"Or if he's still punishing himself over Lara?" Carl asked.

"You would make a good psychiatrist, love!" His intuitiveness surprised her.

Simone heard one single beep, looked over her shoulder, and saw that the defrosting process was over. Then she went to the microwave and adjusted it to heat her dinner.

"I have an excellent teacher at home!"

"Thanks, my love. I've never noticed you paying attention to my lessons."

"I do—I'm always trying to learn something new when you talk about psychiatric stuff."

Behind her, the microwave beeped, and Simone went to open the door and take out her dinner. She set the container on the island.

"It sounds like your dinner is ready. Do you wanna hang up so you can eat?"

"Nope, I can eat and talk. I have more news to tell you" She balanced her phone between her ear and her shoulder while she gathered up a placemat, a dish, silverware, and a napkin. She took a seat on the barstool. "I'm putting the phone on speaker, so let me know if the sound is good," she said while placing the phone on the kitchen island and tapping the speaker button on the call screen. "Can you hear me now?"

"Yes, I can hear you well. So, tell me! New patients?" Carl asked.

"Yes, only one but an interesting case, although I can't talk about that. There's something else... I went to MacDougall this morning. Peter says he knows nothing about bears or pandas, but I can tell he's hiding something."

"Don't dig around in that, babe. He's a dangerous man. And besides, that matter is already in the hands of the police."

"I know... I just thought maybe I could get him to slip up and say something, but I was wrong." Simone took a deep breath and spoke all at once. "When I was leaving MacDougall, that nice officer I told you about, Liam, told me Edward wants to see me." She dropped the bomb and waited for a reaction.

Carl took several seconds to answer. "Well...that's what you wanted originally, right?"

"I really don't know... I think I owe him a visit, but at the same time, it's hard for me to imagine facing him after everything."

"So, don't go. You're not obligated to see him."

"You're right, I'm not obligated... I'm going to think about it."

But deep inside, Simone knew she had already decided to visit Edward. She felt she owed him.

They changed the subject and started making plans for John's visit and the upcoming Christmas holiday. She had never been too fond of Christmas, but Carl absolutely loved the festivities. It would be their first Christmas as a couple, and Carl had been talking nonstop about it, as well as about New Year's Eve.

CHAPTER TWENTY-ONE

Delusions

Chased by some unknown pursuer, Simone raced down a long, narrow corridor. Although she couldn't see who was after her, the sound of his footsteps told her he was close. The tap-tap made her heart race, and despite the heat that brought sweat to her brow, chills caused goosebumps to break out along the skin of her arms. She wouldn't be able to run much longer; her legs felt like they were filled with lead. She reached a set of red-painted doors, a fire exit. She pushed the bars, first one then the other, but they were both locked.

It's supposed to be open!

Hot breath hit the back of her neck, and she pressed frantically on the bar, her entire body trembling. Her legs grew weak, her knees gave out, and she dropped to the floor. Turning to see her pursuer, she widened her eyes in shock. Peter towered over her. He threw back his head and laughed maniacally as she stared at him in disbelief. He leaned over her and wrapped his hands around her neck. Simone opened her mouth, but she couldn't scream. She had no voice...

Bip, bip, bip.

A distant noise echoed through the room. Simone's eyes shot open, and a wave of relief washed over her.

A nightmare!

It was her phone´s alarm, what a relief! She reached over to her nightstand, grabbed the phone, and silenced it.

Thank God that wasn't real!

She blew out a long breath. It'd been a long time since she'd had nightmares about Peter. She needed to schedule a meeting with her psychiatrist, Doctor Edgar. The thought of going back to the days immediately after Peter had kidnapped her when she'd had one crazy dream after another made her skin crawl.

Simone got out of bed, shivering violently. She turned toward the source of an icy breeze and found her bedroom window slid wide open. The ground outside was covered in snow. In another life, when everything had been boring and normal, she would think she had forgotten to close it before going to bed the night before. But after everything she had been through over the last few years, she knew better. Someone had deliberately opened her window, and the icy cold, which had reminded her subconscious of Peter torturing her with freezing temperatures, had caused her nightmare.

Who would do such a thing?

After lowering and locking the window, Simone got her phone and checked the surveillance cameras.

My life is like Big Brother!

No one had been in the rest of the house, but reviewing her room's camera—pointed at the window for privacy—she saw someone outside who had opened it. For a few seconds, the beam of a flashlight had lit up her darkened room.

Someone was outside last night.

Once more, the hairs on her arms rose. She pressed a

button on the phone and checked the external video.

A person, clearly a man, dressed in all black and wearing a ski mask, crouched to attach something to the waterfront deck on the shore in front of the house.

What is he doing? Had he come by boat?

The person approached the house and started trying the windows, finding them all locked, but when the person reached the master bedroom, the window slid slowly upward. After opening the window, the person shined the flashlight inside. Apparently, he hadn't expected to find Simone in the room. The would-be intruder took a quick step back then spun around and strode calmly back toward the water. Obviously, he'd arrived in some kind of watercraft.

Simone downloaded the images and sent them to Officer Carlo Dimario's phone. She would call him later. She went into the bathroom and was getting ready to step into the shower when her phone rang.

"Good morning, Simone." Carlo's voice filled the phone. "Where did you get these images? It doesn't look like your house to me."

"It is. I sold the old one and bought a new one by the shore… Do you believe this nightmare is going to start all over again?"

"Maybe it was just a regular robbery attempt…" he said, but his voice lacked conviction.

"I don't believe that, and neither do you. Do you think it's someone connected to Hay and all those deaths among my patients?"

"It could be anything. Please don't touch anything! I'll get there as quickly as I can—just text me your location."

"Okay. I'm sending the address now."

The phone went silent. Obviously, he'd hung up.

A little bit of courtesy would be great, how about a "see you soon? Or Goodbye?" He sounded rushed.

Simone quickly sent him her address, then hurried to shower and dress. She had just finished when the bell rang. She checked the cameras on her phone, shoved her feet into her shoes, and ran to the door. Carlo had arrived, along with two other people.

"Hello, Carlo. Nice to see you, although I wish it were under different circumstances…" Simone smiled at him then glanced at his companions.

"Nice to see you, Simone." He nodded at the woman behind him... "This is Detective Ava Harkrader, our best forensic expert."

The detective looked a bit like an alien, as her whole body was covered in a white plastic romper. She held something that looked like a tackle box.

"Good morning, Doctor Bennet." The woman's smile was warm, and her voice was kind and sincere.

Simone returned the smile, happy to see sympathy on another person's face for a change.

"Good morning, Detective."

Carlo continued with the introductions. "And this is Officer Elijah Goldstand." He pointed at the man at his side.

The officer mumbled something that sounded like, "Good morning, madam."

Simone nodded. "Good morning."

"Can we inspect your room?" Carlo asked, one foot already on the doorstep.

"Sure. Please come with me."

Simone led them to her bedroom, and they spent at least two hours dusting for fingerprints on the window and thoroughly inspecting the house. The officers seemed determined to follow protocol, doing exactly what one would expect from the police in such a situation. The video footage clearly showed the intruder wearing gloves, making the procedure seem pointless to Simone.

After the police had inspected everything and left, Simone went to every window and door in the house to make sure the place was locked up tight. She set the alarm then left for her office.

I really hope this was a random robbery attempt…

But her instincts said that wasn't the case. She would not mention the incident to Carl.

He would be worried sick, and besides, we don't know anything for certain yet.

Liar, she thought. *You know exactly what's going on.*

*****

Simone faced a full day at her clinic. Her chest expanded with a sensation of pleasure and relief when she saw her schedule and realized she had five patients to see that day. *I'm almost back to where I was before I took time off. I did this once; I can do it again.*

*****

After a blissful, dreamless night—thanks to the sleeping pills she had taken to keep from tossing and turning while her mind fixated on the intruder and her upcoming visit with Edward—Simone woke up with a rare sense of calm. She felt refreshed.

The sensation lasted just a few minutes, however, when she remembered it was Thursday, and that morning, she was supposed to meet with Edward. Thoughts of the day's events weighed heavy on her mind, but they were things she needed to face.

Her stomach contracted and started to roll, but she forced herself to get up and out of bed. She showered and dressed in a dark suit then slipped on a pair of comfortable shoes. In the kitchen, Simone prepared her breakfast and then ate it slowly, calculating the time she would need to leave home to ensure she arrived at the prison on time.

Once she was certain she would arrive fifteen minutes ahead of schedule, and after double-checking all the locks on every door to the house, Simone grabbed her purse and headed to the garage. She got into her car, started the engine, and hit the road.

As she drove toward MacDougall, her hands shook. Talk about being a nervous wreck.

What am I going to say to Ed?

She had no clue. Nor did she know why she was visiting him.

Because he was convicted, and you never gave him a chance to explain what happened. You owe him that.

Throughout the drive, she had imaginary conversations with Edward. In some, Ed shouted at her; in others, she shouted her indignation at him, and in all of them, they ended up giving each other a strong hug, promising to be the best friends they once were. Forever this time.

Even if forever means a visit to a jail once a week.

When she finally arrived at the prison, Simone began to drag her feet. She took much more time to park than she usually did, circling the lot several times until a spot opened close to the door. Inside, she slowly filled out the paperwork, reading then re-reading each question before writing in her answers or signing her name.

You are avoiding the encounter as much as you can, you coward.

Her heart pounded like a jackhammer, and all her thoughts were directed toward forgiving Ed, being forgiven, and happy endings. She just prayed she wasn't living in a fantasy world, and the reality she encountered when she met with him would be much different...

CHAPTER TWENTY-TWO

How've You Been?

Simone entered the infirmary, the same place they held her meetings with Peter. Edward was already there, unhandcuffed, sitting on a metal chair and, looking toward the bar-covered window.

His chestnut hair was now speckled with white, and his torso was more muscular than it had been before. When he turned to her, his face showed new wrinkles, and his blue eyes were surrounded by them. He rose when she approached and walked to the window.

He is keeping his distance…

Simone couldn't stop herself from analyzing his behavior. Suddenly, he turned and pointed at her.

"Stop digging into Hay's motives and activities! He is as dangerous as the most lunatic psycho you ever imagined, so stay away from him!"

A lump formed in Simone's throat. At any moment, she would start to cry, and she took a deep breath and drew on her years of practice to keep control of her emotions.

"Good morning, Ed. Nice to see you, too," she answered in a strangled voice.

Edward didn't return her greeting. "Why don't you take a seat?" he said, his voice low this time. He pointed at the metal chair behind her.

Simone hesitated for a moment but did as he suggested. Even though Edward remained standing, she welcomed the opportunity to sit. She needed a moment to calm her nerves, to gather herself before facing whatever was coming next. The cold metal beneath her felt grounding, yet her heart still raced.

"The FBI visited me on Tuesday while you were visiting with Peter Hay!" His voice rose again. "Seems you've decided to play detective now. Let them do their job, will you? You're going to get into trouble. There are things about those dead girls that can be dangerous, and you must stop digging around in this! Stop visiting Peter Hay. Don't go to the police; just stay away. What do you have in mind? Haven´t you had enough?" When he finally stopped shouting, he had spittle on the corners of his mouth.

Simone trembled, instinctively reacting to an Edward she had never seen before. She clasped both hands tightly together, determined not to let him see how his behavior affected her emotions.

"FBI? What are you talking about?" She lost her patience and shouted back at him. "Yes, I've been visiting Peter. I want to understand his motives, or do you think my life was a delight after our paths crossed?"

"It seems to me you're enjoying yourself now. Were you and that lawyer together when I had the illusion you were my girlfriend?" His voice rose even more.

Simone glanced toward the door. Nobody came, nobody spied through the glass window as they had whenever Peter raised his voice.

Apparently, they don't think Edward is dangerous.

"Stop, Ed!" she shouted back. "Can we at least try to be civil? You're shouting a hundred things at me, and I can't keep up. Ask me whatever you want, one thing at a time. If you want to talk about anger, I can talk about anger. You were not honest with me, but I never betrayed our relationship or our friendship!"

For a while, they both remained silent. Simone's heart hurt for her friend. He stared into her eyes, his lips drawn down into a deep frown, and then suddenly, his eyes were filled with tears. The sight of his pain was too much for Simone to bear, and soon, she began to cry, as well.

Too many things to say, too many unresolved feelings...No courage at all.

Edward stepped forward, grabbed a chair, and placed it directly in front of her. He sat down, his gaze never leaving hers, and for the first time, their eyes were at the same level.

"Let's start with the first thing you said, okay?" She shook her head, turned away, and dried her tears. "What do you mean about the FBI? What is going on with them? I didn't contact anyone at the bureau. I only went to the NYC police station after I found the pictures of the Chinese girls in the middle of your stuff and then heard a report on the radio about the death of a Chinese girl wearing a T-shirt with a panda on it. It seemed like everything was connected, and I couldn't just look the other way."

The silence between them was thick with emotion, as if they were each waiting for the other to speak, yet neither could find the words. Edward took a deep breath and took the first step.

"The FBI was called in after your visit to the station in New York. The police already had three dead girls, and when you handed over more pictures, you added a fourth. You live in one state, the person who was investigating those deaths—

me—is from another state, there are similarities between all those dead women. The panda T-shirts they were wearing, all the girls are of Asian descent or come from Eastern Asia, and none of the bodies had any identification or papers... The FBI got involved immediately, and you told them I was investigating...so...they came here to pay me a visit." He opened his arms, indicating his surroundings.

"Oh, my God, another serial killer like Peter Hay? Or are they linked to Peter? What are the chances of that happening to the same person again?" Simone widened her eyes.

"It is not happening to you. Calm down. You dug around in my stuff, discovered I was investigating, and you just decided to help... Could you stop helping before you consider the consequences? You always do that. Usually, you keep your head and emotions under control, always finding a way to rationalize everything. But the moment you think someone needs you, all that rational thought disappears, and you jump in, ready to play superhero!" he stated. He spoke in an almost normal tone of voice and ran his fingers through his hair.

Simone didn't deny his words.

"I didn't think about it. You're correct, I just wanted to help."

Tears slipped from Simone's eyes. She couldn't control herself this time, and the sobs followed. Edward rose from his chair, gently took her hands, and helped her stand. Without a word, they hugged, holding each other in silence. They stood there until she recovered her control. When they separated, Edward's eyes were wet and red.

"I missed you so much." He spoke in a whisper. "Forgive me."

"You need to forgive me. I abandoned you here and never listened to your side," Simone whispered.

"In a certain way, I am a guilty criminal. I didn't stop him. I could have prevented so many deaths. I should have been trying to prove my innocence instead of worrying about not destroying your feelings for me. I was selfish. And I'm a Doctor—I'm supposed to save lives." He held her hands. "Let's sit down for a little bit again."

They sat, face to face, as he held her hands gently in his.

"We don't have much time, so I'm not going to try to explain everything to you now. I just need you to stop the investigations, okay? You're risking your life. Stay away from Peter. He has tentacles outside, and if he thinks you're digging around in his business, he's going to hurt you."

"So, those girls' deaths could be Peter's doing?" Simone lifted an eyebrow.

"They are, in some way. I got those pictures when I broke into his house to try to find something I could use against him to stop the blackmail. I found them inside a drawer in his home office—he hadn't even bothered to hide them. I started to investigate, but unfortunately, I couldn't finish the job before I ended up here. I thought I would have more time. How did you get them?"

"I convinced Beth to get your stuff from Carlo. One day, I was organizing the things from that box and putting them in your office at the clinic, and the dead girl's picture slipped from the book. I got that magnifying glass you keep on your desk, and the panda on the T-shirt caught my attention. During one of my previous visits, Peter had been talking crazy, going on and on about bears. It was too much to be a coincidence. I knew there was something connecting them both."

"Don't ask him about that. Just don't ask!" Edward shook his head vehemently.

Simone lowered her head before answering.

"Too late… I already did…" She tightened her lips.

"My God, Simmie! You just poked a wasps' nest!" He ran his fingers through his hair, causing the muscles in his arms to flex.

He's had much more time to work out in here, she thought.

"He tried to play it off, as if he'd been talking about the pandas in China. He told me all about how they're fed and about their caretakers, nothing more." She shrugged.

"He will check up on you, see if you continue to have an interest. He's a predator. He studies all his victims, their movements, and he plays with them like a cat with a mouse. He's patient. Do you remember how he approached you and Carl, just for the pleasure of playing you both and to satisfy his curiosity about Lara's half-sister?" Edward took a deep breath before continuing. "I firmly believe he commands something outside these walls. I don't know what or how, but I believe he has connections. He can do you harm. Nobody knows exactly who ordered Maria to kill your housekeeper and tamper with the drugs that were prescribed to your patients."

After Peter kidnapped and tortured Simone and left her to die while he escaped to China, a series of her patients—and even her housekeeper—had been poisoned with cyanide by a woman named Maria. Caught by the police, Maria asserted she had been acting under Deena Hay's orders, but the police couldn't find any real evidence against her. Maria had been taking orders from someone she believed was Deena, but she couldn't recognize Deena's voice. In the end, Peter Hay confessed to the crimes—He had been behind everything all along.

"Somebody visited my house the other night." Simone tensed for the coming storm.

"What do you mean, somebody *visited* your house?" He turned his palms up and opened his arms, but at least he didn't yell. Yet...

"Well, I woke up, and my bedroom window was wide open. I knew it was closed when I went to bed. I checked the cameras—someone came through the water..."

"Through the water?" Edward frowned.

"I live by the shore now..." She didn't want to say more. Not now.

"And how about your dear husband? Was he not there to protect you?"

"He was in the city..." She wouldn't discuss Carl with Edward, so she continued her story. "The person was wearing black, I think a man, and he tried all the doors and windows until he came to the master bedroom. It wasn't locked, so the intruder opened it, turned on a flashlight, and I think he saw me asleep, so they decided to get out of there."

"It was a message, Simone, can't you see? I told you he has tentacles outside these walls. Did you call the police?"

"Yes, I called Carlo, and he came over with a team. I think everything is all right now."

"Please keep your distance. Stop visiting Peter, stop helping the police, just take care of your own life, okay? Promise me you'll be safe? I can't be out there to protect you!" Edward joined his hands as if in prayer.

"What about you? The FBI has been here. How can you help them from behind bars? All you had is in their hands now." Simone looked at Edward.

"No, I have more, and I'm working on cutting a deal... I'll help them if they can get me out of here."

Simone widened her eyes.

"Is that possible?"

"Everything is possible. They want information, I have it, and it has a price. If they think what I have is good, I can be released, or at least, get them to reduce my sentence by a big chunk."

"Let me help! I can talk to Peter, be your eyes outside these walls, follow the leads you've already developed." Her voice rose with excitement. *I can help my friend.*

"No way! I'd rather stay here forever. I can't put you in the middle of another mess. You have no training. You would be dead in no time!" His patience was gone, and his voice rose again.

"And do you have any training to deal with criminals? You're a Doctor, for Christ´s sake!"

"A year living among all kinds of bad guys is the equivalent of a master's in crime," he shot back, eyes narrowed. "I might not have a degree in criminology, but trust me—I know the game."

Simone stared. She could count on one hand the number of times she'd heard Ed raise his voice.

And now, it's like he can barely control his temper. This place must do that to people—they don't have any walls left, except for the ones that physically enclose them.

She squeezed her eyes closed and chastised herself for being so judgmental.

Why don't you try staying in this place for a year and see who you become...

"There must be some way I can help... You're not going to get a good deal if you don´t have a juicy steak for the FBI."

"I have more than a steak. Trust me..."

Someone knocked on the door.

"Doctor Reynolds, it's time for the session." Liam stuck his face in the door opening and smiled. "Hello, Doctor Bennet."

"Hello, Liam."

"I have to go. I promise I'll explain everything to you, but stop digging, okay?"

Edward leaned in and hugged Simone and then got to his feet and left before she could answer.

Just before he closed the door, Liam said, "I'll be back to show you out in a few minutes, Doctor."

Simone stood there, waiting for the guard to escort her out, her heart aching for her friend and the situation he was trapped in.

How long can he keep his sanity in a place like this?

Her inner voice responded bitterly.

That question assumes he was sane to begin with...

*****

Simone walked a marathon around the inside perimeter of the infirmary while she waited for Liam. Her emotions raged out of control. She'd gotten no answers regarding whether Edward had participated in the killings with Peter. In fact, she knew no more than she had when she'd arrived.

You didn't even ask! You both just spilled your guts without thinking!

She paused in her pacing and stared sightlessly out the bar-covered windows.

I don't recognize Edward.

He was different, harder, and yet somehow, he was still the same sweet guy.

A thousand thoughts crossed her mind, and there were still so many unanswered questions. She could come back another day. Even though they hadn't talked about another visit, Simone needed explanations only Ed could provide.

The door opened, drawing her from her thoughts. She turned to see Liam standing just behind her. He nodded a greeting and gave her his usual tender smile.

"Let's go, Doctor Bennet. Sorry for the delay, but I had to

organize the session, and it was crowded today."

"No worries, Liam. I want to help with your sessions. We just need to reschedule with the program director."

"Yes, we do. The problem is, he had an emergency today. I'll try to schedule something for next week," Liam replied, his eyes lowering as he spoke.

Bad, bad liar.

His body language was all too clear—he was hiding something, making excuses to keep her from connecting with the person in charge.

Would Edward have asked him to keep me out of the program? she wondered. *Certainly, he would*!

They started to walk toward the exit.

"Could I see Peter Hay today?" Simone asked as she followed behind Liam.

"I don't think so. His boyfriend is visiting, and the rules state just one person per visit if you're not family members." He looked at his watch. "Besides, visiting hours are almost over, and we'd never get there on time after we filled out all the necessary paperwork."

"His boyfriend? The Chinese guy? His name is Wang something, isn't it?" Simone couldn't remember the man's whole name.

"Yes, Wang Zhang Li. He seems to be the serious type. Never laughs, never smiles. They just sit there, holding hands and talking in Mandarin. The man is very reserved—not all like our friend Hay."

"Some people don't like public displays affection," Simone replied.

Or they have no affection to display.

Her brain argued with her.

"Especially in a place like this." He opened his arms wide

and indicated their surroundings.

"I'll call you to schedule something with the director so he and I can talk about the program."

"Sure, call me. It will be a pleasure to help you." He didn't add anything more.

Now I'm a hundred percent positive. Edward asked him—and probably the director, too—not to involve me in those sessions.

The thought stung, and it hurt to realize just how completely he had shut her out.

As Simone and Liam reached the final door, they said their goodbyes, and Simone went over to the locked metal cabinets to get her belongings. She was walking to her car when she had an idea, so she climbed in behind the wheel, started the car, and drove over to the facility's only exit. She pulled over toward the curb so she wouldn't block traffic and then waited...

CHAPTER TWENTY-THREE

Too Quick

For the tenth time, Simone checked the clock built into the dashboard. Although the heat was keeping her warm, her nerves were stretched to their limit, and she kept shivering. After waiting for more than twenty minutes, she had to pee, she longed to stretch her legs, and her stomach was even rumbling from lack of food—something that rarely happened to her.

Being prevented from doing something makes the whole body want to do it.

But she refused to give up and abandon her mission.

After five more minutes, an Asian man left the building, the first and only Asian person she'd seen leave the facility, despite the droves of people exiting now that visiting hours had ended.

That must be Peter's guy.

The man was young, around thirty years old, but he was not pretty. He had a too-angular face and very high cheekbones. He was short and extremely lean, she noted, as he put a large backpack on the ground beside him and shrugged into a thick leather motorcycle jacket that looked too heavy for his slim shoulders.

Definitely not Hay's kind of man. Maybe his ears outside this place.

Simone had met two of Peter's former lovers—once when she met Hay and again with her own half-brother. Both had been handsome and muscular...a specific type. This guy didn't fit that mold.

The man lifted the backpack and draped it over one shoulder but then seemed to change his mind and instead held it in front of him and dug through the large center section as if trying to find something. He lifted his head and looked around, intently scrutinizing the parking lot for several moments.

What's he afraid of?

Simone lowered her head and pretended to be looking for something inside her car for several seconds. When she lifted her head, the man was already leaving on a black motorcycle.

Without thinking much about what she was doing, Simone decided to follow him. For two blocks he maintained a normal speed, then suddenly, he hit the gas and disappeared in front of her eyes, the bike roared away like a bat out of hell.

Simone didn't know much about motorcycles, but his black bike looked like a powerful and expensive machine.

She pulled to the side of the road and waited for the traffic to clear in both directions, then she did a U-turn and headed in the opposite direction toward work.

*****

Her feelings in turmoil, Simone decided to call Carl as she drove to her office.

"Hello, honey!"

"Hello, my love. Can you talk for a little bit?" She adjusted her phone to connect with the car's stereo system so she could drive safely.

"I can, and I'm curious about your visit. In fact, I was waiting for your call."

"I know just as much now as I did before I went. Edward said he is sort of a criminal. He didn't really explain very much, but he asked me to stay away from Peter. Also Ed said he is cutting a deal with the FBI."

"Slow down. The FBI? Why and how?" His voice sounded louder, intrigued.

"FBI got involved after I delivered the pictures. Thanks to the murderer's *modus operandi*, the agents were able to connect more than three cases involving dead Asian girls, so they think they have a serial killer. I told them where I found the photographs, so they've been visiting Edward. Apparently, he was investigating those girls when he was arrested."

"My God, Simone, are you going to be safe with all that going on around you again?" His voice rose even higher and cracked a tiny bit.

"I think so. Edward told me to leave things to him and to the FBI. Maybe he can reduce his sentence or even get out of that place."

"Doctor Bennet, I can read your thoughts. If the Doctor Frankenstein told you to stay out of it, you must've tried to get involved somehow. Convince me you didn't, please."

"Well, I offered to be his eyes on the outside."

Simone couldn't lie to Carl; their relationship was too transparent for that.

"Get away from this!" His voice on the speaker filled the whole car. "For God´s sake, Simone! Haven't you had enough? That guy is in jail because he deserves to be. He's not an innocent man. He was Peter's accomplice in some horrific crimes! Just stay away!"

Her ears hurt from the volume of his voice.

"Okay, okay, no need to raise your voice. I understand the risks."

"No, you don't! You act like a little girl when it comes to helping others. You never think through the consequences, you just act on impulse!"

He sounds just like Edward.

Although the two men had used different words, they held the same meaning.

"I promise I won't be reckless. Calm down. Do you know if Peter used to have a motorcycle?" She asked, trying to distract him from his concerns.

"No, I don't! Why are you asking that?" He was annoyed and angry, his voice getting louder with each word.

"I saw his boyfriend leaving MacDougall on one, and it occurred to me it could be Peter's."

"Did you follow him?"

"Well…no…we were just leaving at the same time." She bit her lip. Just one little white lie couldn't hurt anything.

A lie is a lie, Simone.

"Thank God, you used a little common sense!" He blew out a puff of air, the sound filling the car.

"He was driving too fast, and—"

"*You tried to follow him!*" he shouted.

"No need to raise your voice. I didn't. He left the facility in front of me. I was in my car, and there's only one way out of that place. But a mile or so down the road, he hit the gas —or whatever they call it when you're driving a bike—and disappeared, and I didn't try to follow him. You know I hate driving fast."

"You hate... So, the only reason you didn't go after him is because you don't like driving over the speed limit?" His high-pitched voice shrieked through the car.

"Stop, honey, you're being rude." She tried to calm him down, but deep inside, she knew he was right.

"Love, please, you are my reason for living. Please, please, stay away from all that stuff. Stop asking questions, stop *not* following people"—the sarcasm was palpable— "and keep yourself safe. Okay? For me?" His voice was back to normal, if a pleading tone could be considered normal.

He is really stressed out.

"Your reason for living?" She smiled. "With a plea like that, how can I say no? Don´t worry, I won´t play secret agent. When do you intend to come home, honey, so I can show you a few other reasons for living?"

*****

When Simone arrived at her office, evidence suggested the presence of Benjamin Taylor-Miller—his fancy car, his bodyguards sitting inside another car, both parked in front of her door.

What the hell? He's not scheduled for today.

Simone climbed out of her vehicle and strode past the bodyguards saluting them with a nod. She opened the door, and Patricia rose to greet her and take her coat.

"Mr. Taylor-Miller insisted on having an emergency appointment with you. I told him how busy your schedule is, but I also know you asked me to find a way to squeeze clients in when it's a serious matter."

Patricia spoke in a raised voice—higher and sharper than her usual calm tone—but Simone could tell she was forcing the drama.

Patricia looked toward the waiting room she had recently created then leaned into whisper.

"He told me he was prepared to pay double, and we do need his money." She shrugged.

"Nice." Simone answered in an equally low tone. "Does he seem suicidal or just impatient?"

"Spoiled, if you want my opinion." Patricia smiled.

"So, I will go to my office, and I'm going to have a strong expresso because I'm really in need of one right now. Just calculate roughly how long it will take for me to drink my coffee, and then send the little man my way."

"I call him Grumpy," Patricia whispered again.

"I know, but...don't." She couldn't hold back a smile.

Or we're going to have the whole Snow-White *story circulating around this office...*Simone went to her office, set her purse on her desk, and went over to the little table where she'd placed her latest acquisition—a state-of-the-art expresso machine, which had been a gift from her husband. She added one of the little premeasured containers, pushed the button and waited for the black liquid to fill the small cup. The smell of fresh coffee gave her immense pleasure.

Carl is responsible for this addiction.

She lifted the delicate porcelain cup to her lips and slowly sipped the hot espresso.

Liquid poison.

When she finished her drink, she took her notepad, sat on her couch, and waited.

Less than a minute later, her patient appeared, entering through the door that connected the waiting room with Simone's office.

Patricia has perfect timing.

Benjamin seemed in a hurry. He went straight to the couch and jumped up to sit on the middle cushion. He looked at her with his sharp eyes, crossed his hands in his lap, began shaking his little foot, and then started talking, his words left his mouth like bullets from a machinegun.

"Morning, Doc." He didn't wait for her to answer. "You can't imagine what that lunatic did to me! I'm a man! I'm offended! I'm never going to see her again!" His face was red, he was breathing quickly, and he had foam on his mouth.

Simone needed to intervene and take back control of the meeting.

"Good morning, Benjamin." She spoke in a calm, sweet voice. There were studies that showed that one person's tone of voice could affect another person's mood. "Please take a deep breath and calm yourself." Simone put up her hand and motioned for him to tone it down. "Relax!"

He seemed to be following her instructions, drawing in several long, slow breaths, so she waited a little bit. When he was no longer panting like a thirsty dog, she went on.

"Now, tell me, calmly, please, who is *she*, and what did she do to leave you in this state of mind."

"She is the woman I'm in love with. The old one I told you about the other day!"

Simone didn't comment on the insult. He needed to get back at the woman by offending her somehow, so he called her old.

"Does she have a name?" Simone raised an eyebrow.

"Yes, but you are not going to like it." He lowered his head. "Chivon, she is one of your patients."

Simone was not being picky about what patients she treated these days since they needed the money, but... couples?

"I don't treat couples." She shook her head.

"I know that, but it's your fault. I wouldn't have said her name, not if you hadn't made me! Besides, we're not a couple.

Not anymore!" He pointed his finger at her.

"Part of being a grown up is taking responsibility, Benjamin, and you misled me on purpose. You knew Chivon was my patient when you first came here, right?"

He didn't need an answer; his red face said it all.

"Will you please make an exception? I really like you, and I don't think she's going to give up on your services, either. So, will you please, please continue seeing us both? I really need you, and I can keep paying double. I don't care!" His small hands were clasped in front of him like a silent prayer.

I have no choice.

She needed his money to put toward the bills while she continued rebuilding her practice. The thought made Simone feel dirty and cheap, as if she were selling out her principles or morals. Under other circumstances, she would never be like that, but now it was her reality. If she wanted to grow her practice again, she had to make one or two exceptions.

Rich man counted as an exception. Her mind answered. *You're becoming a mercenary*!

"I will think about it, but if I do this, and then somewhere down the line I feel as if it's not healthy for one of you, you're out." Simone paused and nodded toward the door. "That's only fair—she came to see me first. How did you know she was my patient? Did she tell you?"

"No." He shrugged. "I had somebody following her, so I knew she'd been here..."

Simone clenched her hands in her lap to keep from picking the man up and tossing him out the door. "That's not healthy for any kind of relationship. You must promise you'll stop having her followed, or we can't continue our sessions!"

She used the same tone of voice she used with her students when she wanted them to sit up and pay attention.

"Okay, whatever you say. I promise! I need you! And I don't want to see her again, so I'm not going to follow her!"

Simone didn't believe him. He was the type of powerful man who would do as he pleased.

"I will accept your promise, but don't try to fool me." Something in his expression told her the idea had entered his mind, and she pointed at him. "Do you understand?"

He crossed his arms, his body language unmistakable—He hated having to promise something he clearly didn't want to do.

"Do we have an agreement?"

"We do." He relaxed on the couch and smiled.

Sometimes, he looks sweet.

"Please proceed. What did Chivon do to make you so angry? You were fuming when you entered my office."

"The crazy woman spent the night at my house. She'd always refused before now—said it's too much intimacy to share a bed, but last night I persuaded her to stay. She was horny, and we were in bed and started kissing. She took off her clothes in that show-off way she has." He put his hands on his suit lapel and opened it, obviously trying to mimic his girlfriend's actions before he continued.

"Once we were both naked, we started to kiss again and touch each other. I fingered her, and she was totally wet. I was ready to fuck her hard, but she asked me to wait and said she had an idea. She asked me to lie down on the bed, told me she had a surprise, and then she retrieved her silk scarf from the floor where she'd tossed it earlier and used it to blindfold me."

Benjamin blew out a long breath, obviously becoming agitated again, so Simone waited.

"The demon jumped from the bed and came back seconds later. I could feel some kind of oil on my back, and she started to massage me with her boobs. She rubbed them on my back and then moved lower as she massaged my buttocks with her hands. I was loving every second of it, when suddenly, out of the blue, she stuck her whole finger into my ass!"

His face was red again, his eyes startled, and he lifted his index finger in the air.

"How did you feel about it? Did you enjoy the experience?" Simone had to ask, but she could guess the answer.

"How did I feel? I threw her out of my room! I told her that I'm the man in that house, not the dog!"

"Sorry, I don't understand what the dog has to do with all that."

"Oh, that's because whenever my dog barks at something in the garden, I always tell him to go out there, see what's going on, and play the man of the house," he said with a chuckle.

Simone nodded slowly. She wanted to laugh, but professional protocol demanded that she keep her composure.

"You felt less of a man because of what she did?"

"Less of a man? That's not a male thing!" He hit the arm of the chair.

"There are men who enjoy that kind of experience," Simone informed him.

"They are not men, and that's wrong. Trust me, Doc!" he answered quickly.

"It's not wrong. Anal pleasure is something normal for all sexes," Simone replied.

Benjamin's face turned even redder.

"There is no pleasure in it, and that's a gay thing," he shouted, determined to keep his convictions.

"No, that´s bias. Many studies have shown that it's

perfectly normal for straight men to find pleasure in such acts."

"That woman was testing my masculinity, I tell you!" He pointed at Simone.

"Did she ask for permission?"

"Yes. But I didn´t understand what ´Can I finger you? meant. I thought it was something different."

"So, you said yes"?

He lowered his head.

"I did."

"In my professional opinion, she thought you were open to new sensations once you said yes. That's how people know what to expect from their partners, how to give pleasure. Your companion must be free to propose things in bed. If you don't like it or don't want to do it, all you have to do is say no, but if you forbid her to try, eventually, she will stop attempting new things and besides, you said yes."

"Do you think it was a kind of test to see if I'm gay?"

My God, how stubborn can someone be?

"That's not what I said. I said, and I'm just guessing here because you will have to ask your partner about it, but maybe she was just exploring another sexual option, as couples often do."

"Couples do that?"

"Explore their sexual options? Always, when they have intimacy."

"No, I'm asking about the woman fingering the man."

"That's an exploration of sexuality, as I said. It's not wrong or right, and nobody needs to know. It's a private thing between consenting partners. To be able to be inventive in bed is a way to make your relationship last longer."

I must try something new with Carl, but I don't think the

finger would work well for him.

"If I let her do that to me, I'll end up turning gay!" He shook his head.

"A gay man likes men—and only men. Are you sexually or romantically attracted to other men?"

"Of course not!" He shouted his indignation at the question, his voice rising.

"So, a little experimentation is not going to convert you into a homosexual. Unless, of course, you have unanswered questions about your sexuality?"

Simone looked into his eyes.

I love a little challenge...

"I know who I am!" He lifted his nose in the air.

"Well, if you do, I think you owe Chivon an apology. Did you really throw her out?"

"I did. I told her to collect her belongings and disappear from my life forever!"

"Flowers would do the job—lots of expensive flowers!" Simone surprised herself with her advice. Then she remembered Chivon and added, "A man in your position should add some jewelry, too."

That's not science; that's crap! Where am I going in my career now? Next step, a radio program telling listeners what to do? I'm disappointed with myself.

*****

Surprisingly, Simone´s schedule was crowded that afternoon, and by the end of the day she had just enough time to go home, take a quick shower, get dressed and grab an Uber to the university. She was expected to give a lecture about the duty of mental health professionals to warn authorities of a patient's potentially violent conduct.

Carl had helped her with the legal part of her speech. She had lectured on that topic a hundred times before, but it felt good to let him in, to let him participate in her life.

"Connecticut statutes do not require psychiatrists to disclose information that would be confidential between a patient and his or her Doctor; however, it allows such a disclosure when the professional believes there's a serious risk that the patient will harm himself or someone else." Simone walked back and forth on the dark wood stage, lecturing to a crowded auditorium filled with post-grads.

"How do you know when your patient represents a risk?" asked a young woman in the audience who appeared to be scribbling notes on a tablet resting on her knees.

"In my experience, it's essential to pay very close attention during an appointment . Focus... Not only on what the patient says, but how they say it. A patient's word choices, tone of voice, and body language can reveal just as much as their statements themselves. We should take note of every movement and anything they say that strikes us as unusual or odd...even if we don't understand the hidden meaning. Trust your gut. Trust your instincts. I like to use a voice-activated recorder with some patients. Later, I can listen to the audio recording and take notes. Our work doesn't finish when the patient's session ends."

"Give us an example, please."

"There are patients who tend to say a lot... I want to kill my mother, husband, et cetera, but in most cases, we can tell the differences between someone who's venting or merely expressing anger or frustration, and someone who's dangerous and making threats. If you listen carefully and trust your instincts, you'll develop the skills needed to judge when a patient is serious about his intent to perpetrate a crime. When they have plans, and they explain to you how they intend to achieve their goal... Those are true signs they might be dangerous."

Simone cleared her throat and took a sip of water from the glass on the mahogany podium.

"When we talk about suicidal cases, usually, depression is on the surface. I had one case I want to share with you. A white man, twenty-eight years old. He was having professional challenges, which were completely normal at that point in his life. He complained about depression, but he always seemed to be in a good mood, making jokes during the sessions, laughing about everything that happened in his life, and yet, I knew he was hiding something."

"Depression?" the same interested student asked.

"No, his sexuality options. After all, he searched me out —a specialist in paraphilias—so he should have some issues in that area. I was trying to make him come clean about his goals in therapy, so I was observing him closely, and little signs started to pop up. He started acting anxious. He was reporting reckless behavior. And he complained about feeling isolated sometimes."

"That´s a small part of the classic symptoms list, but if he was always in a good mood, it seems to me all those other symptoms didn´t add up," a bespectacled man in the front row said.

"The classic symptoms list is just that—a list, the most obvious. A psychiatrist will have to go beyond those basics. That's the reason I'm talking to you about observation. It is key to figuring out what's really going on. What can you tell me about this example and about the symptoms that are not on the list?"

Suddenly, the whole audience began offering their opinions, and Simone turned to the blackboard behind her. She wrote down each symptom as the students shared their thoughts.

The discussion continued for another hour. When the lecture was over, Simone felt invigorated, her mind sharpened by answering all the doubts the class expressed. After the exchange of ideas, Simone had a sense of learned new things.

Simone organized her material, got her purse, and started to walk to the stairs of the stage, trying to find her cellphone in her purse in the process. As she reached the floor of the auditorium, a fair-skinned young man approached her. He wore a black coat, a wool hat, and glasses with thick lenses that didn´t allow her to see his eyes, but he did look familiar.

Was he in the audience tonight?

She couldn't be sure.

"Doctor Bennet?" he asked her.

"Yes, can I help you?"

Simone answered with a smile, but the smile slowly vanished as the ceiling lights caught on something he held in one tight fist. Something shiny...

A knife...

She took a step back and recoiled, trying to protect her body, but the blow was quick. Adrenaline rushed through her. Pain ripped through her chest, and then she was falling.

Before she could think to shout for help, her vision blurred then went dark.

CHAPTER TWENTY-FOUR

Stiches

Simone woke up when she was being placed on a gurney to be taken to an ambulance.

“She is awake,” one of the paramedics shouted at the others. “How are you feeling, Doctor?

“My back side hurts. I was stabbed,” she told him.

“It’s a small, superficial cut. You were lucky. You’ll need a few stiches, so we’re taking you to Yale Hospital,” he said.

“Your name’s Mr. Thompson?” she asked, giving a tiny nod at the nametag on his shirt.

“Sure is!” He smiled down at her.

“Nice to meet you, Thompson. I’m Doctor Bennet.” She tried to smile, but everything hurt.

"It’s a pleasure to meet you. We were given your name by a couple of the students who attended the lecture tonight. If you’ll just lie still, we’ll have you to the ER in no time." His tone was gentle but firm, as the paramedics worked quickly around them, securing her onto the stretcher.

“Mr. Thompson, I need to call my husband. Can you hand

me my purse, please?"

"It seems you were robbed. If you had a purse with you, it's gone now."

Robbed, my ass!

"Robbed? The guy didn't seem to be interested in my purse. He didn't ask for it; he just walked up to me and stabbed me! It hurts!" she said as the paramedic stuck a needle in her arm.

"Sorry for that. There were some other robberies on the campus today. I think he chose you for his next victim, but he must have gotten scared or thought you were reacting somehow, because he didn't stab anyone else. He just stole things."

He adjusted a hanging bottle connected by a tube to her arm.

"Maybe..." She remembered the assailant's words.

She remembered the assailant's words. *"Doctor Bennet?"* Who on Earth would call the name of the person he intended to rob?

She remained quiet. A paramedic wouldn't have an answer to that. She needed to talk to the police.

"Is there a police officer here?" Simone asked, raising her head slightly.

"Yes, there are some, but they'll talk to you at the hospital," the paramedic replied gently. "We've already informed them that you need medical care first."

"Okay, can you lend me your cellphone? I really do need to call my husband."

He reached into the pocket of his white coat and handed over his phone. Simone had to think a few seconds to remember her own husband's number.

A side effect of people's total reliance on cellphones.

"Hello." Carl answered in a tired voice.

Hey honey, it's me—I lost my phone."

"Hey, love. How did you lose it?"

"Well, I didn't exactly lose it, I was robbed, and it seems I reacted in some way that frightened him, and he stabbed me. Nothing big." She hurried to clarify her statement before he panicked. "Just a small cut."

"How small is a small cut?" His voice rose.

That yelling thing he does whenever he's worried or angry really annoys me. I need to talk to him about it.

"Well, I guess I was stabbed, but it was superficial. They're taking me to Yale New Haven Hospital for some stiches…"

"Oh, my God, I'm getting my car and driving there. Are you okay?"

His voice rose even more, forcing her to pull the phone away from her ear.

"I'm just in a little pain, and I'm upset over the loss of everything I had in my purse. Phone, credit cards, my ID. Can you try to cancel my credit cards? The problem is, I don't have the numbers—they were saved on my phone," she said.

"Don't worry, hon. I'll figure it out and handle it on my way. Hold on, I'll be there soon."

*****

Doesn't suck to be treated like a queen!

Simone leaned back on the pillows. As a valued employee of the university and highly sought-after lecturer, she was receiving the best of care. Even some former students working as Doctors at the hospital came to check up on her when they learned she was there.

As soon as she was stitched up, the police arrived to take notes about the robbery and the missing contents from her purse. She chose not to mention her suspicions, keeping them to herself for the time being.

Simone was watching TV when Carl arrived, breathing like he'd run the whole way there. He rushed into her room and hurried to her side.

"Hello, love, how are you feeling?" He took her free hand, avoiding the one with the needle in it. The wrinkles on his forehead deepened.

"Great, just four stiches near my ribs. I was lucky. It could be much worse." She touched her side to show where the stiches were under the hospital gown.

"How come you had to protect yourself from a robbery? Doesn´t the university have a campus security system? Where were you? On your way to your car?"

"Calm down, honey. Sit here, and I'll try to answer all your questions."

She tapped on the bed, and when he sat, turning to her, she put a hand on his arm.

"I wasn´t not outside. I was still in the auditorium, had just finished my lecture when a man approached me. I thought he was a student. I don't remember that I reacted in any way other than to back up and try to protect my body with my purse when I saw the knife. Then I blacked out, woke up in the ambulance, and came here where they stitched me up."

"Why are they allowing a thief access to the inside of an auditorium?" Carl's expression his total disbelief.

"I don't know how they would have known he was a thief. Apparently, there were other robberies before he approached me. But he seemed like a regular student, and maybe he was. There are nuts everywhere..."

Time to be honest with your husband...

She drew a deep breath.

"I don't think it was a regular robbery. When the guy approached me, he said, 'Doctor Bennet?' That seems far from random..."

"Maybe he was inside the auditorium, listening to your lecture..."

"Maybe. I'm not sure about that... but I visited MacDougall before coming here, remember?" she replied.

"And tried to pursue Peter's friend." He was lecturing.

"I didn't try to follow him..."

Yes, I did but I will not confess.

"Anyway, listen...There's something I was going to tell you this weekend... I didn't say anything before because I didn't want you to worry... And please, don't raise your voice—it bothers me insanely!" she added, lowering her eyes to her hands.

"Look at me, Simone, and don't beat around the bush!"

Simone lifted her gaze to him.

My given name... Not love or honey... That means trouble.

"Someone tried to break into our home."

She almost put her hands on her ears, fearing his loud, angry response to her statement. He drew a deep breath and turned to her.

"Our Christmas holiday starts today." He pointed to the first finger on his hand then to each subsequent one as he listed off his requests. "I'm going to be home, and I'd like you to stop visiting inmates, stop collaborating with the FBI or whoever is dealing with those two. And most importantly, don't follow anyone else," he said, his tone firm, but steady.

"So wonderful that you'll be home until Christmas!" she exclaimed, her face lighting up with a smile. "I'm happy to have my husband around even if it takes me getting stabbed for that to happen!"

"Don't change the subject, love, and don't try to make light of this. I'm terrified, and I just can't risk losing you!" He leaned in to hug her, but she stopped him with her hand.

"The wound hurts. I'm afraid the anesthesia has worn off. Let me call someone to see if we can go home." Simone turned slowly and touched a button near her bed. In seconds, the on-call nurse came into the room.

"Hello, Victoria, I want to be discharged, please. Can you call a Doctor who can approve that?" Simone used her sweetest tone with the nurse.

"Well, of course, Doctor Bennet," she said, holding her clipboard. "I'll find the Doctor in charge, but how are you feeling? Do you need anything? Don't you think it's too early to be discharged?"

"I just need a painkiller; those stiches are starting to bother me." She made a face.

Victoria nodded.

"Hold on, and I'll be back in no time."

She hurried from the room.

Only a few minutes passed before she returned, carrying a tray with a small cup and a glass of water. A charming, young afro American Doctor with heavy glasses, and muscled arms showing under his white coat, trailed in behind her.

When I was in med school, Doctors looked like zombies. Now, they look like a Magic Mike´ s character? She had never seen the movie, but the billboards were everywhere.

"Doctor Zane Alexander. I'm happy to meet you, Doctor Bennet."

He introduced himself, obviously proud of his stethoscope around his neck.

Young Doctors need so much to be recognized as real Doctors.

"A pleasure, Doctor. I know it is not standard procedure,

but can you discharge me?"

"Doctor Bennet, I know you're a competent Doctor, but I would really prefer to keep you here, at least for the night."

"I understand, but as you mentioned, I have some knowledge in this area, and the cut is small and superficial. I believe I can take care of myself. And, as wonderful as this hospital is, being home would be even better." She gave him a mischievous smile.

He looked at the papers at the foot of her bed and said,

"You're right, the cut isn't serious enough to justify the discomfort of a hospital bed. I'll sign the discharge papers for you, but promise me—if you need anything during the night-you'll call my private number."

He noted the number on the prescription he was writing for her.

"A pleasure to have you as my patient. I read your books when I was a student, even thought I should be a psychiatrist for a while as a result." He smiled, admiration sparkling in his eyes.

"Thank you. What made you change your mind?"

"Blood... I really love the smell of it!"

He shrugged, and Simone laughed—not at the statement, but at the startled look on her favorite lawyer's face. "I understand!" She nodded.

Thank God he decided not to be a shrink; he'd scare the hell out of his poor patients...

They left the hospital with Carl pushing her wheelchair—an act she found completely unnecessary. She could walk just fine. A nurse followed closely behind, silent but attentive. Outside, they made their way to Carl's car. He opened the door and gently helped her inside.

He was being extra careful, handling her like she'd broken

half the bones in her body.

Obviously, he doesn't understand the extent of my pain.

She had to admit, it felt good to be pampered.

*****

A noisy woke up Simone. She lifted her head as Carl entered the room carrying a tray. From her position she could see steam rising from a cup of something, and a single red rose in a small bottle she had seen before somewhere. Simone had taken a pill to help her sleep the previous night. Her stitches had been throbbing, and she knew she wouldn't sleep well without a little help. But this morning, her head was still a little foggy from the medication.

"Good morning, Sleeping Beauty," Carl said, placing the tray on the nightstand and kissing her forehead. "Let me help arrange your pillows. How are you feeling?" He started to help her sit up, and she grimaced in pain. "Hmm...not that well I see. I have your painkiller here."

He gave her the medicine and a glass of water, and she took it immediately.

"Thanks, love!"

"Don't thank me yet. Wait and see what you have for breakfast." He turned, got the tray, and set it over her legs.

"A croissant? Oh, my God, you are an angel!"

Simone dug into the meal, hoping to show Carl how much she appreciated his efforts. They hadn't had roses or croissants in the house last night, so he must have gone out in the cold this morning to get all this for her.

"I need to get stabbed more often if the reward is fresh-baked croissants!"

"Don't make jokes about that. It's not funny, and you almost ripped my heart from my chest when you told me you'd been hurt!" He wagged his finger at her then sat on the edge of the bed.

“Honey, I called Patricia and asked her to reschedule any patients you have today. The university called this morning to inform us they found your purse inside a trash can, and it seems all your belongings are there, as well as your credit cards and phone. So, if you’re feeling up to it, we need to go get your purse and make sure there’s really nothing missing," he said.

"Great news!" Simone smiled, relieved she wouldn’t have to deal with the hassle of having her driver’s license redone. One less thing to worry about, even though Carl had canceled her credit cards.

“Well, in my opinion, it’s not that great,” he said.

Simone raised an eyebrow and waited for him to explain.

"Obviously, that wasn’t just a robbery; it was an attempt on your life," he said, his voice tense. "So, after we get your purse, we still need to go to the police station to complete your statement and report this as an attempted murder disguised as a robbery. Someone tried to kill you or at least send a warning. Finish your breakfast. When you’re done, I’ll help you get dressed, and then we must go.”

*****

“Simone, in your opinion, why would someone break into your house or stab you? Do you think it has any relationship to the previous crimes? The cyanide or the women´s murders? Could Peter Hay be involved somehow?” Carlo asked, staring at her with his piercing eyes.

Carl and Simone were sitting in front of Carlo´s desk at the New Haven police station, and he had spent the last thirty minutes asking dozens of questions about the details of what had happened to Simone the previous day.

“I don´t know. I can only guess.” Simone shrugged.

“Have you ever seen your assailant before?” Carlo asked

from behind the computer screen.

"I think so. I think he was one of the students who attended the lecture. He didn´t come from outside the auditorium; he was already inside."

"Does the auditorium have security cameras?" Carl asked. He looked at Simone and widened his eyes, as if the idea had just occurred to him.

"Never paid attention to that, but they are everywhere, so I'm almost sure it does." Simone nodded.

"I will try to get those images," Carlos said. "Can you tell me which auditorium you were lecturing in?"

"The Mary S. Harkness in Sterling Hall."

"Did you check your purse to see if all your belongings are in there? Is anything missing?"

"Nothing." She shook her head.

"Are you involved in something I should know about? First someone breaks into your house, then you get stabbed. Doesn't seem like a coincidence, does it?" Carlo frowned.

"Of course not. Just living my regular life. Back to the office, teaching, everything's normal." She shrugged, trying to downplay the situation.

"I think you should stop visiting MacDougall, Doctor Bennet.

He sounded more like a cop issuing a warning than the friendly acquaintance she'd gotten used to.

Simone didn't have time to reply before Carl answered for her.

"She will do that, Officer. Can we go now?" Carl rose.

"Yes, you are free to go. We've done everything we can here for now." He waved his hand. "You have my number. Please call me if anything out of the ordinary happens again," he said, his tone serious yet reassuring, as his eyes locked onto hers.

*****

Simone got to her feet and reached to shake Carlo's hand. Carl did the same, and then they left.

*****

No words were exchanged as Carl and Simone left the police station. In the parking lot, Carl opened the car door for her. She sat and waited for him to climb in behind the wheel.

"Tell me what's bothering you," she said gently, sensing there was more on his mind than he was letting on.

Carl fastened his seatbelt then turned to her.

"What's bothering me? I feel overwhelming guilt because the officer there is right." He turned his head toward the police station. "There's a link between what's happened to you lately—the attack, the attempted breaking and entering—and your visits to the inmates at that prison. And I was the one to tell you to go."

"Honey, there is something weird here... Neither of us told Carlo I was visiting MacDougall..."

CHAPTER TWENTY-FIVE

Promises Made with No Intention to Keep Them

"The police know everything. Once you visit a facility like that, your data is recorded, and if someone broke into our home, you filed a report. Carlos must be snooping, checking up on you."

"Or paying visits to inmates himself. He and Edward used to be good friends."

"That's a possibility, but good friends aren't allowed to visit inmates freely. Relatives and police officers, yes—but if he goes there, he must have a good reason and he must be on the inmate's approved, active visitor list." Carl tapped the steering wheel with his thumb.

"I ´ m visiting as a Doctor..."

"You have some privileges, but you also need to follow a protocol—someone must have registered you in advance."

"Patricia did. Have you never thought about visiting Peter? You're a lawyer; your license also gives you some privileges."

Carl put the vehicle in gear. The engine hummed to life as they started to move forward. He turned to her and then looked back at the road.

"Many times... He was a good brother-in-law, he became a

great friend, and a generous client. I just can't face him again and try to align those things with him being a psychopath. I would have so many questions and emotions to deal with, and I don´t think I can handle all of that. It's still too much for me. I'm tired of grieving."

He is an honest man about his boundaries and limitations. Other men would make an excuse and would never say they couldn't handle emotions.

She felt a pang of love for this man who could bare his heart and soul to her.

*****

The weekend was calm. Simone had to cancel with John because she was supposed to rest, but they invited him for Christmas.

For Simone, this would be a holiday like none she'd ever experienced. Half her life she'd spent with silent parents who were not festive at all. She couldn't remember a family Christmas with her former husband Jack and her daughter. They had divorced when the child was a toddler, so Christmas had been spent with just the two of them, and then lately, she had been spending it with Ed.

The house would be full of guests, as Carl had decided to invite her siblings, and they had accepted. Sean would arrive on the twenty-third, and Deborah and her family would come just for Christmas lunch.

I will have to breathe into a brown paper bag before facing a full house, but Carl is so happy about having guests... We are so different. We were both only children, but he loves to be surrounded by people, and I hate that...

Carl told her his father had always been passionate about Christmas. Every year, they would go out together to find the perfect tree, decorate it, and, even if it was just the two of them, his father would cook a grand meal. The house would be filled with music, and on Christmas morning, they'd sit under the tree to unwrap gifts, cherishing the festive warmth.

When she entered the kitchen that Monday morning, Carl was balancing the phone between his shoulder and his ear while frying something on the stove. He reached over and pressed the button to start the coffee machine. He caught sight of her and gave a quick blink in acknowledgment. He ended the call, turned to her with a slightly apologetic look on his face, and handed her a latte he had just brewed.

"Honey, I'm sorry, but I have to go to the city. There's a huge problem with a client. Do you think you can manage alone? I'll try to come back this evening."

He turned back to the stove, and Simone took a deep breath through her nose.

Mmmm.

Whatever he was making smelled delicious.

"I can, no worries. I'll have Patricia to help me take care of everything, and I really need to see a patient today. I won't feel so guilty if I know you have work to do, too." Simone smiled, blew across the top of her hot drink, and then sipped it.

Thank God!

When she'd woke up that morning, she'd had no idea how she'd get out of the house and to the office with a mother hen watching over her.

"You won´t leave home, right?" He turned his head and looked at her.

"I think I can do my meeting online," she lied.

He smiled and sat down to eat with her, placing a plate in front of her that smelled wonderfully of cinnamon.

"Here you go," he said, his tone warm, as they settled in for breakfast together.

"French toast! You are the love of my life," she exclaimed with a smile, mouthwatering at the sight of one of her favorite foods.

"Anything for my beautiful patient," he said with a playful grin, giving her a quick peck on the cheek before diving into his own plate of food.

*****

Simone stayed seated at the table, sipping her lukewarm coffee, and waiting as patiently as possible. When she heard Carl's car start and the garage door open and close, she leaped to her feet and hurried into her room. She changed into a silver-gray suit, chose a darker gray coat, then grabbed her purse, checked her makeup in the vanity mirror, and then left the house.

Her stitches were hurting, and she wanted to remove them, but she would wait one more day for that. She didn ´t think about going to the hospital to have them removed—they'd be easy to take out by herself.

Simone parked in front of her office, climbed out of the car, and closed and locked the door. After Peter killed Mona and then left the poor woman's body inside Simone's car for her to find, she'd stopped leaving her car doors unlocked.

She entered her office, rubbing her hands together to heat them. The wind was glacial, and she welcomed the blast of warmth that hit her when she entered and closed the door.

Patricia was at her desk, sipping something from a mug.

"Good morning, Doctor. How are you feeling today? Are you sure you're well enough to work here today?"

Simone had sent a message to Patricia on Sunday, telling her the schedule should go on no matter what Carl might say to her.

"Feel like I've been stabbed, but if I stay home, I'll feel every single stitch and go crazy."

Patricia smiled and shook her head. "I have good news! You have two new patients! They would like to start tomorrow. Can I schedule them?"

"Yes, of course. That's great news! How about my visit to MacDugall this afternoon? Did you get it?"

"I did, but Doctoryou can't take food or gifts as you'd like to." Patricia contorted her mouth apologetically. "Sorry, Doctor, I really couldn't fix that, you are allowed to send money orders to the inmate trust fund."

"That's awfull! Did you manage to get me visits with both inmates?"

"Yes, I did," she replied with a smile, and Simone smiled back.

"Good. Now, tell me, who are these new patients?"

"Both were recommended by Chivon. Two men…but honestly, the voice of one of them didn't sound masculine at all."

"Great, schedule them for tomorrow afternoon. And Patricia, could you pick up a scalpel and alcohol from the drugstore for me? I'll need those for tomorrow, as well."

Simone didn't have another patient scheduled for a little more than an hour, so she decided to do some research. She settled in behind her desk and turned on her computer. She needed to check if Peter's lover really existed. Once it powered up, she opened her browser, went to Google, and typed *Brian Gonzales*

A second later, the search engine returned with more than fifteen thousand results in addition to five thousand more when the name was spelled with an S instead of a Z. She thought for a moment, then refined her search by adding another word. *Brian Gonzales missing*. The search came back with ten thousand results, so Simone added *New York* to refine the results a little more. Unfortunately, there were nearly four thousand hits for *Brian Gonzales missing New York*, and Simone gave up. She'd never find out more about the man Peter said he'd killed. Not by doing an internet search anyway.

Knowing Peter, Brian Gonzales wasn't even the man's real name. Peter would realize what a popular name that was... like Jack Smith or Jim Jones. Simone would have to come up with another way to find more information.

She sat back in her chair and closed her eyes, considering the problem and trying to come up with possible solutions. After a couple of minutes, she opened her eyes and smiled.

"I think I've got it," she said. "I think I know who can help."

*****

Doctor Wendy Rafalli, Simone's new patient who was due for a first appointment that morning, had been referred by one of Simone's best friends, Arami, a Paraguayan Doctor who lived in Miami.

Recently hired by Yale University, Wendy was a renowned scientist, researcher, and author of books on stem cells. Her studies had helped thousands of Doctors around the world who were looking for cures for rare genetic diseases.

Simone had expected to meet a woman entirely dedicated to science, someone who paid little attention to her appearance or wardrobe. Instead, a stunning, well-dressed Black woman entered her office, radiating confidence. She wore impeccably tailored clothes and expensive jewelry, revealing not only a sharp sense of style but also an appreciation for the finer things in life.

"Good morning, Doctor Bennet." She smiled at Simone and with scrutinizing honey-colored eyes, she appraised the entire office. "What a beautiful place you have here. May I sit?" Without a pause, she settled onto a couch in front of

Simone's.

Oh, she's a confident one... Apparently, she knows what she wants.

"Good morning, Wendy." Simone didn't use the woman's title. From the beginning, they needed to establish the hierarchy between Doctor and patient. "What brings you to my office?"

Wendy didn't seem like the type of woman who beat around the bush, so Simone got right down to business.

The woman smoothed her immaculate white skirt before answering.

"I'm fifty-two years old and find myself in love with someone other than my husband. This man is almost as young as my son, and I feel like a teenager experiencing her first major crush. I crave him with every fiber of my being, and I'm becoming reckless... Sneaking around, lying... I need guidance. I can't lose my mind now, especially when nothing like this has ever happened before," she continued, her voice trembling slightly. "I've always been so in control of my emotions. And now, here I am, feeling things I never thought I'd feel again, and risking everything. I don't know what to do."

The woman spoke in a composed manner, her tone even and calm. She seemed completely relaxed with her legs crossed and her hands folded in her lap. The vision of ladylike perfection.

"Let's start with some questions first, okay? I need to establish some background before we explore your current issues."

"Sure." Wendy nodded.

"How long have you been married? Is your husband the father of your son?" Simone opened her notepad.

"This is my third marriage. I've been married for eight

years now. My son is from my first husband. He died in a car crash when our child was just a toddler. Then I married a colleague, but that didn't last very long. We couldn't stop competing, and that doesn't make for a good marriage relationship. My current husband is a businessman." She didn't move her hands from her lap, and she didn't seem eager to share her husband's name.

"And now you are in love with a younger man... How much younger?"

"He is twenty-nine, twenty-three years younger than I am." Wendy frowned, and her lips turned down at the corners.

"How did you meet him?"

"Well, I'm addicted to weightlifting, but my cardiologist told me I needed to do more aerobic activities, so I decided to take martial art lessons. I found Shaw on Google—he is a karate instructor."

A woman who primarily engages in intellectual pursuits paired with a man who lives a more physical-focused lifestyle might not be the best match.

Even if she was addicted to weightlifting, that wasn't really her world. As she listened to Wendy talk, Simone jotted down the information in her notebook.

"After taking a few classes, I realized his personality delighted me. He makes me laugh every time I see him, and the classes became one of the few bright spots in my life. My life is tough. I spend almost ten hours a day in a laboratory doing research, either alone or with one or two assistants..."

"How did you end up becoming emotionally involved?"

Simone had enough background. Now it was time to talk about the main reason for Wendy's visit. Simone met and held Wendy's gaze while waiting for the woman to answer.

"I don't know...First, I began to really enjoy the classes and look forward to visiting his place every week. Then I found myself laughing with Shawn and craving that laugh when I wasn't with him." She paused, looked up at the ceiling, and then back at Simone.

"At some point, after a few weeks, I started sharing my problems at work with him, and he began opening up about the issues he had with his wife and kids. We were developing a friendship, I guess," Wendy said, her eyes flickering with uncertainty. "But then one day, I went to one of Shaw's karate tournaments with my husband, and after it ended, Shaw sent me a message."

She paused and took a couple of deep breaths.

"What did his message say?" Simone prompted her to continue.

"He said I looked beautiful." She stopped again and cleared her throat. "He also wrote *I have a dream about spending an entire afternoon making love to you.* The message surprised me. I was impressed by his boldness and courage, shocked that a man his age would want to have sex with me, and nervous because deep inside, I knew I wanted the same thing."

"How did you finally get together?"

"I promised him I'd spend just one afternoon with him, no more than that," Wendy admitted, her voice soft and conflicted. "I didn't even think about the consequences at the time. It just felt so good to be the object of desire…especially from someone as gorgeous as him. We set a date…like a visit to the dentist." Wendy grimaced. "At first, I couldn't find the space in my schedule, or maybe I was deliberately postponing things.

"Then one day, I arrived early for my karate class," Wendy said, her voice lowering as the memories resurfaced. "He was alone, and we couldn't resist the attraction anymore. The sexual tension between us was palpable, so thick you could cut it with a knife. It's still like that between us every time we're near each other."

She paused, taking a deep breath before going on.

"We pretended we were going to spar, getting ready for the fight, but instead, we ended up on that filthy couch in the corner I don't know why we didn't stop. It was like something took over, and we just...gave in."

Wendy fluffed her perfectly curled dark hair and looked at Simone.

"Please continue," Simone said.

"I was wearing one of those kimonos, tied shut with just a belt," Wendy said, her voice trembling slightly. "And then... I opened it. I untied the belt and uncrossed the vest. It was like I wasn't even thinking—I just let it happen." Wendy shook her head. "I pulled it off and threw it on the floor. Shaw followed my lead and took off all his clothes, and I just stared for a minute." Wendy's voice grew softer. "He has a beautiful, muscular body, like something sculpted, all lean muscles. I ran my fingers down his torso, and I remember thinking, *My God! The feel of smooth, young skin is incredible!* But also, I remember thinking I was becoming a cougar, and that disturbed me."

Finally, Wendy's calm, cool, and collected demeanor began to crumble. She was flushed, her voice had gotten husky, and she lowered her eyes.

Simone made a note on her pad.

Buries her emotions. Hides them well. But they are there!

Wendy looked up at Simone again, searching her eyes, as if in a silent interrogation of how to proceed or maybe looking for confirmation she'd been heard.

Simone nodded and gave her new patient a smile of encouragement. "Please continue."

"He caressed me briefly—we didn't waste much time on

foreplay—and when he entered me, I came in seconds. I was soaking wet and ready for him and dying for his touch. I loved his rhythm, the way he seemed to enjoy my whole body, the way he sniffed my skin, touched me…he was totally focused on me. Most guys seem to get lost in themselves after a certain point, but not Shaw. I came so many times I lost count. When I felt his breathing change, I told him to come in my mouth, and he ended up ejaculating all over my face, in my eyes and hair. What a disaster, but we both laughed about it." She smiled, and her face had turned red again.

"And how did you feel after that first time? Your thought about turning into a cougar upset you; did you feel differently when it was over?"

"I felt completely satisfied, and I have to confess, I've had no regrets." Wendy's words were full of confidence.

"After that first time, did you start to meet him on a regular basis?"

"Yes. That first night, when I crossed the street to go to my car, I was already longing for him. I'm finally finding time in my schedule for something I love to do. I hadn't realized how much I missed sex. And at first, I tried to lie to myself and convince myself that's all it was. Just fun, great sex."

"How did you lie to yourself about your feelings?"

"First of all, I thought I was in control. I established several rules for him—don't get attached, don't disturb me when I'm at work or at home, let's talk only through an app that erases the conversations, and so on." She waved her hand, punctuating each rule as she listed it.

"What about him? Did he agree with all of that?"

"He's married and has two kids, so in the beginning, he seemed to agree, but he used to tell me we risked falling in love. Every time he brought it up, I would deny the possibility, and I'd tell him we need be adults…act like professionals. I tried to convince myself we were just having fun. And I told him if we agreed to keep it all about the sex, then that's all it would ever be. He used to call me Elsa, after the girl in the movie *Frozen*."

"What made you fall in love with him? Or finally admit you'd fallen in love?" Simone asked.

How could someone so smart fall for Cupid's arrows, risking everything—her marriage, her reputation—by falling in love with a man half her age?

Simone understood it from a psychiatric perspective, but personally, she found it difficult to comprehend relationships with a large age difference.

"The way he treats me... He is always so kind, so gentle, and he's always telling me how beautiful I am. And of course, I've never had that kind of physical chemistry with anyone in my life. He touches me, and I want to be his."

"Where do you meet?"

"We go to a discreet hotel, and sometimes, we spend three or four hours straight making love with only a couple short breaks. And still, every time he touches me, I want him again!"

Tadalafil.

Simone imagined that had to be Shaw's secret. Tadalafil was the name of the compound found in almost all the prescription medications men used to maintain an erection for an extended time.

As if she'd read Simone's mind, Wendy added,

"I thought he was taking Viagra or something similar, but he ejaculates two or three times, and that's not normal with those kinds of drugs."

"What you have with Shaw...is it different from what you felt for your husband? Not now, I mean, but in the beginning."

"First of all, I don't think I was ever in love with my husband. He was a cerebral choice. *Another* cerebral choice..." She grimaced, as if disgusted by that fact. "He's a businessman, and he was responsible for connecting me with many of my sponsors. He is always recommending my research to various companies, and his company is one of my greatest supporters. We were friends."

Simone zeroed in to Wendy's use of the past tense verb, *were*.

"And you're not anymore?"

"Sometimes, I think I live with a stranger." She shrugged.

"How about your sex life?" Simone asked, keeping her tone and expression neutral.

"It used to be good, but my husband has this recurrent fantasy that I'm with other men and playing along with that started to wear me out and turn me off. Apparently, he can't get a hard-on if he doesn't imagine me with another man. When I'm with Shaw, on the other hand, it's just us, and he makes me feel incredible."

Having a high level of physical chemistry with somebody usually made comparisons more complicated and affected a person's ability to think rationally. That wasn't love; that was lust. Simone nodded thoughtfully, keeping her expression neutral. She needed to gather more details before offering any conclusions. Lust and chemistry could cloud judgment, but she would keep the thought to herself for now.

"Your marriage—would you describe it as a good one?" She leaned in slightly, her tone calm and professional.

"I thought we were friends. I thought we made good companions. But lately, thanks to his erratic behavior and his stupidity in accepting everything his spoiled son does, I've lost the respect I used to have for him."

"Describe the erratic behavior for me please. And how is

his relationship with his son?"

"He is always shouting and losing his temper. He imagines things and has become paranoid about certain things, and he thinks he's the most intelligent man in the world. Whenever he hires someone to work with him, I know it won't last. He's a workaholic, and he expects everyone else to be the same way. He doesn't respect the idea of business hours or holidays; he hires people to follow his orders, not to think. If the person starts to rebel in any way, he starts a campaign of persecution until the person resigns." Wendy uncrossed and recrossed her legs and continued.

"As for his son, he used to work with his father, but he betrayed him, left the company, stole money right out from under his nose, and told him he didn't care about him. His exact words were, 'I don't even like you'. The kid put my husband through hell, made him suffer, and I stuck by his side, pitied him because he's a good father, a good provider, and I was positive I had gotten rid of that little shit forever... But then his money ran out—and that's all he cares about—and now, he's back, playing the repentant son and manipulating his father, turning my husband against the person who took his son's place and did a great job when the kid walked out. I tried to open my husband's eyes, but he just won't listen. And lately, I'm being treated like the evil stepmother in Cinderella."

For the first time since she'd entered the office, Wendy raised her voice, and she slammed both hands down on the couch.

The cat has claws.

"That's a complicated problem. There are all sorts of emotions that come into play when one spouse criticizes the other spouse's child."

"The problem is my husband acts like a needy chick. He needs to feel loved, or rather, he needs constant reassurance that he's loved. His mother, who he believes is just a complicated person, spits in his face, and he still takes care of her. His son acts just like the old woman. I've tried repeatedly to open his eyes, but he thinks he's always right, and I'm tired."

Wendy sighed, her shoulders slumping.

"So, would you say you feel betrayed by your husband's behavior?"

Wendy rolled her eyes to the ceiling and then looked back at Simone.

"It's a mix of feelings, really—betrayal, my loss of respect for him after watching him allow his mother and his son to walk all over him, and yet, he still goes out of his way to get their attention. On one hand, he acts needy and weak, but the way he treats others…especially the people who have worked for him, disgusts me. He's a bully."

"And now, you are betraying his trust, taking your revenge," Simone stated.

"I don't know… I've thought about that, and I question myself all the time. I wonder if I'm not just searching for a way to exit a worn-out marriage."

"Do you consider your lover as a way to escape your marriage?" Simone frowned.

"It is too similar to another situation from my past… a different lover, a different marriage…but the story is the same."

"Do you feel like you're stuck in a loop?" Simone asked gently.

Wendy sighed, rubbing her temples.

"I'm lost here I don't know what to think, and I think until my brain starts to hurt."

"You really need to consider that—and think about the

consequences. What happened last time, in the other story? Did it put an end to your previous marriage? In what ways are they similar, and why are you walking into something so familiar, knowing how it ended before?"

Wendy paused, then glanced at her expensive watch and sighed.

"A lot to think about," she said. "But I guess we'll have to leave the rest for our next session."

Simone gave her a gentle smile.

"That's okay, Wendy. We've made good progress today. We'll pick this up next time. Just give some serious thought to the questions I posed."

Wendy nodded and her shoulders looked more relaxed as she gathered her things.

"Thank you, Doctor. I'll see you next week. I promise I will think about everything." With that, she stood and made her way to the door.

CHAPTER TWENTY-SIX

Helicopters Coming and Going

Simone had become familiar with MacDougall's procedures. Their rules stated inmates weren't allowed to receive any food or gifts from the outside. But Simone had brought some chocolates and cakes in boxes, a few small gifts—a chessboard, a couple of card games, and several books—hoping that since it was nearly Christmas, she could convince one of the security officers to take the items and make sure Peter and Edward received them.

"We are going to verify everything, Doctor. I can't promise you anything, but I'll try. You know once those things come past the gate, they can't leave, don't you?" the penitentiary guard asked.

Simone glanced at his name tag.

"Yes, I know, and thank you, Officer Romano. Please try your best; after all, it's Christmastime."

Simone batted her eyelashes and smiled at the guard, doing her best to act flirtatious, despite not having a flirtatious bone in her body.

Officer Romano smiled back at her. Apparently, she'd succeeded in touching his humanity, but it didn't last long.

"It's going to be Christmas soon for the families of the people those two killed, too, and they can't have their loved ones there to exchange gifts or celebrate," he said, a scowl replacing the smile.

His words and the change in his demeanor hit Simone like a bucket of cold water had been dumped on her head, but she knew he was right, so she nodded and kept quiet.

After that little lecture, Simone didn't bother trying to sweet-talk the man. She waited for him to punch a code into the lock panel then followed him to the infirmary.

Simone had arranged to meet with Peter first and then Edward.

"We'll put you in one of the empty infirmary rooms and escort the prisoners to you. You don't have to do a thing. Just take a seat and we'll take care of everything." He smiled at her again, clearly trying to make up for being so harsh earlier.

"Thank you." She couldn't bring herself to say more. Like most people, she hated to be lectured.

Neither of them spoke for the rest of the walk to the infirmary.

*****

Peter entered the infirmary room like a caroler making his rounds, singing "We Wish You a Merry Christmas" in his deep, baritone voice.

He's really very talented.

Simone admired the smooth, rich tone of his voice as it filled the room.

With that voice, he could have sung professionally.

"Good afternoon, Peter. You seem like you're in a good mood today. How've you been?" Simone forced a smile.

"Oh, yeah, happy as a canary in a cage." He smiled back and plopped down into an empty chair, and his weight hitting the seat sounded like a sack of potatoes being thrown on the floor.

Peter sat quietly until the guard who'd escorted him left the room. As the door closed, he looked at Simone, smiled his mischievous smile, and said, "Getting stabbed? That's no good for your health, Doctor. One of these days, the cut might be deeper, and then there you go…a one-way ticket to the cemetery. Life is so short! Don't you agree?"

He looked into Simone's eyes, his expression sincere and earnest, folding his hands in front of him on the table as if in silent prayer.

"Well, what I think is that you know who attacked me, considering how quickly you learned what happened. Why don't you tell me about that?" Simone mocked his candid expression.

"No, it's Christmastime! I want to give you a gift… I was thinking about it, and since I can't buy anything tasteless, I decided to tell you a little story about your husband." Again, he locked his piercing gaze with Simone's.

"Let's keep Carl out of this."

Despite her attempt to remain calm, Simone's voice wavered a little, and she lost the ability to smile.

Dammit! Why do I let him get to me?

"Well, I suppose I can call the guard and tell him I want to go back to my quarters… I'm missing quite a lot of entertainment to be here with you, my lady," he said, doing a horrible imitation of a British accent. He lowered his head in a faux half-bow, like some kind of lord or king from another time.

"What do you want to tell me about him?"

Simone, do not *let him see how curious you are. That would not be good. Remain detached. No matter what.*

"I want to tell you about Lara's death…"

Again, he looked at Simone, as if he was waiting for a reaction. She didn't blink.

"I know everything about that day," she said.

"I don't think so… Let me tell you the truth."

"If it is important to you, please proceed."

"I will start from the very beginning…" He stretched the word beginning.

"It is your story; you tell it however you please."

"I received a call from Carl. His voice was filled with despair, he was crying like a baby, and the only coherent phrase I could make out was. 'Lara is not moving; Lara is not moving'. I asked him why she wasn't moving, and he said, 'I killed her. I'm going to call the police.'"

He took another look at Simone, but she didn't give him the pleasure of a reaction. After a moment, he continued.

"I told him not to call the authorities. It was late, but I could be in the Hamptons in no time. I had this discreet guy who, for the right amount of money, could take me by helicopter, so in a matter of an hour, I would be there. I was able to convince him to wait for me so we could think together about everything. He continued to sob, but he agreed. Could you give me a glass of water, please? My throat gets dry when I talk too much."

Simone rose and went to the drinking fountain in the corner. She filled a paper cup and then put it between Peter's cuffed hands. He lifted the cup and took a long sip before resuming his story.

"Before I left, I got some money from my safe. If the police got involved, I figured a little cash might prove useful. I called Carl's father—that old homophobic bat was the best criminalist ever—and he joined me on the rooftop where the helicopter and the pilot were waiting for us."

None of this is in Carl's diary. Simone kept her expression neutral, but her thoughts raced.

Was this fact or fiction? If these events had taken place, why hadn't Carl ever said anything?

"When we arrived at Lara's house, all the lights were on, as if someone was throwing a party. The door was open, so we walked inside, and we encountered the most pathetic scene I've ever seen. Carl sat on the floor in a corner of the living room, still sobbing, and he had Lara's head on his lap. She looked so beautiful. He had covered her with a light blanket, and I wouldn't have guessed she was dead. She was glowing, and she seemed so relaxed, at peace."

"Peter, I know Carl accidentally killed Lara while they were having sex, so spare me the drama." Simone sat back and crossed her arms, her entire body rigid.

"I know you think you know that...but you don't know the whole story, do you?"

"I know a lot." She shrugged and tried to pretend she had all the information. But she had stopped reading Lara's journal right before Lara's death and Carl could have a created a fictional account in his diary, so she really didn't know the whole story, only what Carl had told her.

Peter ignored her and continued.

"I asked Carl how he killed her. What happened exactly? But he couldn't answer me because he couldn't stop crying. His father, who had been talking to someone on the phone when we entered the house and was still deep in conversation, prepared a whiskey for his son and handed him the glass. And dear old Dad was still on the damn phone. I sat by Carl's side, put my hand on his shoulder, and let him cry until he was calmer." Peter's eyes were like sheets of glass.

The eyes of someone recalling the details of a previous event, or the eyes of someone making up those details as he went along?

Simone didn't know which, but the anxiety inside kept

building.

"I took Lara from his arms and put her on the sofa. Mr. Lourenzzo, as I used to call Carl's father, approached his son and said, 'Son, what happened?'"

Carl started to sob again. He pulled a small, square box from his pocket and opened the lid to show us a ring...By the way, it was not the same ring you have now. Don't worry." He pointed at Simone's finger.

"While he held the little box in his lap, Carl told us what had happened. 'I asked her to marry me, and she told me she would never belong to anybody! She started to laugh and said that was the most ridiculous idea in the world, so I put my hands around her neck. I just wanted to silence her; I want her to stop mocking me." Peter repeated Carl's confession while imitating Carl's voice.

"'Did you plan to kill her?' Mr. Lourenzzo asked."

Peter used another voice to relay Carl's father's words. Apparently, he'd decided to act out the events, to play the role of every character who appeared in his little story. Like some sick, twisted version of a play.

Is he mocking me or is it part of his mental illness?

"Carl's answer surprised me." Switching to a high-pitched, clear voice, Peter said, "'I wanted to! I killed the woman I loved because I wanted her for myself, but I would never have her. I want to call the cops. I will tell them the truth.'" Peter cleared his throat then went on, adopting the older man's tone.

"'No, you're not! You're going to listen to me. My only child will not waste the rest of his life sitting in a jail cell. That woman—'" Peter paused and shook his head. "He pointed at Lara's body on the couch, and the look on his face indicated exactly how much he despised her," Peter said in his own voice. "I figured he was probably aware of what kind of woman she was."

He nodded, as if he agreed with Carl's father on that point and then continued with his story-turned-macabre-play.

"Mr. Lourenzzo told Carl exactly what he was going to do. 'Everybody knows she's deranged. We're going to warm up her body with hot water, undress her, set it up to look like you were playing a sex game, and say it was an accidental death. And only after we have everything ready will you call 9-1-1 and have them send the cops. I will be in my New York City apartment. You will call me and your dear friend Peter, and we will hire a helicopter and come here.'

"First, we filled the bathtub with hot water and put Lara's body in there so her temperature wouldn't drop too low before we got everything set up. When we were ready, we dressed her in a sexy outfit—she had plenty of those kinds of clothes in her bedroom—and a pair of high heels, I arranged some candles around the house." He made a circle with his index.

There was no need for Carl to pretend to be Dr. Reynolds. Your husband had unprotected sex with Lara before he killed her, so his DNA would already be present—probably compromised by the water, making the timing impossible to pin down." He contorted his mouth. Peter had used his own voice to relay these events, and when he'd made such a clear reference to Edward's necrophilia fetish, laughter had underlined the words. Peter had always managed to entertain himself by making inappropriate jokes at the worst possible times.

Simone sat in stoney, unsmiling silence. Her thoughts were in turmoil, and her heart was racing. The whole story seemed crazy but entirely plausible. She tried her best to control her breathing and not give any sign Peter had managed to disturb her.

No, don't let him get under your skin. He's trying to

manipulate you into turning against your husband.

"We created the whole scenario, and when everything was ready, Mr. Lourenzzo and I took the helicopter back to New York, as the pilot was waiting for us. The rest, you know. Carl called 9-1-1, the cops, and his father, who flew to the Hamptons on a commercial helicopter airline. Skyrock or Skyrain..." He waved a hand dismissively. "I don't remember the name..."

"No one asked why the semen was water-contaminated?" Simone asked.

"No," Peter replied. "Carl's father called an old friend who guaranteed that the doctor performing the cause-of-death exam would be loyal to him."

He smiled at Simone, rose, and using his sweetest voice, said, "*Merry Christmas*!" Then in his regular voice, he shouted, "Guard, we are done here!"

*****

Simone's head was spinning, but she was convinced the story he'd just told her was exactly that...a story. A figment of a lunatic's imagination.

He's just trying to manipulate me.

She took several deep breaths to regain control of herself and prepare for Edward's arrival. She didn't want to appear upset or shaken in front of him.

Edward stepped into the room, and his gaze went directly to her. He nodded a greeting then offered his cuffed wrists to the guard. The sight of Ed in handcuffs sent a shock through her system. On her previous visit, he'd been waiting for her in the infirmary already, and she hadn't seen any cuffs. Peter wore restraints on both his wrists and his ankles, and they stayed in place throughout her visits. Edward must have been allowed certain privileges...

It's not like that, and it wouldn't matter if it was... He's a convicted felon; don't delude yourself.

The guard removed Edward's cuffs then left them alone, closing the door behind him. Edward strode over to Simone, sat right in front of her, and frowned. Simone ignored his grouchy expression and studied his face while she waited for him to say something. *He has a lot more wrinkles now... Then again, we both do.* They were both getting older, and life had been difficult.

"What did that psycho say to you? You're as white as a ghost!" He reached out and caressed her cheeks.

"Good to see you, too, my friend." Simone smiled. "It seems to me everybody knows everything in this prison." She spread her arms to indicate their surroundings. "Do you have spies? Maybe a few hidden cameras?"

"I told you; it's like living in a small town...but one that's sitting right in the middle of hell. What happened?"

"Nothing, Ed. Seeing you in handcuffs disturbed me, that's all." She gave him a part of the truth. Better that than to lie... "Plus, my stomach has been bothering me lately."

"It must be the antibiotics they prescribed after you got cut. Can you tell me how you got stabbed?"

"My God, I was only kidding about the spies and cameras, but now, I'm not so sure I'm wrong. Do you people have an underground prison newspaper?" Simone threw her hands into the air in exasperation. She didn't like having to explain herself every time she came there.

"Actually, we do. Something like that anyway. You don't want to know how it works, but it is more reliable and factual than the news we're fed on television. Just tell me what happened, Simone, and don't beat around the bush."

Simone stared at him for a moment, taken aback by his tone.

Jail has hardened him...

His words were harsh now, and he would have never ever talked to her that way before. Still, she couldn't lie to Edward, so she told him everything she remembered about the attack.

"I will kill that son of a bitch!" Edward said, forcing the words out between clenched teeth.

"How do you know who it was? Who are you referring to?" She knew the answer, but she wanted to hear him say it and confirm her suspicions.

"Peter and his goons. That man has tentacles that reach far outside this place. And you started digging... I knew he would do something. That's why I told you to stay out of this, that I would take care of everything. Please stay away from Peter. Can't you see what he does to people's lives?"

Edward opened his arms, as if to say, *look at me; I'm a prime example*. Even though he'd lowered his voice, she could feel the anger in his words.

"I was out of this, as you say," she responded, genuinely confused. "I wasn't doing anything except lecturing at the university!" She gritted her teeth. How damn annoying! Both Carl and Edward seemed to be saying she'd brought the stabbing on herself.

"But you visited Peter, so you must have asked something —something that put him on guard, or you talked to someone about him, asked about him, and somehow, he found out, and he decided you needed a lesson. A warning. A message! People here are not trustworthy. They'll sell themselves, and they won't charge a high price. Some of them will do anything in return for two or three cigarettes! You must understand, it's an underworld—a parallel universe of survivors!"

Simone mentally reviewed the people she'd asked about Peter. She had only questioned that nice man, Officer Liam about who was visiting Peter. Could he have possibly passed that information on to someone else? She couldn't believe he would do such a thing, but lately, everything she had faith in had begun to fall apart.

"Please tell me what's going on. I won't try to help. I just need to protect myself and my family, and to do that, I need to know what's going on." She begged Edward to fill her in.

The smile he gave her—a kind of sideways, half-smile that lifted only one side of his mouth—reeked of sarcasm.

"By family, you mean your husband and Tammy? Is she back?" He scowled again, deepening the lines on his forehead.

"No, and she won't be. Her life is in France now. She's studying law in Lyon, and she will never come back. She already secured an internship at some fancy firm that specializes in international law," Simone said, her voice tinged with both pride and sadness. "She mentioned she'll be able to visit me during her international trips once she graduates." Simone smiled sadly. "Kids... What a bad investment of time and money."

"Don't I know it! Noah refuses to visit me." Edward's eyes filled with tears, and he looked away.

Simone instinctively wanted to reach out and comfort him, but she hesitated. She wasn't sure how he would react—or if the rules even allowed such a gesture in the infirmary. In the visiting room, touching was strictly forbidden, but they were alone in the infirmary.

Edward's fingers brushed softly against her cheek, and she flinched, startled by the tenderness.

"I didn't know that, Ed. Do you think Beth is influencing him? I could talk to her," she managed to say after some time.

"No..." Ed shook his head. "Beth comes here every week. She told me she's your patient now, and she couldn't be happier with the treatment she's received. She seems more mature, and I thought she would never grow up."

"She's suffering; that's all I can say. Suffering makes the most juvenile of people get in touch with their inner wisdom. She didn't tell me she comes here. What do you talk about? You seemed to do nothing but shout at each other after the divorce."

"Not only after the divorce... Now, we talk about Noah. He's a teenager, and he dominates Beth. She's having a hard time with him."

"She hasn't mentioned that in any of her sessions, either." Simone muttered under her breath, her mind racing as she pieced together the small, hidden fragments.

"She is loyal to her son; she won't complain about him to you. Most of the time, we discuss what went wrong in our marriage." Edward paused for a moment. "To do an autopsy on a previous marriage is like revisiting the chapter on sins in the book of life—not very fun—but necessary for a cleansing of the conscience." Edward's features had tightened, and he swallowed hard.

In Simone's opinion, there were worse events in the chapter on sins in Ed's book of life, such as being a necrophilist and helping a psychopath, but strangely, Ed didn't mention those activities as being a part of his list.

"Reviewing our sins is a good idea; it's the way to start healing." Simone nodded.

Now he'll say something about having a lot to review.

Simone looked into his eyes, waiting. Several moments passed in silence before Ed finally spoke.

"I need you to promise me you're going to stop visiting Peter—or inquiring about anything linked to that man," he said.

"I promise I won't ask anyone about him... but I can't stop visiting him. I won't lie to you. I need to understand things that happened, and there's a lot for me to process.

All the deaths around me, my kidnapping, my daughter's kidnapping, discovering I have siblings—"

"You have to figure out how I'm involved in all that, but you don't ask..." Edward shrugged, his blue eyes locking onto hers with an intensity that seemed to penetrate her soul. "Your need for answers is leading you down a dangerous path. Let me deal with him. I know how. Stop digging! It won't bring any good, you're more vulnerable than you think, and I will prove it to you.He shook his head violently.

"About Peter — he confessed that he killed a lover, Brian Gonzales. I couldn't find anything about him on the internet. Do you know anything about it?" Edward shook his head.

"I don't know everything about Hay's criminal life... but I can check. I just doubt he would kill a man; it isn't his signature. Maybe he was misleading you — it's his specialty."

Simone agreed with her head and simply changed the subject. "Has there been any kind of progress with the FBI regarding the panda girls?"

"Yes, they found another one last week...but this one is alive."

CHAPTER TWENTY-SEVEN

Truth, Lies, or Something in Between

"What? She's alive?" Simone's adrenaline spiked, and she told herself to calm down.

"Whoever tried to kill her gave her enough drugs to cause an overdose, but not enough to finish the job. They left her on a bench in the park—I believe they thought she was dead or at least dying—but she got doubly lucky. The dose wasn't fatal, and a Doctor happened to find her. Now, she's in the hospital, in intensive care. The FBI is praying for her to regain consciousness and make a full recovery, and I suppose with ten armed men at her door, they're going to make sure the killer doesn't try to sneak in and finish the job."

"But I didn't see anything on the news!"

"Thankfully, the local news stations have agreed not to disclose this information for now. In addition to the drugs, there are other horrifying factors. It seems the girl was used in some kind of orgy. She was raped in every imaginable way and has multiple internal injuries and a broken arm. They really brutalized her before discarding her like trash."

"Poor girl. Is she Asian?"

Edward nodded.

“The FBI is investigating the possibility that she, along with the other girls they found, had been forced into the pornography industry," Edward explained, his voice grave. "It would explain the brutality they suffered and the way they were discarded. They’re looking into whether these girls were trafficked specifically for that purpose."

Edward added, his voice heavy with the weight of the revelation.

“How do you know all this?”

He is more informed than anybody outside.

“I have my sources.”

He smiled, and Simone scowled at him. Of course, he wouldn’t tell her.

“I told you I’m cooperating with the FBI to reduce my sentence. I know what I’m doing, and I’m used to dangerous situations. Stay out of this, and let others solve these crimes. That way, no harm will come to you and—" His lips curled into a sneer, and he finished in a sarcastic voice. “Your *family*.”

Simone forced a smile and refused to engage. She wouldn’t be drawn into an argument with him. Being locked up, away from everyone he cared about, had to change a person. Besides, it was Christmas... She and Edward chatted a little more about issues they had to resolve together concerning the office and Ed’s participation as a silent partner. He was pleased Simone was paying rent to Beth, and he didn’t want Simone to change anything about the deal she’d worked out with his ex-wife.

“Maybe I’ll be back one day,” he said with a sad smile.

“I hope so,” Simone told him.

But who would want an ex-con as their psychiatrist? Will I want him as a partner?

Her heart hurt. What a wasted life... Even if he got an

early release, could he ever rebuild his career? Could he successfully appeal the suspension of his license? She forced a cheery smile, glanced at the clock on the wall, then patted his knee.

"Well," she said, getting to her feet. "I guess we're about out of time for now." She leaned down and kissed Edward's cheek. "Merry Christmas, my friend. I won't be able to visit you for several days, so I hope your holidays are as good as they can be under the circumstances." She regretted the words immediately.

As good as they can be... Sounds so stupid.

"Same to you. Is Tammy coming home?" he asked, looking into her eyes.

"No, not this time." Simone averted her gaze. She didn't want to tell him about her siblings and new friends. She didn't feel comfortable sharing the details of her life with Edward like she used to.

"Merry Christmas, Simone."

My whole name... He doesn't consider me a close friend anymore, either.

In the past, Edward always called her Simmie.

"Thanks, Ed."

They said their goodbyes, and Simone left the infirmary. She walked the facility's halls and passed through several locked doors without paying attention to her surroundings. If the guard at her side said anything, she didn't notice or respond. She had a bitter taste in her mouth, and her mind had fixated on what a mess Ed had made of his life. Her chest hurt, and her throat grew tight. Despite his intelligence and years of education, he'd made some horrible choices. Would he ever be able to claw his way out of the pit he was in?

Simone hurried the last few steps to her car, no longer able to hold back the tears. She unlocked the door and climbed into the driver's seat as the first sob broke loose. With her forehead resting against the steering wheel, she cried like a heartbroken child, shedding buckets of tears of pity for her friend. The leather-wrapped wheel grew steamy and wet from her tears, and she lifted her head.

Get it together, girl.

She pulled a tissue from her purse and dried her face then wiped off the steering wheel. She grabbed her water bottle from the center console, took several sips, and calmed herself. But as she reached for the start button on the car´s panel, a thought hit Simone like a thunderbolt.

Who is the source Edward said told him about another dead girl?

Simone shook her head. Even if Edward was cooperating with the FBI, they would never risk their investigation by telling him they'd discovered another victim.

So, Ed had lied to her. Again. The question was, why? What was he up to now?

*****

Simone drove from MacDougall directly to her house. Thankfully, she could practically do the drive with her eyes closed. On that particular day, her mind was like a crazy frog, leaping from one subject to another, and she couldn't even remember how she got home. From Peter's story about Lara's death to Edward's news about the girl who'd lived through an attack, back and forth.

"Thank God, I don't have any patients this afternoon!" Simone murmured to herself; she couldn't imagine going back to the office in the mood she was in. If her brain tried to take on anything else, it might blow a fuse… She couldn't go for a run while she still had stitches, so she would try to meditate. That should help empty her mind and clear her thoughts.

Five minutes from her house, Simone dug her cellphone from her purse and called Patricia.

"Hello, Doctor Bennet, how can I help you?"

Simone frowned at Patricia's direct, no-nonsense tone.

"Hello, Patricia, will you please see if you can find out if there's a helicopter company named Skyrock or maybe Skyrain still operating in New York? Apparently, they fly to the Hamptons, so it must be a smaller, privately-owned company."

"Do you need me to book you a flight?"

"No, just want to know if they're still around and in business."

"Okay, I'll handle it for you."

"Thanks, Pa—" Simone glanced at the phone. "She hung up!"

No, "Goodbye," no, "Have a nice day," nothing... Simone shook her head and tossed her phone onto the passenger seat.

Sometimes I miss Mona. At least she was sweet most of the time, even if Patricia is more efficient.

Simone pulled into her driveway, opened the garage door, and parked the car. After putting the door back down, she grabbed her purse and phone and went to the kitchen door. She reached to punch in her code then froze.

Someone had opened the door to the house and had left it ajar. There were no cars parked outside or in the garage. Her heart accelerated, her legs started to shake, and she slowly and silently tiptoed back to her car. After easing the car door closed so it didn't make any noise, she raised the garage door again, backed out, and sped off.

Two blocks from home, she pulled over. Still shaking like a frightened kitten, she grabbed her cellphone and opened the app for their security cameras so she could find out if whoever had broken in was still there. As she tapped the icon for the first camera, she pressed a finger to her throat over her frantic pulse, willing herself to calm down.

CHAPTER TWENTY-EIGHT

Do You Have Any Secrets to Tell Me?

The first few security cameras showed the exterior of Simone's house, and she searched around the front, back, and sides but didn't see anyone. Then she moved to the first interior camera. There was a man in her kitchen! Her breathing accelerated, her stomach contracted, and her hands shook so much she could barely control her fingers to enlarge the image. Maybe he was looking for a knife so he could kill her. She shook her head.

No, you idiot... If he broke in, he probably brought his own gun!

She made the image bigger and zoomed in.

Yep... You're an idiot, all right. Probably the biggest idiot in the world.

Carl stood in their kitchen, and even with his back to the camera, she would have recognized him anywhere.

She put her phone into her purse, sat back, put the car in gear, and went back to the house. After repeating everything she'd done five minutes earlier, she entered the kitchen to find her "killer" drinking a cup of coffee.

"Can't turn my back and you were out! I bet you went to

work, didn't you?" Carl smiled, his eyes narrowing playfully as he studied her.

Simone loved when he smiled like that. It was his way of saying, *I know you, and it's all right.*

"My God, Carl, you almost gave me a heart attack!" She put her bag on the island and went to him.

He gave her a coffee-flavored kiss on her lips while she tried to calm down a little more. She was still a bit shaky and upset, especially after her visits with Edward and Peter.

He frowned. "Why?"

"Where is your car? When I got here, I didn't see a car, but the kitchen door was open, so of course, I thought we had another intruder!"

"My car broke down, and I ended up having to phone into the meeting I was on my way to attend. I was sitting alongside the highway, waiting on the tow truck, and I could barely hear with all the traffic racing past." Carl's face contorted into a scowl.

"You didn't get a complimentary rental car? What kind of insurance do you have?" Simone gazed up at him. "That's ridiculous. Do you want me to call them?"

"No, babe, it's okay... We're not going to need a lawyer to fight for a rental." He smiled. "They're going to bring me one later. I didn't want to wait around. So, come here and calm down." He put his cup on the counter and pulled her into his arms. He held her gently, like a mother would cradle her newborn. He brushed back her hair and looked into her eyes. "How are you feeling? Where have you been?"

"I'm fine. Stitches are itching a little bit. I went to the office, but I left there to go for a walk in the park. I was feeling suffocated in closed spaces today."

He glanced over her shoulder toward the window.

"It must be freezing out there. Let's stay in our super-warm and cozy home. I'll just finish up a little bit of work I have to do, and then I'll take care of you." He kissed the top of her head.

Simone closed her eyes and rested her head against his chest. Carl was what most people would call a nice guy, the kind of man who loved to be in a relationship. He enjoyed staying at home, and he rarely complained. He wasn't a cold-blood murderer who would kill a woman just because she refused to be his. Simone felt guilty for doubting him.

I'm letting Peter mess with my head!

Simone stood in Carl's arms until her breathing returned to normal, and she was warm, then gently, he moved her away and picked up his coffee cup.

"Love, I'm going to our office. I must finish the work I should be doing in the city. I'll wrap it up as quickly as I can, and then I'll have you back in my arms. Are you okay?"

"I'm fine, honey, don't worry. I'm going to meditate for a little bit."

Simone left Carl in the kitchen and went into the bedroom to change. Dressed in her yoga clothes, she headed to the special room she'd had remodeled specifically as a place for meditation. The area was small, just a little over two square yards, but the back wall had a window overlooking the yard and a partial view of the shoreline. She had the ceiling painted dark blue, and a local artist decorated it with gold stars. The walls were a light shade of lavender, and the floor was dark wood. Several rolled yoga mats stood in one corner, and Simone grabbed one and spread it out at her feet.

After closing the blinds and telling Alexa to find a flute meditation song Simone liked, she pulled her phone out of her pocket to put it on silent mode and saw Patricia had called.

"I'll call her back later."

Legs crossed, Simone tried to focus on controlling her breathing, but her mind was in turmoil. She decided to call Patricia and then meditate. Otherwise, Simone would wonder what her secretary had discovered, and she'd never put her mind to rest.

She picked up her phone and dialed, and her Patricia answered on the first ring.

"Hello," Simone said. "Any news?"

"Yes, Doctor Bennet, I couldn't find a Skyrock or a Skyrain, but I found a place called Flyrock. I think that may be the place you're looking for. Do you need anything else?"

She sighed.

"A judicial order to take a peek at the flights they did in 2014 and 2015." She didn't know exactly when Lara died, but based on all Simone had learned, it was one of those years.

"Can't your husband...?" Patricia was smart, and she didn't finish her question. "No, okay, let me see what I can do. There's a paralegal I know... We used to work together. Maybe he can do me a favor. What exactly are you looking for?"

"I need to know if that company flew Peter Hay or Anthony Lourenzzo to the Hamptons during that period."

"Okay. Let me see what I can do."

"And please—"

"I know. Be discreet. I will. Don't worry."

And once again, she hung up without warning.

Simone went back to her lotus position, and this time, she found her inner peace.

*****

Simone and Carl spent the rest of the day wrapped in the comforting simplicity of being together, indulging in the little things they cherished. They lounged on the couch, watching movies hand in hand, letting the weight of the past few weeks slip away in the quiet intimacy they shared.

Dinner was a joint effort, a routine they both enjoyed when their schedules aligned. Carl had a knack for creating delicious meals, even though his repertoire was limited, each dish was always flavorful. Simone, on the other hand, was admittedly hopeless in the kitchen, but Carl had taught her how to be his *sous chef*, guiding her through the basics with patience. She loved how cooking together felt like a dance, each movement in sync, laughter filling the gaps.

Simone's stitches were still bothering her, and Carl, ever the worrier, was concerned she'd reopen the wound. So, making love was out of the question for the night. Instead, they settled on having dinner, and then afterward, they'd watch a movie.

He'd probably pass out if he saw a drop of blood.

Simone smiled as she put the last dirty plate into the dishwasher.

After the movie ended, they sat on the couch, wrapped in each other's arms, listening to music. Simone drifted, her mind and body totally at ease.

Like floating in a sea of warm, tender emotions...

She sighed and snuggled closer. She could live like this. His embrace was like a soft, cozy blanket made of love, and she would stay there forever.

*****

The next morning, Simone woke up early. She stretched and yawned, amazed at how a good night's sleep could rejuvenate the body and mind. She glanced over at Carl. He was still sound asleep, breathing softly. Quiet as possible, she slipped out of bed and went to take a quick shower. When she finished and realized Carl hadn't moved yet, she went to the kitchen and prepared a nice breakfast for him. After filling the plate with crisp fried bacon and scrambled eggs, she toasted a bagel to a light-golden brown, just the way he liked it, then spread some cream cheese on it. She poured him a cup of freshly brewed coffee and then put everything onto a serving tray. Normally, Carl pampered her.

"My turn." Simone smiled.

Brick by brick, they were building the kind of wonderful relationship she'd always dreamed about.

Simone and Carl spent the next few days doing almost everything together, except when Simone had to speak with one of her patients or Carl had an online meeting he needed to attend. They drove into the city to pick up Tommy, who had been staying at his dog-sitter's place, which he loved, since there were other dogs to play with. They bought gifts, and together, they prepared the house for the coming festivities and their guests.

A few days before Christmas, they went to a nearby nursery and bought a tree. When they got home, Carl set the tree in the stand and cut off the odd branches, while Simone dragged boxes of decorations in from the garage. They spent the next two hours stringing the lights and hanging the colored balls and other ornaments. When they finished, they stood back to admire the results.

"It's beautiful," Carl said, taking Simone's hand in his.

She moved in front of him and put her arms around his shoulders, tilting her chin up for a kiss.

Something brushed against Simone's legs, and at the same time, Carl shouted.

"Tommy! No!"

Simone turned to look just as the dog leaped onto the tree to grab one of the colored balls. He fell back on his hind legs, ball in his mouth, and gave a tug, and the entire tree toppled over.

"Bad dog! You can't touch the tree! See what you did?"

Carl started wagging his finger and lecturing Tommy, and the poor dog seemed ashamed as he gazed up with sad eyes.

Simone laughed at how silly they both looked.

"Don't do that," Carl said. You're spoiling him."

Tommy rolled over on his back and covered his face with his paws, and Simone laughed harder.

"Poor dog, he regrets his behavior. Let's do it all over. I think he learned his lesson, right, Tommy?" she said.

The dog rolled onto his stomach and looked up at her with his tongue hanging out.

Simone swallowed back another fit of giggles. "Why don't you take him for a walk, and I'll finish here. Just help me lift the tree, and I'll fix everything."

"I think that's a great idea. I don't know if I have the patience to hang all those again. Let's go, you big, goofy, mutt. Let's take a walk." He rubbed the old dog's head.

*****

When Carl and Tommy left for their walk, Simone looked at the tree, sighed, and got to work. She picked up an ornament and placed it on an empty branch.

Thank God, the balls are plastic nowadays.

They weren't as pretty as the glass ornaments, but at least, they were Tommy proof!

The sound of her ringing phone interrupted her task. Simone headed for the kitchen. "Where did I leave that darn cellphone?"

She found it on the island.

"Good morning, Patricia," Simone said. "Is everything okay?"

The office was closed for Christmas. Hopefully, none of her clients were having an emergency.

"Morning, Doctor. Everything is fine. I have some news for you about the Flyrock subject. My friend got the records, and you were right. On the night of May 14, 2015, they flew a Mr. Lourenzzo and a Mr. Hay from NYC to the Hamptons at around 10:00 p.m. I'm sending a picture to your phone. That's all she was able to find, and please don't show anyone. If anyone finds about this, my friend will be in big trouble."

Simone stayed silent, her mind racing.

"Another thing, the government closed them down. Apparently, they made a few flights that they failed to include in their records."

Still, Simone didn't comment as she tried to figure out what the information might mean.

"Doc, are you there?"

Simone shook her head to clear it.

"Yes, yes, I'm here. Please don't tell anybody about this."

"That's what I just asked you, Doctor. So, don't worry. Have a nice holiday! Ho, ho, ho!"

Simone laughed with Patricia.

She must be drunk.

That woman didn't have a comedic bone in her body.

Be fair—she just has a dark sense of humor. She gives all the patients weird nicknames.

She was surprised by the warm feeling of friendship she had developed for her peculiar secretary. "

Same to you, have fun." Simone told her then ended the call,

Her head was spinning with the new information.

Maybe all that stuff Peter told me really happened…

But then, was it so unusual for Carl to have called his father and best friend when he realized Lara was dead, why hadn't he included those details when he'd told Simone about the events he'd experienced that night? The information Patricia had found seemed to prove that part of Peter's story… But what about the rest of it?

I'll stop digging into this, or I'm going to go crazy. Do I trust my husband or not? If I do, I need to stop this stupid investigation.

She was in the middle of her mental debate, sitting on the floor, the phone still in her hand when Carl entered the room. Tommy came to her, wagging his tail and panting.

"What happened, honey? Are you okay? You look kind of pale. Bad news?" He pointed at her cellphone.

"A patient with suicidal tendencies. I had to calm him down, but I don't think there's any real risk. He just needed some attention. I'll have to monitor him a little bit over the next few days." She shrugged. "I guess it's that time of year."

"Thank God, I only have clients who've lied to the government and are afraid of going to jail. Then again, it is a little bit suicidal not to pay your taxes in this country."

He smiled at her, but she'd barely been listening. Her mind was too busy She wondered if Carl had been lying to her all along or if he was truly a trustworthy person.

Carl was still smiling, obviously in a better mood since his walk, and he appeared completely relaxed. Could there be a killer behind that calm demeanor?

Is there more to Lara's story than what he told me? Is he hiding something? Listen to your heart!

CHAPTER TWENTY-NINE

Live One Day at a Time

John arrived two days before Christmas. He came up the sidewalk, holding hands with a pretty Black woman. Petite and curvaceous, she had a face that wasn't what most would call beautiful, but her sparkling black eyes gave her a unique charm. They were laughing about something, and they both looked happy. Simone's heart warmed at the sight of her friend and former patient in such a good mood.

Simone and Carl waited on the porch to greet them. John hugged Simone and Carl and then turned to introduce his girlfriend.

"Simone, my dear friend and shrink, this is Ruby King, my girlfriend and a colleague. Ruby, this is Simone, the best psychiatrist ever, who became a dear friend, and this is Carl. He's the rarest of all breeds—a lawyer who has a soul."

"Wait 'til you need my services again... The invoice will have tons of zeros, and you'll rethink that whole idea of me having a soul."

John punched Carl on the shoulder lightly, and they laughed.

"Nice to meet you, Simone," said a smiling Ruby. "John

talks about you and your husband a lot."

"I hope only good things. Let's go inside; it's too cold out here."

Tommy met them as they stepped through the front door. He introduced himself, and like the king of the castle, he stood patiently to receive the caresses and attention from their new guests. He probably thought anyone who entered the house had come to see and pet him. No doubt about it, though, the little guy was a success wherever he went.

Ruby seemed nice and extremely talkative. She didn't stop chattering from the moment they met. In fifteen minutes, Simone discovered Ruby worked as a virologist and was responsible for introducing John to Doctors Without Borders.

"It's volunteer work, and we stay in regions where people need medical care but have nothing." She talked quickly and gestured with her hands.

She has the brightest eyes I've ever seen.

Simone struggled to follow the flow of words, distracted by the woman's physical magnetism.

"I was thrilled when John finally agreed to join us, even if it is temporary. We've never had a neurosurgeon before, at least, not one with John's experience and knowledge. We hope to have him with us for a while so he can train some of the younger Doctors in the program."

"But it is temporary, right, John?" Simone's practical side worried about her friend wasting an amazing career he had built during his years at Johns Hopkins.

"Most regular Doctors have to sign up for nine to twelve months. Lucky for me, they make exceptions for surgeons. So, I've committed to three months, the maximum the hospital will allow me to stay away. I've been out for a while, and they want me back, but my boss also understands my needs, and my position is secure if I come back at the end of three months."

He's saying that for Ruby's benefit, as well as mine.

Good. Simone hoped he'd stay strong and resist any urge he might have to throw away a great career for the love of a woman. Any woman...

Ruby went behind John and hugged him around his waist. She stuck her head around his side so she could see Simone. "I have plans to convince this guy to return every year. After the first experience, almost all Doctors who volunteer for the program come back again and again. It's a transformative experience that changes our souls forever."

"Is that what happened to you?" Simone asked.

"Yes, exactly!" the woman replied with a smile.

Wow. What a transformation...

When she smiled, she turned from merely pretty into a breathtaking beauty.

"Ever since I was at university, I had this dream. I was never drawn to fancy hospitals. For me, it was always about the jungle, poverty, and mosquitoes." Her voice softened and grew more passionate as she spoke.

A poet...

Simone glanced at John. Did he appreciate a woman like Ruby? Or was this just another infatuation?

Let him choose Simone. You're just a friend now, not his psychiatrist anymore.

But as his friend, she still worried, even if she did like the easygoing woman.

"Simone, may I take a shower? I hate to travel and not shower right after. It's one of those simple pleasures not possible to enjoy in some corners of the world, so I take advantage of hot, running water whenever I can!"

"Sure, come with me, and I'll show you to your room."

Simone guided the talkative woman through the house to one of the guest rooms they'd prepared ahead of time.

*****

Carl left Simone and John alone while he went out back to get some wood for their fireplace.

"We decided to keep the classic wood fireplace, to maintain the charm and the romance of the flames. Carl's idea of course," she told John. "How about something to drink, my friend?"

"Not now, thanks, Simone. Actually, I was anxious to talk to you alone for a minute. You've become my best ear." He blinked at her.

"Even if you couldn't wait to escape my office. Doctors...we never need help, do we?"

"Yes, we do, but you're so good, you put me back on my feet in no time, and now, we are such good friends, I can't be as open with you as I was when I was a patient. If I did, you would be disappointed."

"Never. Friendship is not judgmental. At least, not for me." Simone touched John's hand.

"What do you think about my decision to join Doctors Without Borders?"

Simone frowned, but before she could answer, he went on.

"I can read some wariness on your face. As a Doctor, I'm sure you make an excellent poker player, but as my friend, you're too transparent." He smiled at her.

"Not wariness, just some concern. Tell me, how did you meet Ruby? She seems to be a nice girl, and she has been good for you; you're smiling again."

"I met her during one of my travels around the world, in the middle of a small village in Africa, the poorest place I've ever seen," he began, a distant look in his eyes. "She was there—a tiny thing." He gestured with his hand to show her size. "She was shouting at everyone because she couldn't get medicine for a little boy. So forceful, so full of fire. It made me feel so small and selfish." His voice carried admiration.

"So, is she responsible for the smile on your face?"

"She is in part, but what has really made me find joy again was getting out in this vast world. Travelling opened my mind. The world is so big, and there are so many things to see and do, and there I was, locked in my little world, in my surgery room, drowning in my misery, and I was missing so many amazing things." He opened his arms.

"How are you really feeling? Not from patient to psychiatrist, but friend to friend."

"I can answer as both. I'm healing, little by little. I realize nothing will bring Lara back. What I had with her was special and rare, but it's in the past, and I can't live there, or I will lose my life, whatever years I have left. We're middle-aged people, so we have to think about the other half of our time here. And answering the question your transparent eyes are asking, I don't know exactly what I feel for Ruby. She is totally different from every woman I've met, and we are building something together, but I still can't label my feelings."

"Feelings don't need labels. They are just that—feelings."

"Okay, but I can say I was passionate, besotted with Lara for half of my life. With Ruby, it is a growing sort of feeling; every day, I admire her a little bit more. She's a great professional, and a wonderful human with the most transparent feelings. She talks about everything and anything and is open about what she likes and dislikes. With Lara, and in my other relationships, also, I felt I was always guessing what was happening. With Ruby, I just know. She likes this, she dislikes that, and I know."

"Almost like dating a man?" Simone laughed and John soon joined her.

"Exactly, I never thought about that, but yes, the relationship is simple, just like you said." He laughed again.

"I'm happy for you. Relationships based on that kind of openness tend to last."

I thought I had one like that, but now, I have my doubts.

"Do you think you can love her more than you loved Lara?"

You are asking that for your own purposes.

"I don't even want to try to compare; there's no point. Lara will never come back, and if I decided to stay focused on worshiping her memory, that would be no kind of life. Not only that, but it wouldn't be fair to anyone. I decided to live one day at a time, and, my friend, I've been happy many, many days after making that decision. It is about freeing myself."

Does Carl feel the same? Will he love Lara forever but consider me his chance at living? Does he love me at all?

"Hey, shrink… I know exactly what just crossed your mind. That guy"—John pointed to the door—"loves you a lot. You're not some kind of human Band-Aid, okay? What you have is the real deal; I know because he always tells me how happy he is to have you. So, don't put any questions in your mind that don't deserve your precious time." He tapped his forehead.

"Thanks, John, I needed to hear that."

Just then, Carl kicked the door open, his arms loaded with split logs. John ran to help him, and Ruby came into the room. Wet hair, sweatshirt, and sweatpants, and barefoot.

Simone smiled. *I like her.*

CHAPTER THIRTY

The Perfect Mess

Christmas Eve morning, Sean arrived alone. Simone watched him come up the sidewalk, and one word filled her mind. *Magnificent*. All sun tanned and smiles, he carried a bunch of wrapped gifts, balancing them in his arms and with his chin.

"Hello, Sean, you are so handsome! Please tell me the secret of maintaining a tan like that during this time of the year."

"Hello, sister. It's artificial! I'll kiss you right after I find the tree." He moved past her and down the hall.

Simone was so touched and distracted by him calling her sister, she took a minute to realize he'd walked right past the living room.

"Sean? Back this way. Second door on your right."

Sean nodded and carried his gifts in to put under the tree. Tommy followed, wagging his tail, no doubt intent on adding a new admirer to his ever-growing list. Simone went in to make sure the dog behaved himself and didn't tear up any presents, but apparently, she'd worried for nothing. Tommy lay on his back near the tree, paws up in the air, smiling the way only a happy dog would smile as Sean rubbed his belly.

"Let's have a seat." Simone indicated the couch in front of the tree.

As soon as Sean settled into a corner of the sofa, Tommy leaped up, lay down, and rested his head on Sean's lap.

"Hey, you are a gorgeous guy! But how about you let me talk to your mom?" Sean patted the dog's head gently, his hand through the soft fur as Tommy wagged his tail in response.

I'm a dog's mom now!

Simone used to laugh hard when Carl used to say things like, "Come with Daddy, Tommy," and now, she was labeled his mom. She shrugged.

Maybe my canine child won't go abroad and leave me behind.

Sean got to his feet, went to Simone, and hugged her like they'd been together their whole life. Tommy took the opportunity to jump in and join the hug. They laughed together.

They were alone for the moment... Carl had left to run some errands, and John and Ruby had gone to the mall to finish their Christmas shopping. Simone had Sean all to herself for a while, and she would take full advantage of every minute and enjoy getting to know her brother. As an only child, she was delighted by the idea of having siblings.

They chatted for nearly an hour, and Simone discovered a man full of passion for life, ambitious, and in love with his profession. Sean was a chemical engineer from MIT, working now for a large fragrance company in New York.

"I'm a nose!" Sean touched his nose as he explained his profession to Simone. "That's what the perfume industry calls people who can produce a composition made of various essences. I've always loved smells. I think I have my half-French gramma to thank for that. She taught us to smell pretty much everything when we were kids, from flowers to fruits, spices... When it came to aromas, her French side took control." He smiled, and his eyes were wet and luminous as he spoke of his grandmother.

"I've analyzed your sister's diaries, as you know..." Simone said, staring at him intently, searching for any flicker of emotion or reaction on his face.

"Our sister..." He corrected her, pointing back and forth between them.

Simone nodded.

Yes, Lara was my bombshell sister.

"Our sister...She loved your grandma so much, and from what I've read, she was a spectacular woman."

"She was... I believe God compensates us for bad mothers... Emm was so modern, so strong, so fierce. Despite being less than five feet tall, she was really a force of nature." Sean shook his head. "Not many people would go up against Emm. Her life story should be made into a novel. Maybe one day, I'll have the courage to write it all down." He smiled tenderly before continuing,

"She taught Lara to write journals, and Emm always kept one, too. But I still haven't gotten up the nerve to go through them... Sooner or later, I will, though. My heart still aches for her loss." He grimaced, and frown lines creased his tanned forehead. "Reading our sister's journals was like being stabbed repeatedly—so painful. So obviously, I'm still reluctant to go through Emm's."

"I understand. I've been there, too." Simone frowned.

"How about you? Any relatives?" Sean asked.

"I've never had a relative. Both of my parents were middle aged when I came along, and of course, now I know where I came from." Simone scowled. "My mother and father were alone in the world, both only children. I had no siblings, no sweet grandparents, no relatives of any kind. It's like my family was deposited on Earth by a flying saucer."

Sean laughed.

"We have weird stories that somehow crossed."

He touched Simone's shoulder and seemed about to say more, but the sound of a car pulling into the garage interrupted him.

"Someone's here. Let's exchange more details about our life stories later. We have a lot of catching up to do!"

"We will! I would love that!"

Simone's heart warmed. She and her brother had managed to form a tenuous bond. Over time, she prayed it would grow stronger.

Carl appeared at the door, saw Sean, and approached him with a smile.

"Thanks for coming, Sean. Having you here is very important for both of us." He pointed at Simone and then himself.

"It's my pleasure. Thanks for having me."

Carl turned to Simone. "Honey, I got your Christmas gift, but I have to give it to you now. If I wait until tomorrow, it'll be spoiled."

He went back to the kitchen door that led to the garage, and moments later he returned, pulling Tammy by her hand along behind him. Simone's heart almost stopped. Her eyes filled with tears. Her daughter was home!

And my sweet husband must have arranged this surprise all on his own.

Simone went to Tammy, hugged her, and looked at Carl and whispered, "*Thank you.*"

"Babe, I'm so, so happy you're here." Simone caressed her daughter's hair then stepped back to get a good look at her. What she saw made her sad and proud at the same time. How different she seemed—more mature, sophisticated, and she was wearing a French foulard tied fancily around her neck.

Simone blinked back more tears.

"You are so beautiful and so French," Simone said softly, touching Tammy's short, sleek Chanel-cut hair.

"Mom, I'm so happy to be home."

So, it's still home for you?

Simone was delighted to hear that.

"But how…? Last I heard, you'd decided not to come back here for the holidays."

"We have Carl to thank. He convinced me to get some time off from work, sent me the tickets, and voila! Here I am." She opened her arms.

Just then, John and Ruby arrived, and Sean entered the kitchen as Simone made the introductions.

"Oh my God, it's so good to know I have an uncle!" Tammy exclaimed, jumping up to hug Sean.

"My pleasure to meet my beautiful niece," Sean wrapped her in a warm embrace. "And what a great outfit you have here," he added with a smile, admiring her style.

"Hey, everybody, we need to plan our Christmas Eve dinner!" Simone announced, using the same tone of voice she used when dealing with chaos in the classroom.

The room instantly fell silent, all eyes turning to her for direction. For a brief five seconds, there was a peaceful stillness—then, in a flurry of excitement, everyone began talking at once, offering opinions, sharing ideas, and divvying up tasks for the holiday feast.

Carl was in charge of cooking the turkey and the ham, and he would follow recipes he had found on YouTube, Sean would make the gravy, the salad, and the vegetables, John and Ruby had bought beans and pieces of pork, and Ruby promised to cook the best bean casserole ever, *African style*, she explained. Carl had picked up cookies and pastries at a local bakery that morning, and to Simone's surprise, Tammy decided to do the dessert. A classic, French crème brulé.

"Um, Mom? What are you in charge of?" Tammy asked.

"I'm going to supervise and make sure nothing is served raw or burned!" Simone declared with a playful smile. "And in between, I'll keep everyone's glasses filled."

"The most important job, in my opinion," Sean said.

Everyone laughed as they each got started on their self-assigned tasks.

The meal went off without a hitch, and just when Simone thought she couldn't be more surprised or delighted, Tammy dug through her luggage and eventually pulled out a portable torch. After placing the ramekins filled with her dessert on the table, she used the hot flame to caramelize the tops of the crèmes to perfection.

The house, usually silent and organized, was a mess. Dirty dishes and half-empty casseroles covered the countertop, and people kept coming and going from the kitchen, but Simone didn't mind one bit. Their home was full of laughter and joy. Like a perfect Christmas Eve should be.

CHAPTER THIRTY-ONE

What a Real Family Looks Like

The next day, Christmas morning, Simone woke up early. Carl lay on his back beside her, breathing deeply, and she took the opportunity to watch him sleep. He always looked so calm and peaceful…relaxed. When he slept, the lines on his forehead and at the corners of his eyes disappeared.

He is so handsome.

She scooted closer to him, and as always, his smell turned her on.

Amazing. The chemistry between them was strong. All she had to do was get close to him, and the desire to touch him took hold. She ran her fingers along his jawline, which was covered in short, dark hairs. His five-o'clock shadow was more like ten o'clock stubble, and she smiled. She loved how he looked when he hadn't shaved in a day or so. A little sexier, a little more dangerous. She put her nose close to his warm neck and inhaled his cologne. She had never met another man who put on cologne before going to bed, but she had to admit, she kind of liked it. His delicious scent and soft skin called to her, and she leaned in and kissed him just below his ear.

Carl opened his eyes and rolled toward her. He smiled a

sleepy smile and took her hand, guiding her to touch his hard shaft. Guys called it morning wood among other names, but Simone called it a gift.

"A Christmas gift!" she said.

He laughed.

"Not exactly but…" He pulled her closer and kissed her, softly at first then deeply.

When he pulled back, Simone rose and kneeled beside him on the bed. She removed her nightdress and threw it to the floor, and since she was totally awake—and very eager—she helped him out of his pajama top, opening the buttons and kissing her way down his torso as she revealed more and more of his firm, hot flesh. She started to untie the closure of his pajama bottoms, but by then, he was fully awake and removed them himself, showing her that his penis was ready for her.

Simone took his shaft in her hand and massaged it, and Carl gave a deep sigh.

"Wait," he said, "or you're not going to have your Christmas gift." He traded places with her, helping her to lie back on the bed.

Carl leaned over her, taking a nipple into his mouth while running his fingers over her belly and waist. She had a sensitive spot there that made her shiver whenever he touched it.". He knew exactly what to do and how to do things that made her lose all control.

Simone fought to stay quiet so she wouldn't wake up the whole house, but her body responded to his touch like a quivering, tightly wound violin string. He played her to perfection. As he reached between her thighs and found her clit, she jerked at his touch, and as he began caressing her there in rhythm with his mouth sucking her nipple, she came apart and cried out. Carl lifted his head and brought his mouth down on hers.

"Shhh..." He smiled against her lips.

As she had done when she'd removed his shirt, he made his way down her body, leaving behind a trail of kisses, alternatingly loving her with his lips and his tongue. When he reached the sensitive area at her waist, he put his hand on her mouth, muffling her sounds of pleasure as he kissed her there and then moved lower, all the way down to the juncture of her thighs. He drew her clit between his lips and sucked it while penetrating her with two fingers, synchronizing his movements until she came hard in his mouth, shouting her release before Carl could do anything to stop her. She cried out again, even louder than before.

When she returned to reality, she tried to change positions again.

"No, I'm too hard. If you do that, I'll end up coming in your mouth. Not that I'd mind, of course, but I want you to experience more pleasure, too. Open your legs a little wider for me, honey."

She didn't argue, and in the next instant, Carl pushed inside her in one deep thrust, and unbelievably, she came again, her pussy gushing juices all over his hard cock.

They started to move faster, and their kisses turned more frantic until they came, first her, then him.

Carl dropped to lie limply on top of Simone, and although he was a little heavy, like deadweight, she didn't want him to move. She caressed his back while they waited for their breathing to return to normal.

"I think we woke up the whole house," she said, but she couldn't bring herself to care. Not really.

"I'm afraid so," he whispered without lifting his head from her chest.

She stroked his hair until she drifted back to sleep.

*****

After showering and making love again under the spray, they dressed and went to the kitchen to prepare breakfast for their four overnight guests.

Ruby was already in the kitchen, her hair wet, wearing another pair of sweatpants and a T-shirt. In bare feet, she moved from one side to the other, opening cabinets and prepping the island for breakfast.

"Good morning, Simone, Carl." Ruby smiled at them and then pointed at the stack of plates and silverware. "I'm setting up the island for our meal because I think it's cozier…more intimate. I hope you don't mind?" The little machine gun didn't wait for Simone to answer before adding, "Someone had lots of fun this morning." She flashed a mischievous smile and looked back and forth from Simone to Carl. "You must be starving!"

Oh, boy… Simone's face grew warm.

Carl turned toward the window and mumbled,

"Good morning, Ruby."

"Yes, good morning, Ruby, and thanks for preparing breakfast for us. I'm sorry we overslept," Simone said once she'd recovered her voice.

"No worries." She waved away the apology. "I'm used to getting up early in Africa. It's much nicer to work in the mornings; once the sun is high, the heat is unbearable. I work all day, really, and sometimes at night, but I prefer the mornings."

As the rest of their guests started to appear, Carl greeted each of them with a fresh espresso and invited them to sit.

The party started early today.

But Simone surprised herself by smiling, her heart filled with gladness.

I, a woman who prefers solitude, am finding pleasure in the company of good friends and family.

Now, that was a first!

*****

Debbie and her husband Aidan arrived around eleven a.m., and they brought their two beautiful girls with them. They clung to their mother's hands, one on each side, as they greeted everyone. Roberta, the eldest, was a little lady of twelve with fair skin, fair hair, big blue eyes, and a sparkling personality.

Simone bit her lip.

She looks a lot like her dearly departed auntie Lara. Let's hope she doesn't turn out to be as much trouble.

Johana was ten, and she had brown hair and green eyes, and she seemed shy, especially compared to her elder sister.

What amazing genetics this family has!

Easy-going Debbie started mingling right away, wishing everyone else Merry Christmas while her husband, who never seemed to talk much, stayed near his wife, touching her now and then or exchanging a glance with her.

A marriage based on love.

Simone smiled as she observed their interaction. She looked around. The kitchen had gotten crowded.

"Hey, everyone? How about we all go into the dining room and let Ruby and John finish preparing the meal?"

*****

After a delicious meal, the kids went off to play with a happy Tommy. Sean was on the phone on the porch, marching back and forth, Ruby and John had left for a run, and Simone and Debbie sat alone at the dining room table.

"Simone, do you have a nickname?" Debbie asked.

"Yes, my friends call me Simmie. I suppose you can use that

if you'd like." She smiled, but her thoughts went to the only two people in the world who used to call her by her nickname —her ex-husband and Edward.

"Simmie, it is!" Debbie gave Simone a beautiful smile. "I love your house. It's not only gorgeous but also very homey. I had a sense of welcoming warmth the moment I walked in." She waved a hand around the room. "All of this—it's as if every item was chosen for a specific purpose and to complement every other piece. Did you do this yourself, or did you have help?"

"Thanks, Debbie. I did it myself, but it took me forever."

They started to chat like two old girlfriends. Simone didn't know how her sister managed to keep track, but she jumped from one interesting subject to another—nothing deep, nothing cultural, but Debbie had a great sense of humor and a very funny, entertaining personality. Still, Simone focused, trying her best to keep up as her sister darted from one topic to the next, her mind racing with seemingly endless tangents. A thought suddenly struck Simone. Debbie had the same symptoms of ADD that Lara used to have.

When Debbie paused to take a breath, Simone spoke up.

"Can I ask you something?"

Simone held Debbie's gaze.

"Sure, anything." Debbie smiled.

Only people who have nothing to hide would answer that way.

"Does it bother you to see me with Carl? Considering..." Simone didn't want to finish her sentence. Hopefully, Debbie would understand.

"You mean because of Lara...? Well, I met him only the one other time, for the reading of my mother's will. He came with my sister... After that, I hated him, because...you know..." Debbie shrugged with one shoulder and grimaced. "What happened to Lara... But then I read her journals, and

I absolved him in my heart." She put a hand on her chest. "Poor guy, he seemed to be another toy in my sister's—" She paused, pointed from herself to Simone, and then continued. "In *our* sister's hands, but to answer your question, no, it doesn't bother me seeing you two together because I never saw him as Lara's boyfriend. I mean, she never introduced him to us that way. When we met for the reading of the will, she introduced him as Carl and told me he was a lawyer and would be with us for the reading..." She looked up at the ceiling as if searching her memory. She shook her head. "That's how I remember it... It was Lara. She had so many flings, we could barely keep up."

Simone nodded.

"Thank you. I appreciate you humoring me and putting up with me bringing up memories that must make you sad."

In his diary, Carl had described meeting Debbie at the reading of her mother's will and then again later after Lara died, and the details matched Debbie's story exactly.

See, you idiot? You talk to a lunatic and allow him to make you start to have doubts about your husband.

"It bothers me more to see John with another person." Debbie sighed, her normally bubbly attitude turning bleak. "I used to like him, you know, back when he was Lara's boyfriend... That girl..." Debbie pointed toward the door. "She's nowhere near as beautiful as my sister was."

Simone raised a brow. Obviously, Debbie had no trouble speaking her mind, regardless of what she might reveal. She was a very open, stable woman. Nothing like their elder sister.

Then again, she hasn't suffered the same traumas.

"Lara was beautiful, indeed; I saw a few pictures..." Simone said. "I found one in a drawer recently; I'll have to give it to you."

"Don't worry. You can keep it, I have plenty." Debbie said, "I can see your husband loves you. Lara was more like an infatuation for him, but you are true love. And besides, Lara was so fucked up!" Debbie put both hands to her head and twirled her index fingers.

Once again, Debbie had surprised Simone. Could her sister read minds, or had she seen something in Simone's eyes that hinted at her insecurities?

Debbie went on, as if she didn't expect Simone to comment.

"And as for Ruby, when we were first introduced, I felt a bit of petty jealousy at the idea of John being with her, but she's nice, and it seems she might be good for him. Besides, my sister is dead, so their love story can't have a happy ending."

Tears filled Debbie's eyes. Simone leaned toward her, thinking of patting her hand or something, but Debbie came halfway up out of her chair and wrapped her arms around Simone's neck, hugging her tightly. Simone froze for a moment, then forced herself to relax and return her sister's embrace.

After a few seconds that seemed like years, Debbie dropped back into her chair and smiled, but her eyes were still damp.

"Thanks, sis. Holidays are awful for me—I miss my sister, my dad, and my grannie *so much*."

She tried to come in for another hug, but this time, Simone was prepared. She grabbed Debbie's hand and pulled her up as Simone got to her feet.

"Come on," she said. "There's a huge mess in the kitchen. A little physical labor will take both our minds off our troubles."

This holiday season was turning into something special. Simone had discovered the pleasure of being in the company of people she loved and people who were finding a quick way into her heart. She had never had a Christmas like this. The beauty of friendship and having close relatives was new to her, and in two days, they had gifted her with words of solace and wisdom and a warm feeling it would have taken years on her psychiatrist's couch to discover on her own.

Grateful...that's what I am. Incredibly grateful.

*****

Right after Christmas lunch, the doorbell rang. Carl got up to answer it, but a little hurricane in the form of a girl cut him off as she raced to the door.

"Don't worry, Uncle Carl, I'll get it!" Johana shouted.

Simone laughed and glanced at the child's father.

"Johana is going through a phase right now. She wants to be in charge of answering the door at home." Aidan smiled and shrugged.

The girl returned a few moments later, carrying a beautiful gift wrapped in gold foil.

"This was sitting outside the front door," Johana said, a frown marring her pretty face. "The man who left it was already going down the sidewalk to leave when I opened the door." She handed the package to Simone.

"A mailman?" Simone frowned, too. Did the post office operate today? She turned the golden box, trying to see if it had a card.

"No, he wasn't wearing a uniform. He was just a regular guy, wearing a baseball cap."

Carl jumped from his chair and ran to the door. He looked back over his shoulder.

"Simone, don't open that package!"

CHAPTER THIRTY-TWO

Someone who knows me

Simone put the gift aside and faced her guests. They were all looking at her with questioning expressions, but most knew better than to ask.

"We've had a few problems with people pulling pranks lately. Strange neighborhood." Simone gave the first explanation that came to mind.

"Pranks? You mean like kid stuff?" Ruby asked.

John looked directly at Simone, and his eyes showed he suspected she was lying.

"A little less funny." Simone said, but she didn't elaborate.

If you're going to make up a story, it's best to keep it short.

Carl came back to the table completely out of breath as if he'd chased someone a few dozen blocks.

"Whoever it was, he vanished."

"Damn kids." Simone captured Carl's gaze. They had the kind of relationship that allowed them to communicate without words.

"Let's get some dessert. We can open whatever those little demons dropped off later."

Simone went to the fridge to grab one of the pretty cakes Carl had bought. After placing it on a serving platter and getting a cake knife and spatula from the drawer, she headed back into the dining room.

Everyone enjoyed their dessert, and Simone accepted their compliments to the chef without bothering to tell them she couldn't bake to save her life. Roberta, who had grown used to being with her new relatives and friends, started to tell jokes, innocent jokes that made the adults laugh, more for the child's sweet naivety than for their humor. Simone was only half-listening; she couldn't take her mind off the gift box sitting in the corner, waiting.

*****

When the guests left at the end of the afternoon, Simone, Carl, and Tammy returned to the dining room to sit near the fireplace. Carl added more wood, and they settled with fresh cups of coffee.

"Okay, what's happening? I'm sure the thing about kids pulling pranks is bogus, Mom. I know you too well." Tammy pinned her gaze on Simone.

"Your mom has been visiting the prison at MacDougall, and strange things are happening."

"Mom, are you nuts? After everything we've been through? Let those two dangerous felons sit there and rot!" Tammy raised her voice, something she rarely did.

Carl looked at Simone, and in all capital letters she read the words, *I told you so* written in his expression.

"Let's open that box, shall we? Maybe whatever is inside will offer a clue as to who sent it." Simone changed the subject.

"Knowing Peter, it will be a dead bird. He's crazy about *The Godfather*. When he held me captive, he was always quoting from the movie or making me watch it." Tammy shook her head. "I know the lines in that film by heart now."

"I'll open it." Carl got up and retrieved the package from the mantel where he had left it hours before. "There is a card here," he said. "Let me read it first." He took the small card and opened it.

"Everybody knows where to find you. Merry Christmas!"

"Peter, of course." Simone shrugged, but one glance at Carl, and she wished she'd kept her mouth shut.

"You visited with him recently?" Carl's voice rose.

"Well…"

Her husband shook his head and pressed his lips together in a thin line.

"I'll open the package; you two keep your distance. We can't know what's in here." He shook the package and then put it near his ear. "I don't think it's a bomb; it's too light. My money's on the dead bird." He started to undo the bow and then slowly opened the box. A look of surprise on his face, he lifted the package, turning it to show Simone and Tammy the contents.

Twelve perfect pink dahlias lay on a bed of white tissue paper.

"Close that quickly and throw it into the outside garbage please," Simone said, stepping back and keeping a safe distance.

"But it's just a bunch of harmless flowers."

"Mom is super allergic to those flowers, Carl. Better do what she said, or we're going to find ourselves spending the next several hours in the ER."

"Oh, my God." Carl ran to the door and threw the package into the outside trash can.

When he came back to the room, Simone was already holding a box of antihistamines and a glass of water. She took a pill, swallowed it, and took a sip of water.

"Are you okay, honey?" he asked.

She nodded.

"Now I will be."

"How does Peter know you're allergic to those flowers?"

"He doesn't. Edward does."

"Mom, Uncle Ed would never harm you!" Tammy shouted.

"Honey, I don't know Ed anymore... Maybe I never did. I could have never imagined he would be capable of covering up crimes for his own selfish reasons, but he did!"

Simone hated to say the words aloud, and her heart ached at the thought of hurting Tammy, but Simone needed to open her daughter's eyes and try to dispel the image Tammy had of a good and kind uncle. Trusting people blindly could be dangerous.

"You're right, Mom."

Tammy shrugged, and Simone felt a pang of guilt.

Damn you, Ed, for causing so many people so much pain. Tammy shouldn't have to learn real-life lessons like this one.

Simone glanced at Carl, and he nodded, his eyes filled with understanding.

"In my opinion, your mother should stop visiting those people. Clearly, they have connections outside the prison walls, and they're able to reach us with them. The message was clear: Everybody knows where we live and how to find us."

Simone's emotions flipped on a dime. God, she hated him sometimes! How dare he take advantage of the moment to push his opinion?

"I agree with you, Carl. If Edward could send those flowers, knowing how they'd harm you, who knows what else he's capable of doing?" Tammy looked from Carl to Simone. "You should listen to Carl."

Simone felt cornered. Normally, Tammy and Carl didn't display a lot of affection toward one another, yet there was always respect between them. Now, though, they were standing united in agreement against her, and their behavior isolated Simone.

"Well, I don't agree. This isn't just about Peter as an old friend—it's about studying his behavior and developing an understanding of the psyche of a true psychopath," Simone said, her tone defensive. "I need to learn more about the signs, so if I ever encounter someone like him again, I'll be better prepared. Before Peter kidnapped me, my knowledge was purely theoretical. Now that I've experienced his tactics firsthand, I want to dive deeper."

Simone pointed at Tammy, then at Carl. "You both wouldn't question my research if this were about anyone else, would you? I've conducted studies like this for years, and you've never intervened before."

Tammy and Carl exchanged glances then lowered their heads slightly, as if conceding to her point. She had won this round, but she could sense their underlying concern, and part of her wondered if they were right to be wary.

*****

After Christmas, Simone, Tammy, and Carl fell into a rhythm, tackling the post-holiday cleanup together. Tammy, after spending time abroad and adapting to living on her own, had become surprisingly capable around the house. She moved from one task to the next without complaint. There'd been a time not so long ago when she had done more complaining than cleaning, and her favorite line had been, "Can't we leave that for the cleaning lady?"

With a scarf tied around her hair in a classic French style and her Saint-Tropez pants, Tammy looked every bit the Parisian, even in her gestures and posture. She dusted the dining room, singing a French song that Simone didn't recognize, transforming the house into a gleaming, cozy space again. After the cleaning, each of them took a quick shower, and then they regrouped in the kitchen around the island, where Tammy had set up a spread of Christmas leftovers.

"You guys, come here. I just cleaned up the dining room, so we're not making a mess in there!" she called.

Dinner that evening felt warm and close, like a family who had known each other for years. Tammy and Carl delved into a fascinating discussion comparing the legal traditions of common law and Roman law. Tammy was fully immersed in learning, her tone deferential and engaged as Carl shared insights. Simone sat back, observing, and appreciating their connection and the ease of the conversation, happy that, for once, topics like Edward or the prison visits weren't part of the discussion.

For three days after Christmas, they kept up the routine—gathering to talk around the table, cooking together and drinking wine. It was too cold to go out. Before Simone realized it, the time had come to take Tammy to the airport for her return to France.

As they hugged goodbye at the entrance to security, all three found their eyes a bit misty, and Tammy's hug for Carl warmed Simone's heart.

They've managed to form a special bond.

The thought brought a sense of peace.

Simone and Carl drove back to his apartment in the city with Tommy snoozing in the back seat. They were ready to enjoy the remaining holiday days and looked forward to ringing in the New Year together.

Two days before the end of December, Simone and Carl were sitting on the couch together, watching an old black-

and-white movie, when she decided she had to bring up a subject she dreaded.

"Love, what do you want to do for your birthday?" she asked, although she already knew his answer. Carl's birthday was on December thirty-first, New Year's Eve, and for some reason, he'd never separated the two.

"Honey, you know exactly what I want to do. I'd like to—"

"See the ball drop. Yes, I know. You told me you always do that. I was just hoping you'd changed your mind." She sighed.

Oh God, I hate that.

"You know me well." He threw his arms around her. "And I know it's not your favorite thing, so thanks, honey."

She glanced at his face.

Not my favorite thing?

Simone *hated* to be in the middle of the crowd, waiting for a crystal ball to drop and illuminate the new year. She'd had that experience once and swore to herself she'd never repeat it. But now her husband wanted it as a birthday gift.

I can´t deny him that.

Carl told her his father used to take him when he was a little boy and his dad would say all those people were there to celebrate Carl's birthday, which made him feel as if the entire world loved him. Years later, he discovered the truth, but the good feelings were implanted in his heart forever.

Simone glanced up at his handsome face.

I need to hypnotize him to make him forget those things.

She would never deprive him from his good memories. She gave a resigned sigh and snuggled deeper into his embrace. That would never happen. She loved him too much to try to take away anything that made him this happy.

*****

Simone woke up early on New Year's Eve morning. She

slipped out of bed, careful not to disturb Carl, and made her way into the kitchen. On a mission, she pulled out the delicacies she'd managed to secret into the apartment the day before and placed them on the counter. One of her husband's favorite foods had always been fresh-baked bread. He loved restaurants that served warm, steaming loaves with lots of whipped butter, so Simone was determined to make him fresh bread for his birthday breakfast. The only problem…she couldn't bake.

So, instead of attempting to pull something together from scratch, she'd gone to the freezer aisle at their local grocery store and had bought several of the premade, mini, frozen loaves of bread. All she needed to do was pop them into the oven, and in relatively short order, she'd have the tastiest "homemade" bread around.

As she closed the oven door, Simone glanced toward the hallway. Tommy came pattering into the kitchen, no doubt drawn by the prospect of table scraps. He tilted his head from side to side as if to ask, "What are you making?" then sat on his haunches with his tongue hanging out.

"Cute boy. Don't tell me you smell the food already. I just put it in to bake." Simone gave him a stern look. "Besides, you're getting too fat! Every time I turn around, Carl is giving you bites of whatever he has on his plate. But you know better than to come to me…" She touched the dog's nose with her fingertip.

She set the timer on the oven, and then prepared the rest of the breakfast. Tommy watched her every move, but she ignored him. Silly dog would end up with heart disease or something if he didn't lose a few pounds. Simone prepared Tommy's food and set it down for him, but he sniffed it and turned away. He took a few steps then sat where he could keep an eye on the bread inside the oven, his nose twitching. How could she blame him? Compared to the hard, dry kibble he usually ate, freshly baked bread would probably make him drool.

The buzzer on the oven indicated the bread was ready, and as she pulled out the tray, her chest filled with pride. Three small, golden-brown loaves of perfectly baked bread! Her mouth watered at the heavenly aroma.

"Okay, Tommy, let me put all this on a tray, and then you can help me wake Carl and give him birthday kisses!"

Simone arranged everything on a large, colorful wooden tray, found the gift she had hidden in a lower drawer in the kitchen, and put it on a corner of the tray. After taking a moment to make certain she hadn't forgotten anything, she headed back to the bedroom with Tommy on her heels.

"Good morning, birthday boy!" Simone called out.

Carl's lids fluttered, and then he opened his eyes. When his gaze landed on her standing at the foot of the bed, he gave her a sleepy smile.

Simone's throat tightened with a mix of emotions.

I would kill for that smile.

"Happy birthday to my favorite man in the world!"

"I love you so much, woman. Come here with that tray, and let's have breakfast together. Something smells amazing." He sat up and then settled against the headboard, opening his arms for the tray, and lifting his head for her kiss.

They kissed the best they could with a tray between them, and then Simone stepped back so he could eat and open his present.

"Sit here, honey." He tapped the bed beside him.

Simone settled onto the edge of the mattress and reached for her cup of coffee.

Carl pointed at the foot of the bed.

"And you, Tommy, sit *right there*."

The dog trotted obediently to the designated spot, his eyes fixed hopefully on Carl, as if expecting that his good behavior might earn him a treat.

Carl arranged the tray on his legs and stared down at the food.

"Wow! That's what I smelled. Where did you get these wonderful, fresh-baked loaves of bread?"

"I made them!" Simone had to brag. After all, she could count the number of times she'd baked on the fingers of one hand. She smiled and pointed to the square box. "Now, open your gift."

"You shouldn't buy me anything. Waking up to see you and discovering you've baked for me are the best gifts of all! Do you mind if I enjoy the bread first while it's still warm?"

He had a slice in one hand and a butter knife in the other, and Simone laughed.

"As if I could stop you... But please don't give anything to Tommy. He's fat enough."

They ate and joked, and of course, Carl threw a few bites at Tommy. Carl spoiled the dog rotten, to Simone's and their veterinarian's despair.

Thunder rumbled in the distance, and the sky turned dark. When she and Carl finished breakfast, Simone put the tray on the kitchen counter but returned carrying the gift he still hadn't opened. She handed it to Carl.

"Do you know, my dad always did the same thing—brought me a birthday gift in the morning."

"Really? My father used to do the same for me!"

They shared a smile at yet another coincidence, a small but meaningful similarity that deepened the warmth between them.

"It means a lot when people remember early," she said. "It

just feels more intentional, like they really care and couldn't wait to celebrate with you."

Carl nodded in agreement, a soft smile lingering.

"Exactly. It's like being seen, truly remembered." He paused, looking thoughtful.

The gentle moment between them was comfortable and familiar, reminding Simone of the little things that make connections feel sincere and lasting.

He tore the beautiful silver paper with blue stars without care. *Men..* Before opening the green box, with a golden crown on it, he looked up at her.

"I'll love you forever, woman!" He opened the lid, and his face lit up, showing his pleasure with the black Oysterflex bracelet and white gold casing.

Simone used to call Carl, *The Lord of Time*. He was always worried about being on time and hated to make people wait... He was worse than she was, and she considered herself a certified neurotic. He really enjoyed controlling time, so what better, more appropriate gift than a watch? Especially a *Rolex*.

On the back of the watch, she asked the jeweler to engrave the words: *I will love you forever. ~ S.*

Whenever she said or did something that truly touched him, he would say, "I will love you forever," to which she always responded with the words she'd had etched on the back of his new watch. The engraving was subtle yet deeply meaningful, encapsulating her reply in a tangible form that would serve as a reminder of their private, heartfelt exchanges.

*****

The last day of December had to hold the record for the rainiest day on Earth. Simone had hoped Carl would change his mind, and they would stay home, but no...

He was determined to mingle with the crowd of people huddled under umbrellas or wearing raincoats, fun hats, and tall, rubber boots as they stood in the pouring rain. Not to mention, the temperature had turned frigid. Was there anything these crazy people wouldn't put up with to see a stupid ball drop at midnight?

Simone and Carl arrived at the heart of the celebration in Times Square at 11:30 P.M., surrounded by a vibrant crowd of people armed with umbrellas. Despite the rain, a cheerful warmth spread through the crowd. Strangers smiled at one another, exchanging nods and glances that sparkled with joy and anticipation. Hand in hand, Simone and Carl joined thousands of others, swept up in the music, laughter, and the festive energy that electrified the streets.

Simone found herself pausing for a moment, reflecting on the scene around her. *How hopeful everyone becomes at this time of year,* she mused, noting the permanent smile that had settled on her face. New York, typically known for its bustling intensity, now felt like the City of Smiles, transformed by the contagious optimism of New Year's Eve.

As the countdown began on the towering screens of One Times Square, the entire crowd turned in anticipation toward the glowing ball. Simone, soaked from head to toe, felt a wave of relief wash over her—this marked the beginning of the end of her rain-soaked ordeal, and soon she'd be warm and dry at home.

Carl, standing beside her, lifted his index finger to the sky, joining the roar of tens of thousands counting down in unison. His gaze was fixed on the timer as each number flashed, lighting up the crowd's eager faces. When the clock struck two, he clapped and cheered, his voice blending with the chorus of excitement that echoed through the streets.

"Happy New Year!" everyone cried in unison as the ball completed its descent. The numbers *2019* lit up on the stage, casting a golden glow over the crowd as cheers filled the air. Strangers embraced, friends laughed, and couples shared kisses, welcoming the new year with joy and anticipation.

Carl hugged Simone, kissed her with enthusiasm, and seeing him so delighted brought happy tears to her eyes. Despite the rain and freezing temperature, Simone's heart was full. A "Happy New Year" meant starting it off by her lover's side.

CHAPTER THIRTY-THREE

2019, Let the season of all hopes begin!

Smiling, Simone walked her last patient of the day to the door of her office to say goodbye. When the man left, she went back inside to meditate. She'd found ten minutes of meditation helped tremendously when she needed to come back to her reality after another session spent listening to and analyzing other people's journeys. Simone sat on her favorite couch, took off her shoes, and tucked her legs up underneath herself in a kind of kneeling position on the seat. She smiled and then paused, surprised to find she was still smiling. The new year sure brought good vibes this time she'd had a silly grin on her face for much of the week.

All the patients she'd met with that week were also in great moods, full of hope for the new year.

That's insane. What difference does the date make?

As far as she was concerned, the first of the year was just a number—a day like any other day—and if her patients couldn't change on the inside, how would they change their lives?

She considered the feeling of change a new year brought about, a kind of collective hysteria as the whole world seemed to be of the same mindset. Until the fog lifted and people started seeing things more clearly. She grimaced and shook her head.

You're such a shitty Doctor sometimes.

She should be teaching people to manage their reality, not cheering on their delusions.

Then again, she had to admit, deep inside, a sense of excitement for the year ahead was blossoming. After all, her schedule was nearly full for the first weeks of January, the university had invited her to lead a promising new research program, and she was married to a remarkable man. Her daughter, too, was blossoming into an extraordinary young woman. Life seemed to be aligning in Simone's favor, each piece fitting perfectly into place. For the first time in a while, she had every reason to be genuinely hopeful.

Simone felt a pang of guilt; she hadn't been to MacDougall since before Christmas. The flowers had convinced her to keep her distance. Ed´s message was clear. She didn't plan to stop visiting forever—she needed to understand Peter's screwed-up mind. Above all, she felt sorry for Ed, but she couldn't face that misery so early in the year.

Her breathing exercises always helped her to stabilize her emotions, and she used those techniques now to bring herself back to her reality. After a while, she put her feet on the floor, directly inside her shoes, rose, grabbed her purse, and left her office.

"Patricia, I'm going home."

"Doctor Bennet, do you want me to set up a time for you to visit MacDougall this week?" Patricia asked, lifting her gaze from the computer.

"I'm still not sure. I'll think about it and let you know tomorrow."

"Okay, but please decide by tomorrow. I'm filling your schedule, and if you wait, you're not going to have any spare time to go anywhere."

"How did you manage to find so many new patients during the holidays?" Simone pinned Patricia with a questioning stare. No doubt, Simone's full schedule had something to do with her secretary's maneuvering.

Patricia smiled, confirming Simone's suspicions.

"An attorney I know threw a big Christmas party for a hundred of his *closest* friends and colleagues." Patricia rolled her eyes. "I was invited to attend, and you know how it is; those people are mostly depressed during the holidays. Bad or nonexistent relationships, bad end-of-year bonuses, and so on. The whole tribe is fucked up..." She put her finger against her temple. "After I spent an hour listening to nonstop complaining, I took the opportunity to tell some of them what a marvelous psychiatrist you are and about the incredible changes you've made in my life."

"Changes I've made...? Patricia, you're not my patient..." Gaze still fixed on her assistant, Simone sighed. What was Patricia up to now?

"I know that, and you know that, but they only care about the potential advantages. They don't deal in reality—that's why they're lawyers. Isn't that true?"

I hope my husband isn't like that.

"I don't have many acquaintances in the legal field." Simone's one example seemed grounded in the real world, but maybe Patricia had a point.

"Trust me, for them, it's all about beating someone else just to win something else for themselves." Patricia made a looping motion with her finger in the air.

"My schedule is full of greedy lawyers?" Simone didn't know if she should be happy or worried about that.

"Nope, they've already bragged to other people about how they're seeing a shrink who's a professor, an author, and a previous victim of a serial killer. You'll have a variety of new clients. Their rationale is simple." Patricia shrugged. "If my friend can pay someone like that, so can I." Patricia twirled her finger in the air. "Crazy but true!"

"And if they don't like my treatment style after their curiosity about how their friends are spending their money is gone?"

"They are going to brag about you to others... This is no longer about consistency. It's about a full schedule once more." Patricia smiled slyly and turned the computer screen toward Simone, a hint of mischief in her eyes, as she explained, "For those new patients, I've raised your fees and made getting an appointment with you a bit...exclusive." Her voice was soft, almost conspiratorial.

As far as Simone could see, her schedule for the week had just a small space empty on Friday morning.

For once, I'm going to stop questioning every little thing and just let it ride.

*****

A week later, Simone noticed a difference at the office. The good vibes still lingered in the air; however, some of her patients weren't quite as enthusiastic about the New Year's resolutions they'd made to change their lives, and had started slipping back into old habits. Next, they'd give up and then beat themselves up over their inability to stick to their plans.

And then comes January's blue mood.

Chivon came in for her first session of the year, and the first thing Simone noticed was the scandalously large diamond on her client's finger. Having a clinical eye, she never missed anything out of the ordinary when it came to her patients. She was dying to ask who the "lucky man" was, but even though she already had an idea, she wanted to wait for Chivon to share her big news in her own time.

A cloud of perfume filled the office, and although the scent was nice—and no doubt pricey—it was a little bit too strong, too overwhelming for Simone's taste. Chivon's makeup was perfect, and she'd changed her hair. The wild, Farrah Fawcett style had been replaced by a classy Chanel haircut, that made her look younger.

The change in hairstyle wasn't surprising. When people were up against big changes in their lives, often, changing their hair was part of the process. Some people couldn't embrace the real changes they needed but cutting or dying their hair proved they were trying to.

Chivon took off her navy blazer, placed it on the back of a chair, sat, and crossed her legs. In a classic navy pencil skirt and button-front white chemise, she looked impeccable.

So, not only has she changed her hair; she has changed the way she dresses. Less sexy and more professional.

After a minute of polite chitchat, Chivon paused, and then her expression turned serious.

"I'm engaged." She held out her hand and showed Simone the new ring.

"Congratulations! Who's the lucky guy?" Simone raised an eyebrow.

"Benji, of course. Billionaires are not floating in the air…" She waved her hand above her head.

The finger story popped into Simone's mind. Had Benjamin forgiven Chivon for what she'd done to him? He must have if they were engaged…Yet, the man hadn't come back after Christmas, leaving a lingering question hanging in her mind. "How did this come about?"

"After we broke up over me doing the finger thing…" Chivon raised her index finger and rotated it in a circle.

Simone didn't know about the *finger thing* from Chivon's

mouth, but from Benjamin's, so she remained quiet.

"Benji told me he is your patient, and he told you about the finger thing..."

Unperturbed, Simone didn't answer. She wouldn't betray a patient's confidence even if he had talked about coming to her for therapy, but she was proud of Benjamin for sharing that information with his fiancée.

Did he tell her he had her followed here, too?

Chivon looked at Simone, as if waiting for a reply, but when Simone kept mum, Chivon continued.

"After he came here, he showed up at my place, and we talked about our relationship and the sex-pectations we have. I told him I might be able to remain faithful if he was more open to exploring, and he promised me he'd try. We ended up in bed together, as we always do when we fight, but I admit I lured him there that time. I wanted to see if he was really committed to his promises, so I fingered him again."

Oh, no... Does that mean I need to prepare for another of Benjamin's emotional storms?

Simone cleared her throat.

"I see... And how did he react?"

"He was relaxed and open to trying his best to please me, so he enjoyed himself. He told me his boundaries, what felt good, and even asked for more, and now he wants to have my finger in his ass every time we fuck! I think I created a monster."

Chivon's smile did not belong to someone who was ashamed or annoyed about the outcome of their actions. Instead, her expression appeared triumphant and maybe even a little malicious.

"How did you feel about him surrendering?"

"I felt a sort of connection, a complicity with him." Her

smile changed a little, and she seemed a bit surprised by what she'd just said.

"That's a good thing in a marriage, but here's the question... Have you really decided to be faithful? To be in a relationship?" Simone was taking notes.

"I don´t know... Since I was able to teach him to like a finger in his ass, maybe I can get him into a threesome or something like that?"

"I´m not certain. He seems to be a more traditional kind of man, and marriage is not just about sex. It requires a commitment from both parties to work."

Oh my God, she is not my friend, and I just gave her my opinion. Simone was surprised with herself.

"I will take the risk!" Chivon lifted her chin.

"And you agreed to marry for the money and security?"

And now, Doctor Bennet, you're voicing your assumptions!

"No... Of course, not having to worry about money is a good thing." Chivon glanced away, and when she turned back, her expression had grown serious once again. "I'll tell you, but don't let him know." She had lowered her tone to a whisper. "I'm in love with the little guy. He's the only man who has ever been able to surprise me."

And I'm certain you are a daily surprise for him.

"It's good when you can be surprised, but do you know him well enough to marry him?"

"I don't, but if things turn sour, I just have to wait at least two years, and then I can get out a millionaire. Besides, I work in a law firm, and from what I've seen, you never know the person you marry until the time comes for a divorce. That's when their true colors shine through."

In the end and despite any excuses she might try to give, the woman's goals were indeed about money and security.

Simone realized that, to Chivon, a relationship was all about personal interests, sometimes money, other times love, and sometimes just to feel at home with someone.

What are the most important things to me in a relationship?

*****

Simone was having a quick lunch. She had just bitten into a tuna salad on whole wheat toast when Patricia knocked once on the office door then put her head inside the room.

Simone fought for patience.

I hate when she does that. Why doesn't she wait for me to answer?

"Doctor Bennet, sorry to interrupt but Elizabeth is here, and she seems to be unbalanced. She asked if you could see her now. According to her, it's not about therapy." Patricia frowned.

"Well…send her in…" Simone put her lunch aside, cleaned an imaginary crumb off her blouse, crossed her legs, and waited.

Beth, disheveled and panting, rushed into the room like a hurricane. Without bothering to say hello, she drew in a deep breath and then blurted, "Edward is not at MacDougall anymore!"

CHAPTER THIRTY-FOUR

He´s Not Where He's Supposed to Be

"What do you mean, he's not at MacDougall? Was he transferred?" Simone didn't pause to analyze the ache in her heart at the idea of Ed being moved somewhere far away, maybe to the other side of the country where she couldn't see him or speak to him as easily.

Beth shook her head but didn't say more. She stood in the doorway like a deer frozen in the headlights.

"Please come here and sit, Beth." Simone wouldn't get any more information until the other woman calmed down. Leaning back in her chair, she waved for Beth to join her.

Beth sank onto the small sofa against the wall, still holding her purse against her body, and took a couple of deep breaths.

"I have no idea what happened. I went there this morning… I wanted to visit Ed and talk to him a little bit, but when I arrived there"—she pointed over her shoulder—"and I was filling out all those stupid papers, a correctional officer came over to the front desk and said I was wasting my time because Edward isn't there."

"Did he explain what happened? Maybe Ed is sick, and they moved him to a hospital?"

Simone gave an exasperated huff. Any number of things could have happened—an illness, some kind of injury, or her original thought—that they'd transferred him to a different prison... Hell, he could even have escaped or been killed in a fight. But whatever had happened, they should have informed his family.

"They wouldn't give me any other information." Beth hiccupped and her eyes filled with tears. "Well, they did tell me that I shouldn't panic because he's not dead." She began to sob. "I begged them to tell me where he was, but they said they couldn't tell me more."

How dramatic she is for an ex-wife!

Beth let out a strangled cry. Her shoulders shook as tears streamed down her cheeks. Simone got up and went to sit beside her. Simone picked up a Kleenex box from the coffee table. and put it into Beth's hand, took her purse from her and set it aside, and waited for her to calm down.

"It'll be okay," Simone said. She patted Beth's shoulder. "I'll try to find out what happened. Do you know when Ed left MacDougall? Did they tell you that at least?"

"No, but it must have been during Christmas. The last time I was there to see him was the morning of the twenty-fourth. I would have gone for New Year's, too, but Noah wanted to go to New York to see the ball drop, and I wanted to be with him. He asked me to take him, and we have so few opportunities to bond, you know? Teenagers are so strange these days." She blew her nose loudly.

Class... The lack of it shows in many small details.

"I went on the twenty-second or the twenty-third—I don't remember exactly—but everything seemed okay." Simone paused as she recalled Ed's words. *I'm cooperating with the FBI to reduce my sentence.* Was he out of prison so he could help the federal authorities? If that was the case, they would never tell Beth...

"Simone? Are you okay?" Beth touched Simone's arm.

"Yes, sorry, I was just thinking about where he might be. I promise I'll try to find out what happened, and I'll let you know. Whatever is going on here, it's not your fault, Beth, so get that thought right out of your head. The trip to New York with your son was good for you both to bond." Simone patted Beth's shoulder again then stood. "Let me see what I can find out, and I'll let you know."

Simone walked to the door and opened it. Beth had stopped crying, and Simone needed some time alone to figure out what to do next. Beth took the hint and rose to leave. At the door, she paused and hugged Simone.

Standing stiffly in the other woman's embrace, Simone forced herself not to jerk away.

Why did some people need to be so touchy-feely?

Talk about uncomfortable…

"Thanks, Simone, please let me know as soon as you learn something."

"I will; take care." Simone eased her way out of the personal-space-invading hug.

"Patricia, Elizabeth is leaving. Will you see her to the door and then come to my office, please?"

Beth walked out, and Simone closed the door and went back to sit at her desk.

A knock sounded at her office door, and then Patricia stepped inside. "What can I do for you, Doctor?"

Simone gave her secretary a brief explanation of what Beth had discovered and then asked Patricia to see if she could find out anything about Edward's whereabouts from her connections within MacDougall.

Patricia nodded.

"I'll see what I can do. Will there be anything else?"

"No, not right now. I need some time alone to get my head together before my next patient. But thanks."

Once Patricia had gone back out to the reception area, Simone grabbed a notepad and jotted down a few names. If Patricia's contacts didn't know anything, Simone would make a few calls of her own. But for now, she would do some deep breathing and clear her mind of all the troubling thoughts. She had a patient in a few minutes, and she needed to be in control and not be so scattered and upset.

*****

At a little after five o'clock, Simone's last client left, and she immediately kicked off her heels and started to pace the room, back and forth on the plush, Oriental rug. She had always done her best thinking when she moved—not to mention, she needed a physical outlet for the anxiety that had been building up inside over the last hour. What the hell could have happened to Edward? She considered the possibilities, but there were so many, and probably some she hadn't even thought of.

"Control yourself. It doesn't matter where he is. It is not your problem!" she told herself.

Patricia knocked on the door, then opened it and peeked her head into the office.

"Come in, Patricia." Simone stopped pacing and waited.

"Doctor Bennet, I contacted everyone I could think of to check on the status of your friend at MacDougall, but the only thing I learned is that he's not there today, but he is registered there as an inmate. Unfortunately, nobody knows where he is."

"They couldn't even find out if he was transferred, freed, or if he's sick?"

Simone tried to relax. If she kept frowning so hard, she'd need a Botox treatment before this latest situation with

Edward was resolved.

"The only thing one of my friends could dig up is that Ed was in perfect health when he was taken from his cell."

Simone's breath whooshed out, and her shoulders relaxed a little.

"Thanks a lot, Patricia. I'm leaving now." Simone put on her shoes and went to her desk. She got her purse and left the office.

Patricia followed Simone out into the reception area.

"Can you set the alarm please?" she said, turning when she reached the door.

"Sure, no problem," Patricia said.

Simone barely heard the response, distracted as she considered her next move. The answer came to her as she hurried to her car and climbed in behind the wheel. She started the engine and backed out of the parking space without checking her mirrors. Thankfully, she knew exactly how much space she had to maneuver; her mind wasn't focused on her driving.

*****

Fifteen minutes later, Simone arrived at New Haven Police Department at 1 Union Avenue. She found an empty spot and parked her car and then hurried inside the small lobby. At the reception desk, she asked the officer stationed there if she could speak with Officer DiMario.

She paced while she waited, Only a few minutes later, a young officer buzzed open a door leading into the main area of the building and called her name.

"If you'll come with me, ma'am, I'll take you up to see Officer DiMario."

Simone and her escort walked down the corridor until they reached Carlo's gray door. The young man opened it for her, and she thanked him for his help. He gave a small nod and closed the door behind her.

"Simone! It's a pleasure to see you." He smiled, flashing his perfect white teeth. "It's always good to see you, but when you show up here, something bad has usually happened, so, I don't know if it's a pleasure to have you here or the beginning of another nightmare. Please take a seat."

Simone didn't answer right away. She settled into the armchair in front of his desk, thinking how most people weren't usually so straightforward. But as she turned his words over in her mind, she realized he was right—and she shrugged.

"Unfortunately, I think the second option might be the case."

Carlo shook his head.

"Unfortunately, I think the second option might be the case."

Carlo just shook his head.

"Tell me what's going on."

He sat with his hands clasped on his desk and looked at her.

"I don´t know where to start, but this past weekend I received some flowers..."

Carlo tilted his head and smiled.

"Don't tell me you want me to arrest someone for sending you flowers. I'd have to fill the jail with half the men in this city. Besides, we still haven´t identified your intruder. I need to solve that case first." He chuckled at his attempt at humor.

Well, I'm glad someone's in a good mood.

But Simone didn't find much of anything funny lately.

"The flowers I received are like poison to me; I´m extremely allergic to them, and only two people knew that information—my daughter and Edward." To avoid listening to anymore stupid jokes, she hurried to finish. "Today, I discovered Edward is no longer at MacDougall."

Carlo's eyebrows rose until they practically disappeared beneath his hairline, and she choked back a laugh at his extreme, cartoon-like expression.

"Are you sure?" he finally asked.

"Yes, as sure as I can be. His ex-wife went to visit him today, and they informed her he was no longer there. Nobody could tell her where he is, how he left, or why, so I thought maybe you could."

"Simone, I would love to help you, but I have no idea where Ed could be. I'll try my best to find out, but I can't promise anything."

Carlo turned to his computer and rapidly typed away on his keyboard. He stared at the screen, his eyes moving back and forth, and then he ran his finger over the monitor as if he were making certain he was following each line. Finally, he looked back at Simone and shrugged.

"Well, this is weird. Nothing in the system indicates he left MacDougall. According to these records, he's there! The database is updated in real time, and if anyone is released or moved to another facility, that information is put into the system. He's still at MacDougall."

CHAPTER THIRTY-FIVE

Connections

Simone left the police department in a bit of a daze. Carlo had seemed just as shocked as she was by the information he'd pulled up. He had sat behind his desk, glowering at his computer screen. He'd still been staring at his monitor when she thanked him and said goodbye. Maybe he thought if he reread the prison records a few more times, he could solve the puzzle.

As she climbed in behind the wheel of her car, she threw her purse on the passenger seat then reached into the large, zippered compartment and pulled out her phone. As if on autopilot, she started the car and pulled out.

Beep... Beep... Beep...

Simone frowned. What was that annoying alarm? She glanced at the dashboard. A lit image of a car seat and a seatbelt flashed in time with the sound. Simone grabbed the strap over her left shoulder and brought it around in front of her. The moment she clicked the buckle into place, the sound stopped.

"Well, that was crazy." Normally, she fastened her seatbelt without giving it a thought.

Just goes to prove how sidetracked and out of sorts I am.

"Hey, Siri. Call Patricia"

The metallic voice answered she couldn't make a phone call while driving.

"I'm not driving, I'm the passenger."

The phone beeped.

"Calling Patricia," the robotic voice replied.

A moment later the sound of a ringing phone came over Simone's cellphone speaker.

"Doctor Bennet's office, how may I help you?" Patricia answered in a clipped but professional tone.

"Patricia, it's me. I need a favor." Simone merged onto the highway and headed toward her house. "Please switch my schedule around and arrange a time for me to visit Edward and Peter Hay."

She asked to see both men, just in case she couldn't get any time with Edward. Peter seemed to know a lot of information about what went on inside the prison. Maybe he'd have some idea about what was going on with Ed...

"But Doctor, Doctor Reynolds isn't at Mac-Dougall..."

Simone rolled her eyes toward the sky and struggled for calm.

"I know what we've been told, Patricia, but I've received some additional information that leads me to believe he's still there. At the very least, I need to find out for myself."

After a moment of silence, Patricia responded.

"I'll see what I can do."

The line went dead, and Simone tossed her phone onto the passenger seat.

That woman makes me crazy sometimes...

Patricia called back before Simone reached home.

"Doctor Bennet, you can't get into the prison today—it's too late. I can get you in tomorrow, but only to visit Peter Hay. Doctor Reynolds is not available for visitors this week. They have a ten a.m. opening, but that means you'll have to cancel appointments with two patients. Could you see them after five? If so, I think I can arrange that."

"I can see them after five, sure."

"Very well... I'll set things up for ten tomorrow morning at MacDougall."

"Thanks a lot, Patricia, I don't know how you managed that so quickly, but I owe you."

"I'll have to suck someone's dick, but that won't be a problem. Have a good evening, Doctor." Once again, the line went dead.

I really hope she's kidding about sucking dick for information...

A flicker of doubt crossed Simone's mind. How had Patricia made this kind of connection inside a penitentiary, and how was she managing things so easily? Patricia had set up all Simone's visits except for the first one.

She frowned. Had Patricia ever said anything about who was helping her? The only thing Simone recalled was Patricia's original statement when Simone had asked for assistance in getting in to see Peter.

"I know someone who can help us with that." Patricia had sounded certain.

Who is this someone? What kind of influence does he or she have over the daily activities inside the facility? Is the same paralegal who helped us with the helicopter research?

"The next time I see Patricia, I need to find out."

*****

Before she entered the garage, Simone stopped her car in

the driveway and checked the cameras in the app on her phone. Since the day she'd thought there was a burglar inside her kitchen, she'd developed this habit. She didn't want any surprises, and she refused to be a victim again.

The surveillance system showed all clear. Nobody had been there since she left that morning. Carl and Tommy were back in the city. Simone opened the garage door, parked the car, and entered the house.

She had really enjoyed the holidays with her family and the New Year´s celebration with her husband but having the entire house to herself was pure bliss. Still, she had to admit —she missed Tommy.

I'm a lone wolf...

She loved to be by herself. Some might call her selfish, but she took pride in being a woman who knew how to live alone. So many people depended on someone else to complete them, but Simone didn't need anyone else around to be happy. She smiled. How many times had she given the same advice to one of her patients who craved sex, attention, and sometimes even love to be fulfilled?

No one can say I don't practice what I preach!

In her opinion, cultivating the ability to live alone without feeling abandoned or isolated was one of the hardest things a person could do. People tended to seek company all the time to avoid their own thoughts, to avoid examining deep feelings or really getting to know themselves. Simone didn´t have that kind of fear.

Of course, she loved her husband and would love to live with him forever, and she loved her daughter and missed her dearly, but the fact remained she could be perfectly content on her own.

The feeling was so pleasurable she left her things in her room, took off all her clothes, dressed in a warm robe, and in her bare feet, she went to the kitchen to prepare a cup of hot cocoa.

CHAPTER THIRTY-SIX

Art

Peter entered the infirmary followed by a guard who growled a good morning at Simone, led Peter to the chair next to her, and attached his handcuffs to the table. The guard turned and left, murmuring something else Simone couldn't understand.

She stared after him.

He reminds me of a bulldog.

When the door closed, she turned her attention to Peter. He had a relaxed expression—no mischievous smile, no grimace.

He looks almost normal…

"Good morning, Simone. I've missed you!"

Simone raised her brows and cocked her head.

Peter ignored her reaction and continued.

"Someone has good connections… Thank you for the Christmas gifts. I never thought it was possible to send gifts to this jail."

Simone felt glad to know they were delivered.

"I never thought they would be delivered." She smiled.

"They were and the butter cookies were amazing; they really made my day. I was so sad and alone, and when I opened that beautiful box, it was like a balm to my heart. Little things we take for granted in our regular lives are like gifts from God to someone in here." He waved his hand in the air, indicating the room around them.

Is he mocking me?

She looked into his eyes.

Holy shit! Are those tears?

The guy deserved an Oscar!

"You're welcome. I'm glad they gave you the gifts. I wasn't sure if that type of thing went against policy here, or if the guards would eat them themselves or just toss the whole box into the trash."

"Fortunately, they are not all bad, and even the bad ones tend to have softer hearts during the holidays, technically, bringing us gifts is forbidden; only books are allowed. But still, during that season, you can sense a quiet rebellion in the air." He gave a half smile.

"Peter, are you okay?" Simone asked. He seemed sad, and she leaned toward him a little, thought about putting a hand on his arm but then changed her mind.

Bad idea...

"As okay as someone locked in a cage can be." His smile grew a little bit wider. "What do you want to talk about today, Doctor? Your hubby, my alleged crimes, or did you come here just for the pleasure of my delightful company?"

"Have you seen Edward lately?" Simone got straight to the point.

"My dear friend Doctor Reynolds was at last evening's public session of lamentations."

"Here?" Simone pointed to the floor.

"No, they meet in a larger room because his support group seem to become more popular and adds more members every day. He is a total hit!" His voice turned high-pitched and feminine.

Simone barely resisted the urge to roll her eyes.

The nut is back.

"Do you attend, too?" she asked.

"No, I'm not crazy!" He grimaced. "I just saw a notice on the bulletin board. Why? Your eternal subject doesn't want to see you anymore?" He raised an eyebrow and scrutinized her. "I don"t blame him. You were like two turtle doves, and then suddenly, you fall in love with another guy, and before you really know who he is, you go and marry him!"

He snapped his fingers and continued.

"Honestly, I think you're better off with Carl. The idea of you and the Doctor fornicating...well, it simply bores me." He faked a yawn. "I can imagine him asking: Can I penetrate you now my dear?" He laugh at his own joke.

"So funny...I didn't try to visit Ed; his ex-wife did, but they told her he wasn't at MacDougall anymore."

Peter narrowed his eyes and stared at Simone as if he were trying to extract some hidden information beyond her words.

"I don't have any information. and I know everything about this place. He's here." He pointed to the ground. "Again... I can't blame the guy for avoiding his ex-wife. If she's an ex, she should stay in the past...just like you. But that's just my advice; take it or leave it."

"Well, but I'm here to visit you." Simone smiled.

"You are not, and we both know it. You lost track or control of your former lover, and you were trying to extract information from me. But don't worry, I will forgive you." He pointed at her and did his imitation of a mob boss from *The Godfather* movies. "But only because I'm in need of intelligent company today. They're all morons in this place."

A compliment? I better watch out. He wants something...

"So, what do you want to talk about today?" She slipped into her psychiatrist persona.

"I will let you lead, Doctor."

There was no doubt Peter was a smart guy. Very quick...

"Well, where did you go when you disappeared after you kidnapped me?" Simone shot the question.

"I didn't exactly kidnap you, Doctor. Let's say I retained you for my pleasure." He nodded.

His body language indicated he agreed with her assessment and his words were a lie.

He's distracted today.

He usually had better self-control.

"That's not what happened, and we both know it," she said. "Where did you go?"

"To China, to tend to my business. I had to visit my merchandise suppliers and decide what to send back here to our beautiful country. You know... China has many degrees of quality; I couldn't risk importing a disease." He shook his head.

"You disappeared instantly, Peter. Don't give me this bullshit about traveling on business."

Peter started to laugh.

"Oh, my God, the perfectly composed Doctor is losing her temper?"

Yes, I am, and I must learn to control myself around him.

She took a deep breath and relaxed her shoulders.

"We both know you're not telling the truth."

"The worst thing is, I really am. I bought the ticket a month earlier. My lawyer already added the evidence to my case file. That day, after we had our last...conversation...I was already late for the airport. I left for China, and that's the truth."

He was smiling again.

He smiles like that when he wants to pretend he's a human being.

"But you left me in that damn place, feverish, hurt, weak… I could have died there. Was that your plan? You just left me there, hoping I'd die?"

Images of being tied up and the torture he'd inflicted on her ran through Simone's mind like a horror movie, and she shivered.

"You are ungrateful. Didn't you get help from your beloved Edward? Who do you think called him?"

"He and the police discovered where I was. He was searching for me…" Her voice sounded strangled; her throat had grown so tight.

"Are you sure about that? Because it would take years to discover my special place… I called him and let him know. He was my assistant. I wouldn't kill you because when someone is loyal to me, I take care of them and the people they care about."

He really believes he is the Godfather.

"Do you consider Edward a kind of unpaid employee? Is that what you're saying here? That he was your servant?"

"Not my servant. More like an operator. An asset." The smile was there once more.

"Operator of what? Your killing business?"

"Dear Doctor, you are so naïve… You really don't know who you were in bed with, do you?"

Simone didn't answer, her mind spinning, trying to decode Peter's words.

Every time I come here, he tries to control my mind and turn me against someone I love.

Simone focused on quieting her thoughts. Since he'd brought it up, she'd explore the subject. She schooled her features to keep him from reading her thoughts.

"I was surprised to find out Edward had helped you, but I thought his role in your crime was just that of a sperm donor, isn't that correct?" She looked directly into Peter's eyes, unwavering.

"Doc, I talk about *my* life; I'm not going to disclose other people's secrets, you know? If he didn't trust you enough to talk to you about his business during those pillow talks lovers have, who am I to say anything?" Peter pointed at himself and smiled again.

"You talk about everybody's life, Peter!" She raised her voice, impatient with his stupid game.

"I'm not a gossip girl, Doctor! You're hurting my feelings." He grimaced, and his voice turned feminine and filled with indignation.

"Do you have any left?"

"Any what?"

"Feelings, of course." Psychopaths could have feelings, but nobody knew exactly what kind of feelings and for whom or what.

"I do. I blame you for my conviction, so, sometimes, I hate you. That's a feeling." He moved his head as if trying to decide if it was a feeling or not.

"I was not responsible for your sentence. You were. You killed those girls," Simone said.

Peter ignored her and continued following his own train of thought. "I have feelings for my cat, but now he's living with my sister..."

"How do you know that? Does she visit you?"

"I have my sources."

Of course, he always does.

"I love and miss your husband, but I also hurt because of his behavior. We were close friends, intimate even, and now, nothing. He is a lawyer; he could visit me here, the ungrateful bastard. I introduced him to Lara. I gave him my legit business to tend to. I was his friend and listened to all his complaints and now… Nothing. It's like I died." He lowered his head, then raised it to look at her. "I even brought you two together."

Legit business…

Simone zeroed in on those words. Had he used that phrase on purpose to provoke a reaction? She made a mental note, just in case she needed to follow up at some point.

When Simone looked back at Peter's face, he had tears in his eyes again.

He's trying to play me.

"Don't you think you deserve to be here?" she asked, waving a hand to indicate the prison.

"With you or in this place? I don't deserve either one. You, I can't get rid of because you decided to visit me and use me as your lab rat, and being put in here was totally unfair, but this world doesn't understand art and beauty."

"What do you call art? Torture? Do you think killing is beautiful?" Simone ignored the remarks about her. After all, minutes ago he'd sounded happy to see her, so his words now were pure bullshit and contradictions.

"Ridding the world of ugly people…that's all I did…" He blinked in a feminine way, fluttering his eyelashes. "Those women were all ugly; they didn't have a place in this world, you know? If more people thought like me, only masterpieces would remain." His sinister smile seemed fixed on his lips.

Simone leaned toward him a little, searching his eyes,

which were like twin green ice cubes.

He's serious...

"So...you know...you survived because you are dear to your former *lover.*" He prolonged the word lover. "Not because you fit into my plan of a world filled with perfect artistic specimens." A look of disdain crossed his face, his lips twisting into a sneer.

"Did you intend to get rid of everyone you considered ugly? Don't you know beauty is in the eye of the beholder? Who are you to judge?" Simone didn't care if he found her attractive, but if that was the plan he'd come up with, how horrendous.

"I know beauty better than most, but that was not the main goal..."

"What was the main reason then?" Simone raised an eyebrow.

"You are so smart, Doc, so full of shitty, useless knowledge, aren't you? Solve this puzzle, or I will devour you!" Peter dipped his head toward Simone's face, like a striking snake, and snapped at her, teeth bared, trying to bite.

Simone jerked back in her chair, and he missed by a few inches.

"Ever since I watched *Silence of the Lambs* I wanted to do that to someone. It's not personal, but I don't receive many visitors.

*****

Simone rose and left the infirmary without looking back at Peter. He still sat chained to the table, but his loud laughter seemed to bounce off the surrounding walls to echo around her.

What is he up to now? Perfecting his impression of Hannibal Lecter from Silence of The Lambs?

She didn't care; right now, she needed to put some distance

between them.

Legs shaking and heart racing from such a close encounter, she left the facility. Only after she'd driven several miles away from the penitentiary did she manage to calm down.

So many questions bounced around inside her mind like popcorn kernels. Legal business...as opposed to...? Did he operate some kind of criminal enterprise? What had really motivated him to kill? And the biggest question, one Simone had almost forgotten—her main reason for visiting MacDougall.

Where in the hell is Edward?

CHAPTER THIRTY-SEVEN

Dirty Thoughts and Acts

Simone had a new patient that afternoon. Walter was the son of a former patient and twenty-nine years old, but he looked like a teenager. He was tall—probably six-foot-three—and lanky, all skin and bones.

He entered her office looking like he wanted to hide somewhere, his shoulders hunched as if his stature bothered him, It seemed like he wished he could shrink.

"Walter, it's a pleasure. Please have a seat." Simone smiled and pointed at the couch across from her chair.

The young man sat, legs tightly closed, rubbing his hands and avoiding her gaze.

"A pleasure, Doctor Bennet." His voice cracked.

Simone looked at his hands; they were peeling, red, and raw in some spots.

"What brings you here?" she asked. *Besides OCD.* She couldn't tell him that right out of the gate, but his hands showed definite signs. No allergic condition—only the palms were peeling. Most likely, he was washing them too much, which usually indicated disgust, guilt, or shame over some sexual behavior. Many young men his age grappled with similar emotions as they navigated their developing habits and boundaries, often coping through frequent masturbation. Either that, or an intense fear of germs and contamination.

"My dermatologist told me to see a psychiatrist for the problems with my hands... He says it is not a dermatological condition."

Bingo.

Simone nodded.

"Okay, that's good. Can you tell me more? Who referred my services?"

Walter lowered his eyes and stared at his hands. He lifted them, turning them to show her his palms.

"My father referred me to you."

Simone would not admit to the existence of a specific former patient, but she smiled.

"Please thank your father for the reference." She took her notepad, the patient's file folder, and a pen from the table beside her chair. "I need to ask some questions to determine where we're going to start with your therapy. Is that okay with you, Walter?"

"Yes, that's fine." Despite his words, he sounded as if he'd rather have a tooth pulled.

Simone gave him an encouraging smile.

"Okay, we'll start with some basics. What's your profession? It says here in your file that you're an engineer. What kind of engineer?"

"I'm a programmer. I design apps and games for phones."

He gestured with his hands as if he was holding a phone and pressing buttons.

I'll bet he spends all day alone, hiding in his room playing video games or inventing them.

"Do you work for a company or—?"

"No, I design at home, and I sell to several different companies." He smiled for the first time. "I love my job."

"That's the secret to having a successful career—loving what you do." Simone smiled back.

"I can say I'm successful, I'm on my way straight to the top! I've had my own apartment for a year now. I haven't depended on my parents since I left home for college, and I think I chose the right field for my degree." He flashed another smile, straightened his shoulders, and thrust out his chest.

He's proud of his achievements and isn't shy about sharing them, and that's as it should be.

At just twenty-five, he'd accomplished things it took most people years to achieve.

"What do you think is causing the problems with your hands? It seems you're washing them a lot... True?"

Walter nodded and shrugged, but he didn't offer anything more.

"Are you afraid of germs and contamination of some kind?" Simone pushed him to talk as she took a few notes.

"No... I-I... It's not like that." Head down, he looked as if he were studying his shoes.

"Do you know exactly *when* you wash your hands?"

"No." He turned his head, avoiding her eyes. "Well, maybe..."

"Let's do a little brainstorm session. Think back to the last time you washed your hands and then try to recall what you were doing right before that. Usually, the handwashing is related to something you did right before."

"I'm addicted to fucking whores!"

The outburst didn't shock Simone. Not a bit.

Always a sexual problem… Why are people so dramatic about something as natural as sex?

"Why those types of women? Don't you feel as if you're able to have a normal girlfriend? I assume you like girls?"

"I do like girls—only girls. I have a beautiful girlfriend, but I can't do the same things with her that I do to the whores."

"What do you mean? What you *do* to those women? And there's more than one, right?" Simone raised a questioning eyebrow.

"Yes, always more than one… I don't want to have a relationship with any of them. It's just sex…" He grimaced as if he found something sordid about the whole thing.

"What do you do with those women? Can you tell me?"

"Lots of things… Like…" He seemed to have a difficult time talking about what he'd done. His hands moved a lot, and he couldn't meet Simone's eyes.

"To help me help you, just describe what you did with the last one. Pretend like you're telling a story. Nothing will be judged."

"Well, I got this beautiful Russian girl from a catalog, and she came to my place. First, I ripped off her clothes, and then I ran my hands all over her body. Then I slapped her face, and she landed on my couch. She was small, and I held her hands over her head and…" He lowered his head again.

He's ashamed.

Simone stayed quiet and waited for him to gather his courage and go on.

He swallowed hard, and keeping his eyes lowered, he said,

"I penetrated her ass, and she started to cry, and that excited me so much. I pumped more and more 'til I was about to come, and then I pulled out of her ass, got rid of my raincoat, and spread my seed all over her body… When

I finally looked at her, she was all dirty and had blood on her legs. I had some on mine, too. She was sobbing, and her makeup was all smudged. I threw her clothes at her—I'd already paid her...they all ask for money in advance—and I told her to leave. She looked at me with deep, ocean-blue eyes that were filled with pain, and I felt dirty."

"Then you washed your hands?"

"Yes. After she left, I washed them many times. And after telling you this story, all I want to do is find a sink and wash my hands again." He started to rub his hands as if he was trying to scrape off his skin.

"Walter...stop that... Just relax your hands on your knees and breathe in deeply."

He did as she advised, but his eyes remained frantic.

"Now, release the air slowly...good...and take another deep breath in again." Simone did the exercise with him until he seemed to regain his control. After all, she couldn't talk to him while he was in the middle of a panic attack.

After several minutes of focused breathing, his expression softened a little, and his body seemed less rigid.

"How do you feel?" she asked.

"I'm okay...but that happens all the time. Right after I do these things...and then it'll happen again if I think about what I did."

"Can we talk about your relationship with prostitutes a little bit more?" Simone leaned toward him, showing she was open to listening.

"I think so..." He shrugged.

"How often do you have sex with prostitutes?"

"Three to four times a week..."

"Do you have sex with your girlfriend?"

"I do when we're together. She's still in college, so she

doesn't have much time during the week...but what I do with her is nothing like what I do to the others… I love my girlfriend; I wouldn't hurt her."

"So, I assume you always hurt those other girls?"

He inclined his head in kind of a half-nod.

"I do. I like to make them submit, and I feel immense pleasure in humiliating them. I always slap them, and I always go directly to the ass…" He punched the palm of one hand with his other fist, and his features turned hard as he clenched his teeth.

Lots of repressed anger…

His gestures indicated too much bottled-up negative emotions.

"How long have you been doing that? And by that, I mean, how long have you been using sex as a weapon to punish women?"

"Since I got my own money and apartment. Well…about that long."

"I must ask…how is your relationship with your mother?"

"Can't blame her...she died when I was two. Barely remember her."

"Yes, of course, I remember now." Her client—Walter's father—had said he'd lost his first wife and still mourned her, even though he'd remarried two or three times since.

"How was your relationship with your two stepmothers?"

"It's been a long time since my father last saw you… He's on his fourth wife…"

CHAPTER THIRTY-EIGHT

In Open Spaces

By the end of the day, Simone's back hurt, and her ass was sore from sitting for so many hours. For the first time in a long while, she'd worked a full schedule, and despite being tired and sore, she smiled. There was no elevator to help her rise to the level of a successful psychiatrist. She'd have to take the stairs—one step at a time—and work hard. Eventually, her efforts would pay off.

Simone stood up, grabbed her purse, and left her office. At the front door, she stopped and glanced over her shoulder. Patricia moved from one window to the next, double-checking that each lock was engaged. The soft clicks of the latches sounded like the finishing touches on a long day, sealing away the work until tomorrow.

"Have a good evening, Patricia. Please make sure you set the alarms. I'm leaving." Simone gave the woman a tired smile.

"Have a good evening, Doctor Bennet. I will. Get some rest; tomorrow, the party continues." Patricia smirked. "Your schedule is full," she added, already turning back to her end-of-day tasks.

Simone gave a quick nod and headed out. The weight of

such a busy day still lingered. She paused in the cool night air and lifted her face into the breeze. The light wind cooled her skin and helped revive her tired mind. The cobwebs cleared, at least for the moment, and she made her way down the steps and to her car.

Once she settled into the driver's seat, she started the engine, checked her mirrors, and then backed out, using the vehicle's rear-facing camera. As she left the parking lot, she hit the *seek* button on the radio. Her mood had lightened considerably. Nothing like getting her professional life back on track to make a woman feel less exhausted and more capable. She stopped scrolling on a local station and turned up the volume. The song "Havana," by Camila Cabello, blared from the speakers. She liked the tune but didn't know the words or have the voice to sing it properly, so she hummed along instead.

Suddenly, something pressed lightly on her shoulder, and an electric current of cold fear raced along her skin. Someone was in the seat behind her!

"It's all right. It's just me."

Edward! At the sound of his familiar albeit serious voice, she blew out her breath in a woosh. Blood rushed to her head, and her ears rang from the intense pounding of her heart. Simone drew in another long, deep breath then let it out—slowly this time—trying to regain control, but her legs shook so badly she had to pull onto the shoulder of the road and put the car into park.

"Do you want to kill me?" she managed to say when she recovered her voice. She turned to him. "You scared me to death!"

Ed scowled. "Act normal and keep driving.. I couldn't approach you any other way. There's a park nearby, and it used to be pretty deserted this time of day. Let's go there."

"No way. I'm staying right here, and you're going to tell me what you're doing inside my car!" Her voice rose.

"Move the car, Simone. You don´t want a police officer stopping and asking why you're parked on the side of a busy street. Please drive. I promise I'm going to explain everything. It's not as if I'm kidnapping you."

Simone put the car in gear and eased back onto the road. Her legs were still shaking. She glanced up at Edward's reflection in the rearview mirror.

"You better explain! I went to MacDougall to look for you after Beth came to my office and told me you weren't there anymore. I talked to Carlo, and he said you *were* there. I went to see that crazy nut just to try to get some information, and he said you were there too—but here you are, hiding in my car!"

"It was easy to unlock your car. Prison teaches a lot of useful things... You should be more careful after Mona—turn on the alarm, for example, not just lock the vehicle."

Simone scowled at his reflection in the mirror. Simone shivered as she recalled the horrific sight of her secretary's corpse inside her car.

"That was a long time ago," she said. "I thought I was safe now..."

"Why? Because Peter and I are locked away? *Are* you safe? Did you enjoy the flowers?"

Simone jerked her head around to look at him again.

"I Knew it was you! Are you nuts? Why?"

"Please watch the road," he said.

She turned her head, and he went on.

"I knew you'd recognize what type they were right away, and you wouldn't get close enough to them to get sick. I just wanted to show you how easily someone could reach you and convince you to listen to me and stop digging, but apparently, you don't learn. Beth tells you I've gone missing, and what do you do? Start asking the whole world about my whereabouts!" He raised his voice.

"Of course, I did. I worry about you! Do you know how many people get killed in prison every year?" Simone asked, her voice shaking.

"If they get killed, the corrections department notifies the family and releases the body. Simone, next time, just think before you act, okay?"

She pulled into the small, paved lot adjacent to the park Edward had mentioned. She parked and looked around. Hers was the only car there, and the place was silent, almost too quiet, with only the faint rustling of leaves breaking the stillness.

She chose a bench under a tall oak tree. Long branches cast shadows in the fading light. Simone and Ed sat down as the last warm hues of daylight slipped away.

Edward turned to look at her, his expression softened by the dim light filtering through the trees.

"Simmie, I told you I was cutting a deal with the FBI, so sometimes, I'll be in MacDougall, and sometimes, I won't. But if you start making a fuss and letting everyone know I'm not where I'm supposed to be, you're going to blow my opportunity to get out early."

"You're my friend. I was sick with worry," Simone said.

She put her hand on Edward's, but he shook his head and pulled away.

"Friend? I'm not your friend, Simone, and I never will be. I've been in love with you since the day we met. Do you think that has changed?" That it ever will?"

He looked at her, his blue eyes intense with emotion, and Simone dropped her gaze. She wasn't up to dealing with his feelings.

"You must understand; I was worried," she said in a whisper.

"I know, and that's why I asked permission to be here today. So, please"—he turned to her and put his hands on her shoulders—"This is dangerous. We're not only talking about a psycho with a few connections. The MOB might be involved. The FBI is trying to piece everything together. But those people…they're going to smash you like a bug if they even suspect you're connected to anything under investigation. So, please, stay out of all this, for you…for your daughter, for me, and even for your husband…"

He twisted his lips into a look of distaste as if it pained him to include Carl on that list.

Simone nodded her agreement.

He's right; I can't put my family at risk again.

"I promise," she said softly, her gaze steady. "But…do you think Peter is involved in something?" She hesitated then clarified. "In some crime outside the jail?"

"I believe he's probably involved in a lot of things—none of them good. The fact that he's a psycho is just the tip of the iceberg."

"You should know I went to see him again—"

"I was already aware of that." Edward frowned.

"Peter was talking about feelings, and he said my husband is ungrateful. Apparently, Peter is upset because he introduced Carl to Lara and to me, and let him do the legal work for some so-called legitimate business Peter owns…" She shrugged. "Or something like that. I never know if he's trying to mislead me by telling half-truths or if he's spewing more of his lies to cause trouble, so I didn't take the bait."

"I was working on uncovering his connections to less-savory enterprises before everything fell apart and came crashing down around me the way it did… I'm certain he's a part of at least one or two criminal ventures…"

"Let me help! I can try to talk to him. Maybe, I can lead him where I want him to go."

"Absolutely not. Stay out of this. I'll handle everything with the help of professionals, and please don't tell your husband about anything we talked about today, okay?"

Lie to Carl, again?

Simone looked at him, her eyes wide. Edward smiled.

"I always wondered how you manage to maintain a poker face when you're working with a patient, and yet, you can't manage to mask your thoughts or emotions and maintain a tranquil expression when you're dealing with someone you're close to or in a relationship with. The words are written on your face. 'I´m not going to lie to my hubby'." He spoke mockingly then shrugged. "Okay, then don't think about it as lying. Instead, tell yourself you're leaving a few things out—like an omission for the sake of his safety. And yours!"

He tapped her lightly on her chest with his finger then rose. Leaning down, he gave her a peck on the cheek before turning and walking away.

"Hey!" she called after him, her voice laced with concern. "Where are you going? How are you planning to get out of here?" She gestured to the empty lot. They had arrived together in her car—how was he planning to leave the park? Walk?

"Stop asking questions. Be safe. And please call Beth and tell her I'm okay, and she can visit me on Friday," he said without turning.

Simone sat on the bench for some time, her mind racing as she reviewed Ed's words. At least, he was alive. As the cold began to seep through her jacket and into her bones, she decided to head home. On her way, she would call Beth and reassure her.

Simone glanced at the clock on the dash. Seven p.m. She hesitated to disturb Patricia so late, but Simone had an idea, and Patricia was the only person who could help. All Simone needed was a phone number, and then maybe she could uncover some details that might indirectly aid Edward…

*****

Even with all her connections, Patricia couldn't obtain Deena Hay's phone number right away. But on Thursday at noon, the secretary came to Simone's office with news.

"Talk about a woman who seems to be hiding from the world!"

Patricia had the unfortunate habit of diving into topics without context, as if she believed the other person could read her mind and understood exactly what she was saying.

Simone shook her head.

Talk about attention deficit issues!

"Patricia, please start from the beginning. Who is this woman?"

Simone removed her reading glasses, set aside the book she'd been engrossed in, and looked directly at Patricia.

"Deena Hay of course… She's no longer a prosecutor. She has no LinkedIn, no social media presence whatsoever. It's like she vanished! Unfortunately, up until now, I haven't been able to find her phone number or address. However, one of my friends in the legal field knows someone acquainted with her. Have patience, Doctor. We'll find out where she is." Patricia was wringing her hands, her fingers twisting together.

"Don't worry, Patricia. It's not urgent. Stop putting so much pressure on yourself. You'll come through in the end. I have complete faith in you."

Simone smiled at the secretary, but a wrinkle appeared between Patricia's eyebrows, a sign she was deep in thought, trying to piece together the puzzle.

"I'll locate her." Patricia gave a firm nod. She started to leave the room then turned back to Simone. "You have another patient in ten minutes. She was referred by one of the lawyers I mentioned. He never made an appointment himself, but as I told you before, they can be quite pretentious. The woman looks like she's straight out of Transylvania or the cast of the Addams Family. Very Morticia-like."

Patricia and her bad habit of nicknaming patients. I wonder if I ever told her that… or if she did the same to me…

*****

Amber Nelson entered Simone's office a little over ten minutes later. Struggling to keep a straight face, Simone coughed to cover a sharp laugh. The woman had long black hair, deep black eyes, and the fair complexion of someone who had never seen sunlight. A simple black pencil dress slimmed over her lithe body, and she wore tasteful jewelry and a pair of Louboutin heels. Morticia, indeed, albeit a bit younger.

"Good morning, Miss Nelson, please take a seat wherever you like." Simone pointed to the sofa and armchairs in front of her.

"Thank you, Doctor Bennet. Call me Amber, please."

She settled into an armchair and crossed her legs in an elegant manner.

The epitome of a lady… Ms. Nelson radiated an air of refinement. *Undoubtedly, old money*.

Before the meeting, Simone had reviewed the woman's file, as was her practice with all her patients. At age thirty-four, Amber served as a financial director for a prominent liquor company and was an alumnus of the Stanford School of Business.

"What brings you to my office, Amber?" Simone asked, her gaze fixed on the woman.

Amber looked intently at Simone for a few seconds before responding.

Is she weighing whether she can trust me or simply gathering her thoughts?

"My boss caught me in a...compromising situation." Amber began. "She said I needed to see a psychiatrist if I wanted to keep my job. Your name was mentioned." She gestured toward Simone. "After I heard about you, I did some research. You're a renowned professor, and I trust individuals with a solid academic foundation."

Amber sat with her hands clasped together. She held Simone's gaze with an intense expression.

"Can you elaborate on this compromising situation you found yourself in?" Simone asked, poised with her notepad open and pen in hand, ready to jot down the details.

"I have this...compulsion to put myself in risky situations," Amber said, her gaze dropping to her hands. She began rubbing her knuckles.

"I can't make any suggestions without specifics," Simone responded gently. "Given my expertise, I can assume it's related to a certain sexual behavior. But I need you to describe it in detail. What were you doing when you were caught? The more precise you are, the better I can help you."

"It's really embarrassing. I'm a very private person, and I avoid drawing attention to myself whenever possible. But in certain moments of intimacy, the thrill of a public setting can be...intoxicating."

Private, my ass!

Simone thought but kept silent and allowed the woman to

continue.

"And that's precisely the trap I fell into recently. We'd been collaborating with representatives of another company, and one of the men had been noticeably attentive toward me throughout our meetings that week. At the end of yet another long workday, he approached me. He waited until everyone else had gone and then leaned in close and asked if he could accompany me to my office. His breath on my neck gave me chills..."

Amber examined her hands, as if they suddenly held the answer to the meaning of life.

"I thought he wanted to discuss something about the meeting. When I closed the door to my office, he took the remote for the blinds from my worktable and closed them. I watched him, my mind blank. I guess I was a little slow at discerning his intentions. He approached me, pushed me against my desk, and kissed me. His hard shaft pressed against my belly, and in that moment, I had to have him. The chemistry between us was intense, and I grew wet just thinking about fucking him. However, we couldn't do anything in my office. There were too many people around. I told him to meet me in the stairwell, and he agreed. I freshened up in my office bathroom, and fifteen minutes later, I met him on the staircase."

"And?" Simone prompted the woman to go on, even though Amber had yet to lift her head.

"When I joined him, we didn't waste any time. We helped each other disrobe, and in seconds I was totally naked. I put my legs around his waist, and he supported me with my back against the wall. By that point, I was blind with lust, and I begged him to give it to me hard and deep. I was moaning, and we were fucking like two teenagers out behind the high school. I came in seconds, but when I opened my eyes, one of the interns was standing there staring at us. She'd just entered the stairwell, and she looked like she might faint. Her mouth hung open, her eyes were wide, and her skin had turned white. No doubt, we'd shocked her. I knew I would be in deep shit once the girl started talking, but the orgasm made up for the fact I'd gotten caught... At least, in that moment."

Amber raised her gaze to look at Simone—*finally*! Blotchy red spots stood out on her otherwise uber-pale skin, and a fine coating of sweat covered the flesh above her upper lip. Patients often reacted physically when they recounted details of the events that had caused them to seek counseling. Almost as if they relived the experience and received a thrill from the retelling. Amber, apparently, was one of those patients.

"Would you categorize this as a one-off, impulsive act—a fatal attraction, so to speak—or is this a pattern? You told me you like risky situations; does that include having sex in public places?" Simone asked gently, observing Amber's body language closely.

The girl's shoulders were hunched, nearly touching each other, as if she were trying to make herself smaller.

"Unfortunately, it's all about sex in public places and it has become a pattern." Amber sighed. "I'm addicted to the thrill of taking a risk. Even though I always hope to remain unseen, deep inside there's a part of me that craves to be seen having an orgasm with a huge dick inside my body! But this last time, I genuinely believed we were safe. I wouldn't risk my job; I worked too hard for that position." Her voice trailed off as a look of regret washed over her face. She sighed then drew a deep breath. "And there have been other occasions, not always with the same outcomes but with the same urges driving me."

"Can you describe the other occasions?" Simone asked.

"Yes—making love to someone while he's driving, in the

front seat of a car, on a park bench in broad daylight, even in a supermarket parking lot… That time, I had just taken him into my mouth when a lady walked by carrying her toddler on her hip, I just kept going as the horrified mom tried to cover her baby's eyes."

Her dark stare sparkled with a hint of mischief.

"The most mundane places become charged with an illicit thrill when seen through the lens of possible discovery. Each instance brought an adrenaline rush, a thrill at the thought of being seen, and fear over the possibility of getting caught. What I feel… Well, it's indescribable."

Simone kept her expression neutral, letting her patient continue without judgment.

"I see," she replied calmly. "It's clear that these public encounters provide you with a powerful adrenaline rush, almost acting as a counterbalance to your otherwise extremely private nature. The act you described in the supermarket parking lot, especially, seems to suggest an escalation in risk and a disregard for the comfort of those around you."

Amber looked away, clearly embarrassed. "I know it's not right, and I don't want to be the kind of person who makes others distressed or uneasy. It's just… The thrill is overpowering at times, and I'm unable to control my instincts."

Simone nodded as she added a couple of notes to the patient file, and then she lifted her head.

"Are you really as composed as you appear, or is it just a façade? How do you perceive yourself? You seem totally professional…"

Hey, Simone, stop adding your opinion to the mix!

Simone paused and gathered her thoughts, waiting for the other woman to respond.

Amber gazed at Simone for a moment before replying.

"Yes, usually, I'm quite composed, and I always try to behave professionally. That's how I was educated, but these situations are like out-of-body experiences. In those moments, I'm not the reserved and polished businesswoman everyone knows. I'm someone else entirely."

"Do you like that version of yourself? The one who takes risks?"

"Since professional me hasn't ever had an orgasm, let's say I've come to appreciate my darker nature. I can only climax when I know there's a chance I'll be seen or watched or caught."

"So, you never find release in normal sexual intercourse, is what you are telling me?" Simone lifted an eyebrow.

"Exactly. When I'm with a guy in a so-called normal setting, say a bedroom, having a climax is like a distant dream, no matter the duration or intensity of our encounter. Yet, shift that scene to a daring public locale, and ecstasy is mine in moments."

"Can you recall when this…inclination began?"

Amber remained silent for a moment, gazing at the ceiling as if she might find the answer written up there. She shook her head. "It's hard to pinpoint exactly when, but I suppose it was a gradual progression from simpler acts to these more daring ones. An old boyfriend, who was just one in a string of many brief and unsuccessful relationships, noticed I couldn't climax."

Amanda fell silent and lowered her head. Was she ashamed of not being able to have an orgasm?

"Go on…" Simone prompted her.

"He suggested experimenting…trying different alternatives for sex. Back then, my desperation for an orgasm was so intense, I was open to anything."

"So, did he suggest the two of you try having sex in public spaces?"

"Not exactly—at least, not at first. We initially hired a male escort, but that wasn't the answer. We then ventured into one of those exclusive, private swingers' clubs. The thought of running into someone I knew unnerved me, but my boyfriend reassured me and helped me to unwind. He reminded me that if we stumbled upon a colleague, we'd share the same secret, erasing any cause for concern."

"And was a swing club the answer for a while?"

"Yes and no... I have vivid memories of that first visit. Initially, it was strange. I was uneasy, a bit unsettled by the sight of people openly pursuing and swapping partners amidst all the moans and cries of pleasure. Once I surrendered to the intoxicating atmosphere, the experience turned into something indescribable."

Amber's words brought back memories of an experience Simone had.

I know exactly what she means...

"We didn't swap partners or invite anyone else to join us that night, but the potent sexual energy of those around us was inescapable. I felt as if I was electrically charged, alive with an insatiable desire. We made love in front of at least ten other guests. Having all those people watching me...well, I had an orgasm for the first time, ever, and for me, there was no going back."

"The first time? Did you ever have an orgasm with masturbation or other women?"

"No, I'm not attracted to women. I've only dated guys. As for masturbation, I've brought myself release that way, but only when it happened in a public place." She shook her head.

"So, did you continue engaging in sex in public to achieve orgasms, or did you eventually manage to climax in private places, as well?"

"No...never." She shook her head and dropped her gaze to the floor. "It seems I can't reach a climax within four walls..."

"Well, Amber, it's too soon to say for sure, but typically, people who find pleasure in public intimacy are dealing with a form of paraphilia known as exhibitionism. We need to delve deeper, explore your childhood, and uncover any potential traumas or significant experiences to understand this fully. I have a hunch you're not here just because you wish to conceal your sexual activities or because your employer insisted you get therapy. My guess is that you aspire to experience orgasms without being tethered to risky, public settings. Is that accurate?"

"Initially, I agreed to get help because my boss made it clear that my job was on the line if I didn't address this issue. But yes, you've hit the nail on the head. This is something I need to face and resolve, but I never had the courage. The inability to sustain a normal relationship due to my current condition is not just a hurdle but a source of immense frustration."

Simone flashed a subtle smile.

Bingo! *She is an exhibitionist*!

She'd hit the mark again. There was a quiet gratification in identifying a behavior as the first step toward healing.

"Let's work together to find a path to reach your goals," she said warmly. "We'll meet once a week. Does that work for you, Amber?"

Amber returned a faint smile.

"Yes, if we can keep this same time, that would be great."

"Absolutely. This will be your time," Simone reassured her.

They both rose, and Amber extended her hand, giving Simone a firm, grateful handshake.

"Thank you very much, Doctor. I really believe you can

help me."

Simone nodded as they said their goodbyes then watched Amber leave. As she had when she'd entered Simone's office, the young woman walked with shoulders squared and steps measured. She projected that polished, composed image she seemed to cherish, the carefully constructed armor she wore so well.

Not one minute later, the door flew open again, and Patricia hurried into Simone's office.

"I got her!" She grinned. Hand in the air, she waved a small piece of paper like a tiny white flag.

CHAPTER THIRTY-NINE

Some Nasty Secrets, and Some Serious Arguments

The walls are too high to climb.

Simone had been inside her car for almost two hours, parked near the entrance of Deena Hay's residence on Simons Lane in Greenwich. The immense house was encircled by tall walls and trees; only the top of the roof was visible from the street. The structure appeared more like a fortress palace than a residence—untouchable, imposing, and silent.

There was no sign that someone even lived there—no lights visible from this vantage point, and no cars entering or exiting the tall, iron front gate. Simone had considered all her options.

She rang the bell, but nobody answered.

She could keep waiting, but her bladder was starting to hurt. The thought of climbing the wall crossed her mind, but it was a stupid idea. She was no parkour athlete, and what would she do once she was inside?

Simone had left the office around four that evening, and it had taken her almost an hour to get to Greenwich. It was time to head back home; hunger pangs were making her stomach rumble. Simone returned to her car and glanced at the dashboard clock, Carl would be calling any minute.

What am I going to tell Carl if he calls me before I get home? That I've been out stalking his ex-wife?

Simone started the engine and had put the car in drive when an ultramodern black Tesla approached her from behind. The other vehicle turned and came to a stop before the gate.

That's her!

Deena Hay's face had been all over the news for a while the year before following her arrest. Even though she had cut her hair short, Simone recognized her instantly. She killed the engine, climbed from her car, and while Deena waited for the dark-green iron gate to open, knocked on her car window.

Deena jumped in her seat then looked at Simone and nodded once in what Simone took to be a gesture of acknowledgment.

My face was on the news a lot, too.

Deena rolled down the window.

"Doctor Simone Bennet, I was distracted. Good evening. I suppose you want to talk to me?"

"Good evening, Prosecutor. Yes, I would like to. Do you have a few minutes right now?" Thank God she wasn't a stunning beauty like Lara. Carl's ex-wife, was just a regular woman like Simone.

Maybe he was attracted to her brains. She must be smart.

Simone caught herself musing and cringed inside. As if it wasn't enough to compare herself to a dead woman, now she was assessing how she measured up against a woman Carl hadn't been involved with in over a decade!

Simone offered a shy smile; she was not used to pursuing people and judging them at first sight.

"Please follow me with your car. There's some distance

from here to the house."

Deena closed the car window before Simone could respond. She returned to her vehicle, a little more optimistic about her visit.

At least she's open to listening to me.

She climbed behind the wheel, started the engine, and followed Deena along the gravel road. They crossed through another wall of tall pines, and Simone's mouth opened in awe at the grandeur of the house before her.

The Tudor-style home looked as though it had been renovated recently. Simone looked up at the second story and counted the windows across the front. Twenty-two.

I wonder how many bedrooms and baths this place has...

Several other smaller buildings stood off to one side. A guesthouse? A couple of garages? There was no way Deena bought all that on a prosecutor's salary alone.

Her husband must be as rich as a prince...

The moment the thought formed in her mind Simone scowled. "Can you be any pettier?" she murmured. "You sound like a jealous bitch."

Deena parked in front of the house, and Simone pulled up beside her.

"Let's head inside. It's a bit chilly out here," Deena suggested.

She gestured toward one of the many doors, unlocked it, and held it open for Simone. As they entered, Simone took in the surroundings—a warm, inviting kitchen filled with the gleam of copper and stainless-steel pots and pans hanging from a classic Italian-style holder suspended from the ceiling. The scent of herbs lingered in the air, adding a cozy charm to the room, where every detail seemed carefully chosen to create a welcoming, homely feel.

“Sorry to welcome you in the kitchen, but I really need a cup of tea,” she said with an apologetic smile, moving toward the stove. She picked up the kettle. “Would you join me?”

“Sure, but first, may I use your bathroom? I was waiting outside for a while before you arrived, and I really do need to go. But after that, I would love a cup of tea.”

Deena chuckled.

"Of course! There’s a powder room near the staircase." She pointed down a short hallway. “I’ll wait for you here.”

Simone nodded then hurried down the corridor to the little bathroom across from the stairs. No sign of the cat Peter had mentioned…

Moments later, she returned to the kitchen feeling much more at ease and ready to converse with Carl’s ex.

Deena had set out two fine China cups and a plate of biscuits on the large wooden table.

Before she sat, Simone took a moment to survey the kitchen. The room had an old-world charm with its mix of natural and water-green patinaed woodwork. Sheer curtains draped the windows, and fresh flowers adorned the center of the table, creating a warm and inviting space on a chilly day.

Deena began to pour the tea. Once the cups were filled, she looked up, her gaze steady, and asked,

“What brings you to my home, Doctor Bennet? And how did you find my address?”

Her even tone and neutral expression masked her emotions. Such skills must have served her well in her former role as a prosecutor. But Simone had spent a couple of decades perfecting talents of her own, and she sensed a layer of tension beneath Deena’s exterior. And if she was irritated or disturbed already, that wasn’t likely to get any better when Simone mentioned Peter. Simone sighed. Although she didn’t want to cause the other woman any added stress, she hadn't come this far to just walk away without at least trying to get some answers.

"I'd like to ask you about your brother. I'm trying to understand everything that transpired between him and me..."

"My brother?" Deena asked, still maintaining her neutral tone. "I have no interest in talking about him. To me, he's nothing more than a cruel, selfish, poor excuse for a human being."

"His actions had a profound impact on my life," Simone continued. "A dear friend of mine went to prison because he made the mistake of getting involved with Peter. I lost my secretary, patients, and I came very close to giving up my medical career. He manipulated me and used me like a pawn in his sadistic little game. But I wanted to get past all of that, so, I decided to confront him. I visited him at MacDougall, hoping to obtain more information, but he remains an enigma."

"He's not an enigma. Even as a child, he'd throw a tantrum if he couldn't get his way, and he'd never do anything unless he benefited from it in some way. I don't think he has a selfless bone in his body... He never considers the consequences and has no regard for other people's feelings. I sometimes wonder if he has any feelings at all. You're the Doctor—aren't the traits I just described those of someone who's been diagnosed as a psychopath?"

"That's the question I've been trying to answer," Simone replied, moving her hands in thoughtful gestures. "He exhibits all the hallmarks of psychopathy: he's intelligent, quick-witted, highly manipulative. And yet..." She paused, searching for the right words. "I'm hesitant to pin him down with a diagnosis or label him too quickly—it feels almost... too neat, too convenient. There could be more at play here, something more complex."

Deena scowled, spread her arms, and said, "If I can help you by answering some of your questions, go ahead and ask them. Please, feel free to explore the house, too... Maybe you can understand him better by taking a look around here."

"This is Peter's home?" Simone's voice rose.

"Yes, it is. Or rather, it was. Now, according to the government, it's mine to keep. This house, the New York apartment, several other properties around the world, that modern car you just saw and his business which I'm trying to manage as best I can. I'm not sure how long I'll be able to hold onto them, as his victims' families are suing. In the end, we'll see what remains of his empire." Deena smiled sadly. "Go ahead, Doctor, ask your questions."

Simone sat up straighter in the chair, adjusting her posture. She'd been slouching a lot lately, and the muscles in her back, neck, and shoulders were paying the price. "Could you share details about Peter's childhood?"

"Sure." She nodded. "I was almost ten when he was born. I think he was an accident—my parents never talked about it, but I don't believe they wanted or needed another child. They were both intellectuals, and raising children was not their strong suit. When Peter arrived, they were already middle-aged. My mother was vying for a chair on the Supreme Court, having already established herself as a tough judge, and my father was deeply involved with his books and students. He was a professor and had been a prodigious bestseller since he was in his twenties."

Deena paused to sip her tea, and Simone went on to her next question.

"Who is your father?" Simone searched her memory but came up empty. "I can't recall an author by the name of Hay."

"He used the pen name Simon West—his mother's maiden name. Let's just say he didn't have much appreciation for his father."

Simone gawked in surprise.

"Are you serious? That's amazing. He's one of my favorite fiction writers!" She couldn't hide the excitement in her voice.

"Everybody else's favorite...but not mine... To me, he was just a distant figure, lost in his own world, and I believe my brother had even more trouble relating to him."

"What was Peter like as a child?"

Deena's eyes rolled upward, as if she was sifting through memories from the distant past. "My complete opposite. He was talkative, constantly causing trouble at home and perpetually breaking the rules. I think he was lonely and wanted attention and affection from our parents, but Mother and Father weren't very loving. I didn't interact with him much, either. I was on the cusp of my teenage years, and children annoyed me, so I paid little mind to the bothersome boy."

"You say he was a lonely boy. Did he not have any friends?"

"Peter didn't have any close friends. In fact, I don't recall him ever having a sleepover. His only companions were his nanny's grandkids. He was homeschooled until high school because my parents believed it was better for him to have a tutor at home. Looking back, I think they realized he was different and wanted to keep him away from society as much as possible." She crossed her hands on the table.

"Did you know his nanny? He confided in me that she abused him, but your parents didn't believe him. As a result, he was sent to a boarding school to learn to stop telling lies."

Deena unfolded her hands and opened her mouth but paused before answering.

"Really?"

Simone nodded. Where had Deena been that she hadn't known about such a horrible event?

Deena shook her head. “That’s absolutely not true. As I said, he had a tutor and never went to boarding school. My parents wanted to keep a close eye on him.”

Simone’s mouth fell open. “While I was in captivity, in Peter’s hands, he told me he had been abused by his nanny, but your parents didn’t believe him. He couldn’t talk to you about it because you were at boarding school, and he was sent to a boarding school himself because your parents thought he was a liar.”

Denna laughed dryly. “Peter is such a good liar! Neither he nor I have ever been to a boarding school. His nanny was a wonderful lady—she had grandkids and loved children. She worried about Peter spending so much time alone, so sometimes, she got permission from my parents to bring her grandchildren over to play. But Peter inevitably found ways to harm the kids or scare them with his stupid pranks, so it didn’t last.”

“Did he have just one nanny?”

“The first one lasted until he was four years old. After that, he had a procession of sitters because he scared them, and none of them lasted more than a week. But when Carmen took charge, he was around six, and she seemed to know exactly how to deal with him. Perhaps she’d taken care of difficult children in the past. She stayed until he reached an age where he no longer needed a nanny.”

Deena paused and with steady hands poured herself more tea. Without asking, she refilled Simone’s cup, the faint clink of the teapot against porcelain filling the silence.

“He used to love her; she was tender, and I witnessed his affection for her myself, the kind he never gave to anyone else. Peter would sit on her lap and tell her stories, and they often laughed together. He would caress her face, just the way a child might show tenderness toward a beloved grandma.”

Simone scratched her head, feeling the weight of yet another puzzle settling into place. Deena's account was so at odds with what Peter had shared with her in confidence, not to mention what he'd testified to in court during his trial. More questions churned through her mind.

"You told me you weren't close to your father, but Peter said you were 'Daddy's girl'."

"He said that?" Deena scoffed. "Another lie. My father and I were basically strangers; I was close to my mom and admired her a great deal. I studied law because I wanted to be like her and even tried to follow in her footsteps. But my dear brother destroyed all of that for me."

Deena's statement brought another question to Simone's mind.

"How do your parents feel about what he did?" Simone raised an eyebrow.

Deena shifted in her chair and lowered her eyes.

"Fortunately, they died in a car crash a long time ago. They didn't live to see what became of their children. Peter had graduated the year before with honors, and for the first time, I think, they were proud of him. I was experiencing success in my career as an attorney and was even considering becoming a judge. My mom was supporting me in this endeavor, but then, suddenly, they were gone." Deena grimaced.

Simone reached out and put her hand on Deena's. Imagine spending years getting an education and establishing yourself in your career, only to have everything destroyed.

"I'm so sorry. Not just for the loss of your parents but for everything you've lost due to your brother's crimes."

"Thank you, Simone. But I was seriously considering quitting my pursuit of becoming a judge when everything happened. I was being considered for a federal judgeship; I was ready to turn it down to pursue something different in my life. I lacked the courage, but I had come to realize being a judge wouldn't make me happy."

Simone recalled an entry in Carl's journal. He'd met with Deena and had noted she'd expressed a similar sentiment. She'd said something like, "A person must have the courage to change course when they need to. I want to do that now. Every day, I'm becoming a little more courageous...a little braver."

Another thought struck Simone—*Whenever I think back on Carl's journal and compare it to what I'm hearing from the people he mentioned, everything he wrote seems remarkably accurate.*

Simone smiled at the thought, and across from her, Deena gave her an inquiring look.

Simone shook her head and changed the subject.

"Do you know what type of business Peter runs?"

"An import company. I don't know much about it. After Peter went to jail, I had no one to ask about his business. I hired a company to deal with it."

That's weird... Hadn't she just said she was taking care of it...?

Maybe she'd meant she was handling Peter's personal business.

"No one?" Simone asked. "What about his boyfriend, the Chinese guy?"

Deena jerked back in her chair and ran her fingers through her hair. Her face took on a pained look, as if the question hurt her physically.

"I don't know about any Chinese boyfriend. He had countless men in his life, but I don't recall him dating an Asian guy..." She shrugged. "Apparently, I don't know as much about my brother as I thought."

"I know it doesn't offer much consolation," Simone said, her tone turning from casual to professional, "but oftentimes, we don't know ourselves very well, which makes understanding others even more complicated."

"You are completely right, Simone. In a way—and as twisted as it might sound to someone on the outside looking in—deep down, I'm glad Peter forced my hand. His actions provided the catalyst for the changes I needed to make in my life and the means to achieve them, as well."

Deena smiled, her lips curling just enough to reveal faint wrinkles etched around her mouth.

Here stands a woman who couldn't care less about society's obsession with aesthetics.

"Have you resigned from your position as a public prosecutor?"

"Yes...I did, but not just because I needed to change the direction of my life. After everything Peter did, I realized my career in the world of law would never go anywhere. I knew I wouldn't reach the Supreme Court, and I didn't want to remain stagnant, but back then, I lacked the courage to make changes. As I indicated, I'm not sure I could have achieved anything without Peter's... Let's just call it his *intervention.* Now, I'm happy pursuing my passion as an artist."

She smiled again, but Deena's tone and attitude lacked real joy, and Simone got the impression the other woman was putting on a front.

"If you manage to find your true path in life, you are fortunate indeed. Not everyone is so lucky."

"Well, in my case, it's more like my path was found for me." She offered another forced, insincere smile.

Simone glanced at her watch; in fifteen minutes, Carl would call, and she didn't want to have to explain her whereabouts. She looked back at Deena.

"It's getting late. I don't want to impose on you anymore, but I have one last question. Do you have Carmen's contact information?" Simone pulled her phone from her purse to take down the number in case Deena had it.

"Peter's nanny? No, I don't have any way to get in touch with her, sorry." Deena shook her head. "I haven't seen or heard from her in years...not since she stopped working for us."

"How about her last name? Where she used to live?" Simone refused to give up so easily.

"Di Lucca, Di Lacca... Something like that. And when she first came to work for us, I think she said something about growing up in Sleepy Hollow. But I'm sorry...I'm not sure. I wish I could be of more help," Deena said, rising from her chair. Her actions sent a clear message—it was time for Simone to go.

Simone got to her feet and followed Deena to the door. "Are you taking care of Peter's cat?"

"Peter never had a cat, or any other pet."

Peter is a liar.

"When you get to the gate, just wait a moment, and I will have it opened for you. No need to use your horn."

As if I'm a savage and would sit there blasting my horn!

Before Simone responded, Deena went on, "Please extend my best regards to your husband. He is doing an exceptional job in court, defending my family's interests. So far, no defeats!"

This time, her smile lit up her entire face, and her eyes sparkled with a mischievous quality. No doubt about it; Deena took great pleasure in telling Simone that Carl was working for the woman and her family.

She knows he never told me that.

Making certain her emotions didn't show on her face, Simone nodded. "I will. Thanks a lot for having me, Deena."

"My pleasure." There was no trace of pleasure in her words or her body language. Her tone was flat, her posture rigid, as if every syllable she uttered was weighed down by an invisible burden.

Simone had barely made it through the door before Deena closed it.

She's impossible to read. One moment she's the gracious hostess, kind and warm...and the next moment she's cold and close-lipped. Or worse, vicious and hostile.

Simone pulled her car up to the gate and barely resisted the impulse to honk her horn just to annoy the bitch, but she had worked hard at refining her behavior and took pride in her ability to hold her own in any situation and with people from all walks of life. But boy, that woman had gotten under her skin...

Why in the hell didn't Carl tell me he was working for them?

Simone couldn't think of a single excuse he could give her that would explain away withholding that kind of information.

She had driven only a few miles when her phone began to ring. Glancing at the digital screen display on her dash, she saw it was Carl calling.

"Hello, hon—" She couldn't finish her sentence.

"What the hell are you thinking, Simone? Now you're visiting Deena to pressure her for information about her brother? What's the purpose of all this? Why didn't you tell me about your plans?" he shouted.

"Excuse me, but you need to stop shouting at me right now!" Simone replied in a firm voice, the kind she used whenever she needed to calm an emotionally out-of-control patient. "I don't think I need to report every move I make, just as you don't tell me about all yours. For instance, you've been acting as her attorney for what, more than a year now?"

"Who hires me and who doesn't is none of your business."

Her hands started to shake. She hated to fight, and it seemed the clouds were closing in over their heated conversation.

"Likewise, it's none of your business who I choose to visit," she replied in a harsh tone.

Carl drew a deep breath then let out a long sigh that sounded loud over the car speakers.

"Let's calm down, honey. Sorry for shouting, but Deena called me, and it disturbed me to know you are still digging into Peter's background. That's dangerous, and you know it! I didn't tell you I'm working for my former wife because I knew it would upset you, but I owe it to Deena to help her. She lost her career because of Peter, and all she has now is his real estate to support her. Meanwhile, the vultures are circling overhead."

"It's absolutely not about you working for your former wife; I'm not that kind of woman! It's about you working to defend Peter!"

"I'm not defending him! Please be reasonable. I've never been to MacDougall. I'm simply assisting my ex-wife. We divorced amicably. While we no longer love each other, we maintain a great deal of respect for one another. Defending her was my obligation, something I'd do for anyone I've had a relationship with. It's a matter of respecting my own history."

"You're right; it is the right thing to do, but you should have informed me." Simone tightened her grip on the steering wheel. "It's not as if you need to tell me about every single client. But you should have mentioned you'd been retained by this particular client."

"Maybe you're right, but I was concerned you might get upset. I've dated women in the past who would have been extremely angry if they found out I was working for an ex."

"Are any of your ex-girlfriends renowned psychiatrists?"

"Ouch! That was arrogant of you!" His voice rose again.

"It's extremely unfair of you to compare me with your previous girlfriends," Simone stated.

"Hey, love, are we having our first serious argument here?" He laughed, but she knew him well enough to know he was forcing the humor.

"It's not funny." Simone said.

"I'm so sorry. I really don't want to argue with you. We are not naive youngsters who know nothing about life," he said, her voice steady and resolute. "We are adults, and what we have is a deeply mature relationship, built on understanding and respect. As you said, revisiting the feelings that made me act poorly, it's my worry about you. Your investigation into Peter and his past might put you at risk, and that concerns me." Carl's voice was back to normal.

"I'm not investigating anything; I'm just trying to understand the motives behind his actions to aid my own healing. After my kidnapping, I felt vulnerable, which was a sensation I never experienced before and don't wish to feel again."

She shared only part of the story. She considered herself healed, but if fibbing a little would ease his worries about her, she was willing to bend the truth. But a nagging thought caused her to chew on her bottom lip.

Hiding things is never a good idea in a relationship but it seems we're both going down that path.

"Okay, honey, why don't we drop the subject for now. We can always discuss this some other time, face to face."

As Simone drove the remaining thirty minutes from

Greenwich to New Haven, she and Carl talked about their day, carefully avoiding any sensitive topics. However, Simone sensed a barrier between them, a distance that could threaten their relationship now that they'd had their first serious argument.

CHAPTER FORTY

The Worst Kind of Solitude

Wendy Rafalli was the kind of woman who would never go unnoticed when entering any room. She was the epitome of power and self-confidence. At least, that was the image she projected to the world.

Now, as she entered Simone's office, Wendy wore a bright smile. She went directly to the couch beside Simone's and sat.

"Good morning, Wendy."

The woman made herself comfortable and ran her fingers through her perfectly coifed hair before responding to Simone. "Good morning, Doctor. How have you been?"

"Fine, how about you? How are you feeling after our last session?"

Simone opened her file on the woman, although she had read it minutes before Wendy's appointment. In their last session, Wendy had said she had ended her affair with a younger man, and now, she had taken up with another man, one closer to her age this time. But once again, she had chosen a man far beneath her own social class.

In Simone's professional opinion, Wendy was engaging in a sort of revenge against her husband. Feeling betrayed and angry at his behavior, she would have an affair with someone to humiliate him and demonstrate he meant nothing in her life.

"My feelings are under control this time. I haven't fallen in love with Gabriel; our relationship is purely about sex, good sex." She smiled.

"The sex was good with your previous lover, wasn't it? Do you think it's the same now? And why haven't you fallen in love this time? Do you have any idea why?" Simone searched Wendy's eyes.

"I really don't know... Maybe because he has a blue-collar job. He works in construction you know..." She lowered her head.

"Are you ashamed of his profession?"

The woman lifted her gaze to the ceiling and then looked at Simone.

"Let's just say I would never walk hand in hand with him in public." Again, she appeared to study her shoes.

"How about the karate teacher?"

"Nope." She shook her head.

"And your husband? Are you ashamed of him, too?"

"Oh, no, not at all. My husband is a respectable man, intelligent and clever. People see him as powerful, and nobody would pity me for being in a relationship with him." Wendy spoke in a proud tone, lifting her head and meeting Simone's eyes.

"How about sex? Is it better with your husband or with Gabriel?"

"With Gabriel it's all new; it's about discovery, experiencing new tastes and scents, and he gives me pleasure I never thought was possible. When I'm around him, I'm in a constant state of arousal. The mere contact of our bodies when he lies beside me or on top of me makes my pussy quiver." She drew a deep breath as if she could feel what she'd described, but then she seemed to sober, and her voice took on a matter-of-fact tone. "Sex with my husband is pretty good, but with him, I know all the moves, and I don't feel that desperation..." She moved her hands nervously while she talked.

"Desperation?"

"Desperation to come! I never felt this way before! Gabriel is a nobody to me. I have no respect for him, but the moment I'm in his space, everything changes. His fingers on my skin, his lips on my body—it's as if he knows precisely where to touch me. He has this way of teasing me. He never removes my panties; he simply pushes them aside and penetrates me...hard and deep, and I'm overwhelmed. I climax instantly."

"I understand. It's called chemistry." Simone kept her voice from betraying her emotions, but Wendy's description had struck a chord. Simone understood how chemistry could overwhelm the senses and leave a woman with no control over her body or reactions.

That's how I feel with Carl. I never experienced anything like that with Ed, my first husband, or any other man in my life.

She shook her head to chase away the thoughts.

"Would you leave your husband for any of the men you've had affairs with?"

"Never!" Wendy slapped the arm of the couch.

Simone nodded. "According to your own words, you touch the guy, and you're aroused. His touch drives you insane, makes you feel like you're on the edge, ready to lose yourself. With the simplest gestures, he makes you climax." Simone leaned forward slightly, her gaze steady. "In my opinion, that's not just attraction—that's chemistry, raw and undeniable. And whether you admit it or not, that's what's steering your behavior."

"I...I think you could be right..." She lowered her head "I can't stop craving Gabriel's body."

"You said the same about the other guy..."

"I know—I thought that was the best sex of my life, but Gabriel topped it. Completely."

"But do you understand the risks involved? What if your husband finds out? Are you ready to face a difficult divorce if you're caught cheating? Can you stop seeing Gabriel for the sake of your marriage?"

Wendy raised her head sharply, the motion charged with intensity, before locking eyes with Simone. There was a fire in her expression, an unspoken challenge simmering just beneath the surface.

"To be honest, Doctor, at this moment, I can't, and I wouldn't. It's like I've lost all self-control. I'm just living for the next orgasm. I really don't understand myself! I don't want a divorce, but here I am, taking risks that could lead to one! I'm that stupid! I feel like a hormonal teenager."

"No, you're not stupid. Just human. Doctor Dylan Selterman, a renowned researcher from Johns Hopkins, has conducted extensive research on the motivations for infidelity. Many factors influence this behavior. A major reason many people give for cheating is anger, often over a desire to punish a partner for a transgression. When you first came here, you mentioned how your husband's behavior was hurting you. If I'm not mistaken, that was around the time your infidelities began, correct?"

Wendy nodded her agreement.

"Now, you seem to be less hurt by his behavior, but the sex has become routine. So, you haven't fallen in love; you are simply enjoying the sex. You aren't expressing a desire to get revenge on your husband but are simply following your instincts and fulfilling your desires. Maybe that's why you have no feelings for this one."

Simone maintained a neutral expression as she tried to explain what was going on in Wendy's life.

"You don't respect this guy, Gabriel. However, the sexual tension between you is very evident in your voice and your description of how you interact with him. It seems to me, your connection with him is all about uncontrolled desire. It's up to you to decide whether to pursue that desire or to suppress it. You also need to consider whether it's worth the risk. And by risk, I mean the potential for a divorce—and the pain and loneliness that would accompany a split with your husband."

Wendy's eyes filled with tears. "Pain and loneliness? Aren't you essentially describing my marriage?" she retorted with a bitter smile.

"The worst kind of loneliness is feeling alone and lost even when you're with someone. Are you saying that's happening in your marriage?"

Simone leaned toward Wendy, maintaining unbroken eye contact. A single large tear rolled down the woman's face. She didn't bother to dry it or to conceal it.

"It seems to me you're scared of being alone, even though you just said that you feel alone within your marriage. You also seem worried about public opinion, from people who don't offer you any kind of solace."

"I really don't know what I'm feeling, and I certainly don't know what to do," Wendy said. She closed her eyes, sat back, and rested her head on the couch as tears trickled slowly down her cheeks.

Simone reached for the Kleenex box and then set it on Wendy's lap.

"You don't need to have all the answers right now. What's important is to connect with your true feelings and confront what you truly need to find happiness. If it means staying with your husband, try to envision your relationship in ten years—with his kids and all the issues that bother you currently. Don't say anything to him; avoid any criticism for a week. Just observe his behavior toward you and yours toward him. Be fully present in your marriage for one week. That's not a long time; I think you can manage to stay away from Gabriel for such a short period."

"That's fine. I'll do that. But only after one more round of sex with him this afternoon."

CHAPTER FORTY-ONE

Facts, Foes, and a Hug

The sun had already begun to set when Simone's last patient departed. As she put away the files she'd used that day and gathered up her purse and car keys, she glanced at a scribbled note lying on her desk. She'd almost forgotten. Before she left for the night, she'd wanted to try to find a phone number or address for Carmen Di Lucca… or Di Lacca or whatever the woman's real name is."

I had so many more questions for Deena…

Simone had begun to feel as if she was imposing, and she wouldn´t do that.

Simone glanced at her watch and then buzzed Patricia, certain she would still be at her desk since she never left the office if Simone was still there.

"Yes?" Patricia's voice sounded over the intercom speaker.

"Can you come to my office?"

Less than a minute later, Patricia came bustling in, her long skirt swirling around her tall leather boots. Today, she wore a dark-red sweater and had applied matching lipstick with a heavy hand. Simone couldn't take her eyes off the woman's blood-red lips.

"Can I help you, Doctor?"

Patricia smiled, revealing she had as much lipstick coating her teeth as she'd smeared on her lips.

"Patricia, you have lipstick on your teeth."

Simone said, pointing to her own teeth. Patricia made a small sound of surprise then imitated the gesture, effectively removing the red mess from her teeth.

Simone checked her watch.

"You're leaving, right? We can talk in the morning. I wanted to ask you for a favor, but it's not urgent."

Patricia shook her head.

"I'm not in any rush. Just tell me what you need, and I'll get right on it first thing in the morning. My cat isn't going to care if I get home five minutes later."

Cat, my ass…

Nobody put on red lipstick just to go home to their cat.

"I think it's time for us to hire that friend of yours who can find a needle in a haystack… I need to locate another person, and by now, he or she probably doesn't owe you any more favors."

Patricia pulled her phone from her pocket and unlocked the screen.

"Who do you need to find? I'll talk to my friend. If she thinks it's too much for a favor, she'll set a price for her services." She shrugged.

"I need to find information on a woman. I don't know her age, but she must be quite old. The person who told me about her knew her about thirty years ago, and back then, she referred to her as a granny, so by now, she must be ancient. Her name is Carmen, and her last name is something like Di Lucca or Di Lacca. The only other thing I know is she might be from Sleepy Hollow."

Patricia finished tapping on her phone, locked the screen again, then put it back into her pocket. She nodded.

"Let me see what I can do."

"Thanks a lot, Patricia. One more thing—can you arrange a visit with Peter Hay tomorrow at MacDougall?"

"I will try my best!"

"Very good. Good night, Patricia. See you tomorrow. Please go home to your cat now and...I hope the two of you have fun."

Patricia's eyes widened, but she didn't respond to the insinuating tone of Simone's statement. "Good night!" Patricia waved and rushed from the room.

No argument about not wanting to leave me alone here... She's meeting a man.

Simone shrugged, closed her purse, and draped the strap over her shoulder.

"Simmie, wait, I need to talk to you."

Edward's whispered words made her freeze. She turned slowly toward the window. Was he outside? The long drapes moved a bit, and she glanced down at the floor. There, peeking out from beneath the hem of the curtains, were a pair of men's leather shoes.

She sucked in a breath and shook her head. "Stay where you are. I don't think Patricia is gone yet. I didn't hear her car."

Simone went to the door, locked it, and then leaned her ear against the wood and listened. A few noises came from down the hallway, so Patricia hadn't gone. Finally, the sound of the front door closing—followed by silence—told Simone she and Ed were alone.

"You can come out now. But really, Ed, you must stop scaring the hell out of me. Can't you just tell me when you're going to drop by?"

Edward came out from behind the curtains and walked toward her. "Sure, I'll give you a call from jail next time to say I'll be out and stopping to pay you a visit." He shook his head. "I can't do that. Sorry."

He gave her a smile and tilted his head. Still annoyed by his intrusion, Simone ignored his attempt to tease her into a better mood. He had dark circles around his eyes, as if he hadn't slept for several days, but she fought the urge to feel sorry for him. Instead, she pointed at the couch. "Please, have a seat."

Edward shook his head and stayed put in the middle of the room. Arms crossed, he stared at her.

"No, thanks, I'll stand. This won't take long."

"Well, I need to sit down. My legs are still shaking from your surprise visit." Simone slumped into a nearby chair.

"I must remind you to be more careful. You're still reckless when it comes to your safety, and obviously, you're still neglecting to lock the windows. The one in my office wasn't latched. I entered easily, then I came in here when you went to the kitchen... You need to start paying more attention to your surroundings." He spoke rapidly, the words flying from his lips like bullets from a machine gun.

Ed being Ed! He will never stop trying to protect me.

Those thoughts led quickly to a question—the same one that always came to mind when she tried to analyze Edward's current situation.

How can he possibly be a criminal?

Before she could focus her attention on his accusations and defend herself, he went on.

"I didn't plan on talking to you. I came by to get something from my office, but I can't find it. I thought since you collected my stuff from the New Haven Police Department and arranged things in my office, you might remember where you put them. However, while I waited for Patricia to leave, I overheard your conversation about trying to find someone...and from what I heard, this isn't the first person you've been searching for. So, can you explain to me what you're doing? Should I assume you're in the private detective business now?"

Simone raised a hand, gesturing for him to stop. "Hold on, Ed. You're asking too many questions at once. What were you looking for in your office? Everything that belongs to you is in there... The envelope I found in a box is in the small drawer under the desk, the books are on the shelves, the pictures from your work with the FBI..." Simone shrugged. "It's all in there."

"Damn, I forgot about the small drawer," Ed muttered.

The drawer was almost invisible, like a secret compartment. Ed had never used it before, but Simone had felt compelled to place some of Ed's things in there.

"You want the envelope?" She frowned. "It contains a bunch of old invoices...nothing important. I only kept it because it is yours."

"It is precisely what I need. I'll go get it, and then we can talk about your private investigation business..."

Edward exited her office through the connecting door and returned a few minutes later, holding the envelope. "All here," he said, holding them up for her to see. "Now... Tell me about this Carmen you were asking about, and why are you using the services of a detective so frequently? Something tells me you're digging into Hay's business."

Simone glanced at the floor and didn't respond.

"How can I stop you from putting yourself in danger, Simmie? Please tell me!"

Edward looked deeply into Simone's eyes, but she quickly

averted her gaze. "I'm not in danger. I'm just seeking some answers... I have a few personal questions about Hay that I need answered so I can understand...that's all," Simone replied.

"Or maybe you're trying to clear your husband—because deep down, you suspect him?" Ed leaned forward. Provocation laced his voice. "After all, he did kill his girlfriend, didn't he? And let's not forget—his best friend was a murderer. That's quite the company to keep, isn't it? Maybe you're wondering if you've been sleeping with the enemy this whole time. Is that the question you're really trying to answer?" His words were sharp, cutting through the air like a blade.

Simone sought and held Ed's gaze, her muscles turning rigid from shock. His questions sparked a sudden awareness of the motivation she'd hidden deep inside. Ed had managed to shine a light on the truth.

Truth... That was precisely what she wanted—the entire truth. She needed to know who her husband really was and how his connection to Hay might implicate Carl in criminal activities.

Simone shook her head. N-no...never... I trust my husband... I'm only interested in learning more about Peter so I can understand what motivates him."

"I understand..." Ed's tone oozed condescension, and he gave her a patronizing, insincere smile.

Grateful he'd decided to let the topic go, at least for now, Simone remained silent.

Let sleeping dogs lie...

Edward finally settled on the couch and released a sigh. Clutching the envelope to his chest with one hand, he leaned down and carefully removed his shoes. He closed his eyes and sank his feet into the thick pile before releasing another deep sigh.

After a few seconds, he opened his eyes, meeting Simone's gaze.

"Small pleasures take on a different meaning when you've gone without them for a while," he said, a faint smile flickering across his lips. The warmth in his tone was fleeting, quickly replaced by a sharper edge as his expression hardened. "But we have something important to discuss," he added, his voice steady and serious, pulling them both back into the gravity of the moment.

"I'm certain your visit has another purpose besides hunting for an of envelope," Simone said, her gaze sharp as she pointed to the envelope Edward still clutched protectively to his chest.

He held it with one hand, his fingers curling around it. Leaning closer to her, he dropped his voice.

"It was just the envelope," he said, a flicker of something unreadable in his eyes. "But then I overheard you speaking with your secretary. I understood enough of what you said to realize you're not planning to end your little private investigation anytime soon."

The air between them seemed to shift, heavy with unspoken tension, as if each was waiting for the other to make the next move.

"If I can't convince you to give up this misguided investigation, let's at least share the information we've gathered. Perhaps we can help each other. We can start by you telling me who Carmen is and why you need to find her."

Simone took a deep breath as she weighed her options. She could lie—make up some story he'd have no choice but to believe—or tell him the truth. Her innate honesty prevailed, and she crafted her response carefully.

"During those long hours I spent under Peter's control

when he kidnapped me, he kept having these psychotic episodes or, he seemed to regress to some point in his childhood. He spoke in a childlike voice, and even his word choices and mannerisms were different. He said and did a lot of crazy stuff, but one thing he said made me wonder... He told me he had been abused by his nanny, and when he told his parents, they didn't believe him. Instead of protecting him, they sent him to a boarding school. To me, that story made perfect sense, in that it offered a reason for those psychotic episodes. Of course, you would know better than I do when it comes to this stuff."

Simone shrugged. Having spent years working as a criminal profiler, Ed had much more experience in this regard. She had no problem admitting as much and bowing to his superior knowledge when it came to psychopathic bad guys...

"So, you set out to find Carmen?" Ed asked.

"Not exactly... I went to see Deena Hay yesterday," she said, turning her head to conceal her expression from Edward.

To her surprise, Edward didn't blow his top. Instead, he gave a long, weary-sounding sigh then said, "I suppose she wasn't much help, considering you're now chasing after the nanny."

"On the contrary, we had a lengthy conversation. She refuted everything Peter said. According to her, Peter adored the nanny, whom she described as sort of a nice, grandmotherly type of woman, and he never attended a boarding school. In fact, he was partially homeschooled."

Edward searched her eyes. "What else did you discuss? Did she provide any particularly revealing information?"

He appeared genuinely interested, leaning toward her and focusing his attention on her face. For a moment, the envelope in his hand seemed to have been forgotten, as he casually placed it on the sofa beside him.

Simone thought a moment, searching her memory for anything Ed might find important. But her time with Deena hadn't yielded very much Simone could use. She made a dismissive sound and shook her head.

"Hardly... She's a tough woman and comes across as deeply private and reserved. She answered my questions, but in my opinion, she mulled over her responses and weighed every word before she spoke." Simone scowled but then tipped her head and smiled a self-congratulatory smile. "There's nothing spontaneous about Deena Hay, but I'm used to pulling information from unwilling patients, and she revealed some interesting information."

Edward raised an eyebrow, a familiar sign that he expected her next words would be significant. Simone's smile grew into a grin, and she chuckled, enjoying the easy way they'd slipped back into their previous roles as partners...

Careful, Simone... You don't want to allow yourself to get drawn into forgetting what this man is alleged to have done.

"At the beginning of our conversation, maybe two minutes after we sat down to talk, she told me she has been managing Peter's businesses and estates, through a firm. Also, she revealed that my husband is her lawyer, and he's been working to defend her from any lawsuits brought by Peter's victims." She gave an embarrassed chuckle. "Obviously, I had no clue about that."

Ed opened his mouth as if he was about to say something, but Simone reacted quickly, holding up both hands and gesturing for him to stop.

"No. Please don't. Nothing you could say right now would be beneficial, and I wouldn't want anything to tear a hole in the tenuous fabric of our current relationship."

Instead of getting angry or remarking on her use of the word *tenuous*, Edward mimicked the action of zipping his mouth shut and twisting a lock in a playful signal of his willingness to go along with Simone's request. His eyes gleamed with humor.

"I'm guessing she didn't mention what specific type of business she may or may not be managing?" Edward asked.

Simone shook her head. "No, she didn't. Do you think that's important? What type of commerce he engaged in, I mean..." Simone pointed toward her desk where she still kept Carl's old diary. "From what I recall, Peter owned a clothing import business. Fast fashion from China. I'm almost positive that's what Carl wrote, but again, that information comes from Carl's diary and not from Deena's mouth."

"You still have Carl's diary? Does it mention anything else about Peter's business?"

Simone nodded. "Yes. I keep it here, but the only thing I remember is that Carl wrote about importing clothes of questionable quality. There was even a girl—I need to look at the diary again and find her name—but she owned several stores and was a regular buyer."

Simone rose and walked to her desk, took her keys from her purse, and unlocked the drawer she used to keep some of her private documents secure.

She pulled out Carl's diary and began flipping through the pages. The faint rustle of paper filled the room. Edward sat silently; his gaze fixed on her movements. He didn't rush her, didn't speak—just watched.

"Here it is!" Simone said. "Keyra. No last name mentioned, but he says she owned a chain of fast fashion boutiques called Planet Teens."

"That's invaluable information, Simmie! More than I've managed to gather in days! Thank you so much." Enthusiasm evident in his tone, Edward stood. "I'm sorry to rush off, but I really must be going now."

Simone rolled her eyes, partly amused, and partly

annoyed.

"Right. Of course, you must..."

"Please keep me updated on any further leads you discover. Don't worry about how to reach me... I'll be in touch with you, and we'll work out a way we can communicate, just let me know if you want to visit me in jail, and don't do anything else." he said, moving toward the door. "I need to leave now. Goodbye, Simmie. Be careful—there are certain areas of this investigation where you don't want to delve too deeply. People have been dying around us ever since you got your hands on that damn diary. We're not dealing with ordinary folks here; we must be up against some of the worst kinds of criminals." Hand on the doorknob, he turned. "I'll use the kitchen door to leave. Remember to lock it after I'm gone."

"Ed?" Simone said and then hurried to complete her question before she could change her mind. "May I give you a hug?"

The look on his face said her request surprised him just as much as the need to ask had surprised her.

Edward swiftly closed the distance between them and enveloped her in a warm embrace. Simone lingered in his arms, her heart aching with the nostalgia of missing her best friend. But the moment ended quickly. Edward gently pulled back from the hug, kissed her forehead tenderly, and then left without another word.

*****

Simone lingered on her office couch, reflecting on the myriad feelings coursing through her. Each encounter with Edward left her with a mix of emotions. Guilt was predominant; she had accepted his conviction without question...a fact he had bitterly reminded her of. But deep within, she harbored doubts. The image of him as a serious criminal didn't align with her knowledge of his personality and her experiences with him over the years. She had sincere doubts in her heart about his culpability, she had no proof, only a feeling.

A sense of loss plagued her, as well. Being near him brought back memories of the strong friendship they'd shared. They had been intimate, yes, but they'd also been best friends.

Do best friends turn their backs on each other when things get ugly? It was so easy for me to believe he was a criminal…

Almost as if she'd wanted it to be true.

Simone shivered at the thought. Could that be possible? Was she really that…evil?

Did I want him to be a criminal so I could freely begin a romance with Carl?

Simone made a panicked sound at the unbelievable direction her thoughts were taking.

She put her hand on her stomach and massaged the growing knot. Remorse, most likely, eating away at her from the inside out.

No, stupid, you must be hungry; you haven't eaten in hours.

Outside, darkness had caused the streetlights to come on, but Simone was too agitated to consider going home. She slipped off her shoes and began pacing around her office. She adored this space; Edward did, too. These offices had been their joint venture, their creation. They'd pooled their resources to purchase the property and personally oversaw its remodeling. In the beginning, they'd even painted some walls themselves to save money.

She paused and looked around, studying her surroundings, imagining how things must have looked to him. How difficult had it been for him to see the place, knowing he was no longer a part of it?

Simone halted her hundred-mile pacing in front of her desk. She turned on her computer, which she had already shut down in preparation to leave earlier, but too restless to sit, she simply leaned over the keyboard, opened Google, and typed in "Carmen Di Lucca." She came across several women with the same name, but they were too young to be the one she was searching for. Then, she tried "Carmen Di Lacca," The results appeared almost instantly, but they were just as disappointing.

I'm a terrible detective. Simone chastised herself. *I should leave this to Patricia and her friends.*

Simone had no training in the fields of crime analysis or investigations, but as always, her curiosity got the better of her, and she couldn't resist checking out Keyra's shop. Simone typed "Planet Teens" into the search bar. Even without Keyra's last name, this was Simone's only decent lead.

To her surprise, she struck gold. She discovered a brand called "Planet Teens", owned by Keyra Zanandrya. Originally from Australia, Keyra was a renowned businesswoman with a reputation for innovation and an enigmatic past that seemed to intersect with the mystery Simone was trying to unravel.

In one of the Google articles Simone read, it was reported that Keyra had the Midas Touch and raked in millions annually with Planet Teens and other fashion ventures.

According to Carl's diary, Peter had introduced Keyra to Carl, hoping the woman would help Carl move on from Lara. But Carl had never taken to the woman—or her overpowering perfume, which he found too strong for his liking.

"My husband turned down a multimillionaire," Simone mused aloud, a small smile playing on her lips.

In order to pursue me, an average, working-class Doctor? If that was the case, he must have really loved me.

She clicked on the images tab, intending to view the woman's picture.

She clicked on the first photo to enlarge it and stared, struck by Keyra's piercing, honey-colored eyes. Her dark skin appeared naturally sun-kissed, not artificially bronzed, and her hair was shiny and styled in a modern fashion. Self-consciously, Simone ran her fingers through her flat, unkempt tresses. Her cheeks heated, and a little voice inside her head whispered in a scathing tone.

Stop being such a slob and start taking better care of yourself.

Simone's phone jingled, interrupting her self-recriminations. She retrieved it from her purse, glanced at the number, and smiled tentatively, hoping Carl was in a good mood.

"Hello, honey," she answered.

"Hello, love. May I ask where the most beautiful woman in the world is? I'm here preparing our dinner, and my beloved hasn't gotten home yet." A blend of affection and light-hearted humor filled his voice.

Simone's smile widened. Relieved and pleased that their recent quarrel seemed to be behind them, she responded to his banter.

"What a surprise! You're at home and cooking!" she exclaimed. "That's the man of my dreams!"

"Well, it was meant to be a surprise, but since you haven't come home yet, and my beef wellington is about to turn into ashes, I decided to summon you." His tone, though teasing, hinted at his eagerness for her return.

"I'll be there in a few minutes! You know how much I love that food" Salivating at the thought, she grabbed her purse and hurried out of the office, still chatting with her husband as she made her way to the car.

CHAPTER FORTY-TWO

Forgiveness and More

As Simone reached to punch the code into the electronic lock, the door swung open, revealing what appeared to be a walking bouquet of the most exquisite red roses. She smiled as Carl lowered the flowers and offered her a warm smile in return.

“Please forgive me! I hope these flowers, as well as a perfectly cooked filet, might form a path to your heart and earn me your forgiveness for my earlier harsh words and for not disclosing my role as Deena’s lawyer.” He handed her the bouquet. “Here…he said. “Let me take your coat.”

Simone placed the flowers on the kitchen island, shrugged out of her heavy jacket, and then turned to find herself in her husband’s arms. The coat fell to the floor as they stood wrapped in a tight embrace for a moment.

“No worries, my love. I’ve thought about it, and I understand your point. Let’s put all that behind us,” she lied in a soft tone. She still burned with a sense of betrayal accompanied by an unfamiliar rebelliousness. But she would address the issues surrounding these feelings later.

Before Carl could respond, the beep of the oven timer signaled that their meal was ready.

“Just in time, honey. Please take a seat at the table, and I’ll arrange these flowers in a vase and serve your dinner.”

“All in the blink of an eye.” She murmured to herself.

He winked at her, then bent down to pick up her coat from the floor. With casual ease, he draped it over the stool by the kitchen island, then turned his attention to the flowers. The bouquet rested there, vibrant against the marble. A hand towel was slung over his shoulder, its edge brushing against his shirt as he reached for a vase, his movements unhurried and purposeful.

Carl had set the table with their best china and crystal glasses. Another vase of fresh flowers sat in the middle, flanked by two candles. The warm, glowing flames flickered and danced, creating an atmosphere of intimacy.

Simone settled into her usual chair. A lighter laying on the table drew her attention, and she picked it up and rolled it over and over in her hand. Carl came up behind her.

“Here you are, my love,” he said softly, handing her a glass of Bourgogne. “I’ll be back with the food in just a second.” He headed back to the kitchen.

“It smells delicious, even from all the way over here!” Simone called out to him. The wonderful aromas delighted her senses.

Within minutes, Carl returned and set a plate before her. He’d sliced the beef wellington, revealing the pink perfection inside the golden crust coated in a velvety wine sauce.

I’m a lucky woman… All the men in my life know how to cook, and more importantly, they enjoy it!

Ed had done this same type of thing for her, even when they had just been good friends.

Simone took her time and savored the meal, enjoying each delicious bite. Despite the surprise and the romantic ambiance of the beautiful dinner, though, she sensed a bit of awkwardness between them. Most likely, Carl was wondering how to further address their earlier argument or if he even should. After all, he'd already apologized, and she had told him she wanted to put the whole thing behind them. But she knew him well, and he would need to bring up the subject again. Probably sooner rather than later. As a result, tension rippled through the air between them.

They ate in silence until Simone finally had enough. Summoning her professional resolve and drawing on her skills as a psychiatrist, she turned to Carl, determined to put him—and herself—at ease.

"Carl, thank you for this superb dinner," she said, her tone warm and appreciative. "I was bracing myself for some kind of frozen, premade meal, but coming home to a homemade dinner, prepared by my favorite person in the world, is truly an amazing gift!" Her words, sincere and heartfelt, aimed to bridge the gap that their earlier disagreement had created.

Carl's response came with a mixture of happiness and lingering frustration.

"It makes me happy to hear that, love. But I must admit, I was quite angry to learn you'd started playing Sherlock Holmes again. I was worried about your safety and annoyed because you went to bother Deena. She has suffered a lot since her brother went to jail, and all the turmoil surrounding her because of his actions has been overwhelming. Her husband left her, you know. Coward! I just didn't want you to add to her troubles or put yourself in a risky situation."

Determined to show her understanding, Simone kept her tone soft.

"If you had told me that you were defending her and helping to protect her from some of the challenges she's been facing, I would never have gone to her house. I was just trying to find a few answers regarding why Peter does what he does, and she is his only relative," Simone said. At some point, a hint of defensiveness had crept into her voice. "I didn't mean to intrude or exacerbate her difficulties. I just... need to understand."

She hoped her words conveyed the sense of regret she had, as well as her wish for better communication. Somehow, she needed to highlight the importance of sharing intentions and information in their relationship.

"Did you?" He lifted an eyebrow.

Simone frowned as she tried to decipher his meaning. "Did I what?

"Get the answers you were looking for?" He clarified.

Simone responded with frustration.

"Nope. In fact, I ended up with even more questions. He's a liar but a very convincing one. Even with all my experience, I couldn't tell he was making things up, misleading me. In fact, Deena seemed like *she* was hiding things. But he's a manipulator, capable of creating elaborate stories and possibly even believing his own lies. Deena, on the other hand, seems to be a normal person. I think he has some sort of schizophrenia mixed with psychopathy."

Her assessment reflected a deeper understanding of the personalities involved, distinguishing between Peter's manipulative tendencies and Deena's apparent sincerity. But despite her outward confidence in her analysis of the situation, Simone harbored lingering uncertainties about both siblings. Aware of the tension that already existed and not wanting to fuel the fire with her unresolved suspicions, Simone chose not to voice her doubts to Carl just then. Her primary desire was to return to a sense of normalcy in their relationship, preferring to keep her uncertainties to herself. This decision underscored her wish to protect their relationship and maintain harmony in their home.

Carl offered a more cautious perspective, blending his experience with a touch of his natural skepticism.

"Well, if I were you, I wouldn't be so certain about either of them. Remember, she was a lawyer for many years, and you know what people say—are they lawyers or liars? I was married to her, and I know from experience that when it suited her, she could lie to me flawlessly." He made a sweeping motion with his hand while nodding in a way that left no doubt about the accuracy of his testimony and previous experience.

Carl's caution served as a reminder for Simone to approach the situation with a balanced view and to consider all possibilities.

How about you, my beloved lawyer? Other than working for Deena, what else have you lied to me about?

She kept that thought to herself, but the suspicions echoed in her mind.

After dinner, they decided to take separate showers—Carl opting for the guest bathroom while Simone used the master one, and meet in their home theater, possibly to watch a movie or the first few episodes of a new series. The problem with watching a series revolved around the promise they'd made to each other not to watch any episodes alone. Since they were apart most of the time, Simone had gotten the urge to go back on her word. But that would mean she'd have to watch the same episodes twice. Since she wasn't the kind of person who enjoyed re-reading the same book or watching the same movie repeatedly, that was enough to make her keep her promise.

*****

As Simone stood underneath the warm spray and rinsed her hair, her thoughts turned to Carl's kind gesture... the surprise dinner he'd made for her as a sort-of olive branch.

"I should do something for him in return," she murmured. But what? Considering the short notice, she didn't have too many options. Anything she'd order online would take at least a day to arrive, and they'd just eaten, so food was out of the question. She turned off the water and reached for a towel from the warmer against the wall. As her gaze fell on her image in the vanity mirror across from the shower stall, inspiration struck.

"That's a perfect idea!" she told herself, flashing a grin at her reflection. She wrapped one towel around her hair and the other around her body and hurried into the adjoining bedroom.

Simone rummaged through her bureau drawer until she found the lingerie she had recently purchased. She wasn't what any man would call a typical bombshell, but she had promised herself she'd try to do more to spice up her love life and please Carl. And since she hadn't mustered up the courage to wear the sexy, little outfit yet, her husband hadn't seen it.

The lacy blood-red bodysuit still had the price tags attached. She grabbed a pair of scissors from her vanity and snipped them off, handling the garment carefully so as not to snag the thin, delicate fabric. Making certain she didn't do any damage with her nails, she stepped into the bodysuit and pulled it up and over her torso, then went to her closet and chose a pair of super-high, glossy red heels.

Simone dried her hair quickly, the warm air from the dryer banishing the last traces of dampness. Once done, she brushed her hair with practiced ease, smoothing out any tangles. Then with a playful tilt of her head, she leaned forward and gave her hair a vigorous shake, letting the strands fall naturally as she straightened. She added a few drops of her favorite perfume and found one of the few red lipsticks she owned and applied it meticulously. She took a step back and studied herself in the vanity mirror.

Wow...

She barely recognized herself. Amazing what a tiny scrap of fabric could do for a woman's ego, not to mention her desires. She rarely felt sexy, but the woman in the mirror looked ready for some hot and heavy action. Simone laughed softly as she twirled in front of the mirror.

Even my ass looks great in this outfit.

She still needed to walk out there and show Carl, so she gave herself a mental pep talk before she could lose her nerve.

Now, gather your courage and go play the seductress.

With a determined stride, Simone walked across the room, the carpet muffling the sound of her heels.

In their home theater, she found her husband already on the couch. Remote in hand and dressed in his old navy-blue pajamas, he was flipping through the onscreen program guide, browsing for a movie.

I really need to spice up our marriage, or we'll soon become a couple of boring, old fogies.

Positioning herself in front of him, she coughed softly then said,

"I want your opinion on my new outfit."

Carl turned his head, his gaze sweeping over her body, and she shivered at the desire that gleamed in his wide eyes. His mouth had fallen open, and Simone had to swallow back a laugh at his shocked expression.

"You are stunning... I've never seen you like this before," he murmured.

"Do you like it?" Simone asked in a low, husky voice that fit her new persona.

Carl nodded rapidly, leaving her with no doubt that he liked what he saw. Gently taking the remote from his hand, she positioned herself on his lap, straddling him. She leaned in close, initiating a deep kiss, their tongues entwining in a dance of passion. As she shifted her attention from his mouth to his neck, he rewarded her efforts with a moan of pleasure.

She led one of his hands to her breast, whispering, "Touch me."

He responded with eagerness, substituting his hand with his mouth, fervently suckling her nipple. Simone's arousal intensified with each flick of his tongue.

While he focused on her nipples, she pressed herself against his shaft, but their garments created a barrier. With a small sound of frustration, Simone rose from his lap, pulling Carl to his feet beside her. She began to unbutton his pajama top, gently tracing her nails along his chest. Carl grabbed the waistband of his boxers and slid them down and off along with his blue sweats. As he straightened, his desire for her was evident.

Simone began to remove her bodysuit, but Carl halted her by gently taking her hand and moving it away.

"No, let's keep it on. It's so beautiful. I want to have you while you're wearing it," he whispered.

Buoyed by her newfound confidence, Simone moved to a nearby chair, placing one knee on the seat and one foot on the floor for support, she was aware that her buttocks looked amazing in that position, round and firm.

She turned her back to Carl and issued a playful challenge. "So, come over here and do your job."

Carl approached her, pushed the fabric aside, partially exposing her sex, and began to caress her clit.

"God, you're so hot and wet. I need you. Place both knees on the seat and open your legs for me," he told her, impatience underlining every word.

Just as hot and ready as he seemed to be, Simone complied without hesitation.

Adjusting the little tab of lace between her legs a little more, he exposed her completely, opened her with his fingers, moved to stand between her legs, and then entered her in a single fluid motion. She climaxed immediately, and their surroundings faded away as they both lost themselves in a frantic desire to satisfy each other, their movements intensifying in a crescendo of passion.

The sound of Carl's ragged breath near her ear as he leaned over her told Simone he was about to climax. Longing to prolong this amazing connection between them, she straightened and stepped away. They both moaned as his solid length slid from her body, but Simone followed through with her plan. She gently guided him to sit on the couch. His rigid shaft rose in the air, slick and shiny with her juices and as hard as marble.

Simone straddled him, making sure he was fully inside of her, and then started to ride his erect penis. Her legs were spread wide, moving in a rhythmic, ecstatic dance until she reached a second climax, a cry of ecstasy escaping her lips.

Carl followed with a shout of agonized pleasure.

They remained entwined, their bodies locked in an intimate embrace, still connected, their passion evident as traces of their desire dripped onto the couch. There was no rush to separate, as they reveled in the amazing sensations of pleasure and belonging.

Long after they had finished, Carl tenderly kissed her forehead and whispered, "You have no idea how much I love you and how much I crave you all the time. It's like an insatiable hunger that never fades..."

CHAPTER FORTY-THREE

A Missing Girl

Simone didn't awaken the next morning when Carl got ready and left for the city. When she finally did, she found a note on the nightstand.

I love you. Thank you for being the incredible woman you are. I'm a lucky man.

She smiled to herself, the memory of the night before warming her. Simone longed to stay in bed a little longer, letting the morning drift by. Her body still carried the pleasant soreness from their passionate lovemaking—a fiery connection that had, to her surprise, turned into an unexpected second round.

Simone left the room with a smile lingering on her lips, her steps light and confident. She felt ready to face whatever the day had in store for her. In her opinion, a person who has had mind-blowing orgasms isn't looking for a fight—they're grounded, energized, and more than prepared to take on the world with grace and a touch of boldness.

I'd love to teach that to my patients.

She flashed a mischievous grin, amused by the idea of prescribing pleasure as the ultimate remedy for life's stresses.

*****

Simone entered the office front door and removed her coat, still grinning over thoughts of her time with Carl the previous night.

"Someone had a happy, happy evening," Patricia said in a melodic voice.

Simone didn't bother to confirm or deny her secretary's insinuation. Instead, she smiled and shrugged. "Good morning, Patricia. And how about you? Is your cat doing well?"

"Good morning, Doctor. My cat is good." Patricia rose from behind her desk and came over to take Simone's coat, chattering nonstop. "Your woman, Carmen, doesn't exist. There are no records with that name. We've dug into both last names and found nothing. The name you gave me must be incorrect."

Simone had to do a mental readjustment to keep up with her secretary's quicksilver change of mood. *Patricia is back to her no-nonsense, professional persona.*

"Can you tell me more about her? Who is she connected to? My friend needs more information to be able to trace her, because so far, his databases have yielded no results." She slashed a hand through the air. "Zero. Nothing. Nada."

"Databases? Your friend has access to *databases*? Are you referring to nonpublic ones, like government records? Is that even legal?"

Simone had never considered the origins of the information Patricia's contact provided. The possibility of being involved in something illegal caused her to frown with worry.

Patricia laughed, and Simone gave her a startled scowl.

"Sorry, Doctor, but your expression was priceless." Patricia put a hand over her mouth as if to suppress another chuckle. "Let's just say it's better if you don't know who we're talking about or how he does his job, okay? Please, just try to give me more clues about the woman. For example, what does she do for a living?"

"She was Peter Hay's nanny. I think she quit when he was a teenager, so maybe about thirty years ago. I just have this feeling…this woman could be the key to understanding him." She paused for a moment before adding, "And don't forget, Peter's mother was the famous Judge Olivia Taylor Hay."

"Good, now we're getting somewhere," Patricia said as she took out her phone and quickly typed something. "I just sent that information to my friend." She smiled and made her way back to her desk, where she checked her computer screen, gliding her finger across the monitor. Casting a glance at Simone, Patricia smiled. "Your first patient is about to arrive, but you still have time for a coffee. Should I make one for you?"

"No, thanks. I think I'll use the expresso machine in my office. Did you manage to schedule the appointment in MacDougall for today?" Simone wanted to go there and confront Peter about a few things.

"Yes, it's all set. You'll need to leave the office around one. Your meeting with Hay is at two, but you must be back here by four o'clock because I couldn't rearrange your schedule," Patricia replied.

"Thanks a lot Patricia, I need to ask that lunatic a few questions."

Patricia just nodded and left.

Simone walked into her office and gave a satisfied sigh. The familiar space always made her feel at ease, like being welcomed by an old friend. She placed her bag carefully on the desk before heading straight to the espresso machine.

With a practiced hand, she pushed the button and waited patiently as the lights flickered, signaling it was ready. Moments later, the rich, nutty aroma of freshly brewed espresso filled the room.

She took the cup to her lips and savored the first sip as the warmth spread through her. She took her time, appreciating the bold flavor, then placed the empty cup neatly on the tray beside the machine. With a satisfied sigh, she made her way to her favorite spot on the couch and sank into its comforting embrace, ready to take on the tasks of the day.

Another day, different patients, more crazy stories.

I'm not sure I'm in the mood for that today.

But another voice, that of her more responsible side, spoke up, reminding her of her duty.

As a Doctor, your role is to heal people. What you're in the mood to do doesn't matter... I think you're having a midlife crisis. You need to figure out what that void inside you really means.

The idea gnawed at her. Maybe she did need another purpose in life. Her once-rewarding work no longer sparked the joy or fulfillment it once had.

Her thoughts wandered from the deeper questions about her purpose in life to the more immediate matter of her upcoming meeting with Hay that afternoon. What would he reveal this time? Would it lead to answers or only more questions?

Patricia knocked on Simone's door.

Simone glanced up, taking in her secretary's wide-eyed look of alarm.

"What's wrong?"

"There are two policemen here; it appears one of your patients is missing."

A chill ran through Simone, like her blood was freezing inside her veins.

Please, God, not again!

She prayed silently. Before Peter had been arrested, there had been a series of murders involving Simone's patients. She prayed this wasn't the beginning of a similar ordeal.

"Who?"

"Your first appointment for today—Miss. Milford. It seems she vanished about thirty hours ago, and the police have come to see if she might show up."

The girl with rape fantasies... Simone shoved that thought from her mind, refusing to believe there was a connection.

"Let them in please," she said.

Setting her mug on the side table, Simone rose from the couch, bracing herself to meet the officers.

They entered her office, following Patricia.

"Good morning, Officers. Please take a seat."

"How can I assist you?"

She asked, managing a polite smile despite feeling weary of the constant tragedies in her life, yearning for long, boring, event-free days.

"Good morning, Doctor. I'm Officer Klabyn, and this is Officer Odin, we are police officers.

And not the smartest of their kind- their outfits make obvious.

"We've been investigating the disappearance of Keanne Milford. She's been missing for twenty-four hours, and we haven't been able to find any leads as to her whereabouts. We received a copy of her schedule and decided to check with the people she was supposed to see this week. We're hoping she's living her normal life...and maybe she just decided to lie low for a while or something." Officer Klabyn shrugged.

Nothing normal about that one.

Simone bit her lip to keep from saying anything unprofessional. What was going on now?

"She is not here as you can see." Simone waved an arm, indicating the empty office. "She was supposed to meet with me right now, but she hasn't arrived yet."

Simone checked her watch; a five-minute delay was not significant. However, her patients were aware they had fifty minutes of her time. As a result, they typically arrived a few minutes early or precisely on time for their appointments.

"It's unusual for a patient to be late." Simone frowned.

"Doctor, do you have any idea where she might be?" Officer Klabyn asked.

"A friend of hers called to tell us she seems to be missing," Officer Odin said before Simone could answer. "This friend said he went to Ms. Milford's home after not being able to reach her by phone for almost two days. He has a key, so he let himself inside, but no one was there. He said nothing looked out of place, but she didn't leave a note or anything. He found her schedule on her kitchen counter."

Officer Odin huffed and puffed like the big, bad wolf in *The Three Little Pigs*, and his cheeks had turned a deep shade of pink. Was he out of breath or about to have a heart attack?

"I have no idea where she might be. I'm sorry." Simone gave Officer Odin a concerned look. "Can I get you a glass of water, or would you like to take a seat?" She pointed toward a chair.

"Oh, no. Thanks ma'am, but we' re not going to be here that long. We just needed to check with you and see if there's anything you can add to the investigation."

Simone shook her head. "No. There's not. Everything seemed fine during our last session. She hasn't contacted me since then, so I assumed she was okay."

As okay as someone with rape fantasies can be...

Again, Simone held her tongue. She couldn't divulge that

information, anyway…even if she wanted to. Not unless she wanted to lose her license.

But what if the woman is in danger?

Didn't a Doctor have a duty to say something in that type of situation?

"When we got her schedule, we saw she had met with you previously, so we assumed she must be a regular patient. We've already checked with everyone she scheduled appointments with in the last twenty-four hours, and she didn't show up for any of them. You were last on her list for this week." Officer Klabyn's expression had turned grim. "Can you help us with some details about her? Maybe she's told you something that would help us track her down?"

"Unfortunately, I can't provide that information; it's confidential. I would need a court order to disclose anything she told me." Simone paused, debating with her professional conscience. Maintain her duty to secrecy or reveal information that could lead to the girl's whereabouts? If she didn't think they had cause to worry, she would never break her oath, but Miss. Milford had the kind of fantasies that could lead her down a dark and deadly path.

"I don't want you to get into any trouble, but when someone goes missing, the chances of finding that person decrease over time, so it's crucial to act quickly."

Officer Odin sounded upset, and his melancholy expression tore at Simone's resolve.

"Okay." She sighed. "I'll probably regret this, but I think she told me she has a boyfriend—or a close friend who's male, anyway. Let me get his name for you. Maybe he's the guy who went to her apartment and then reported her missing."

Simone moved to her computer and opened Keanne's file, searching for the name of the man she'd mentioned during the previous session…a man who liked rape fantasies almost as much as Keanne did.

"She never mentioned his last name, but she did use his first name. Ah, here it is. Remy."

Simone wrote the name on a Post-it, got up, and handed it to Office Odin.

He accepted the piece of paper, his broad smile illuminating his gratefulness for Simone's assistance.

"Thank you very much, Doctor. This will give us something to investigate. I'm afraid we're about out of other leads. Don't worry, we won't mention your name."

Officer Klabyn nodded and smiled at her, too. Both men seemed grateful she'd agreed to help them.

They should be... I could lose my license for this.

"You're welcome. Both of you."

Simone glanced at her wristwatch and went to the door. She had to prepare for her next patient.

The officers took the hint and followed.

"We'll be on our way now but allow me to leave this with you." Officer Klabyn dug into his shirt pocket and pulled out a business card. "Here you go," he said and handed it to her. "If she contacts you or if you think of anything else that might help us, please do call me."

"Thanks, Doctor, and have a nice day." Officer Odin opened the door and stepped out.

Simone closed the door after them then retrieved her phone from her purse and attempted to reach Keanne, but the call went straight to voicemail.

What happened to her?

Could Keane's disappearance have something to do with her dangerous sexual fantasies? Or was something more sinister going on?

CHAPTER FORTY-FOUR

Are You Sure?

Every time Simone looked at Peter's face, a bad feeling swept through her. Like being choked by a poltergeist, the sensation started at her feet, swirled around her body, and swept upward to wrap around her neck and squeeze. Upon entering the infirmary, she found him there, waiting for her and whistling some nonsensical tune that likely originated from somewhere deep inside his deranged mind. His broad smile did nothing to alter her perception of him; he was the embodiment of evil. Everything about him—his actions, his words, and his thoughts—was aimed solely at causing other people pain.

Although she'd opposed the death penalty her entire life, not due to religious beliefs but because of her oath as a Doctor to protect life, each encounter with the whistling monster made her question her stance. Maybe some people didn't deserve to live. Maybe some people had nothing positive to offer humanity.

I should view him as a victim, a man shaped by his circumstances and molded by the suffering he experienced.

After all, he could be the victim of child abuse. Simone was not sure Peter was solely to blame anymore. His life sentence was deserved, but the roots that led him to that weren't clear.

Maybe I should rethink these visits...I´m starting to believe Peter is a human being.

Simone set her purse beside the chair she intended to sit in, maintaining her distance from Peter. She tried to make herself comfortable in the chair, gathering the courage to initiate what usually turned out to be an unpleasant conversation. However, Peter was quicker to start.

"I've missed you, Doc." A familiar, dark and mocking undercurrent infused his words. "But you seem to prefer visiting my relatives. I can guarantee I'm much more interesting than my incredibly boring sister. What did you want with her, anyway?" He paused and leaned toward Simone conspiratorially. "You know," he continued in a softer voice, "I don't think she's been fucked in decades. You should ask Carl about that..."

His mischievous smile reminded her of a child snitching on his sibling just for the pleasure of seeing them get into trouble.

"Good morning, Peter. Yes, as you already know, I did visit your sister, and as you seem to be omnipresent or omniscient, you must know what we talked about."

"Unfortunately, as you can see," he told her, showing his cuffed hands, "I'm a little tied up right now. I get bits and pieces—a little gossip here, and a little gossip there... So, I count on you to provide all the *spicy* details."

The emphasis he put on the word *spicy* made him sound like a hissing serpent, and he ended his little speech by flashing her another forced smile. Instead of softening his expression, the grin made him look menacing, like the Joker in a Batman movie.

"My visit was part of my research. I'm trying to gain a better understanding of you and your motives," Simone replied, maintaining her professional demeanor despite her growing discomfort.

"You offend me, Doctor." Peter's voice deepened as he shifted into his macho man persona and pointed to himself. "You could have just asked me. Here's a tip for you; I know myself better than anyone else!" Again, the hissing viper surfaced to finish his words.

"I might disagree, Peter. Sometimes, we don't have the slightest idea who we really are. I deal with people all day long who are unaware of their true selves," Simone responded, gently challenging his assertion with her professional insight.

His tone then shifted back to the high-pitched, softer voice he often used when he wanted to appear more amiable or less threatening.

"And what did you and my darling sister talk about?" he asked. His raised eyebrow indicated his curiosity, but his tapping foot spoke of his growing impatience.

"I'm still surprised you don't know what we discussed, considering you seem to know everything," Simone retorted with a hint of sarcasm. "By the way, your house is charming. You must miss it. This place"—she gestured broadly with her arms—"doesn't quite have the same fancy air."

Simone was deliberately provoking him, her words carefully chosen. She leaned back slightly, maintaining a calm and a bit amused expression, daring him to respond.

"Ouch, the cat has claws!" Peter exclaimed, a mix of amusement and mock surprise in his voice. "But yes, Lara knew her job like no one else. My house is beautiful, just as she was—perfect in the way she presented herself."

His gaze swept from Simone's feet to the top of her head, and his expression revealed a clear disdain, or at least, that's what he seemed to want her to perceive.

His intentions are becoming increasingly more transparent.

"I've never met the architect. When all of you stormed into my life, she was already dead, but indeed, her work there was impeccable. A fine choice of a professional." Simone smiled, her composure unshaken by his evident comparison between her and her husband's deceased girlfriend. "However, I didn't see much, just the kitchen and a part of the living room. Your sister and I were too busy discussing your childhood, which seemed quite different from what you've told me..."

Let's wait for his curiosity to surface...

Peter was a skilled poker player, yet he seemed a little off his game today. His foot-tapping had come to a halt, and there was a flicker in his eyes, a brief sharpening that betrayed an emotion. Was it curiosity? Fear? It was hard to discern, but the slight reaction hinted that her words had reached him, stirring something beneath his composed exterior.

Now, we are going to play.

"Different how? She wasn't even around for the most part..." Peter countered, managing to come across as both defensiveness and dismissive at the same time, as if he hoped to undermine the credibility of his sister's account.

"Well, the part about the boarding school," Simone said, her gaze unwavering as she looked at Peter. "She said you never attended, and we discussed your nanny, too, the one you claimed abused you? The woman you said you hated? And yet, your sister kindly informed me that you adored her because she was the only one who could tolerate your mood swings."

She trailed off, leaving the implication hanging in the air, directly challenging his narrative with the contrasting information she had acquired.

"Did I tell you I hated Melinda? When? Are you crazy? I loved her; she was so sweet and took good care of me!" Peter retorted, feigning surprise and confusion. "You're the one sounding crazy here. And what boarding school? I never attended one..."

I know your game, Peter. You're not going to make me believe I'm losing my mind.

"You've never mentioned anyone named Melinda to me. You told me her name was Carmen Di Lucca, remember? When you had me as your so-called guest, you told me about Carmen Di Lucca or maybe Di Lacca... I was a little bit disoriented at the time, so I'm not certain which one."

She held her ground, her expression steady as she pointed out the discrepancy. Peter had never once mentioned the nanny by name—had always referred to her as "the nanny." Yet now, Simone deliberately slipped the name into the conversation, her tone casual but her mind sharp.

She was gambling on his reaction, hoping he'd take the bait and unwittingly confirm the woman's name. The pause that followed felt electric, her heart pounding as she watched him carefully, waiting for the moment he'd either fall into her lie or catch on to her ploy. Either way, the truth was bound to surface.

Peter leaned his head back and laughed heartily.

"Oh, you are good! Nice try. I never mentioned the name of the nanny, but again, nice try! "

His laughter suggested a mix of admiration and mockery, acknowledging Simone's effort to catch him in a lie while also reveling in her inability to pin him down on the details.

He looked at her directly, his normally sparkling green eyes swirling with dark shadows reminiscent of an approaching thunderstorm.

"Who do you think is lying to you? Me or my dear sister?

You're better than this, Simone!"

Simone smiled to herself. He'd demoted her status to plain-old *Simone*. What happened to "Doctor"? Was this an attempt to forge a personal connection and sway her?

Good luck with that!

"Put your brains to work; you've got a fine mind there," he said and pointed to her head, further attempting to flatter and manipulate her into doubting her conclusions.

"So, I should doubt your sister… I should trust the words of a confessed murderer over those of a distinguished former prosecutor, known for her commendable work, who is now grappling with a multitude of issues you've caused? Is that what you are advising me to do?"

"Open your eyes," he said, his voice low yet filled with venom. "Consider those so-called troubles she's facing. She's profiting from my business, and as you saw for yourself, she's living in a splendid house. For the first time, she's free to do whatever she wants. Money is not a concern now. Do you truly believe my sister is the victim here? That she's incapable of lying? Or is it possible she was complicit in my endeavors, and we're merely pretending to despise each other?"

"First and foremost, she's in deep shit because of your actions. She lost her job and is now facing legal cases brought by the victims of your crimes."

"Ask her about the other activities she's been involved with for years."

"What kind of activities?" Simone raised a brow.

Peter stood up slowly and shouted,

"Guards, I'm ready." He then turned to Simone and said, "That's for you to find out, Sherlock Holmes. Perhaps your beloved husband could assist you."

As one of the guards entered the room and approached, he

avoided any eye contact with Simone and simply waited. A moment later, as he walked out, he whispered something to the guard. The man laughed as he escorted Peter from the room.

CHAPTER FORTY-FIVE

Too Real to Handle

Simone buttoned her coat then stepped out onto the front stoop. As she turned the lock to engage the deadbolt on the front door to her office, someone touched her shoulder. Simone jumped, her blood pumping and her heart racing as she turned.

Keanne! The woman had dark circles under her eyes and bruises covered most of her face.

"My God, you almost gave me a heart attack. Are you okay? Where have you been? The police are looking for you. They came here, and I had no idea where you could be! What happened?" Simone spoke quickly, a reflex of her nerves.

"Sorry, Doctor, I didn't mean to worry anyone. I don't have an appointment right now, but can you spare a few minutes? I really need to talk. I need help!"

Tears filled Keanne's eyes, and her trembling lips and obvious anguish worked like a torch, firing up Simone's protective instincts. The girl was so young and seemed so lost. Simone unlocked the door, opened it, and gestured inside.

"Come on in. Let's talk."

Without thinking of removing her coat or turning the heat back up, Simone followed Keanne inside. She pulled her phone from her purse and sent a message to Carl, telling him she'd be late due to a medical emergency with a patient.

"Have a seat. Would you care for some tea? Coffee maybe?"

Simone regretted the offer immediately.

She needs her Doctor, not her mother or a best friend.

"Just a glass of water, please." Keanne sat on the couch next to Simone.

Simone hurried to the minibar hidden inside a cabinet, opened it, and took out a bottle of mineral water. She grabbed a glass and returned to the woman.

"Here you go. I'll let you pour for yourself if you don't mind?"

"Just the bottle, please."

Simone held the bottle out to Keanne, and the girl's hand shook when she took it.

"Thanks," Keane whispered.

Simone picked up the notepad she'd left on the coffee table earlier and then took a seat in her chair opposite Keanne.

"Tell me everything. Why did you disappear?"

Simone studied the girl's face. Keanne had several scratches on her cheeks and one on her upper lip, and a large bruise on her left temple. The rest of the bruises were smaller, but there had to be a half dozen of them. Had she been beaten? The bruises had turned a pale shade of green, indicating that whatever happened must have occurred around the time she disappeared...about ten days earlier.

"I disappeared because I was ashamed of my situation." She lowered her head and continued speaking while staring at her shoes. "My fantasies are out of control, and I'm afraid I'll end up getting hurt if I don't stop, but I can't do it on my own."

Simone looked at the ugly bruise again.

I'd hate to see what she considers getting hurt! What could possibly be more dangerous than the violence she must have submitted to make her look like that?

As Keanne kept her head down and her hands folded on her lap, a single tear rolled down her cheek and dropped onto her leg. Simone reached for the box of tissues she kept on the end table.

"I met a girl at a bar. Her name was Liz. She was nice...a bit wild but funny. We got to talking, and she mentioned she was going to this kinky party, one with public sex. She told me all about it, and I was turned on and asked if I could join her. She hesitated at first and said she didn't think I was ready for something like that. So, in a bid to convince her, I shared my fantasies with her. I figured that would convince her to take me along."

"Did you share your fantasies with someone you just met at a bar?"

Keanne paused and twisted off the cap of the water bottle. She took a long sip.

"Yes, you are right, I didn't think..."

She kept her head down, her hands knotting and unknotting.

She is gathering her courage.

Bracing herself to reveal what she had done or experienced, but the number of marks on her face gave Simone a pretty good idea of what had gone on.

"The party was in a huge mansion, a classy place. I think there were like fifty people there, maybe more." Keanne shrugged and then went on. "Everyone was friendly, dressed sexily, and I felt comfortable. Liz introduced me to the hostess, Ophelia, a middle-aged woman covered in caked-on makeup. Liz told Ophelia she thought I should be one of their girls that night because I had some fantasies that fit... Then Ophelia caressed my shoulder and said, 'If you're ready for a public display of affection from both men and women..."

Keanne altered her voice slightly to mimic the two women, allowing Simone to picture the scene herself.

"Did she explain what this 'public display of affection' entailed?" Simone inquired.

Keanne shook her head. "I won't lie to you, Doctor, I'm addicted to porn, and I thought I knew what to expect."

Again, she shrugged, and Simone made a quick note about her new revelation: a pornography addiction.

"And then what happened?" she asked, resting her pen on the notepad.

"The party was pretty normal...People drinking, chatting, music in the background. But at midnight, when one of those old cuckoo clocks went off, the guests were invited to the basement. The walls were draped in burgundy velvet, and the room had very little lighting. Ropes hung from the ceiling over an old rug." She continued after a small pause.

"There was a circle of chairs around the area with the ropes, and people began to sit down like a bunch of spectators surrounding a stage. Ophelia welcomed everyone and asked, 'Who wants to be the first?'I was already intoxicated by the idea of public sex and the thought of people watching me. Not thinking clearly, I decided to volunteer to go first. Ophelia introduced me to the others. 'A newcomer is ready to experience and provide as much pleasure as we or she can bear,' she said." Again, Keanne changed her voice to a huskier one.

"Ophelia led me to a room where she provided a brief description of what would happen. After I agreed with the terms, she asked me to undress then handed me a silk robe.

Once I was ready, she escorted me back to the stage."

Keanne's voice had dropped to a whisper. She took another sip of water and cleared her throat. Simone waited patiently.

Something ugly is coming...

"Ophelia helped me out of the robe and secured my wrists with one of the suspended ropes. She adjusted another one, wrapping it around my belly in such a way that I was arched, leaving my ass completely exposed. She gave me a safe word and told me to say 'enough' if things escalated beyond my comfort."

Keanne paused again, took another sip of water, and sucked in a few deep breaths before she went on with her story.

"Ophelia picked up a whip and began hitting my buttocks, caressing and praising my ass to the audience between every few strikes. Murmurs of appreciation came from every direction. Ophelia invited the spectators to come closer, and gradually, hands reached out, some gentle, others not so much. Unexpectedly, someone came up behind me and penetrated me, hard and deep and brutally quick. Despite the intense pain and my inability to see who was treating me so callously, I was really turned on. The entire scenario reminded me of my rape fantasy, and I came."

Keanne paused again. Finally finding the courage to lift her head, she looked at Simone.

"If you feel comfortable, please proceed." Simone gave the young woman an encouraging smile.

"As the man behind me continued fucking, another guy positioned himself in front of me and started to hit my face, and not in a kind way."

Simone maintained a neutral expression, but her mind rebelled.

Is there a kind way to hit somebody?

"He used his open hand." She lifted her arm and held up her palm, fingers splayed. "And he hit me *hard.* Someone moved below me and twisted my nipples, and they weren't there to pleasure me. They seemed hell-bent on causing me as much pain as possible. The pounding in my pussy stopped, but a second later, someone entered my ass with no warning and no lube. I was in so much pain; I forgot all about my safe word, and I was helpless to make them stop. Overwhelmed by what I'd allowed to happen to me, at my inability to hide my most secret desires from a room full of strangers, at the humiliation I was suffering I started to cry. It was too much for me."

Keanne's emotions overflowed, and tears streamed down her face as she struggled to regain her composure. Choked by sobs, she attempted to press on with her account.

"Take another drink of water, Keanne. Calm yourself." Simone urged her in a gentle voice, modulating her tone to a soothing cadence to induce calm. "Deep breaths, in and out. You don't need to continue if talking about this causes you pain."

Simone's presence and the simple act of focusing on her breathing seemed to help Keanne to slowly find her equilibrium amidst the turmoil of her emotions. Her breath slowly returned to a normal rhythm.

"I need to tell everything."

That's fine... Continue when you feel ready."

Keanne drew a deep breath, exhaled, and then continued,

"The ordeal seemed endless, and with all the chaos it was hard to tell if anyone noticed my desperation. Before long, I couldn't even cry or scream because a man grabbed me by the hair and stuck his whole penis inside my mouth. Eventually, the relentless activity stopped. I don't know if it was another girl's turn, or if someone realized I was crying and gagging. Someone untied me and led me to the room Ophelia had taken me to earlier. They had to support me while I walked because my legs felt like jelly, and I was as weak as a newborn kitten. I have no idea if the person who helped me was male or female...all I recall is them guiding me with a gentle hand." She cleared her throat.

"I settled onto a bench, and all I remember thinking was how cold the room seemed compared to the heat of my body. As I sat, trying to gather my strength, the world around me felt distant, surreal... Only my soreness seemed real. When I finally lifted my gaze to the mirror, I barely recognized the reflection staring back at me. The evidence of what I'd endured showed in my face, a testament to my recklessness. My cheeks were swollen, my lips were bloodied, and horrible bruises covered my entire body. Blood dripped from between my legs and rolled down both thighs. Every single inch of me hurt. And in the quiet of that room, my injuries were more than skin deep. I don't know... I can't explain!"

"Can you tell me which sensation was most dominant? Pleasure, pain, or shame?"

"Pleasure, and that's what frightens me most. I couldn't go to work for ten days; I got a room in a disgusting motel where I knew no one would find me. The shame came from the exposure, but ultimately, I reveled in the entire experience. I was there in that filthy room"—she pointed behind her, as if Simone could look and see the motel where Keanne had stayed—"and every time I thought about what happened to me, I needed to masturbate! Doctor Bennett, I need to address this issue, or I'll end up finding myself in worse situations. Things are spiraling out of control."

Simone nodded. She completely agreed.

"Your fantasies involving abuse and domination are sexually masochistic in nature. But this wasn't a fantasy. You placed yourself in a real situation where you gave control to those around you. You emerged injured and humiliated, yet it appears you have no boundaries regarding what you permit others to do to you. At some point, this recklessness could lead you into a life-threatening situation."

Just like Lara.

Keanne's story was so similar, and the more she talked, the more Simone thought of her half-sister.

"I had a patient once. His girlfriend was a lot like you, and he wanted to please her... During a masochistic encounter, he unintentionally caused her death. She needed pain... begged him to play the role of her sadist, and in fulfilling that request, he killed the woman he loved."

Keanne's eyes went wide.

"I can't go on like this. I need your help. I don't want to die or to live as a freak!"

Another flood of tears rolled down her face.

"You are not a freak. Fantasies are normal—you just need to understand your real needs and set boundaries so you don't get hurt beyond what you can handle."

"I don't know...I can´t see a way out of this."

"Do you want a way out?"

The girl just nodded and lowered her head.

"I understand that you don't recall any childhood abuse or events that might have shaped those fantasies, but we must explore your past; something significant may have occurred. Perhaps we could consider hypnotherapy to uncover any buried memories. It's common for people who've experienced abuse as children to repress those painful memories. However, the effects linger, regardless of how deeply they're hidden."

*****

Simone drove distractedly, her thoughts moving back and forth between Keanne's erratic behavior—and trying to find ways to assist her—and Peter's revelations about his sister and how his story varied from Deena's account of events. The events Simone had experienced that day, not to mention the fact she should have been home hours ago, weighed on her system, and her head began to pound. She rubbed her throbbing temple with one hand while steering with the other, but the pain didn't subside. Desperate for relief, she pulled off the road and cut the engine. She sat for several minutes, focusing on her breathing, until the pain in her head faded a little, and she regained her composure.

By the time she pulled back onto the road, the pain in her head had disappeared, but she'd only driven a short distance when her thoughts started drifting into disturbing territory once again. The silence in the car felt suffocating. Simone turned on the radio, connected her phone, and synced it with her song library.

The pain in her head had disappeared, but she'd only driven a short distance when her thoughts started drifting into disturbing territory once again. The silence in the car felt suffocating. Simone turned on the radio, connected her phone, and synced it with her song library.

I need some music. It always lifts my spirits.

The clock in her car indicated her husband should be off work. She needed to call him, to hear his voice and allow him to distract her from the whirlwind of disturbing thoughts. She touched the car's multimedia screen and selected her husband's number, affectionately saved as "My Love."

"Hello, my beautiful, workaholic wife."

Carl's deep voice gave her chills, and the way he wrapped each word in warmth and affection made her smile.

"Tell me you're home, lounging on the couch in your pajamas, and I will gladly accept the title."

He laughed hard.

"No, honey, I guess we'll have to share it. I'm still at the office. My back is aching from sitting all day, and my eyes are red, hardly a charming sight. I'm feeling my age, babe, and seriously, I think I should scale back my activities. Maybe it's time we took a trip somewhere beautiful, just you and me." He sang the last few words.

"Not a bad idea; let's think about it. I'm feeling the weight of fatigue and age on my back, too."

And in my feet, and my shoulders, and especially in my head...

"Can you talk about the emergency? Someone try to off themselves, or just the usual craziness?"

She might've bristled at his words about her patients in the past, but she'd come to recognize the insanity of her job a long time ago.

"You remember that patient who vanished? Well, she popped up out of thin air in front of my office just as I was locking up. Nearly scared me half to death! I had to take her inside and talk to her. She was in a mess, way beyond anything you'd imagine."

"I do remember, and babe, you work in a madhouse. Seriously, I can't wrap my mind around how you deal with all that craziness. You're my hero."

"Well, your hero just wants to come home to a hot bubble bath and a foot massage... But I'm out of bubbles, and I'm too tired to stop somewhere and buy some, and my favorite masseur is away. So, it looks like I'm stuck with taking a quick shower and going straight to bed."

"Sounds like my night, too, minus the dog walking part. Still gotta take the pooch out before I can even think about hitting the sack."

"Hey, don't call my best friend a pooch!"

"I thought I was your best friend."

They continued talking until Simone arrived home. She

treasured their nightly exchanges; they might have been casual and silly sometimes, but they filled her with warmth. Their conversations provided a slice of normalcy and the comfort that came from belonging to someone in the vastness of life's routine.

CHAPTER FORTY-SIX

So Soon?

The following morning, Simone entered the front door of her office building, her thoughts already on the day ahead.

"Good morning, Doctor," Patricia said as she came down the hall from the direction of the kitchen.

Is she psychic? How does she always know the moment I come in the door?

"I heard you pull in," Patricia added, as if she'd heard Simone's thoughts.

Simone smiled and accepted the steaming mug of coffee her secretary offered.

"Thanks a lot, Patricia. I really need a shot of caffeine right now."

She took a sip of the hot, fragrant brew, closing her eyes in delight. Patricia must have learned how to use the espresso machine... This was no regular coffee.

"I have good news and bad news. We managed to find Hay's nanny; her name is Carmen Luccese. She's quite elderly, a real old bat, and she's currently living in an expensive retirement home."

"What's the bad news?" Simone steeled herself.

"The bad news is, she's dealing with an advanced case of Alzheimer's disease."

"Damn, how can a woman with Alzheimer's communicate effectively? There's no way we can talk to her. Can your people try to locate any relatives?" Simone scowled, struggling to keep her composure. What dumb luck! All her attempts to investigate Peter had ended with her hitting a brick wall.

"We're working on that, but we still don't have anything concrete. My guy visited the home she's staying in, and it's quite nice and kind of fancy, which raised red flags pretty much immediately. After all, a retired nanny can't afford to live like a queen, right? So, he hacked into the clinic's computer system and discovered an interesting fact... The clinic's records list the Hay family as responsible for her nearly fifteen-year stay. He couldn't access the bank accounts to trace the source of the funds; he lacks the necessary technology."

Simone struggled to process all the information at one time.

Hacked into the computer system? That's a crime. The Hays have been paying for the care of someone who supposedly abused Peter? Totally bizarre. Maybe Deena is right and Carmen never abused Peter.

Simone shook her head.

"I don't want to know if your guy is hacking into computer systems, okay? If he does stuff like that, just don't tell me, Patricia."

Which won't exactly guarantee me a Nobel Prize for being a good person, but at least, I'll have plausible deniability.

Patricia's lips twitched as if she was trying not to smile.

"Hacking? What is hacking? I have no idea." Her tone had a mischievous quality, and she shook her head firmly, only to follow up with several nods.

She's a terrible liar!

But she'd still done a lot to help Simone with her investigation.

"Keep up the good work, Patricia. You're doing a great job, and I really appreciate it! Let's talk about your friend's billing hours, okay?"

"He already told me how much you owe; it's right here." She turned to her desk, picked up a Post-it note, and handed it to Simone. "Sorry, but it's not the kind of thing he can send an e-mail about. Can't leave a paper trail…"

I ask myself why…

Simone sighed, glanced at the number on the note, and then handed it back to Patricia.

"It's a fair price. I'll transfer the money to you, and you can pay him. Will that work?"

"That's fine."

Simone glanced at her watch. "I'll do the transfer, but then I need to review patient files before their appointments today."

"I've placed today's files on your desk. The Millers are up first."

"Thanks, Patricia," Simone replied, only half-listening as she went down the hallway to her office, her thoughts drifting to Carmen Luccese.

Settling onto her couch for a moment, still clutching her purse, Simone thought about what Peter had said about his former nanny. Deena was right; Peter was lying. The realization irked her. *Damn liar!*

*****

What sounded like a heated exchange brought Simone out of her thoughts. She tilted her head and listened. The raised voices of three individuals, one unmistakably Patricia, came from out near the front entrance, and then abruptly, the office fell silent. Rising from the couch, Simone placed her purse on her desk, took a deep breath to compose herself, and then picked up the receiver and punched in Patricia's extension.

"What is going on, Patricia?"

"Nothing to worry about. Just a little discussion between a couple. I'm sending them to the waiting room." Patricia whispered her response.

Simone set the phone down on her desk, walked over to the connecting door, and opened it. Chivon and Benjamin stumbled through the door to the adjoining room, nearly colliding with each other as they both tried to enter at the same time.

"You clueless man, don't you know it's customary for women to go first?" Chivon snapped.

"That's precisely the courtesy I've extended to you since the day we met. I always allow you to go first—or should I say *come* first!" He raised and lowered his eyebrows comically.

The undertone of their bickering was unmistakably intimate and sex-related, and Simone had to suppress a chuckle. Suddenly, she recalled a detail from her earlier conversation with Patricia, a detail Simone had conveniently overlooked. The Millers—a couple—had booked Simone's first appointment of the day.

As they attempted to sit down, Chivon and Benjamin simultaneously chose the same spot on the couch, sparking yet another squabble over seating arrangements.

"Good morning, Chivon... Benjamin." Simone greeted them with a nod as she entered the room and took a seat. She spoke in a measured tone, but a hint of irony laced her words. She allowed herself a deliberate pause before continuing. "What a pleasant surprise to see you both here...at the same time." Simone hoped one or both might be able to tell by her tone that she was being sarcastic.

Her patients had managed to sit without bowling each other over, and Simone looked back and forth between them, waiting for someone to respond.

Finally, Benjamin gestured between himself and Chivon.

"We're married! And we believe our marriage is already facing challenges, so we decided it would be best to visit you together."

"Congratulations to you both, but let's establish something here. First, you're not 'visiting' me; this is a Doctor's appointment, not a social call." Simone turned to Chivon. "Second, when did you get married? The last time you were here, Chivon, by *yourself*, you mentioned considering marriage, but it seemed far from decided."

Benjamin crossed his legs and leaned toward Simone.

"You see, I proposed, she accepted, and neither of us are children. We didn't see the point in a prolonged engagement filled with unnecessary delays… So, we got a license, paid a visit to the JP, and got hitched!"

With a hint of pride, Benjamin extended his hand toward Simone to display his wedding ring, then he gently grasped Chivon's hand and lifted it. A giant diamond adorned her ring finger, sparkling in the overhead light.

Simone considered pointing out that the purpose of an engagement was to allow couples to truly get to know each other. However, considering how quickly she'd gotten married, she opted to hold her tongue.

"How long have you been married?" Simone asked,

"Today is our ten-day anniversary," Benjamin replied with a smile.

"And what makes you believe you're already in need of couples' counseling?" What problems could they be having so early in their marriage?

As the newlyweds turned to each other and began to speak simultaneously, their words overlapping into an incomprehensible cacophony, Simone cleared her throat.

"Okay, let's put a halt to that!" Simone spoke firmly, determined to regain control and facilitate a productive session. "From now on, you'll speak one at a time and only when prompted. Otherwise, we won't be able to proceed. Remember, this is a professional office, not a local bar."

Her voice carried a commanding tone that brooked no argument. The couple appeared chastened, at least for the moment, and they resumed their seats on the couch like scolded children. They faced her, their eyes wide and startled.

"Now that we've established some ground rules, let's begin," Simone said, turning her attention to Chivon. "Chivon, could you share what's on your mind?"

As Benjamin scooted forward in his seat and started to speak, Simone raised her hand, signaling for him to wait as she shifted her body toward Chivon.

"It's simple," Chivon said in a tight voice. "Since he placed this ring on my finger, he's been trying to control every aspect of my life. He demands to know where I'm going, who I'm with, when I'll return, and even why I need to go."

As she spoke, her hands moved expressively, punctuating her rapid words with gestures that underscored her irritation.

After Chivon concluded, Simone turned to Benjamin, giving him the floor.

With a flushed face, he pointed at Chivon.

"That woman doesn't understand the meaning of marriage. She acts entirely as she pleases, showing no regard for my position. She constantly causes me worry, coming and going without any explanation. She fails to recognize the kind of man she's married to and the dangers she's exposing herself to by walking around alone and refusing the protection of a bodyguard. I'm at my wits' end; I don't know what to do!" He raised his hands in the air.

Simone, aiming to cut through the tension and reach the heart of the matter, glanced at Chivon and then at Benjamin.

"All right, you two... Let's start with a fundamental question; do you both still love each other?"

As Simone spoke, she couldn't help but think about how absurd this was, given the couple's brief marriage.

"I'm crazy about her, but she drives me insane!" Benjamin admitted, his voice softening to reveal the underlying affection amidst his frustrations.

"How about you, Chivon?"

"I've never loved anyone the way I love Benji, but he's obsessively controlling!" Despite her criticism, it was evident that beneath her cool exterior, Chivon harbored genuine feelings for the man she'd married.

Benjamin moved closer to his wife, gently placing an arm around her shoulders. He leaned in close. "I love you," he whispered in her ear.

"I love you more."

Encouraged by Chivon's immediate response and the couple's display of affection, Simone smiled.

"You have the perfect foundation to make this marriage work. Now, let's address your issues. You say you love each other, and it certainly appears genuine, so you can work through your differences." Simone pointed from one to the other. "First and foremost, Benjamin, you must realize that Chivon has spent her entire life alone, fending for herself, and she never had to give anyone any explanations. You can't expect her to change overnight, can you?"

He shook his head but remained silent, so Simone went on.

"She needs time to adjust, to learn how to share her life with someone else. Trust is something that can't be forced; it must be cultivated over time. You're trying to lock a wild fox in a cage. If you persist, the only outcome you'll achieve is fostering resentment and unhappiness."

Chivon's small smile indicated she agreed with Simone.

Turning to Chivon, Simone gave the woman a firm stare.

"As for you, Chivon, it's important to understand that marriage comes with certain responsibilities. One of those obligations concerns keeping your partner informed of your whereabouts—not because he wants to limit your freedom, but because he needs to know you're safe, especially since you've declined a bodyguard and, given your husband's wealth, there are inherent risks involved with you going off alone. You could easily become a target. A simple phone call to let him know where you're going and that you've arrived safely at your destination is not an infringement upon your independence; it's a gesture of respect and consideration all marriage partners deserve."

Chivon lowered her head.

I hope that´s a sign she recognizes her responsibilities...

"If you've both chosen to build a life together, it's crucial to understand that boundaries and cooperation matter for both of you." Simone pointed at Chivon and then Benjamin. "Forcing your will on each other won't earn you anything but an unpleasant divorce. Think of your marriage as a boat; if you work together, you can reach the shore. But if you paddle in opposite directions, you'll end up going nowhere."

The nods of agreement and the silence that followed made Simone feel like a teacher giving a lecture to a very small class of students. The sensation grew stronger when Benjamin raised a finger.

"You can talk, Benjamin." Simone suppressed a smile.

"I understand what you're saying. My challenge is that I'm accustomed to giving orders, and I'm not sure how to change that approach."

"And Chivon is a fighter by nature. She's a lawyer. Remember, your marriage isn't a corporation or a courtroom —it should be a sanctuary where love and peace prevail. It must be your solid rock. The answer is both simple and challenging: learn to express what's in your heart. Talk to each other, don't dictate—"

"That's what I did, and she didn't like it."

God, give me patience.

"Please don´t interrupt me, Benjamin. Let me finish. When you speak, it's not just what you say, but how you say it. It's one thing to ask, 'Where are you going now? Why? Who's going with you?' Those kinds of questions, especially delivered in a bossy tone, sound confrontational. But if you approach her with concern...if you say something like, 'Chivon, I'm worried about you. You're out alone—could you share where you're headed? Is it safe?' it opens the door for communication rather than conflict. Tone of voice is also important."

For several moments, no one spoke. Simone cleared her throat again and looked back and forth between her two patients.

"Changing lifelong habits is indeed challenging," Chivon said, finally voicing her thoughts, in a soft tone of voice. "Every time he asks me where I'm going, it's as if my mother has reentered my life. I struggled to gain independence from her and escape her claws for years." She curled her fingers into the shape of talons and made a sour face that conveyed her deep distaste for her mother's controlling ways.

Mommy issues, again and again.

"It seems that's a trigger for you, Chivon. Perhaps your

mother demanded too many explanations, and obviously, you hated that, and Benjamin's manner of questioning revives those feelings. That's why it's so important for both of you to learn new ways to communicate."

"It's interesting how well we communicate when we're making love..." Benjamin rolled his eyes.

And I remember a man who was very upset about the sexual explorations his girlfriend had introduced into their lovemaking.

"That's a significant point." Simone nodded. "Understanding boundaries and being open to exploration are key when it comes to thriving in that aspect of a relationship, too."

They both nodded again but neither commented.

"You had the chemistry but lacked balance, so you worked to build it on a foundation of trust and exploration. The same principle applies to other aspects of your relationship. You love each other. By letting each other know what you enjoy and what you dislike, you can find equilibrium. Life, much like intimacy, revolves around respect and learning to understand each other's needs."

They continued discussing the intricacies and challenges of marriage, and eventually, the couple left Simone's office hand in hand, completely at peace with each other. For now, anyway. As they left, Patricia opened the door, peeked her head into Simone's office, and waved a long, rectangular piece of paper back and forth.

Simone stared. "What is that?"

"It's a check." Patricia grinned. "I'm not sure what you did, but he just covered a month's worth of office expenses. He said you deserve every penny."

Huh...

By "he", Simone figured Patricia meant Benjamin.

Well, maybe treating couples isn't that bad after all...

*****

When office hours ended, Simone sat on the couch for a few minutes and reveled in her sense of peace and gratitude. It was truly satisfying to see her office bustling again, to know that her patients, both returning and new, appreciated her work and that she was genuinely able to help people rediscover their sense of normalcy, whatever that might mean for each person.

More than ever, Simone understood that normalcy wasn't a concrete reality but rather a state of mind where individuals could find peace with who they were. Coexisting in society, then, meant navigating this understanding and finding harmony within oneself and with others.

Simone stood up, walked over to her desk, and placed the last patient's file in the wire basket. She then meticulously organized her pens, pencils, and anything else she'd used during the day. The sight of her orderly desk filled her with immense satisfaction. She chuckled to herself.

My OCD is getting worse. I should see Doctor Edgar about that.

Simone opened her planner and wrote a note to herself. *Make an appointment with Edgar.*

A knock sounded on her door, and then Patricia stepped inside carrying a tray of mugs filled with something steaming hot. Simone snapped out of her reverie and gave her secretary an inquiring look. For the first time, there were two cups of tea on the tray. Had Patricia taken the liberty of inviting herself to a "tea party" with her boss.

That's not like her.

"Sorry, Doctor, I brought my cup, too. Here's yours," Patricia said as she handed Simone the cup and saucer. "You deserve some tea, and we have news on Hay."

"No need to apologize, Patricia. Have your tea with me. Let's sit down." Simone gestured toward the couch.

Patricia raised her brows, as if surprised, but said nothing as she placed the small tray on the coffee table and took a seat on the couch. She picked up her teacup.

"The Hay family estate hasn't been funding Carmen Luccese's treatment in the Autumm Clinic. The money comes from an office; the account books report "NYC office on behalf of the Hays family," and there's more...

CHAPTER FORTY-SEVEN

A Pink Note and Hot Surprises

Patricia's news consumed Simone for the rest of the day. She almost called her husband but knew Carl—whether he knew anything or not—was too ethical to discuss any client, past or present. To keep the peace, she let it go—for now, she'd have to find another way to learn the truth.

*****

Simone went about her work in the office the next day, attending to patients while Patricia arranged another meeting with Peter. However, it appeared Peter would not be available until Monday. Something related to bad behavior.

Edward didn't want to meet with her, and Simone had no desire to meet him in jail, either, yet who else could she talk to? Their communication was a dance of shadows and whispers. Letting him know she wanted to visit him would serve as a veiled message that she needed to speak with him. Ed would understand her silent signal and realize she needed his help.

Around noon, Simone received the confirmation she'd guessed correctly. Her ringing phone showed a call from an unidentified number, and her pulse rate spiked.

"Go to the plaza for lunch; it's an invitation from the doctor."

Simone didn't recognize the voice of the male who delivered the instructions, but she took her purse and hurried to the front door.

Patricia sat at her desk in the reception area.

"I'm leaving for lunch," Simone told her as she crossed the room. "I'll be back shortly."

"Enjoy your meal, Doctor," Patrica said without looking up from the novel she was reading.

Simone made her way to the square. She settled on her usual bench, and within a few minutes, Edward emerged from behind the trees.

"Good afternoon, Simmie." He handed her a sandwich. "I figured you wouldn't have time to eat."

"Good afternoon, and thank you, Ed." She accepted the sandwich but placed it beside her on the bench. Aware of their limited time, Simone couldn't waste a second on food. "I have some news," she said quickly. "I've managed to locate Peter's nanny. She has Alzheimer's and is living in a high-end retirement home. Peter covered her expenses for years. Not only that, up until his arrest, he visited her at least once every ten days. Staff at the home assumed they were relatives because he was always so kind and attentive toward her, even when she didn't recognize him. So, the narrative about her abusing him doesn't hold up."

The revelation seemed to hang between them for a moment, laden with implications. Edward's expression shifted subtly, a mix of surprise and calculation passing over his features. Simone presumed that this piece of the puzzle could unlock new avenues in his quest for truth.

"It seems I can't keep you out of trouble, but that information will help me a lot. I'm also making progress in my quests, but for your own protection, I can't share details with you, Simmie." He touched her nose with his finger. "Please give me the name and address of the place and let me and the FBI handle it from here. I know you won't stop digging but just play it safe. I'd never forgive myself if anything were to happen to you, especially after all the trouble I've caused already."

Edward's plea, laced with determination and vulnerability, highlighted the depth of their connection and the gravity of the situation they found themselves in. The concern in his gaze tore at her resolve to keep a wall between them. He ran his finger gently across her face, his eyes mirroring the enduring love he still had for her.

Simone looked down and reached for her purse. She took out her phone, a pencil, and the small block of Post-it notes she always carried. After double checking the name and phone number of the care home she'd programmed into her phone earlier, she scribbled the information down on one of the notes. Simone handed the folded piece of paper to Edward and said,

"Be careful. My instincts tell me there's much more beneath the surface than we can see. Peter is more demented than we thought."

"My experience tells me you're right," Edward said, taking the note and slipping it into his jeans pocket. "Peter tried to attack one of the interns this weekend. The regular Doctor at the facility saw he was in a psychotic crisis, that he mistook the guy for a former boyfriend or something along those lines. I couldn't dig much deeper." He shrugged. "Have to go now, Simmie."

Edward stood up, gave Simone a quick peck on the cheek, and left her sitting there.

As he disappeared into the landscape from which he had emerged, the silence enveloped Simone once again, granting her only the solitude of her thoughts.

Why does my heart ache so much whenever I meet with him?

Every encounter left her with an overwhelming urge to cry.

Simone decided to eat before going back to her practice. She unwrapped the sandwich he had given her, and a lump formed in her throat. Crazy, how the little things could bring on the tears. The sandwich was one of her favorites, authentic French street food… The bun overflowed with goat cheese, Iberic ham, and Italian tomatoes. She brought it close and sniffed, and her mouth watered.

Where did he get this?

As Simone bit into the sandwich, the rich flavors momentarily diverted her from the consuming thoughts of the complex web of events they were entangled in.

*****

Even though she thrived on a busy schedule, Simone had begun trying to keep her Friday afternoons free so she could travel to the city and spend time with her husband, a source of balance and happiness in her life.

During her previous relationships, Simone had never considered reducing her patient load to make more time for her personal life. This realization brought a twinge of guilt, as she reflected on the changes she was willing to make now for her husband that she hadn't contemplated before.

You've been a bad girlfriend.

Patricia drove Simone to the station and dropped her off. Since Patricia had purchased the ticket for Simone earlier, she went directly to the platform where the train was waiting for passengers. She found her car, boarded, and settled into her window seat.

As they left the station, Simone reclined in her seat and gazed out the window, watching the scenery pass by. A sense of calm washed over her as the rhythmic sound of the train on the tracks provided a soothing backdrop. She reached into her bag and pulled out the notepad with her notes on Edward's investigation.

Ever since Simone had begun assisting Edward with his investigation, she had taken to meticulously jotting down every detail about the case in a journal. Her list of discoveries, made both independently and through their collaboration, had grown extensive. Despite Edward's reluctance to share information with her directly, Simone managed to gather insights simply by listening to him talk.

The brief journey to New York City provided an opportunity for Simone to piece together the intricate puzzle of the Peter Hay case. She meticulously reviewed all her notes, revising and underlining points she believed were essential to discuss with Ed. The rhythmic clatter of the train served as a comforting backdrop as she focused intently on her work, barely noticing the time passing by.

As she heard the train approaching the station, she closed the notepad and sent a message to her husband. Even though she was aware he couldn't leave the office yet and that she'd have to take a cab to his apartment, she wanted to reassure him that she was safe and back in the city.

Finding a cab this time of the day on a Friday always proved to be a challenge and today was no different. Simone opted for the subway and headed to Saks. She needed to pick up a few items for a surprise she had planned for her husband.

After a quick shopping spree at the enormous store—and a small battle for a cab—Simone finally caught one to Laight Street, stopping at her favorite deli on the way.

*****

As the sound of the apartment lock clicked, Simone was fully prepared to welcome her husband. She had lit all the scented candles she'd picked up at the store, creating a mysterious atmosphere. She sat on the couch, posing in a way that was sure to catch his attention. Especially dressed as she was in a black corset accentuated by a garter belt worn over a thong, and lace, thigh-high stockings. She looked amazing, if she did say so herself. Her slim body was a testament to her dedication to running.

I feel sexy and powerful.

"Don't turn on the lights, please," she said, using a deep, sultry tone. "The candlelight should be enough for you to see to make your way here."

Leaving the couch, she strode across the room in her impossibly high heels to fill two crystal glasses with ice-cold champagne. She turned and, champagne in hand, went to meet her husband as he stepped into the room.

"Enjoy your champagne but don't do anything else," she said, handing him a flute.

Carl set his briefcase on the coffee table, took the glass of champagne, and looked at her without uttering a word. He stood in the middle of the living room, holding his glass, his gaze roaming over her from head to toe.

She circled to stand behind him, leaning in to kiss his neck and tracing a path across his sensitive skin with her lips, tongue, and nails. His soft moan signaled that she was on the right track. Simone then moved around to face him, balancing her flute in one hand as she lifted her face to his, seeking his lips. With her other hand she began to work at opening his shirt, the tension between them heightening as they lost themselves in the moment.

Simone dipped her index finger into the champagne glass, moistening it, and then ran the wet finger across his lips. Just as she was about to replace her finger with her lips, Carl caught her hand and drew her finger into his mouth, sucking gently until she moaned. Slowly, she withdrew her finger, replaced it with her mouth, and softly licked his lips with her tongue.

"Someone missed me," Carl whispered.

Simone caressed him over his pants.

"I've missed you both so much."

Her confidence grew as she became increasingly at ease in her role as a seductress.

All I need to do is dress like a sexy woman, and suddenly, I become that woman.

She embraced the transformative power of her attire and attitude.

"You seem different tonight," Carl said, his voice laced with desire.

Simone placed her glass on the coffee table and gently pushed him back onto the sofa. His shirt hung open, revealing his well-defined torso. The noticeable outline in his pants confirmed that her efforts had been successful. A sense of satisfaction washed over her as she admired him, feeling the chemistry between them intensify. She leaned closer, brushing her fingers teasingly along his chest, savoring the moment they were creating together.

"I'm your fantasy tonight," she told him.

Simone positioned Carl's hands above his head and secured them with his tie. The knot wasn't complex; he could free himself if he chose to. But this gesture was symbolic—it was about asserting control and dominance, about her owning the moment.

Encouraged by his moan, she grew bolder. She kneeled near him, unbuckled his belt, unzipped his pants, and carefully slid them off, along with his shoes. There he was, bathed in the soft glow of candlelight, wearing just his boxer briefs, which seemed like they might burst at any moment. His eyes were fixed on her, full of desire, as if devouring her presence.

Simone stood up and selected one of the candles. They were specifically designed for massage, ensuring the wax wouldn't burn the skin. Carefully, she tipped the candle over Carl's chest and drizzled the warm wax over his pecs. He moaned deeply in response.

Simone kneeled next to him on the sofa once more and gently took one of Carl's nipples into her mouth, teasing it with her tongue before deciding to experiment with a not-too-gentle bite. This was something she'd never tried, but she was curious to discover what he enjoyed.

"Oh, my God, that's good!" His response provided all the feedback she needed. Encouraged by his reaction, she repeated the process on the other nipple, simultaneously massaging the first one with her fingers.

In a bold move, Simone lowered her corset, exposing her breasts. She began to rub her against his chest, brushing his nipples with hers. He moaned deeply and shrank away, leaning into the back of the couch. Simone lifted her head and looked at him, concerned.

"Stop, or I won't be able to hold back any longer, and I'll pop the champagne before it's time."

Carl freed himself from the tie and cupped one of Simone's breasts in his hand. His tongue followed, circling one nipple while he gently pinched the other between his fingers.

"Pinch it harder!"

He obeyed her command and, while pinching her nipple, slid his free hand inside her panties. She was thoroughly wet, ready to welcome his caress.

"Touch yourself. I want to watch," he said.

The request made her a bit shy, but she chose to embrace her bolder side. Standing with her legs slightly apart, she lowered her panties to the middle of her thighs and began to caress her clit. Meanwhile, he inserted another finger inside her, moving it rhythmically in and out.

Her orgasm hit her like a burst of light, and she cried out as sensations surged through her body. Lost in the moment, she didn't notice Carl withdraw his fingers and replace them with his cock until he began to thrust deeply and strongly inside her. His thrusts brought her fully into the moment. They were standing, making love in a position they had never tried before, her back against the wall, and she had no idea how she had ended up in that spot.

The violent strokes were slightly painful yet immensely pleasurable, and as the crescendo of their movements overwhelmed them, they climaxed together. Simone dug her nails into Carl's back for support. He carried her to the sofa, their bodies still entangled and pulsating with the aftershocks of pleasure. The air was thick with the scent of their passion, their skin slick with sweat.

As their breathing steadied, Carl withdrew from Simone and gently positioned her head on his shoulder as he caressed her hair.

"Woman, you're going to kill me this way," he murmured.

Simone felt a surge of pride, her pleasure mingling with a sense of victory. She settled comfortably in Carl's lap, and they remained there in silence, soaking in the aftermath of their lovemaking. The flickering candlelight cast shadows around them, enveloping them in peaceful relaxation.

I can be better than her.

The sudden thought came out of nowhere and abruptly pulled Simone out of the moment.

"I'm starving. Let's order something, okay? I bought a cheese board from the deli so we can have an appetizer while we wait," she said. With that, she got off his lap and stood up, her playful attitude not fading.

"Yes, honey, because I don't know if I have the strength to even make it to the bathroom, let alone leave the apartment tonight. But first, let me just look at you."

Carl's soft voice reassured her she had completely satisfied her man, and she smiled a bit shyly at his request.

He held her hand and ran his appreciative gaze from her head to her toes. "You are the most beautiful wife a humble husband could ever imagine. It's like living a dream to come home after a hard week of work and find a goddess waiting to please me."

Simone smiled, satisfied yet aware that her true self was signaling it was time to change clothes and leave the character behind.

"Let´s take a shower."

She pulled him up from the couch, and he rose reluctantly.

"Yes, go ahead," he replied. "I'll order the food and then take Tommy for his walk. He's scratching at the door as if he wants to break it down."

Simone headed to the bathroom. She removed her clothes and turned on the shower, only to realize there was no soap. Leaving the water running, she returned to the drawer where she kept the toiletries. She chose an almond-scented soap she loved, but as she picked it up, she noticed the corner of what looked like a photo peeking out from beneath the other products.

She pulled it out, and her heart nearly stopped.

*****

Simone's gaze darted between the image of Carl and the unfamiliar Asian girl seated comfortably on his lap. The girl's tiny eyes were wide open, her lips pressed together, radiating a sense of innocence that only intensified Simone's discomfort. A cold wave of realization washed over her. Every detail in the photo—Carl's carefree smile directed at someone just out of view, the ease with which the stranger perched on his lap, and one of his hands casually holding her waist—pierced Simone like a jolt. The intimacy captured in that moment was undeniable, leaving her heart racing and her mind spiraling with questions.

With the photo in her trembling grasp and her heart pounding, Simone contemplated her next steps. The sound of running water in the background became a harsh reminder of the reality crashing down around her. She needed answers, but confronting Carl seemed increasingly daunting. Deep inside, she knew it wasn't the best option. Quietly, she placed the photo back inside the drawer, tucking it under the soap.

Steeling herself, Simone stepped into the shower. The water cascaded over her, but she barely felt the warmth as her thoughts raced. She spent a long time under the spray, needing to calm her nerves and settle her mind. Finally, she turned off the water and wrapped herself in a towel. The image of the photo was etched in her mind. As she dried off, she wrestled with what to do next, each option more troubling than the last.

Simone chose a comfortable bathrobe from the cabinet under the sink, quickly slipped into it, and took the photo out of the drawer. She slid the picture inside the robe's deep pocket just as Carl entered the bathroom.

He smiled and kissed her forehead.

"I'm going to take a shower now," he said. "Our food should be here soon. I ordered your favorite Thai. Will you please answer the door if it gets here before I'm done?"

Distracted and disturbed, she answered without thinking. "Yes, I can."

As she was about to step out and close the bathroom door behind her, Carl called out from inside the shower.

"You were so perfect tonight. I think we were made for each other. We fit together so well. Love you, babe. Thanks for the surprise."

She barely turned her head, her response mechanical. "Love you." Her heart felt heavy as she stepped out, her mind a whirl of confusing thoughts.

*****

That evening, dinner passed in silence. Simone's mind raced as she tried to decide what to do next. In the past few months, she had seen a bunch of photos featuring Asian teenagers engaged in what appeared to be illicit activities—potentially prostitution and drug use.

She had never imagined her husband could be the type of man to use the services of a prostitute. As far as she knew, he wasn't like that.

Really? How long have I known this man?

She recalled how he used to frequent swing clubs. Would anyone else be able to tell he'd participated in activities like that just by looking at him? Simone weighed her options carefully. The idea of doing nothing went against every fiber of her being, and a persistent whisper urged her to act. The girl in the photo with Carl had been alive, but the victims in the other pictures hadn't been. Meddling in potentially dangerous affairs could mean taking deadly risks.

I'm going to leave this to the police; I've already given them the pictures I had. I'm not getting any deeper into this mess.

She needed to talk to someone, but who? Ed harbored a strong dislike for Carl and could be biased. She could go back to the police station where she had dropped off the other photos, or maybe the FBI, since they were handling the case now. But Ed's former girlfriend Carla was the only contact Simone had there, and she highly doubted Carla would be involved in this specific case. Each option swirled in Simone's head as she tried to decide the best course of action.

"You handle spicy food marvelously, but tonight, it seems to have scorched your tongue. Or is something on your mind? You've been quiet for over half an hour. Is something wrong, honey?"

Carl's words snapped her back to reality. She was at the table, eating, and she needed to focus before he grew suspicious. Caught off guard, she was unsure of how to respond. She quickly fabricated a plausible excuse.

"Sorry, honey, I'm just really concerned about a patient. He called while you were in the shower, and I'm worried he might be a suicide risk. I managed to calm him down, but I'm still trying to assess the danger and figure out what to do next. Maybe I should go back to the office for an emergency appointment or something." She looked directly into Carl's eyes, using all her poker face skills so he would believe her.

Carl stood and moved to stand behind her. He gently kissed the top of her head.

"Or maybe you could be available for an online call with him, and stay here with your needy husband just for the weekend..." He whispered in her ear.

"Yes, you're right. I'll let him know I'm available for any support he needs so we can enjoy our weekend together."

As if I wouldn't have done that already if someone really needed me.

Her voice in her head sounded sarcastic and angry.

Excusing herself, she stood and walked over to her purse and retrieved her cellphone. She quickly typed a message to Patricia.

I need to talk to Doctor Reynolds on Monday. Please check if I can visit him at MacDougall.

*****

For the remainder of the weekend, Simone went through the motions, her actions mechanical, though Carl seemed not to notice. To avoid confronting her feelings directly, she filled their days with numerous activities—visiting the theater, attending a ballet performance, and going out for dinner—ensuring they were rarely alone and reducing the need for intimate conversation.

Simone had planned to leave Monday morning, but Sunday afternoon, she fabricated a phone call from her distressed patient and then told Carl she needed to return early. The image of that damn photo kept filling her mind, and she felt on the brink of saying or doing something she might regret. Carl didn't argue; he seemed to understand her concern was too great to ask her to stay.

Carl drove her to the station, with the city's Sunday afternoon traffic still calm. They enjoyed the drive, listening to music and talking about their plans for the upcoming week. In front of the train station, Carl found a spot to pull over and park for a moment. Turning to her, he held her hand, leaned close, and kissed her tenderly.

Just before she stepped out of the car, he said, "I love you to the moon and back. Never doubt that, my love."

"Love you, too."

She responded quietly, speaking through her teeth as she left the car. She needed some time away from Carl to think things over and find clarity.

*****

From Sunday night to Monday, Simone barely slept. At six in the morning, her phone buzzed on the nightstand.

"Can you turn off the alarms and open your kitchen door for me, please?" Ed asked.

Simone leaped from her bed, quickly put a robe on over her nightgown, and hurried to the kitchen door. After disabling the surveillance system, she opened the door and left it ajar. Moments later, Edward walked in.

He glanced around the kitchen. "Good morning, Simmie. Your new home is beautiful. I would love to cook in this kitchen. Could you make me an espresso, please? It’s been a long time since I’ve had one."

He’s quick. He’d scanned her kitchen in seconds and had spotted her espresso machine.

“Good morning, Ed.” She greeted him then walked over to the counter to prepare a cup of coffee for him and one for herself. “Please have a seat.” She gestured to the stools at the island.

Edward nodded and settled onto a stool. A few minutes later, Simone sat next to him and handed him a cup of coffee. They were silent for a while, just savoring their coffee. After he had finished his espresso, clearly relishing every sip, did Ed began to speak.

Edward nodded and settled onto a stool. A few minutes later, Simone sat next to him and handed him a cup of coffee. They sat in silence for a while, just savoring their coffee. Only after he had finished his espresso, clearly relishing every sip, did Ed begin to speak.

“Sorry, but we don’t have this in jail. I’ve really missed drinking fresh expresso. What’s so urgent?” he asked, setting the cup on the countertop, and looking directly into her eyes.

“First, I need you to promise you’ll remain unbiased, and you won’t take any action against my husband,” Simone said earnestly.

“I only act based on solid evidence, and I strive to remain impartial. You should know that about me after all these years,” Edward replied. “Your husband may have taken you away from me, but I wouldn’t use that as a reason to go after him in a criminal matter.”

Simone scowled.

"Even after all these years, I'm still uncertain if I truly know you. Or anyone else, for that matter. It seems we barely understand ourselves."

"You're right, but you sound so bitter and disillusioned. What happened? What did your husband do?"

Simone walked over to her purse, which she'd carelessly left on the kitchen island the day before, and retrieved the photograph hidden between the pages of a book.

"Some pictures have been appearing out of nowhere in my husband's apartment. He seems unaware of them. Some, he claims, he doesn't even recognize. Two were pictures of Lara, but on Friday, I found this one." She handed the picture to Edward.

CHAPTER FORTY-EIGHT

Footage and Coffee

Edward held the photo, studying it for a moment before lifting his gaze to meet Simone's, his eyes narrowing.

"My friend, I can imagine the thoughts that are running through your mind right now." He shook his head. "I bet you've already decided that your husband is some sort of criminal, or that he betrayed you in some way, just like you did when Peter told the world I was his accomplice. You were the first one to turn your back on me."

His bitter words hit her like a slap to the face, and her eyes filled with tears. He was right; she had never given him the benefit of the doubt.

She lowered her head and took a deep breath.

"Maybe you're right. My thoughts are in turmoil, and everything feels confused. I don't know who I can trust anymore. I'm afraid of facing another disappointment."

"In my experience as a Doctor, I would advise you to trust yourself and your instincts! Do you think I'm a criminal? Do you think your husband could be involved with minors? This girl is clearly underage." He pointed to the picture. "How confident are you in his feelings and the relationship you're in?"

Simone put her hand over Ed's and fixed her eyes on his.

"I really don't know, Ed. To be honest, I fell in love with him. I tried to push him away; I even stopped working with him. We only reconnected after the trial, and then it was impossible to stay apart. We married in a rush. I know I love him, and I can feel his love for me, but I don't truly know him."

"That means you fell in love while we were still together. Wow, Simmie, that hurts."

Simone tried to interrupt, but he put a finger on her lips and went on.

"I know you would never betray me; you're not that kind of woman. It just hurts to hear you confirm what I've sensed deep down—you never loved me. Maybe as a person loves their best friend, but not the way they feel about the love of their life."

"It wasn't like that, Ed... I thought I could love you. I do love you. Oh, I don't know! I can't explain the difference..."

"I get it. You love me as your best friend. I don't give you butterflies in your stomach. I made a mistake thinking that could change."

"I get it. You love me as your best friend. I don't give you butterflies in your stomach. I made a mistake thinking that could change."

"The intimacy between us was always electric, transcending the typical bounds of friendship. It wasn't merely good; it was great," she said.

Nothing compared to what I feel in Carl´s arms...

A pang of sadness flickered across his eyes, and Simone felt as though her heart was shattering into pieces. The realization that she was the source of her friend's suffering weighed heavily on her soul.

Simone stroked Ed's hand. He cleared his throat, a subtle gesture betraying his discomfort.

Lowering his head, he glanced at her fingers resting over his. With a gentle yet resolute motion, he lifted her hand and placed it back on the table. Then, looking up to meet her eyes with a mix of resignation and resolve, he said, "I shouldn't be helping your husband, but I love you, and I will do this even if it means helping him." He placed the picture he was holding in front of her. "I've met your husband just once or twice, and he was older than he appears in this picture. That means he hasn't betrayed you. After all, you only met him a few days before I did."

Simone looked at the picture. He was right; in the photograph, Carl's face had fewer lines than it did now, and when the picture was taken, he didn't have gray hair.

Edward continued, analyzing the body language in the photo.

"His posture says he hasn't been intimate with the girl. She's sitting on his lap, yes, but he's placed a hand on her waist, perhaps just to prevent her from falling. His attention is directed at someone in front of him; his torso is turned at a different angle from his legs."

Edward was the best profiler she had ever met, and Simone knew he was right about everything. She felt terrible about her poor judgment.

Maybe Ed is innocent, and I was just desperate to condemn him?

She grappled with the unsettling realization that her emotions might have clouded her better judgment.

"If I can give you one piece of advice, it's to talk to your husband about that picture," Edward said as he placed the photo on the countertop and pushed it toward her. "I don't think this means he's a criminal. What I think is that, somehow, people around him are involved in these crimes. And who was his best friend?" He raised his eyebrows.

"Peter Hay." Simone whispered as a chill ran down her spine. "I've asked myself if and how Hay managed to put all these pictures inside Carl's apartment."

"I have no clue, but that man has long tentacles. So, be aware, and talk to your husband about the picture. I'll continue doing my job, and I'll catch that worm. Don't worry." Edward reassured her, his determination evident in the strength of his words.

"Would you like to have the picture? Maybe you will know what to do with it." Simone slid the photo across the counter toward him.

"I'll take a photo of it," he said, pulling a cell phone from his pocket, adjusting it near the photo and snapping a picture. "You keep the original. I'll wait for your command. And if you decide I shouldn't use it, I won't." He gave the picture back to her.

"Thanks, Ed. I will let you know, but now tell me... How ´ve you been, my friend? Going in and out of MacDougall all the time...that must make you crazy!" Simone tilted her head.

"You can't imagine what it's like—That place is always a nightmare, even with the protection I've secured. It's a relentless challenge. I'm doing everything in my power to fulfill my deal with the FBI so I can leave that place behind forever."

"I hope you can manage it. If anyone can uncover the truth and navigate through this, it's you. I don´t know the details of your deal with the FBI, but stay safe."

Edward leaned forward and enveloped her in his arms. They remained like that for a while, lost in the moment. Being in the embrace of the man who was once her best friend was deeply comforting, yet the conflicting emotions of tenderness and pain warred within her. She felt a profound helplessness, agonizing over her inability to ease his burdens.

Edward was the first to disrupt the moment. He released her and hopped off the stool.

"I have to go." He spoke in a rush as he pulled a piece of paper from his pocket and handed it to her. "Don't call MacDougall anymore. From now on, I won´t be there. Use this number instead. When the man answers, just say, 'Good morning, I'm Doctor Bennet.' You don't need to say anything else. I'll know you need me, and I'll get in contact with you, okay?"

He touched her nose with the tip of his index finger, a tender gesture that warmed her heart.

Simone took the piece of paper, her hands trembling slightly as she rose to her feet. They embraced once more, lingering in the moment. Then, with a final squeeze Edward stepped back and walked away.

*****

Throughout the day, Simone's phone rang several times. Each time, Carl's number showed on the screen, but she hadn't a moment to answer. Busy with patients, she asked Patricia to call Carl and find out if there was some kind of emergency. If not, Simone asked her secretary to tell him about how full her schedule was and to suggest he call her back at the end of the day. Carl assured Patricia there was no emergency.

Simone attempted to put the calls out of her mind, but Carl never phoned her repeatedly like that. Especially not during working hours. Anxiety gnawed at her insides, and staying focused on business became a struggle as the minutes ticked by. Finally, at five p.m., after her last patient departed, she went to her car, free to return his calls.

"Hello, my love, I'm so sorry I couldn't talk to you earlier. I had several complicated issues to work out with patients today, and I just couldn't break away."

Recalling the story she'd created about the potentially suicidal patient, Simone hesitated for a few seconds before continuing her lie.

"The one I told you about last night seems okay, but today was still tough. I had some truly difficult cases."

She felt a twinge of guilt for deceiving him. Not so much over the story she'd told him the night before, but because she had met with Ed that morning and hadn't told Carl anything about her former lover's recent visits.

"I suppose talking to your old boyfriend was one of those difficult cases you had to handle today. Am I right? From what I could see, he was quite comfortable sitting in *our* kitchen." Carl's tone dripped with sarcasm and anger.

Simone's eyes widened, and she had to swallow back a gasp. Oh, no... Carl had watched her while she'd talked to Edward that morning. How much had he seen? She couldn´t remember if the camera in the kitchen had a voice system.

Had he heard everything or only a portion?

The flickering glow from the streetlight cast shadows across the car, and in the dim illumination, the rising tension in his voice made her skin prickle.

"And what a surprise it was to discover a convicted felon in our home, chatting with my wife!"

Simone understood Carl's moods well enough to recognize when he was truly upset. He still carried the scars from Lara's repeated betrayals, which made it hard for him to fully trust her.

Edward is right. Carl and I don't trust each other, and that's not a good thing in a marriage.

"First of all, love, I'm not Lara, okay? If you had looked

at the footage carefully, you would have seen that I only talked to Edward and nothing more. I wasn't screwing some stranger! Have some faith in me!"

She strove for a commanding tone, hoping her forceful confidence would convince him she had done nothing wrong. At least, nothing like he must be imagining.

"I'm sorry, honey. You're right, I have no reason to doubt you," Carl said, much calmer now, "but that is the last man I would ever have expected to see in our home this morning. What is he doing out of jail, Simone? Did he scape?"

She took a deep breath, her mind working frantically to find the best explanation.

"It's too complicated to explain over the phone. I can tell you one thing, but it must stay between us. The FBI offered him a deal. I don't know the exact terms, but from what I understand, he's helping with some investigation. In exchange… they'll give him an early release.

"Simone Bennet Lourenzo, I hope you're not helping him in any way!"

"I'm not helping him exactly…"

"Love…"

He took another deep breath, and Simone could picture how he looked right then. With his emotions hidden behind a neutral mask he'd maintain control with an iron grip.

"I'm the lawyer here, the one who knows just the right word to use to avoid getting my clients into hot water with the IRS. What do you mean by 'exactly'? How much are you helping that man?"

"Not much. He just wants me to look through some of his things again because there's a picture he needs, and I still haven't found it."

I'm becoming a great liar, and I hate it!

"Did he tell you where to find it? I hope it's nothing risky."

"Nothing dangerous at all. I just need to go into his office tomorrow and unlock a desk drawer I didn't know existed. I would have done it today, but I was too busy, and now, I'm too exhausted, and I wanted to call you back as quickly as possible."

"Great. Please promise me, once again, that you're not going to play Sherlock Holmes."

"I´m not; I don't have the necessary skills, and I have an office full of patients who need my help. I'm so happy with my schedule, honey. It's nearly full, and most of my former patients have returned. It feels wonderful to know that I'm still highly regarded, even after everything that's happened."

She infused a fake tone of happiness into her voice. As she'd expected, Carl took the hint and let the subject of Edward's visit drop. At least for the time being. She steered the conversation to a safer topic.

"Tell me about your day," she said.

Carl talked animatedly about a new client he'd taken on that afternoon, and Simone listened, grateful for the reprieve. She'd managed to convince him all was well. This time. But how long would her luck hold out?

CHAPTER FORTY-NINE

Through Windows

Simone stood in her kitchen, the morning sun streaming through the windows and casting a warm glow over the countertops. She was finishing a cup of coffee, savoring the rich aroma, while giving Gina, the new cleaning lady, instructions on where to put the clean clothes after she'd finished the wash or picked them up from the cleaners.

"Please put all the blouses in one section, in order of their color, then all the skirts in another section, and group those by color, as well," Simone told the woman.

She set her coffee cup down on the marble countertop and turned to Gina.

"I need the closet organized in a specific way." she said, her tone firm but polite.

Once again, Simone explained how she wanted things to be arranged.

Gina turned toward the sink, her hands submerged in soapy water, her back to Simone. She nodded, and the gesture spoke volumes. Simone could sense the woman's resistance, the tension in the air thickening between them. The soft clinking of dishes being washed echoed in the small kitchen, a stark reminder that perhaps Gina wasn't paying attention. Simone clenched her hands at her sides. She opened her mouth to ask for Gina to please look at her and not to the sink while she was talking, but the phone rang. Simone blew out a frustrated breath and picked up her phone from the island. She glanced at the number. Why would Patricia call so early? Simone's first patient wasn't scheduled for another two hours.

"Good morning, Doctor Bennet," she said in her husky voice.

"Good morning, Patricia, what's up?" Simone imagined one of her patients knocking on her office door, begging the secretary to phone and ask Simone to come in early for an emergency appointment.

"Doctor, I think we should call the police. I decided to come in early today, and the place is a mess. Somebody tore everything apart and—let me see… Yes, one of your windows is open in your office. Somebody broke in. Please hurry, and I'll see you when you get here. I'm calling the police right now."

"Try to get Officer Dimario, please. I'm on my way."

Patricia hung up the phone without saying goodbye, and Simone shook her head. Sometimes, her secretary acted as if she had no manners. But there were more important matters to address this morning. She imagined her office torn apart, all her papers and books scattered and destroyed.

Heart racing, Simone left her mug on the island countertop.
She grabbed her purse and car keys and without saying goodbye to Gina, headed out the kitchen door to her car.

*****

Simone's thoughts were spinning like a carousel. She gripped the steering wheel tightly as she drove, the shops and offices lining the city streets a blur as she flew past.

Did I set the alarms before I left the office yesterday?

She didn't know—couldn't remember performing that specific task. Of course, if she had, she no doubt did so without even thinking about it. She'd gone through the two or three steps of activating the alarm system dozens of times. The thing was, Simone wasn't always the last to leave. Sometimes, Patricia stayed late, and then she'd take care of activating the surveillance cameras. So, who left first last night?

And why would someone break into her clinic? Her gut told her this wasn't a random case of vandalism or robbery. The possibilities churned in her mind, adding to her anxiety.

Simone parked in her usual spot in the lot and jumped from the car. A police cruiser sat parked in front of the clinic's front door. She entered, heard voices coming from Edward's office, and headed down the hallway, she paused to check her office and drop her bag on a chair before joining them.

As Simone turned to leave her office, the dancing curtains at the open window caught her attention, but nothing else in the room seemed out of place. Sunlight streamed through the gap between the velvet panels, illuminating the neat stacks of papers and perfectly arranged furniture. The sound of muffled voices from down the hall spurred her into action. Heart pounding, she hurriedly closed the window. She left her office, but instead of going directly to Ed's old office, she did a quick tour of the single-story building. She opened every door, turned on lights, and checked for any sign of disturbance, but everything looked just as it always did, and nothing seemed out of place. She finished her inspection and ended up outside the door of Ed's office, took a deep breath, and stepped into the room.

Simone froze. A lump of fear formed in her throat.

"Oh, my God..."

Papers and books were strewn across the floor, drawers hung open, and containers of paperclips, staples, and thumbtacks had been emptied, the contents strewn from one side of the room to the other. Someone had been searching for something very specific, and they'd turned the whole place upside down looking for it. Carlo and Patricia were there, deep in conversation, and Simone nodded at them. Carlo held a notepad and was asking Patricia about the alarms. They both stopped talking and turned to Simone.

"Good morning, Carlo, Patricia," Simone greeted them.

They both wished her a good morning, but their tones lacked enthusiasm.

Carlo placed the pen inside the notepad.

"Not that good of a morning, Simone. I'm beginning to believe someone is either trying to send some kind of message to you, or they're after something you have...or they think you have. First, someone tries to break into your house—now this mess in your office."

As Simone kneeled to pick up a smashed portrait from the floor, he interrupted her.

"Please don't touch anything. Forensics will arrive soon. Can we talk?" He pointed to the door.

Before Simone could answer and invite the officer into her office, Patricia excused herself and left the room.

"From what I see, everything seems to be in order except this room." Simone pointed to the floor. "This is...was Ed's office, so if someone is looking for something, they must believe Edward had it."

As Simone finished her sentence, she remembered the lie she had told her husband the evening before, about how Edward had wanted her to check in a drawer in his office. Simone hadn't told anyone else that fabricated story. Only Carl...

She glanced around the room, taking in the disarray. The sunlight streaming through the blinds cast eerie shadows on the overturned furniture. Her gaze settled on the drawer she had mentioned to Carl. A pang of guilt mixed with fear.

Don't do that to him again...

She had been wrong about the photo and had jumped to conclusions, convicting her husband without listening to his side of things.

Should I tell Carlo about this?

No... First, she needed to get some answers. At this point, she didn't trust anyone.

"Do you know what might have been kept in here that would interest someone?"

"As you can see," Simone said, lowering her gaze to the floor, "what he has is here—his books, some portraits, and the items you gave to Beth that I put away in the drawers and on the shelves. I can't imagine what whoever did this was looking for."

Voices in the hallway interrupted their conversation, and a moment later, two crime scene techs—a man with a camera dangling from a strap around his neck, and a woman carrying a large tool-bag type of tote—entered the room.

"Do you think your team can be done and out of here before ten? I have a patient." Simone glanced at her watch.

Nine o'clock already...

Her first appointment would be here in less than an hour.

"Your secretary already asked me that," Carlo replied with a smile, "and I asked her to change your schedule and bump everyone back an hour. If your first appointment is at eleven, that will give us enough time in case this takes longer than I expect."

Simone nodded and left the room. Back in her office,

she sat on her sofa and spent several minutes going over the events of the last day or so. Frowning at the thought solidifying in her head, she got up to get her phone out of her purse. She dialed the number Edward had given her and followed his instructions. Less than ten minutes passed before she received a call from an unidentified number.

Simone pressed the button to answer and put the phone to her ear. "Hello."

"Miss me already?" Edward asked in his familiar, teasing tone.

For some reason, Simone's eyes filled with tears, and with her voice shaking, she began to fill him in. Speaking at barely above a whisper, she told him about Carl checking the surveillance cameras, about the lie she'd told him, and how someone had made a wreck of his office.

"Were you two alone? Are you sure nobody overheard your conversation?"

Simone admired Ed's ability to look at all sides of a problem before jumping to a conclusion.

Unlike me. But he isn't personally involved.

When she was not involved, she could do the same thing.

"No, Ed, I was inside my car, all alone!" Simone exclaimed, her frustration boiling over. "I think Carl was alone, too, but I can only speculate."

Edward blew out a long breath.

"Okay. Listen closely. This is what we're going to do..."

CHAPTER FIFTY

Anonymous Sources of Pain

A day that starts badly will probably end worse.

Was that the saying? Simone tried to remember as she climbed behind the wheel and began her trip to the city. Even though she hated driving her car into New York, she had no choice. Joseph, one of Carl's partners and a criminal lawyer, had called to deliver some disturbing news. A couple of officers had taken her husband for questioning. Before Simone could ask Joseph for more information, he'd apologized for having to upset her, said he had to go help Carl, and then hung up.

Simone had done a quick Google search for the train schedule. Although the next one left an hour later, it stopped at every station along the way, which would mean traveling for almost two and a half hours before reaching the city. Simone had dismissed that option as unacceptable. Carl needed her, so she'd grabbed her keys and purse, told Patricia to reschedule the rest of her appointments, and hurried out to her car.

Twenty minutes later, Simone gripped the steering wheel with sweaty hands. Her mind raced. What had happened? Why did the police want to speak to Carl? And why drag him down to the station like some common criminal? The car's engine hummed as she sped down the highway, the GPS guiding her toward her destination. Streetlights flickered on as the sun sank below the horizon, and headlights from oncoming traffic reflected off the windshield. She glanced at the clock on the dashboard.

Time sure doesn't fly by when you're in a hurry.

Finally, the New York City skyline filled her line of vision, looming in the darkness up ahead. Simone's anxiety grew with each passing minute as cars crawled along the congested road. The vibration of her phone startled her, breaking the tense silence in the car. She quickly glanced at the caller ID before answering, hoping for news about Carl.

"Hello, Joseph, please tell me what's going on!" Simone exclaimed, gripping the steering wheel tighter. She cringed. She barely knew the man. He probably wondered if she'd been raised by a pack of wolves.

The sound of Joseph's voice crackled through the car's speakers, mingling with the hum of traffic around her.

"Hello, Simone. We settled everything. Carl and I are heading to his apartment," Joseph said in a calm and reassuring tone.

A wave of relief washed over her. The tension in her shoulders eased slightly as she continued to navigate the traffic.

"I'll head there, too." She tapped the GPS screen, rerouting to Carl's apartment. "Can you pass the phone to Carl, please?"

A brief silence filled the line and then the muffled sounds of conversation, but Simone couldn't make out everything they said. A second later, Joseph came back on the phone.

"Simone? Carl doesn´t feel like talking. Meet us at the apartment, okay?"

"Okay..." she whispered as the line went dead.

Simone sat in silence. She took a deep breath, trying to calm the storm of emotions swirling inside her. Her thoughts were chaotic...guilt and fear intertwining as she considered the possibility that her actions had led to Carl's predicament.

She replayed the events in her mind... her dialogue with Edward, the photo, her talk with Carl inside the car, the break-in at her office, and Carl's unexpected detention. The pieces of the puzzle were there, but they refused to fit together in any coherent way. She needed to be rational and composed, but the weight of her actions and their potential consequences bore down on her.

Simone couldn't help but wonder if her actions had somehow led to this. Overwhelming emotions made it hard to focus.

What should I do next?

As she drove, the enormity of the situation settled in. She needed a plan, a way to untangle the mess and find out the truth. But for now, all she could do was keep driving.

The heavy traffic of the final miles pulled Simone away from her swirling thoughts, but they returned with full force as she parked in her spot in the garage. Her heart started to race as she entered the elevator, the journey to their floor feeling interminable. The quiet hum of the elevator only intensified her anxiety.

Each floor passed slowly, the glowing numbers barely registering as she worried over what had happened, and what it all might mean. Her tension grew with every second. By the time the elevator doors finally opened, she was barely holding herself together. She stepped out, her footsteps echoing in the empty hallway, amplifying her sense of isolation and dread.

Simone took a deep breath before opening the door with a trembling hand. As she pushed the door open, the familiar scent of their home did little to comfort her. She stepped inside. Tommy came to her, tail wagging, and she briefly caressed his head and closed the door behind her.

Across the room, Joseph sat at the dining table, his briefcase open and papers strewn about in a disorganized mess—to Simone's displeasure. She wanted to put everything in order before talking, but then he turned toward her. She glanced around.

Where is Carl?

"Hello, Simone." He rose. Meeting her halfway, he gave her a quick peck on her cheek. "Carl is resting. I gave him one of my sleeping pills. The guy was a mess. He has this deep trauma associated with police stations, ever since... You know..."

"Yes...ever since Lara."

A mixture of relief and unease washed over her. It was good not to face Carl right now. She glanced toward the closed bedroom door and then back at Joseph. His calm demeanor did little to ease her nerves.

"Thank you, Joseph," she said, her voice barely above a whisper. She took a deep breath, trying to steady her nerves. "Tell me everything, will you please? I'm a wreck."

"Please sit." Joseph gestured toward a chair at the dining table.

As Simone obeyed and took her seat across from him, Joseph resumed his position, near his briefcase, his eyes fixed on her with an intensity that made her uneasy. She clasped her hands together on her lap. The atmosphere grew heavy with tension, and she resisted the urge to squirm under the weight of his gaze as he silently examined her. Finally, Joseph started to recount the events of the last several hours.

"The police arrived at the office with a court order in hand to search the premises and question him on behalf of the FBI. Someone had sent a photo, clearly from years ago —Carl estimates it dates back about ten years—that showed him with an Asian girl sitting on his lap. Considering they've discovered five dead young Asian girls in the last few months, the agents wanted to know the connection. Since you're his wife and you took some photos to the police station, they're trying to piece everything together."

Simone's heart pounded as she absorbed Joseph's words. Her mouth went dry. The situation was worse than she'd thought. What could she do now?

"The photos I gave to the police didn't have Carl in them. Who sent the photo? Why question Carl? Surely, he's not the only man in New York City who may or may not have flirted with a pretty Asian girl, right?" she asked, her throat tight.

Hard to speak when you feel like you have sand in your mouth...

She glanced toward the kitchen.

I wish I had a glass of water.

Joseph sighed.

"The source of the photo is still unclear. It came anonymously, which complicates things. The FBI is trying to trace its origin, but it's not an easy task. Whoever sent it knew exactly what they were doing, and their goal seems pretty obvious—they want to link Carl to those recent murders." He paused and met her gaze.

Simone forced herself to stay calm and not look away.

Did Ed send the picture? She remembered that he took a snapshot of it.

"What should we do now?" she whispered.

"The situation seems to be resolved, at least for now," Joseph said, his voice steady. "Carl explained the photo was taken at a party he attended, and the host had an annoying habit of hiring women to 'please the guests." He made quotes in the air with his fingers. "Carl said the more he rejected the girls' advances, the more persistent they became, like flies around honey. And they barely spoke English, so it was hard to explain he wasn't interested. After a while, he just gave up and let one of the girls sit on his lap while he discussed something with a friend of his who attended the same party. Carl can't recall what they talked about, but he swears that's all that happened."

"Do you have a copy of the picture?" Simone asked.

Joseph took his phone from his pocket and opened it. After swiping the screen several times, he handed the phone to Simone.

"What in the...?"

Simone stared at the screen in stunned disbelief. For a moment, her brain struggled to process what this could mean. It wasn't the same photo. Of course, it was the same girl, the same day—perhaps taken just a moment or two after the photo Simone had found—but this one was captured from a different angle. The Asian girl had shifted slightly on Carl's lap.

This is not the photo I gave Ed! Someone is playing a dangerous game!

Lost in a fog of confused thoughts, Simone shook her head.

"I've never seen this picture." She handed the phone back quickly before he noticed how badly her hands had started shaking.

Joseph stood, put his hands against his lower back, and arched into a stretch. He shook his head and frowned.

"Man, am I stiff. I need to get going, Simone. Now that you're here, my friend is in good hands, and I need to rest a little bit."

He gathered up all his papers and folders and stuffed them into his briefcase. When he finished, he put a hand on her arm.

"Everything will work out."

She nodded and watched him walk to the front entry. A moment later, the door clicked shut, and Simone got to her feet. She wouldn't wake him, but she needed to see Carl and make sure he was okay for herself.

A small, plug-in style nightlight cast the bedroom in a dim glow. Carl seemed to be sound asleep, his breathing deep and slow. She tiptoed to the side of the bed. She leaned down to touch his forehead, in a caress. She didn't like the idea of taking someone else's prescription medication, and she had forgotten to ask Joseph what type of sleeping aid he had given to her husband.

"I need to stop stressing every little thing," she whispered.

Most of the sleeping pills she'd prescribed to her patients stayed in their system for at least four hours, ensuring a deep sleep. Carl would be fine...

She watched his peaceful face for a moment, a mixture of love and worry filling her heart. She gently brushed a strand of hair from his forehead.

Simone crept back out of the room, closing the door behind her. In the living room, she sank onto the couch, her phone in her hand as she tried to decide what to do next. After a moment of hesitation, she dialed the number she had saved in her contacts as, "The Guy".

The phone rang a few times before he answered, speaking in a low, gravelly voice.

"Hello?"

The word came out in a strange, tense tone.

"Simone, it's me.""

The familiar washed over her like a physical caress. Still, she couldn't speak right away and swallowed repeatedly to get rid of the tightness in her throat.

"What's going on?" he asked.

"I need to know more about the photo you took a snapshot," she said, her voice low. "It was morning when I showed to you, and then this afternoon at about five o'clock, several police officers went to Carl's office with a court order to search the place and take him in for questioning. They took him down to the station to make a statement or something like that. They wanted to ask him about a photo they had received from an anonymous tipster. But it wasn't the photo I showed you. It was another one, very similar—same day, same place, same everything—but this time, the girl was facing the camera and smiling."

Simone tried her best to keep her voice low, and every few seconds, she glanced at the closed door to Carl's bedroom. Hopefully, he'd sleep for several more hours.

"That's very strange. Let me check something and get back to you. I didn't send the picture to the FBI. I told you I wouldn ´t without your consent."

Before Simone could process his words and respond, the line went dead.

While she waited, Simone tried to make sense of what she knew. The person who had those photos must have gone to the same party Carl had attended. And they'd taken multiple shots of the girl on Carl's lap, as if they'd wanted to capture the scene from every angle. But why...? Had someone wanted to paint Carl in a negative light? Even as far back as ten years ago, had someone hoped to set him up? Make him look like he was a pedophile?

After a few minutes, the phone vibrated again. Simone answered the call and then got up to pace the living room as she talked to Ed.

Edward got directly to the point, his urgency evident.

"They got the picture from an anonymous source. They know something about your husband that we don't know yet, but I'll figure it out."

Simone's heart raced as she listened. "What do we do now?" she asked, trying to keep her voice steady.

"I need to find out who had access to that event and took those photos," Edward replied. "I have a few leads, but it's going to take some time. Those pictures were taken a long time ago, probably around five years."

"Ten years ago, according to Carl's lawyer," she said.

"Some people hold onto things for a long time… I'll check. In the meantime, keep a low profile and make sure Carl doesn't suspect anything."

Simone hesitated then said, "Ed…can I ask you a question? Do you think Carl is involved in the death of those girls?"

"Simmie… I really don't know. Take care."

The line went dead again.

"Do *you* think I'm responsible for those girls' deaths?"

Carl's angry voice came from behind her, and she jumped, nearly dropping her cellphone. She spun around.

"Do *you* really think I'm capable of such evil acts? You, of all people, were the one who helped me prove to myself that I had no intention of killing Lara, and now, you're whispering with your former lover and discussing the chances of me being guilty of those disgusting crimes? I don't think I know you anymore!"

Simone's heart ached at the pain and betrayal in his eyes.

"Carl, it's not like that," she began, her voice trembling. "I'm just trying to understand what's happening. Someone is framing you, and I'm trying to find out who and why."

Carl shook his head, his expression a mix of anger and hurt.

"How can you say that when you're talking to a criminal behind my back? If you really believed I was innocent, you wouldn't need to sneak around."

Tears welled up in Simone's eyes.

"I wasn't. I was whispering because I didn't want to wake you up. I didn't know what to do, and Edward was the only one I thought might have some answers. I never doubted you, but I need to find the truth to help you."

Carl sighed, running a hand through his hair.

"I don't know, Simone. First, the police invade my office, and now, I catch you whispering with that man behind my back. It's all too much. I need some time to think."

Simone reached out, but Carl stepped away.

"Please, Carl. We can get through this together."

He looked at her for a long moment before nodding slightly, but his eyes still blazed with a mix of anger and pain.

"Maybe yes, maybe not. Without trust, love can't survive, and it's clear you don't trust me. You trust a convicted felon, but you don't trust the man you say you love. I know it's late, but I'm going to get some of my stuff and find a hotel."

Simone's heart sank as she watched Carl turn and walk toward the bedroom. The pain in his voice echoed in her mind.

"Carl, please," she pleaded, her voice breaking. "I was trying to protect you, to find out who's framing you. I never meant to hurt you."

Carl paused at the door but didn't turn around.

"But you *have* hurt me, Simone. I need time to process this."

Tears streamed down her face as Carl disappeared into the bedroom. She listened to the sounds of him packing, each rustle of clothing a reminder of the growing distance between them. She wanted to rush in, to make him understand, but anything she said now might only make things worse.

After a few minutes, Carl reappeared, a small bag in hand. He looked at her, his expression less furious but still filled with hurt.

"I'm being chivalrous right now, but please, can you leave my house in the morning? I don't want to see you here when I come back!"

His words caused a sharp pain in her chest, as if he'd stabbed her with a knife.

"Carl, please, don't do this," she whispered, her voice breaking.

But he shook his head. "It's too late, Simone. I need time to think, and I can't do that with you here. Just leave me alone for now."

Simone stared after Carl as he walked out the door, the sound of it closing behind him echoing in the quiet apartment. She stood there for a moment, trying to process what had just happened, her chest contracted with the same unbearable pain she had felt when Peter kidnapped her child. That void, that feeling that nothing she could do would make things right again, tortured her.

As Simone sat on the couch, Tommy, who had been watching their discussion attentively, came to her side and put his head on her lap. The gentle, familiar weight of her loyal companion was both comforting and heart-wrenching. She cried harder, her sobs shaking her entire body, until she could hardly catch her breath.

The apartment felt emptier than ever. Every corner, every piece of furniture reminded her of the happy times they had shared. The emotional weight was almost too much to bear.

Eventually, exhaustion took over, and she fell into a restless sleep with Tommy by her side offering the only solace in her distress. When she next opened her eyes, the early morning light filtered through the curtains.

With a heavy heart, she began to pack her things. She had to honor Carl's request and leave.

"But I won't stop fighting for us," she promised herself. "And somehow, I'll prove to Carl how sorry I am for not trusting him."

CHAPTER FIFTY-ONE

Silence is Annoying

Her patient could have confessed to murder, and Simone wouldn't have noticed. She hadn't heard from Carl in five days. She was trying to give him some space, but her desperate need to resolve things had begun to mess with her ability to focus on work.

We need to talk! I'll give him one more day, and then I'm going to call him.

After all, issues between a couple didn't get resolved on their own. Not without communication.

To make matters worse, she hadn't seen or heard from Ed in five days, either. If her head wasn't filled with worry over her husband, her thoughts were preoccupied by why Ed had disappeared suddenly. The uncertainty and silence had grown unbearable. She had to force a conversation with Carl soon and find out what was going on with Ed, as well.

"Doctor Bennet, are you alright?" Benjamin asked.

"I'm fine. Please proceed. I'm sorry I've been silent. I've been analyzing the situation," she said, trying to sound composed and attentive. As her patient always complained about his savage wife, she figured she hadn't missed anything important.

Benjamin nodded and continued speaking, and this time,

Simone made a huge effort to keep her attention on him.

"Chivon is crazy, you know... Everybody knows me. I'm practically a celebrity! The more I try to be discreet, the more she becomes an exhibitionist," he said, but his sarcastic smile indicated he wasn't very disgusted by whatever Chivon had done this time.

He must have said something important while my mind was wandering.

Simone nodded in response to his statement.

"I understand, Benjamin. It must be challenging to balance things when your personal life conflicts with your public image. Have you considered discussing boundaries and expectations with Chivon?"

I feel like I've asked that same question a thousand times...

She saw Chivon and Benjamin, together and alone, and this same conversation played like a recording during every session...

Benjamin leaned back in his chair, a hint of amusement in his eyes.

"Oh, we've discussed it. Multiple times, but she just follows her quote-unquote *instincts*."

"Tell me in detail this time. What exactly did Chivon do?"

Simone held her breath. If he'd already given her the details while she'd been spaced out a few minutes earlier, he'd think she needed the psychiatrist! Luckily, he didn't seem too disturbed by her question.

"*All* the details?" He frowned, raising his eyebrows. "Okay." He nodded and settled back in his chair.

"Well, we were trying out the new car I gave her for her birthday—I gave her this beautiful black machine. She loves to drive, so we went to an isolated backroad to put the Lambo through its paces." His expression couldn't have been prouder if he'd been talking about his newborn son.

"She was acting like...what's that Indy racer's name...? Ah, yes! Mario Andretti! She kept revving the engine, slowing down, and then hitting the gas to bring the car up to speed in just a few seconds. And then she slowed down a little bit. Just a little bit." He held up his hand, bringing his thumb and forefinger close together but not touching. "Then with one hand she managed to open my trousers and get my shaft out. She started masturbating me, and then she stepped on the gas again. To say she was fast is an understatement."

"Who? Your wife or the car?" Simone asked, intrigued. She was sure the story, like nearly everything that happened between the couple, was going to be funny. She repressed a smile.

Benjamin chuckled.

"The car! But Chivon blew my mind, as well. I was amazed by her ability to hold it together and focus on two different things, but I was terrified, too." He shook his head. "There I was, covered in sweat—from fear and from horniness—so, I closed my eyes and tried not to think about how fast we were going. Instead, I focused on the sensation of her hand on me. Stroking, pressing, caressing..." He moaned as if he was reliving the scene. "She made me come so hard I covered half the dashboard in my ejaculate! When I opened my eyes, there was a bus next to us. A dozen or more people had their faces plastered against the windows, just watching us! Can you imagine what would have happened if that bus had been carrying reporters or the paparazzi?"

Simone choked back a laugh and nodded.

"Or it could have been the police... How did you feel afterward?"

Benjamin leaned back, still smiling.

"Conflicted! A part of me was embarrassed and angry, but

I admit, another part of me was thrilled by such a crazy experience. I love her spontaneity, but sometimes, it goes too far."

*****

A long procession of boring patients didn't help take Simone's mind off her troubles, and the day seemed endless.

I just want to go home, open a bottle of wine, sink into the bathtub, and wash away the pain.

She glanced at her watch. Even if it was only three in the afternoon.

She finished her last appointment, drained and emotionally exhausted. She gathered her things, said goodbye to Patricia, and left the office, her mind fixed on the thought of a quiet and lonely evening. As she drove home, the weight of her feelings pressed heavily on her shoulders.

She stopped just to pick up her bath products—she needed to spoil herself today.

Once home, she headed straight for the kitchen and pulled out a bottle of her favorite red wine. The soft pop of the cork echoed in the quiet space. She poured herself a generous glass. Bringing it to her nose, she inhaled deeply, the rich aroma momentarily grounding her. Then she took a large swallow, savoring the fleeting sense of relief it offered. For a moment, the weight of the day felt just a little lighter.

A wave of guilt swept over her as she stared at the glass, the deep red of the wine stark against the gleaming countertop.

Nothing like drowning my sorrows in alcohol.

The uneasiness only deepened when her gaze drifted to the kitchen clock—it wasn't even five yet. Her thoughts wavered between the desperate need to relax and the image of the composed, wise woman she aspired to be.

For a moment, she froze, her hand hovering near the glass. "You need solace," she murmured to herself, "and one glass isn't going to turn you into a raging alcoholic."

"So, to hell with it," she muttered, snatching up the glass again with a resolve that felt more like defiance. After topping off the glass, filling it all the way to the brim, she pushed her doubts aside and made her way to the bathroom. The soft click of her steps on the floor broke the heavy silence as she entered. She set the wineglass carefully on the edge of the tub and reached for the faucet.

She ran the bath, adding her favorite scented bath salts and bubbles, and watched as the steam filled the room, creating a soothing atmosphere. She took off her clothes, put them inside the laundry basket she kept inside the sink cabinet, and was stepping into the water when she heard her phone.

Carl!

She ran naked to the kitchen to get her cellphone.

Unknown number.

She hesitated for a second, wanting to keep the line free for a call from her husband.

"Cellphones don't work that way, dummy," she said. If Carl called, she could just click over and talk to him. Besides, an unknown number meant Edward, and she needed to know his whereabouts. Her finger hovered over the accept button before she finally pressed it and brought the phone to her ear. "Hello?"

"Hi, Simone."

Hearing Edward's familiar voice was like a balm to her frazzled nerves. Relief flooded through her, but anger boiled up to replace it.

"Hi, Ed. What's going on? Where have you been?" she asked, her voice sharp and brimming with frustration.

The days of silence and the constant worry finally boiled over. Her hand tightened around the phone, knuckles whitening as she paced the kitchen. She paused and slammed her free hand down on the countertop for emphasis.

"Do you have any idea what it's been like not knowing anything? I deserve an explanation!"

"Sorry, I can't explain now," Edward replied. "I'm out of town doing an investigation, and you might receive notice that I was transferred from MacDougall after a fight, okay? If you do, don't worry."

"Transferred after a fight? What happened?"

"It's a long story, and I can't go into it now. But it's all part of the plan. There was no real fight. How are you?"

She would love to confide in her old friend, but he cared about her—loved her. It wouldn't be fair to talk about how hurt she was.

"I ́m fine."

"Did you find any information about the photo?"

"Nothing yet, but I'm working on it, among other things. I need to go now. Take care."

"You take care, too, okay? And E...if you think it is important, use the photo."

No answer—the line went dead. Simone hung up, feeling a jumble of emotions: a sense of betrayal mixed with the need to do the right thing and uncover the truth. A chill ran through her, and she glanced down at herself.

No wonder I'm cold.

There she was, standing naked in the middle of her kitchen with cameras all around her.

I'm going to end up on Big Brother one of these days...

CHAPTER FIFTY-TWO

Saturday Night Troubles

Simone lit some candles and placed them around the bathtub, creating a serene and soothing atmosphere. The soft glow combined with the lavender scent from the bath salts added to the calming ambiance. She sank into the bath, but the soothing water did little to calm her racing thoughts.

The conversation with Edward left her with more questions than answers, but at least he had called. Carl's silence was becoming unbearable.

She closed her eyes. How long had it been since she'd meditated? No wonder she felt so adrift and anxious. She leaned back and focused on her breathing—in through her nose and out through her mouth, counting each breath. After several seconds, her mind went blank of all other thoughts. Just as she began to feel tranquility seep in, she was startled by the sound of the door clicking open and pulled from her meditative state. She turned to see what had happened, and her heart skipped a beat.

"Carl?" she whispered, her voice filled with a mixture of hope and surprise, her stomach already full of butterflies.

I've never felt this way about any other man. I don't know who he really is, and yet I love him madly. Did I repeat the same mistake of too much trust, as I did with Ed?

He stared down at her, his sharp features gradually losing

their edge. The emotions in his eyes shifted, and the tension in his jaw eased.

"I couldn't stay away any longer," he said quietly. "We need to talk." His expression had turned tender, and his gaze caressed her from head to toe.

Simone nodded, the tension in her chest easing slightly. "Yes, we do."

Carl chuckled softly, shaking his head.

"I just don't think I can talk to you while you're sitting there naked, looking like a damn siren ready to pull me into deep water. This chemistry we have makes it impossible for me to think rationally." A wry smile tugged at his lips.

"All right, let me get dressed." Simone supported herself on the sides of the tub and started to rise.

"I'll be in the kitchen," Carl said. "I need some wine, too." He glanced at her half-filled glass of red. He took her robe from a hook on the wall near the sink and handed it to her. "Take this."

Simone stepped out of the bath, foaming bubbles covering her body. Desire burned in her husband's eyes as she took the bathrobe from his hand.

There is hope for us!

He turned and left, and she stayed behind to take a quick shower to rinse off the bubbles. She dried off quickly then wrapped the towel around her hair and made herself presentable. From her dresser, she chose a sexy black nightgown with a matching robe that made her feel both alluring and confident.

Gathering her composure, she walked to the kitchen. Carl stood by the counter, holding a glass of wine, his shoulders slightly slumped, his movements slow and deliberate. He seemed lost in his thoughts but looked up as she entered, and for a moment, he simply smiled at her. The dark circles under his eyes told her his week had been as bad as hers.

Carl handed her a fresh glass of wine.

"To us," he said, raising his glass.

Simone raised hers in return.

"To us," she echoed, feeling a surge of warmth and optimism.

"I'm so sorry for being silent these past few days," Carl began.

Simone tried to respond, but he put a finger over her lips and shook his head.

"Let me finish. Everything was so intense and quick between us, and I don't think we had time to really get to know each other. So, we're tainted by our past experiences, having dragged them into our marriage. I suspected you were betraying me with your ex-boyfriend because I saw you two talking on the footage. You suspect I was involved with those dead girls because you saw a photo. We both were so damn betrayed by the people we were in relationships with before, that we can't see clearly." He shook his head.

Simone's eyes glistened with unshed tears as she listened to him. His words resonated deeply, striking a chord she hadn't fully acknowledged until now. He was right. Her chest tightened with the weight of realization.

Our pasts are shaping our current fears and suspicions.

"Carl, I never meant to hurt you. I was just so scared and confused after what happened in my clinic, and then Joseph showed me that picture, and I—."

"Wait... After what happened in your clinic?" Carl's forehead furrowed deeply.

He's not lying.

His body language told her he didn't know anything about the break-in.

She took a deep breath and began to explain.

"There was a break-in at the clinic. Someone ransacked the place—specifically, they targeted Edward's office—after I told you Ed had asked me to look for something there. The only person I talked to about that was you. Whoever broke in, didn't just look in the obvious places. They also broke open the hidden drawer I told you about!"

Carl's eyes widened.

"Simone, I swear I didn't tell anyone. Is there any chance someone heard you? I was alone at home when we talked."

"And I was inside my car," Simone replied in confusion. "I didn't think anyone could hear me, but maybe someone did. Or maybe my phone's been tapped. I just don't know."

Carl didn't say anything. Instead, he got his phone from the kitchen island and quickly typed a message to Simone. He held it up so she could read it.

We need to get someone to check the apartment and our phones.

Simone nodded.

"For now, just come into my arms. I need you, and this last week has been hell," he said, his voice raw with vulnerability as he opened his arms wide.

As she approached, he pulled her gently toward him, taking her glass from her hand and setting it on the countertop. He hugged her tightly as if he never wanted to let her go.

Simone melted into his embrace, reveling in the security she had been missing. For the first time in days, a sense of peace and hope lifted her spirits. Their love would grow stronger, and they would grow more confident in their relationship.

They stood there, wrapped in each other's arms, the silence between them filled with unspoken words of comfort and reassurance. The moment was broken by Carl's phone ringing.

"I'm not going to get that," he said, continuing to caress her hair. But the annoying sound persisted.

"I think you should answer. Things are a little too crazy right now to ignore a phone call," Simone said.

Carl hesitated for a moment, his brow furrowing as if he was weighing her words. Finally, he let out a small sigh, shook his head, and picked up the phone.

"It's Joseph. You're right; I need to answer." He took the call and spent a few minutes talking with his lawyer, a grave expression causing his eyes to darken.

Simone watched his face, reading the concern in his eyes. A knot formed in her stomach.

Now what?

The moment Carl disconnected from his call, she put a hand on his arm.

"What did he say?" she asked softly.

"The FBI just knocked on the office door. They were looking for me…" His voice faltered as he exhaled sharply, running a hand through his hair, the gesture revealing his mounting frustration. "Joseph says they've got some new evidence against me. He said he'll explain later. But the FBI wants me for more questioning- and this time, not at the police station."

Simone's sense of calm evaporated.

It must be the copy of the photo Ed has and the information about my office being ransacked.

If she wanted to have a marriage based on trust, she needed to be honest with him…

Even if he decides to divorce me.

She was sure he hadn't heard her whole conversation with

Ed at the apartment. Simone's heart pounded as she prepared to confess everything.

"Carl...I think it is about... There was another photo... I found it in our bathroom drawer in our apartment in the city. It's very similar to the photo the FBI already has, but this one was taken from another angle, and I was totally confused. I called Ed to show it to him. That's what you saw through the footage."

Carl's expression was a mix of shock and confusion as he listened.

Simone took a deep breath and continued.

"I lied to you about Ed wanting me to find something in his office. Someone broke in, and you can imagine how everything looked from my perspective. Ed used the camera on his cellphone to take a picture of the photo." She lowered her head before finishing her confession. "So, I think it's possible they want to talk to you about those things. Maybe Ed gave them the photo."

Carl sighed deeply, his shoulders dropping as he pulled her into a gentle embrace. His warmth enveloped her, offering a fleeting moment of comfort amid the storm brewing around them. After a pause, he pulled back slightly, his hands sliding down to hold hers.

"Thanks for telling me, honey. We need to trust each other. No more secrets. You should have come to me first, but I understand."

Simone nodded. "I promise, no more secrets. We'll get through this together."

"Joseph hired a helicopter to take me to the city," Carl said, glancing at his watch. "It'll be at the airport in about thirty minutes. They don't just want to question me. There's a court order for my arrest, honey. I need to turn myself in."

Simone's heart sank. "Carl, no... Just because of an old

photo?"

Carl shook his head vehemently.

"I don't think so. I think there's more to it, but Joseph doesn't know what this is all about. He thinks the best thing to do is to go there and speak with them in person."

""Is Joseph a good lawyer?" Simone asked, keeping her tone as neutral as possible. She didn't want to add to Carl's worries, but the question lingered in her mind. She didn't know Joseph personally, and with everything on the line, she needed reassurance.

"He was my father's pupil. Other than my father, there's no one I trust more," Carl said. "We need to trust him, Simone. I'll be okay. We need to believe that the truth will come out. I ´ve been in this situation before..."

The sad look on Carl's face told her he was referring to Lara's death. He had faced not only the police but also a trial.

"I'm coming with you. I won't let you face this alone," she said, determined to stand by her man. "I´m going to get dressed."

*****

When they landed at the private airport in the city, Joseph was already there, waiting near the hangar. His posture was composed, as always, but the tension in his eyes betrayed the gravity of the situation. He strode forward purposefully, extending his hand to Carl first with a firm grip. Then he turned to Simone, offering her a polite but restrained smile as he shook her hand.

"Hello, Simone." Joseph greeted her, his tone brisk yet courteous. "I've arranged a car to take you to the apartment. It's parked just outside." He gestured toward the private hangar behind him. "The driver will be holding a small sign with your name. Carl and I will take my car, and I'm afraid we need to get moving."

Joseph turned to Carl, his expression tightening with urgency.

"Let's go, buddy."

Carl nodded.

Simone's chest tightened as he turned to her. Without hesitation, she stepped forward, wrapping her arms around him. She pressed her finger firmly into his back, trying to anchor him to her, even if just for a fleeting moment. Their lips met in a brief but poignant kiss.

"I'll see you soon," Simone whispered. She managed to sound calm, despite the storm of emotions swirling within her.

"Yes, I´m going to be back home soon," Carl said, his hand lingering on her arm before finally pulling away to follow Joseph.

Simone stood there, watching as they disappeared around the corner of the building toward the lot where pilots and passengers parked their vehicles.

Taking a deep breath, she crossed the tarmac and entered the back door of the private terminal. The small waiting room was deserted except for a man who stood behind the customer service desk. Simone nodded to him as she proceeded out the front entrance where only one vehicle was parked. The driver was holding a sign with her name printed neatly on it. She approached and introduced herself, and he nodded in acknowledgment before gesturing toward the car.

He opened the door for her, and she slid inside, her mind spinning with a thousand thoughts. The soft thud of the door closing felt like an exclamation mark in the overwhelming quiet. She fastened her seatbelt, her movements automatic, her gaze unfocused. The driver settled in and started the car without a word, leaving them enveloped in silence as the cityscape passed by.

Simone didn't register the details of the short journey; her mind was too preoccupied with Carl, the FBI, and the unsettling possibilities that hung over them. Before she realized it, the car came to a gentle stop and didn´t move again. She blinked, pulled from her thoughts, and looked out the window to see the familiar facade of their apartment building.

The driver stepped out and opened her door. Simone got out of the car. She smiled politely and handed him a tip.

"Thank you very much."

"Thanks a lot, ma'am," he replied, touching the brim of his cap in a courteous gesture.

Simone turned and strode toward the apartment building entrance. Her heels clicked softly against the pavement.

She pushed the door open and stepped inside.

*****

Over the rest of the evening, Simone paced around the apartment, too nervous to sit. She'd set her purse and cellphone on the counter, and as the hours dragged on, she kept glancing over, worried she'd miss a call from Carl or Joseph. But the phone remained stubbornly silent, and Simone kept pacing from one side of the room to the other. Finally, she stopped.

"I'm going to wear a hole in the floor," she mumbled.

A low whine made her turn. Tommy sat right behind her, looking up at her with his sad brown eyes.

"It's okay," she said, as much to reassure herself as to comfort the dog. She leaned down and caressed his silky head.

The man who had been taking care of Tommy had brought him back home at Simone's request. She needed some company, and Tommy's presence was just the comfort she hoped for.

As she wandered through the apartment, lost in her thoughts, she couldn't help but laugh softly as she noticed Tommy trailing behind her with unwavering loyalty. His nails clicked against the floor, and his curious eyes followed her every move.

"Have you been following me this whole time?" she asked him, certain he'd been doing just that. She smiled. "How about if I take you for a proper walk?"

As if he understood every word, Tommy raced to the door then back to her side, before twirling in circles, chasing his tail.

Simone laughed softly. She felt the same way. It would do them both some good to get out of there for a while before they went stir-crazy.

*****

Simone spent all night and most of the following day, Saturday, worrying. Around dinner time, Tommy trotted toward the front entry. He stopped a few feet away, sat on his haunches, and stared.

The beep of the electronic code unlocking the door brought Simone to her feet, her heart racing. She rushed toward the entrance but stopped beside Tommy and waited, her hands nervously clasped together. When the door opened, Carl stepped inside, his presence filling the quiet apartment.

He was alone. Dark circles beneath his eyes made him look older, and the wrinkles on his forehead seemed more pronounced, deepened by the weight of whatever he had been through. His clothes were wrinkled, and he looked as though the last twenty-four hours had aged him far more than it should have.

"I need to get cleaned up before we talk, honey. I'll go take a shower." He skirted both her and Tommy and strode down the hall to their room.

While Carl was getting cleaned up, Simone ordered some food, choosing a nice risotto from a nearby restaurant Carl loved. She'd gotten him into this latest bit of trouble. The least she could do was provide him with some comfort food.

Had they fed him?

Even if they had, she doubted he'd had the stomach to eat much...

She set the table with their best dishes and crystal glasses. Some people reserved their finest pieces for guests, but Simone had always believed they should be used for the most important people—themselves. And right now, if anyone deserved a nice table, it was them.

*****

The restaurant's timing was perfect. They delivered the food just minutes before Carl finished his shower.

When Simone heard the water stop, she called out,

"Honey, food is on the table."

"I'm coming," he called from the bedroom, his voice heavy with fatigue.

Carl came out of the room in pajamas and looked at the table. The silverware and crystal shimmered in the soft candlelight. A tender smile formed on his lips as he took it all in.

"I love you. Thank you so much for being here, honey. I'm sorry I'm not dressed for the occasion."

"You're perfect. The occasion is to celebrate that you are home."

"Barely..."

Carl pulled a chair out for Simone, and after helping her to sit, he sat beside her and took a deep breath. "Let me explain what's happening."

"There's no rush, love. Let's eat first. Once you get some food into you, you'll feel much better."

The aroma of the creamy risotto wafted through the room, mingling with the soft glow of the candlelight. Simone carefully served them both, the tinkling sound of the silverware bumping into the China faint against the quiet backdrop.

Concerned for Carl´s welfare, she kept the conversation light. She told a funny story about something Tommy had done earlier that day, and then shared small, inconsequential details about the errands she had run that morning. She hoped the familiar rhythm of her voice would create a safe, calming space for him.

Carl stayed silent, his fork methodically moving from plate to mouth. His silence wasn't dismissive, but heavy, as if he were lost in thoughts too tangled to share. Simone resisted the urge to press, choosing instead to let the quiet comfort of the moment and the delicious meal soothe him. Sometimes, she knew, being present was more powerful than words.

As they finished their dinner, she stood and gathered the plates into a neat stack but ultimately left them on the table. The weight of the day lingered in the air, and she followed Carl to the sofa.

Once they were seated, Carl leaned back, running a hand through his hair. Simone turned to him and frowned.

"I need to ask," she said gently, though the tension in her voice was unmistakable. "All that time just to talk to you about the photo and my office being ransacked?"

Carl put his hand over hers. "Don't worry, honey. Those things were just small parts of why they wanted me. They are investigating the deaths of the Asian girls—by the way, they were Chinese. They asked me repeatedly why I had one of those young girls on my lap, where she came from, and so on...as if my answer would be different the fiftieth time they asked. The biggest issue seems to be that they discovered money transfers to my office account and from there, the funds were sent to some other places they're investigating. They didn't tell me where the money came from or where it went. They assumed I know everything that happens in accounting."

She widened her eyes.

"Transfers?

Carl sighed, rubbing his temples.

"I don't have a clue, and the agents didn't explain anything to me. They wanted me to give them answers, not ask them questions," he said, giving her a tired smile. "I had a hard time convincing them I didn't know anything because we have an accountant who handles the money and bank accounts. She's been working for me for years now."

"Do you trust her?"

He shook his head.

"I don't know. I don´t want to believe she's a criminal," he said, his voice low and strained, "but we need to consider every possibility. Joseph is digging into the financial records. He's going to see what else our accountant knows. The FBI has copies of everything, so we need to understand what they're basing their claims on before they drag us further into this mess."

And if Carl is involved?

A tiny voice inside her—the one that still had a bit of doubt —asked.

Can I trust him completely?

Simone pushed away that thought. Her husband was a good man; there must be an explanation for the transfers.

She took a deep breath, trying to rationalize. Her feelings were like grasshoppers, jumping from one emotion to another.

Be steady!

She ordered herself.

She moved to the table and gathered the stack of plates she had piled earlier. With deliberate care, she carried them to the kitchen, gave them a quick rinse, and then arranged them neatly in the dishwasher. She repeated the process with the glasses. The rhythmic clinking of dishes and glasses offered her a momentary distraction as she took her time, hoping the simple task would help mask her swirling emotions. The last thing she wanted was to add to Carl's already overwhelming troubles.

When Simone returned to the living room, a sense of calm had washed over her, though it was tentative, like a fragile veil holding back her worries. She sat beside Carl. He remained quiet, his eyes unfocused, gazing into the distance.

Simone reached out, placing her hand gently on his knee.

"Let's try to have a calm Saturday night, love," she said softly, her voice a deliberate mix of warmth and encouragement. "How about a movie?"

Her words were purposeful, an attempt to draw Carl out of his lethargy.

"I'm too tired for that, honey. I'm going to pass out in bed," he replied, getting up.

Simone nodded.

"You've been through enough. You need to rest and recover. " She rose and touched his shoulder.

The intercom buzzed, and Simone jumped, her heart racing for a split second. She placed a hand on her chest and exhaled, shaking her head at her own reaction.

I'm a little too stressed with everything going on.

She took a couple deep breaths to calm herself before she

had a heart attack.

Carl went to the intercom in the kitchen.

Simone strained her ears, trying to catch snippets of his conversation, but his answers were brief and clipped, giving her no clues. Her heart sank as she watched him stride back into the living room, his movements brisk as he headed toward the door. A tight knot formed in her stomach. Unannounced visitors on a Saturday night rarely brought good news.

"Who is it?" she asked, her voice tinged with unease.

"Joseph is coming up. He has some news," Carl said from the door. "It must be bad. Otherwise, he would have waited until tomorrow."

Simone forced a smile.

"Let's hear what he has to say. Maybe it's something that can help us."

But her thoughts had grown frantic.

No good news is urgent. What's so urgent that it couldn't wait?

CHAPTER FIFTY-THREE

The Lake of Oblivion

Joseph walked in, his briefcase clutched tightly, the tension in his body reflected in his tight lips and sharp, piercing eyes. He greeted them with a quick nod.

"Hi, Carl... Simone. I have an update, and I'm afraid it's not good." He tossed his briefcase onto the table. "I tried to call you, but it seems you turned off your phone." He glanced at Carl and pulled an iPad from his briefcase. "Here." He held it out to Carl. "Take it. You need to see this."

Casting aside her usual discretion, Simone moved to Carl's side. Normally, she would never pry into other people's business, but the gravity in Joseph's demeanor drew her in. She leaned closer, fixing her gaze on the screen.

Carl looked at the iPad, his expression grim. "What is this?"

"It's a video from RNA Broadcast, some breaking news that's been looping for almost two hours now," Joseph replied.

Carl pressed play on the video. The screen showed the front entrance of some kind of medical building. FBI agents exited the double doors, pushing an elderly lady in a wheelchair. A reporter, holding a microphone, explained the situation.

"This is a significant development in a secret FBI investigation we still don't have much information about. One of the agents, disguised as a Doctor, was working undercover at Autumn Gardens, a state-of-the-art clinic in the Hudson Valley. While there, and thanks to DNA testing, the agent discovered that a woman they believed to be Carmem Luccese was Olivia Taylor Hay, the renowned federal judge. Judge Hay had supposedly died in a car crash years ago."

Simone and Carl exchanged shocked glances as the video continued.

"The investigation has revealed that Judge Hay had been admitted under the name Carmen Luccese. She had been kept drugged and was unaware of her location or what had happened to her. Doctors still don't know her real situation or if she can recover her mental health after spending so many years in apparent captivity and under extreme sedation. The investigation has also uncovered a series of financial transactions linking the judge's family with a well-known New York law firm. Authorities are working to untangle this complex web and identify all parties involved."

The video cut to a series of clips that showed Peter Hay in cuffs after being found guilty. A voiceover stated he was the judge's youngest kid, a convicted serial killer who'd been sentenced to life for his crimes. Another image showed police escorting Deena Hay when they'd considered her a suspect in the cyanide acid murders, with the voiceover noting she was the judge's eldest child and a former public prosecutor.

The old footage ended, and the camera returned to the clinic, where agents were placing the lady into an ambulance. Simone's breath caught. One of the men assisting the agents was dressed like a doctor, but he looked remarkably like Edward. Even though he wore a cap and sunglasses, she'd swear it was him.

"My God, that's crazy! Damn press! They're making Deena look guilty!" Carl exclaimed, running his fingers through his hair. "I never met Deena's mother. When we got married, she was already dead, and Deena talked about her constantly. She missed her. A lot. She was Deena's role model!" Carl shook his head. "I can't imagine how Deena must feel about this."

"That´s not the worst part!" Joseph spoke up. "The worst thing about all this is that they're implying the office is connected to this crime in some way. Thankfully, they aren't reporting the name of our firm yet. At least, I don't think so. I don't know if they did earlier, but it's only a matter of time until they disclose that information." He pointed to Carl. "We need to solve this mystery immediately." His voice grew tight, a sharp contrast to his usual cool demeanor. "That clinic must have been on the receiving end of some of the money we've had going in and out of our accounts." He glanced at Carl, his gaze intense. "If we don't figure this out, you, the firm, all of us will be implicated in this crime, and our good name will be ruined forever!"

"Did you talk to Ophelia?" Carl asked. He set the iPad on the coffee table and began pacing the room.

"No, I couldn't find her. Her phone is off. After I leave here, I'll go to her apartment, but I have a bad feeling about this, Carl. When I started working at the office, Ophelia was already there. Where did she come from? How did you end up hiring her?"

Carl stopped pacing, a worried look crossing his face.

"The business was growing, I couldn't take care of everything, and Deena referred Ophelia to me. She had worked for Deena's father or something like that. She had great references."

"But linked to the Hay family," Joseph said, his wrinkled forehead conveying his concern.

"Maybe she just decided to rest. It is a Saturday," Carl said. "She's a quiet person; She must be home."

"I'm going there now. I have her address." Joseph scooped up the iPad and put it back inside his briefcase then grabbed the bag and headed to the door. Before he stepped out, he turned and said, "Buddy, please don't leave home, and for God's sake, turn your phone back on, okay?"

"It must be charged by now. I will...promise," Carl said as he reached for his phone.

Joseph pointed at Simone. Same goes for you, Simone. I tried to reach you, too."

Simone nodded. "I put it on silent so it wouldn't disturb Carl."

Joseph sighed but gave a quick nod. "I get it. Just make sure both of you keep your phones on and close by. We can't afford to miss any updates."

*****

Once Joseph had gone, a heavy silence filling the room. Simone wrapped her arms around herself to ward off a chill and turned to Carl, who was standing and looking through the window, and went to the sofa.

"Ed was on that video. He told me he was out of town, doing some kind of investigation. I gave him the address of the clinic because I got news Peter's former nanny lived there..."

Carl swung around to look at her.

"How did you know about the clinic?" he asked, raising his eyebrows.

Simone took a deep breath.

"That's a long story."

"It's past time for you to stop keeping secrets from me, Simone. I'm in deep shit, here, and more and more, it seems to me you're doing things behind my back in partnership with that criminal."

Simone lowered her head and gripped the edge of her seat. A wave of guilt rushed through her, hot and unrelenting.

"Carl, I'm sorry. I never meant to keep things from you. I was trying to protect you and find answers. But you're right." She nodded. "I mean it. No more secrets. You are not going to like this. Will you come here please?"

She tapped the cushion, and Carl went to sit beside her. Turning a little, so she could look him in the eye, she took a deep breath and swallowed hard.

Here goes nothing...

She grabbed his hand and started talking.

"I've been visiting Peter..." Simone paused, waiting for Carl's reaction.

His eyes widened, but he didn't say a word.

"He told me about his nanny. There were contradictions between Peter's story and his sister's, so I decided to ask my secretary to investigate—"

"Your secretary? What is she? Some sort of secret agent?" Carl asked, his voice rising.

"No, she has a friend who's some sort of paralegal or something like that," Simone replied, trying to keep calm. "Whenever I need information, she talks to him. I don't know who he is or what exactly his profession is, but he's... quite good. He uncovered the real name of the woman—Deena couldn't remember it—and Peter tried to mislead me. This friend of Patricia's also tracked the nanny to a clinic, found out she has Alzheimer's, and learned that Peter's family has been paying for her room and care. That raised red flags for me because Peter said he hated her, and Deena claimed she hadn't had any contact with the woman since Peter was a teenager. That's when I told Edward everything

I'd found out."

Carl looked at her closely, as though he was processing the information before reacting.

"So, your secretary's friend found out about the nanny and her condition, and you passed that information on to Edward?"

""Exactly. The nanny's name is Carmen Luccese," Simone continued. "Edward told me he would be out of town for a while but didn't tell me where he was going. When I saw that video, I recognized him immediately. He was dressed as a Doctor. He had on a cap and dark glasses, but I'm sure it was him. He's a psychiatrist, so the FBI must have had him go into the clinic undercover."

"And of course, you didn't tell me about it," he said, his voice rising with anger, each word sharp and cutting. "There are too many things we haven't discussed, and they're affecting our lives deeply."

"I was trying to find answers, Carl. I didn't want to burden you with more worries until I had something concrete, but you're right, we need to be more open with each other."

"We certainly do… I can't think clearly right now. I've been up for twenty-four hours. I need some rest." He looked and sounded exhausted.

"Go get some rest. I'll watch the phones. I'm too restless to go to bed now," she replied.

Carl nodded. "Thanks, Simone. Wake me if anything comes up."

He made his way to the bedroom, his steps heavy, and Tommy trailed along behind him. Simone watched him go, her mind racing with all the unresolved issues they were facing.

Once he'd shut the bedroom door, Simone settled back on the couch with their phones by her side. The silence of the apartment was a stark contrast to the turmoil in her mind.

What was the connection between Carl's office and Peter Hay? Simone's thoughts churned as she pieced together the fragments of information she had. Carl had once been Peter's tax lawyer, and her husband was still helping Deena—Peter's sister and Carl's ex-wife. Her imagination began to run wild. Could there be a direct link between Carl and the crimes involving the Chinese girls? The thought sent a chill through her, especially as she recalled the damning pictures of her husband with the girls on his lap.

But how is Peter Hay connected to these crimes? What role did he play in this sinister web?

Simone tried to call the number Edward had given her, but there was no answer.

At least I know he's alive and well.

To distract herself, Simone turned on the TV and chose a news channel. However, there were no updates on the Autumn Clinic case. All the major networks kept playing the same video Joesph had shown to her and Carl. The lack of updates from the media about such a significant development was both puzzling and unnerving. Then again, when she had been in the eye of the hurricane that had been the cyanide crimes, the FBI had cut some sort of deal with the press to control the flow of information. That control lasted until everything broke down with more terrifying news.

Two hours passed as Simone switched from one news channel to another, seeking updates. Finally, RNA began providing more news on the case. They reported that Olivia Hay was now in the intensive care unit at a local hospital. They didn't reveal the hospital's name.

Which one? Local to New York City, or near the Autumm clinic?

No images of the judge were shown, further deepening

the mystery. However, they did show her daughter, Deena, arriving at the hospital. The camera focused closely on her face, blurring the background. Deena did not make any statements to the press.

"Poor woman... her damn brother has put her through hell," Simone murmured. During the cyanide-poisoning investigation, Deena was implicated, detained by the FBI, and eventually cleared. Her career was wrecked by the scandal, and now she had discovered that her mother was alive—and that her name had likely been used to send money to the Autumn Clinic. Simone was convinced Deena hadn't known anything about it, and she wished she could offer her psychological support, but she wasn't the right person for that.

Simone picked up her phone to call Joseph and let him know about the latest news...just in case he hadn't heard. She dialed his number, and he answered after a few rings. She told him what she'd heard about the hospital and Deena.

"Thanks, Simone," Joseph replied. "I haven't seen the news. I'm trying to find that damn accountant, but the woman seems to have vanished. She's not at home, and her neighbors said they saw her leave with a suitcase."

"That's bad!"

"It is and worse of all, she has no friends at the office who might know where she went, and if she has any relatives, I have no idea who they are. The woman is a total mystery. I just told the FBI about her disappearance, and they're going to get a court order for her arrest. I'm going to the office now, and I'm taking an accounting expert with me to deal with the numbers.

"It's late, Joseph. You should go home and rest."

"I can´t. The expert won´t be free in the morning, and I don't know anything about accounting. Before the FBI knocks on our office door again, I need see if I can figure out how deep in the shit we are."

"Do you want me to wake up Carl?" Simone asked, sensing the urgency of the situation.

"No, he knows as much about math and bookkeeping as I do, which means zero. I'm going there now. Take care, Simone, and keep me posted please."

"Thanks a—" Before she could say goodbye, the line went dead. "Damn unpolished people!" She murmured to herself.

CHAPTER FIFTY-FOUR

Numbers Never Lie

After spending several minutes fighting with the computer to connect to the internet, Simone finally managed to enter the remote session with Wendy Rafalli. She had decided to work from the city for a few days; she couldn't leave her husband alone to face the FBI.

Carl was under a sort of house arrest. He didn't have to wear any kind of monitor, but the terms of his bail were clear—he couldn't leave the apartment. Simone decided to stay with him as much as she could to support him through this difficult time.

Even if it meant treating her patients online—something she despised—Simone was willing to adapt. She much preferred face-to-face sessions, where it was easier to read their body language and connect on a deeper level.

"Good morning, Wendy." Simone smiled a greeting, trying to keep her voice steady despite the stress she was under.

"Good morning, Doctor Bennet." Wendy smiled, too, but even through the camera, small wrinkles were visible around her eyes, and she had dark circles beneath them.

"Is everything all right?" Simone asked warmly. "You look

tired."

With a faint smile still gracing her lips, Wendy nodded.

"It's been a long week, but I'm managing."

The way Wendy moved, swaying like a quick pendulum, sharply contradicted the calm certainty of her words.

"What's going on? What's robbing you of your regular energy and balance? Is it work, health, or relationships?" Simone asked.

Wendy sighed, and her faux smile finally slipped.

"Honestly, it's a bit of everything. Work has been overwhelming, and I haven't been sleeping well."

"Not sleeping well... Seems to me it might be linked to personal problems or hormones."

"My hormones are fine. I have this implant now, and so far, it's working great," Wendy said.

"That's good. So, the problem is related to emotions? How is Gabriel, and how about your husband? Have you had a chance to reflect on your relationships with both?" Simone asked, gently probing.

Wendy's expression tightened slightly, her lips pressing into a thin line.

"My husband and I are going through a rough patch. We don't talk anymore. It feels like we've lost our connection. I don´t know what I feel for him anymore." As she spoke, her hands moved rapidly.

"How about Gabriel? Are you connecting with him? Did it evolve into something deeper, or are you still maintaining a sex-only relationship?" Simone watched Wendy as closely as she could to analyze her movements.

Wendy breathed in, rolled her eyes, and said,

"It has been the most amazing sex I've ever had. I rented a small apartment, and we sneak off once a week to meet there for a few hours of pleasure. I can't describe how he makes me feel. He's like a slave; he never comes until he's sure I'm satisfied. We experiment with all kinds of positions, all types of touching, everything two people can think of. I'm open with him. I'm not afraid to masturbate while he fucks me, and I'm not too shy to ask him for what I need. I feel free to do whatever works best for our mutual pleasure. I'm so connected to him, whenever I leave him, it's like I leave behind a part of myself," Wendy said, her eyes sparkling with the intensity of her emotions.

"Do you think you're in love with him?" Simone asked. She had her suspicions, but Wendy needed to reach a conclusion on her own.

Wendy sighed deeply.

"No, I don't think so. It's more like a physical craving, you know? I feel like a drug addict searching for my dealer. I want his body, his sex, his mouth, everything." She paused as a hint of sadness colored her voice.

"Everything except the man himself," Simone said.

Wendy raised her head and frowned; her forehead furrowed as if she was struggling with a thought.

"We'd never work out." Wendy explained. "We're too different. Like oil and water. He's the sun, and I'm the moon. He loves nature, fresh air, people, going out dancing and drinking. I'm the opposite. I love peace and quiet...solitude, and I don't need a lot of human contact. I prefer to stay home with a good book, not go out all the time."

"For someone who claims not to be in love, it seems as if you've given a great deal of thought to the possibilities."

Wendy looked up, a startled look on her face.

"I guess I have. It's just that the physical connection is so strong. It makes me think about what might be possible if we were more compatible in other areas."

"It's natural to consider all aspects of a relationship, especially when one part is so fulfilling," Simone said. "But recognizing the differences is important, too. Do you think the differences are insurmountable, or is there a way to bridge them?"

Wendy sighed.

"I think they might be insurmountable. As much as I enjoy our time together, I can't see us ever finding common ground in our everyday lives. Life is more than just a few hours of sex, and it feels like we're only meant to connect in that one way."

Simone nodded. "Understanding that can help you make more informed decisions about the relationship. Sometimes, acknowledging the limitations of a connection can be freeing. It allows you to appreciate what you have while being open to finding what you need in other areas of your life."

Wendy seemed to relax a bit, her expression softening.

"You're right. Maybe it's okay to enjoy what we have without expecting it to be more than it is."

"How about your marriage? Do you think it's possible to find that sort of connection again?"

Wendy stayed silent for a while. Finally, she shrugged. "I want to believe it's possible, but it feels like we've drifted so far apart. Sexually, it was never like what I have with Gabriel."

"Rebuilding feelings takes time and effort from both partners," Simone said gently but firmly. "It's about finding common ground and making the effort to understand each other's needs and desires. When it comes to sexual desire, it's harder, but there is a chance to improve things in that area, too. What I see is that while you're sailing other oceans, like spending time with Gabriel, you're not going to be able to rebuild your relationship with your husband."

Wendy answered so quickly it took Simone by surprise.

"So, I'm not rebuilding anything! I need Gabriel, his gentleness, his body. Sex with him is surreal. I've never experienced anything like it and I won´t give up."

Simone leaned closer to Wendy; her gaze intense.

"If I can give you one piece of advice, consider your feelings for Gabriel with more caution," Simone said. "It seems to me that what you have with him is not just sex. You just told me your souls are involved. That's bigger than what you've admitted up to this point, and there is another point I want you to consider: Have you ever had an orgasm with your husband?"

Wendy didn't respond, but the way her mouth hung open and her wide, startled eyes locked on Simone spoke volumes.

*****

Around noon, Simone took a break to have lunch with her husband. Carl had ordered something for them, and the table was set when she went to the dining room. Tommy was eating his lunch nearby, and Carl was on the phone. When he saw her, he finished his conversation and joined her at the table. He pulled a chair out for her and then sat, placing the phone near his plate.

"Bad news from Joseph," he said, nodding toward the phone with a grim expression. "It seems that before Ophelia left, she erased a significant portion of the archives. What remains isn't exactly reassuring. There's money coming into the office account from several untraceable sources. We need to talk to the bank, and that takes time, and there are funds going out for expenses that have no connection to the office at all. Apparently, this has been happening for quite some time—probably since she first started working with us. Joseph has already contacted the bank to retrieve older records, but so far, they've only been able to access data from the past year."

Simone frowned, absorbing the information.

"Like payments to the Autumn Gardens Clinic?"

Carl nodded.

"The problem is, the FBI has the files. We don't know if what they have is from before or after Ophelia erased the data, so it's hard to say what they've got that we don't."

"They probably have full access to everything," Simone suggested.

"That's exactly what Joseph said." Carl pointed his fork at the phone. "I don't have an opinion either way. My head is spinning."

"That video Joseph showed us mentioned a connection between the Hays and a law firm," Simone said, reasoning things out in her mind as she spoke. "I think they shared that information intentionally—to see who would panic and scramble to protect themselves."

Carl leaned back in his chair.

"You think they're setting a trap to see who in my firm reacts—or if another firm does?" he asked, skepticism flickering in his voice. "I don't see the point, though. They approached me already. They have the data from the office, so it's clear to me they already know our law firm is involved. But...could there be another firm in play?"

Simone nodded.

"It's a possibility. It seems it's a tactic to flush out anyone involved, or to get someone to panic and make a mistake. Like the accountant probably did... She probably panicked when the FBI got involved, and that's why she vanished."

Carl sighed, rubbing his temples.

"That makes sense. We need to be extra cautious and make

sure everything we do is transparent and documented. We can't afford any missteps. Besides, they said the money was sent in Deena's name, but she has no idea about it."

"Maybe this is just another trap from Peter, to harm his sister even more..."

He turned, shifting in his chair to face her.

"That´s what I think! You would be a great FBI agent, Doctor Bennet!" He smiled at her.

"I´m a mind´s detective."

"Yes, you are. Let's eat. The food must be cold by now."

But before they finished their meal, Carl's phone rang. He put it on speakerphone while chewing. Deena's name appeared on the screen.

He has nothing to hide from me.

"Carl," his ex-wife said with a sob, "I need help!"

CHAPTER FIFTY-FIVE

More Than Ten

To give Carl some space, Simone left the table, took her plate, and went to their room. He kept the phone on speaker, but she didn't try to listen to his conversation with Deena. If someone wanted to be with their ex, they probably would be, so whatever they needed to talk about was their business.

Simone took a deep breath and finished her dinner. Building trust was crucial if they were going to make their relationship work. Carl hadn't told her he was defending Deena, but he had chosen to be with Simone, and they were working through their challenges together.

She was finishing brushing her teeth when the sound of Carl's voice startled her.

"My God, you almost gave me a heart attack. I was completely lost in my thoughts."

She turned to him, her mouth full of foam. Carl chuckled softly, though his face was tense and lined with concern, a look Simone recognized all too well. She grabbed a towel and wiped her face clean, determined not to let anyone—especially Carl—see her like this. The thought of her husband catching her in such a state, looking more like a foaming dog than a charming woman, annoyed her.

"Sorry, honey—I didn't mean to scare you. I just wanted you to know Deena's in a bad place. She's overwhelmed and terrified about the implications of all this. She had no idea about the clinic, let alone the money being sent there in her name." He looked down and went on, "She needs a lawyer, but I can't help her with this. Joseph is defending me, and at some point my interests are going to conflict with her family's." Frustration edged his voice. "I'm thinking about resigning as her attorney, too."

He stopped and ran his fingers through his hair.

"I talked to Joseph, and he thinks we must worry about the associates, the office, and of course, about myself. Joseph gave me the name of a colleague, and I passed it on to her." He sounded determined, but there was some other emotion there, too. Guilt, most likely.

"Joseph is right," she told him. "It's for the best. But I know you, and you're feeling awful for not helping her." Simone put a hand on Carl's arm.

He sighed deeply.

"You're right. Joseph is right. But I hate not being able to be there for Deena, especially with everything she's going through. She was a big part of my life once. Our marriage ended, but our friendship didn't." He paused, appearing to struggle with his emotions. "I've always been there for her until now, just when she needs me the most."

Simone nodded, even though her experiences with her irresponsible former husband had never allowed for that kind of lingering bond. But as she studied Carl, a shadow of unease curled in the pit of her stomach.

Simone couldn't shake the feeling that her husband wasn't telling her everything about Deena's current situation—and more importantly, why he felt he had to step down as her lawyer. His words were careful, too careful, and the hesitation in his voice hinted at something unspoken.

He's not telling me something.

*****

Between her last two patients, Simone finally got someone to answer Edward's phone. A man whose voice she didn't recognize told her he would pass her message on to Ed. It was almost nine p.m. when her phone rang. She answered quickly.

"Hello?"

"Hi, Simmie. It's Ed."

"Edward! I've been trying to reach you for days. I´ve been so worried. Where have you been? I saw you at the Autumn Clinic. The news had a video..."

"Damn machine!" Carl's voice echoed from the bedroom as he cursed at his computer. He had decided to work from there to give her privacy with her patients.

"I'm sorry, Simone. Things have been chaotic. I've been trying to gather more information about the Hays and the clinic. I couldn't risk any communication that might compromise the investigation. Based on how many phone calls our guy said you made, I guessed you already knew I was inside the Autumn Clinic," Edward said.

"Yes, I did. Plus, it's been all over the news," Simone replied. "And since I recognized you, I'm guessing others might have, too."

"I hope not! I think you know me better than anyone."

Simone didn't reply to that. Just then, she wasn't sure she even knew herself.

When she stayed quiet, Edward continued.

"I'm working with the judge right now, hoping to help her regain her senses. In my professional opinion, she doesn't have permanent brain damage; it's just the drugs keeping her in a state of disorientation. That's how I discovered who she was. One day, out of the blue, she looked at me and said, 'I'm a judge!'"

"It sounds to me like a cry for help."

"I'm sure it was."

"So, you called the cops and took her out of that place?" Simone asked.

"No, I got some hair samples and asked for a DNA test," Edward explained. "Peter's genetic information is already in the government's database, so it wasn't that difficult to get a match and confirm her identity."

"Do you have any information about how she got there?" Simone asked.

"Right now? No—nothing," Edward replied. "Since she seems to trust me, I'm working with her at the hospital. A lot is happening. The Chinese girl who survived is recovering well. The FBI has a translator—she doesn't speak a word of English, and, well, she isn't speaking at all. She seems too scared to tell us what happened to her and to the girls in the photos." Simone listened intently, her concern deepening.

Simone listened intently, her concern deepening.

"Do you think she'll be willing to talk eventually? Her testimony could be crucial."

Edward sighed.

"It's hard to say. Trauma like this can make it very difficult for victims to open up. You know how it is."

"Yes, I do."

"What's so urgent you were trying to find me?" He abruptly changed the subject, as if he were in a hurry to move on.

"What's so urgent you were trying to find me?" He abruptly changed the subject, as if he were in a hurry to move on.

"There's been a breakthrough regarding the financial transactions tied to the Hays and my husband's law firm. There are unexplained transfers—no one knows where the money came from or where it went. At least, that's what Carl and his lawyer told me. But I have a feeling the banks might have a report on that.

"The bank would definitely have reports showing everything."

Simone ignored his comment.

"One of the transactions involves the Autumn Clinic, as you know, which his office was apparently paying on behalf of the Hays. My husband and his partners had no idea this was happening. It seems his accountant was behind these maneuvers, but now she's fled—and she erased some critical files before disappearing."

Simone blurted everything out in one breath, her words tumbling over each other in a rush.

Edward didn't answer right away. After several moments he said,

"I didn't know that. I heard something about it on the news but didn't link it to Carl. The FBI doesn't report to me about their investigations; they just ask about mine. I'll see if I can discover something for you, but I can't promise anything. I'm still a convicted inmate, trying to do a good job so they'll commute my sentence."

Simone sighed, her tension easing slightly. "I understand. It's just been tough here. Carl is under house arrest, and we're dealing with so many uncertainties."

"Simmie, try to relax a bit. I think we'll sort out the bank operations issue, and it won't take long. Just stay safe. I know it isn't possible for to stay out of the investigations, so please keep me posted. I'm here to handle it." Simone took a deep breath, trying to heed Edward's advice and calm down a little. "I know you're right, but it's hard not to worry. I just can't shake the feeling that people aren't telling me everything—that this goes way deeper and is far more sinister than we know."

While she spoke, Simone noticed someone was trying to reach her, their persistence evident in the repeated buzz of her phone.

"I'm sure," Edward said. "Just focus on supporting Carl. Leave the investigative work to me and the professionals. I need to go now. Take care."

"You, too," she said, but the line had gone dead.

Simone checked her phone to see who had been desperately trying to call her. At first, she didn't recognize the number, but then it hit her.

Keanne...

With a sigh, Simone hit the button on her phone to call back.

"This might be important," she said aloud. "I just hope she hasn't gotten herself into some kind of trouble again."

She dialed the number and waited as it rang. Keanne answered quickly.

"Doctor Bennet! Finally! I've been trying to reach you all evening. I'm in deep shit. Could we have a session...like right now?"

Simone consulted her watch. *Nine fifteen.* It was already late.

"Hold on. I need to check something, and then I can answer that question for you. I´m not at the clinic. I´m in New York, so we'll have to do a virtual session."

"That's fine with me," Keanne answered.

Simone put the phone on mute and went to speak to Carl.

Holding the phone in one hand, she found her husband still working, sitting in front of his computer, balancing his phone between his shoulder and his ear, and typing furiously on his keyboard. She waved her hand to get his attention.

"I have an emergency with a patient," she said when he

looked over at her. “Do you mind if I work for another hour?"

Carl shook his head, giving her a reassuring smile.

“No, honey. I’ll probably be busy longer than that. Don’t worry,” he said before turning back to his phone conversation.

Simone nodded, grateful for his understanding. She released the mute button and put her phone to her ear.

“Okay, Keanne. I’m sending you a link for our session right now.”

Simone went back out to the living room where she’d have quiet. After settling on the couch and putting down her phones, she sent the invitation link to Keanne. A moment later, they were face to face in the virtual meeting room.

What had this crazy girl done now to create yet another emergency?

*****

Simone tried her best to take stock of Keanne’s physical condition. The girl’s last adventure had left her with bruises all over her body. But Keanne’s heavy makeup and the poor-quality image on the camera made it impossible for Simone to identify anything out of the ordinary.

“What’s the urgency, Keanne? How’ve you been?” Simone asked softly.

Keanne lowered her head.

Oh, boy…

That was a bad sign.

She’s either embarrassed or she’s about to lie about something.

But Keanne raised her head and fixed her gaze on Simone.

“Doctor Bennet, I’m in trouble,” she blurted. “And I won’t lie… I went back to that place.”

“The house where you took part in the orgy?” Simone held

her breath, waiting for Keanne's explanation, bracing herself for whatever chaotic tale the girl might recount.

"Yes, that one... But this time, it was a new experience, totally irresponsible, and now I'm afraid I might have caught a disease or something."

And since when has a public orgy with strangers been a responsible experience?

Simone's concern deepened, but as always, she kept her emotions from showing on her face.

Keanne continued. "There were more people this time, and it got really out of hand. I didn't use protection, and now I'm terrified about the possible consequences. I know it was a huge mistake."

Simone took a deep breath.

"Keanne, I need you to be completely honest so I can help you," she said, keeping her tone gentle. "What exactly happened?"

Prepare yourself for another trip to the madhouse.

Keanne lowered her head and kept it there.

"I had sex with multiple people, and no one used a condom. It was reckless, and I wasn't thinking clearly."

"I understand."

No, I don't.

"You're afraid you might have a disease because someone ejaculated inside you?"

"Not exactly." Keanne's voice was barely a whisper now. She seemed to be sitting on her hands. "We didn't stay in the main room—the burgundy one I told you about before. There was another one. They asked me if I was ready for an adventure, and I was. You know, when I get horny, I don't think... They took me to this room that had dark walls and one of those blacklight lamps that barely illuminated anything. There was one of those gynecologist tables..."

Simone's imagination followed the girl into the dark room.

"Please go on. You don't need to be ashamed with me." Simone moved her hand in a sign for the girl to continue, though Keanne probably couldn't see it.

"Well, I laid there, completely naked. They put my feet on those metal supports, tied them, and a procession of men—I lost count, but I think it was around ten or twelve—fucked me. A few stood in line, masturbating, waiting to put their dick in my mouth, and they all came inside me. Inside my mouth and my pussy... Some of the guys were just watching and masturbating on my body. I was covered and soaked in cum when I decided to use the safe word because I couldn't handle it anymore. I had come so many times, and I was beginning to feel pain."

She raised her head, her eyes locking onto Simone's with intensity.

Simone kept her composure.

"How did you feel when you stopped?" she asked gently.

"I felt so proud of myself," Keanne admitted. "I made so many men come; I finally felt complete. And I can't lie to you, I'm going back to another session. But right now, I'm scared. I could have a disease, and if I do, I brought it on myself."

"How about pregnancy, did you think about that?"

Keanne's eyes grew wide, and she shook her head.

"Let's hope for the best. Keanne, you will have to get tested, but HIV usually doesn't show right away, so you'll have to get tested monthly for a while. If you keep going back, you'll be living in constant worry because you'll be continually renewing the risk. In my professional opinion, you need to regain control. Try to understand why you feel the need to be used by men to feel proud and complete and consider not going back to that place."

Keanne raised her head.

"I was not used by men!" Her voice was sharp and defiant. "I used them, too! And I can't stay away from there."

"Why not?" Simone asked, trying to remain calm. "I can help you with that."

"No, I don't want to be helped to avoid the best orgasms, the most real and most sensational orgasms I've had in all my life. If I need to die to keep experiencing those, then I will, gladly!" Keanne replied, her voice firm.

"So, are you telling me you need at least ten men for you to have an orgasm? Or could you climax with every man that was with you?" Simone asked, taking notes.

Maybe she has problems with having an orgasm.

Keanne hesitated before answering.

"No, I don't need ten men to make me come. It's just...the intensity and the thrill of the situation. I can reach an orgasm with one man, but the whole experience together makes it more...overwhelming."

"If you don't want to stop, it means you don't want to change anything. So, you don't need a psychiatrist. You just need to get precautions and a regular Doctor to give you a prescription for blood tests. I can do that for you, but I can't treat you anymore if you don't decide to change, to find the reason behind your behavior, and commit to adopting healthy habits."

"Please don´t abandon me. I need you!"

"Before our next session, I want you to think carefully about what you want and why you are coming to see me. If you don't want to change your behavior—and I'm not judging you—it's up to you to decide what feels right or wrong for you. If you decide you don't want to make any changes, then you don't need to come to our next session, because it would be a waste of your time and money."

CHAPTER FIFTY-SIX

Who to Trust?

Lights danced chaotically, casting long, shifting shadows across Simone's vision. Faceless figures surrounded her, their muted moans mingling with the oppressive hum of an unseen force. Masks concealed their features, their hollow eyes glinting in the fractured light. Suddenly, she felt herself lifted off the ground, cradled in the arms of a man whose face she couldn't discern. Her bare skin prickled against his rough touch, her vulnerability a tangible weight pressing down on her chest.

He placed her on a cold, unyielding table. She tried to push herself upright, but her limbs were heavy, unresponsive. Darkness clawed at the edges of her vision as hands emerged from the void, gripping her wrists and ankles, pulling her down. Her muscles screamed for movement, for strength, but she was paralyzed, her body betraying her in the moment she needed it most.

She opened her mouth to cry out, but no sound escaped. The silence was deafening, swallowing her screams before they even formed. Fingers ghosted over her skin, their touch sending jagged bolts of sensation that danced precariously between terror and a twisted thrill. Lips pressed against her, leaving behind trails of heat that burned and froze in equal measure. A mixture of fear and an inexplicable, forbidden pleasure surged through her veins, overwhelming her senses.

"Honey, wake up. You're having a nightmare," Carl whispered in her ear while shaking her gently.

"Oh my God, that was so weird!" she exclaimed, sitting up abruptly in their bed. Her chest rose and fell with deep, uneven breaths as she tried to steady herself. The vivid remnants of the dream clung to her like a second skin, every nerve alive with the lingering echoes of her desire. Her skin tingled, each sensation amplified, yet the abrupt end of the dream left her with an ache she couldn't place—a mix of longing and frustration.

"Ending your workday with a heavy session must have caused you a lot of stress. Are you okay?" Carl sat up beside her and held her hand.

"I am now. Good morning, honey." Simone turned to him and pressed her lips to his, her kiss lingering, filled with a yearning she couldn't suppress. Her body ached for connection; her skin was alive with sensitivity. Her breasts, tender and expectant, longed to be caressed, and her entire being craved the warmth of his touch. The remnants of her dream pulsed through her, unfinished, leaving her desperate to bridge the gap between fantasy and reality. She needed Carl—needed to feel him, to have him, to complete what her subconscious had left undone.

She kissed her way along his jawline and to his neck, but he moved away and left the bed, running his fingers through his hair.

He's worried.

Simone observed him, her gaze lingering on his furrowed brow and distant gaze.

What could possibly be wrong at this time of the day?

"Sorry, babe... I swear, there's nothing I'd rather do than

make love to you. But with everything that's happened lately, my head is spinning. I couldn't get a hard-on right now if my crazy, out-of-control life depended on it. Not to mention, I barely slept, and when I did manage to drift off, I had a vivid nightmare. A couple of big guys with biceps like tree trunks tossed me into a cell in some Medieval-style dungeon, and I landed on my ass in the dirt. The place was pitch black except for the thread-like beam from one of the guard's flashlights. His partner slammed the cell door closed while I sat there like a statue, staring up at them." He paused to catch his breath then took a sip of water from the bottle on his nightstand.

"A second later they were gone, taking the only bit of light with them. The darkness swallowed me up, and suddenly, I sensed I wasn't alone. Behind me, someone—a man—laughed. It was soft at first, but he quickly grew louder, until his maniacal cackling surrounded me, and I realized what they had done. Using bogus evidence, they convicted me of killing all those girls, and worst of all, they'd sentenced me to spend eternity in that tiny, dark, dirty cell with Peter Hay!"

Carl took another sip of water and shook his head as if to chase away the details of his dream. He glanced at Simone, and the shadows beneath his eyes looked even darker in the pale morning sunlight.

"Maybe I can just make you come?" he asked.

Although the dream scenario he'd just described sounded like a fate worse than death, Simone had to smile. Finally, a person who had a normal reaction to stress, instead of using it as just another excuse to get their rocks off.

"Don't worry, love, your body's reaction is absolutely normal. Please don't feel bad. Science—and my many years of practice—shows that men often can't achieve an erection under pressure. Don't let it bother you; everything is perfectly fine."

"It's so nice to be married to someone who understands all

the complicated human emotions."

He smiled down at her then turned and went into the bathroom, leaving her there full of desire.

Yes, I do understand, but that doesn't change the fact that I'm still horny.

Resigned, Simone decided she'd just have to spend a few extra minutes in the shower to take care of herself. Her eyes flicked toward the closed bathroom door. The moment Carl stepped out, she slipped inside, a small vibrator discreetly in hand. It wouldn't be the same as the real thing—the firm press of a hard shaft—but it would do. She was determined to start her day with an orgasm. After that, she could face the turmoil of the world around her.

Simone closed the door behind her, making sure it clicked shut. The last thing she wanted was for Carl to walk in on her masturbating—it would seem selfish after what he had just been through. Taking a deep breath, she turned on her little device, positioning it delicately on her clit. The gentle hum combined with the warm water cascading over her skin and sent electric currents coursing through her body. She bit her lip, stifling the moans threatening to escape, her breaths coming in shallow bursts. The orgasm hit her quickly, an intense wave that left her legs trembling and her body humming with residual pleasure.

After her pleasurable shower, Simone dressed in a pair of loose, wide-leg pants in a gray cotton-rayon blend, a white tank top, and a long, flowing, open-front cardigan that matched the pants. The soft fabric draped over her figure like silk, striking the balance between professionalism and ease.

The sound of clinking plates and cups came from the kitchen, the familiar noises of Carl's morning routine. Simone followed the enticing aroma of freshly brewed coffee. Entering the kitchen, she found Carl standing by the counter, holding a steaming mug and talking to someone on the phone. His voice was low and measured, his expression unreadable.

Simone tried not to listen, but she couldn't avoid overhearing his conversation. She turned away to serve herself a fresh cup of coffee.

"I understand that, Joseph, but—"

His lawyer.

Simone glanced at her husband over the rim of her mug. Once again, his frown lines looked like canyons.

Carl said goodbye and ended the call. He set his cellphone on the counter and then took a couple of steps to stand by her side. He put a hand on her shoulder.

"Sorry I didn't get a chance to make breakfast," he said, gesturing toward the coffee pot. "I just managed to brew some coffee, and then Joseph called, and I completely forgot about the rest. The FBI wants me to give another statement about the accountant and the firm's bookkeeping. I feel like an idiot for not paying closer attention to my finances. I trusted too much."

"Calm down, honey. You were teaching and working as an attorney, not to mention all the time and energy you put into being a great husband. Where do you think you would find the time to handle the bookkeeping, too? It's hard to control everything. How bad are things with the FBI?" she asked, her back to him as she prepared bowls of cereal for them both.

"I don't know. I feel like they're playing a game of cat and mouse with me. I'm not under arrest, but I can't leave home. I was invited through my lawyer to go give another statement, but of course, if I decide I don't want to accept their kind invitation, I could be arrested… Things are messy right now."

Simone turned and set a bowl of cereal on the bar counter in front of him.

"We'll get through this together, Carl. It's going to be

tough, but we'll manage. You're not alone in this. Eat something." She pointed to the bowl.

Carl nodded and picked up the spoon. "Thanks, love. It means a lot to have you by my side."

He took a big bite of cereal and chewed slowly. His gaze stayed fixed on some distant point, and his expression went blank. Simone shook her head. He probably had no idea what he was eating... She could've served him Tommy's food, and he would have cleaned his bowl.

Is he still worrying over his upcoming meeting with the FBI or remembering the details of the dream he described to me earlier?

"We'll figure it out step by step." She reassured him, settling in the chair beside him to eat her cereal before it got soggy. But even though she managed to keep a smile on her face, inside she didn't feel so confident.

*****

A full schedule helped Simone pass the hours Carl was away; otherwise, she would have done a marathon, pacing around inside their apartment.

As she opened her laptop for another virtual session, the sound of a key turning in the lock caught her attention. She glanced at her watch—4:30. He had been out for more than six hours, but she wouldn't be done with her last patient of the day for at least another fifty minutes.

*****

When her last session ended and she was finally ready to talk to Carl, she found him standing in the living room, staring out the window, lost in thought.

"Honey?" She called out to him in a soft, sweet tone, careful not to startle him. "How did everything go?"

He turned to her and pointed at the sofa.

"Let's sit."

She followed him, and they settled side by side on the couch. He took her hand and gave it a soft squeeze.

"They found Ophelia. She didn't go far. She admitted that when she heard the news about the Autumn Clinic, she panicked, and she fled without looking back. She was frightened someone might kill her, but she didn't say who. She's under protection now."

"Is she going to cooperate?" Simone raised her eyebrows, her mind conjuring the image of an accountant she had pictured in her head—a woman with a severe chignon and thick glasses with heavy, dark frames that obscured her expression.

"I think she must. If she wants protection, she needs to come clean. But anyway, the FBI had been monitoring the office for some time, and they already had all the data she erased. It seems since she started working for me, money has been coming into the office from different sources. She would then attribute those funds to income from various nonexistent clients...clean it, I guess it's called...and then she used the money to pay all sorts of bills for the Hay family, including the damn Autumn Clinic."

Simone squeezed his hand.

"So, she worked for you and the Hays at the same time?"

Carl nodded.

"The FBI doesn't know if she worked for Peter and Deena or just one of them. The only thing I know for certain is that Deena recommended her to me when we were married." Carl shook his head. "I refuse to believe my wife betrayed me."

Disbelief and sorrow colored his voice. But he cleared his throat and continued.

"Joseph told me that Ophelia confessed to the FBI that her father is seriously ill with some kind of degenerative muscular disease. The information hasn't been confirmed yet because he lives in another state, but apparently, the illness keeps him confined to his home, and he needs constant care. That costs a lot of money," he said, his tone heavy. "Since the Hays couldn't pay her enough, they recommended she come work with us. She made about the same salary, but she supplemented her income by following the Hays' orders. It seems like a match made in hell: I needed an accountant, they needed a way to launder cash, and Ophelia needed money."

He smiled sadly, a faint, bitter curve of his lips, and shrugged as if to say, *Hey, no big deal, right?*

The Hays...

Was he blaming both Peter and his sister? Simone decided to find out.

I can't believe Deena is involved in this... or I'm the worst psychiatrist ever. She is just a bitter solitary woman.

"Do you think Deena knew what Ophelia was going to do, or do you believe Deena concocted the entire scam?" Simone asked.

Carl's lips twisted as if he'd just tasted something extremely sour or gross.

"I hope she wasn't involved because it was during the last days of our marriage, and I trusted her completely. Now, I don't know anymore." He shrugged. "Ophelia is still cutting a deal with the FBI. I hope they can reach an agreement and the truth comes out. For now, this is what we have. At least, I'm not forced to stay home anymore. But I do have to stay in town or let them know in advance of any trips I need to make. They wanted me to confirm some of Ophelia's statements, but she cleared me. She said I didn't know about the stuff in the office."

"That's fantastic, honey!" Simone hugged him. Thank goodness that woman had decided to be honest. Carl didn't deserve to have his life turned upside down like it had been.

I can go home.

Simone felt a twinge of guilt. But she couldn't help it that she preferred working from her office and seeing her patients face to face. Besides, the air in their apartment was too stuffy for her taste.

"Are you going back to the office tomorrow?"

"Yes, I planned on it," Carl replied and added, "I figured you would want to head back. I know how important your patients are to you. So, if you need to go, then go. I'll be fine. I intend to stay busy. We'll see each other on the weekend. I'll get authorization and come home to you."

I will go...but not just to tend to my patients.

Although she wouldn't tell Carl—at least, not now—she had some other business she wanted to handle.

CHAPTER FIFTY-SEVEN

No Pain, No Gain

MacDougall always gave Simone chills. She parked her car, stepped out, and closed the door. Leaning against the cool metal, she wrapped her arms tightly around herself, bracing herself against what felt like an invisible force pressing down on her.

I would go crazy if I had to stay inside those walls for more than a few hours...

She really needed to talk to Peter. She was convinced he was the key to everything: his mother being locked in the hospital, the murdered Chinese girls, and the accounting issues in Carl's office. Were all those things part of a big plan or just the random actions of a psycho? Simone didn't have all the answers yet, but she planned on solving those mysteries as quickly as possible.

With a deep breath and her purse clutched tightly in her hand, she marched toward the entrance, firm and determined.

Simone approached the prison's main door, forcing herself not to glance up at the cold, foreboding structure looming over her. Her resolve hardened as she walked through the security checks, each step bringing her closer to the man who might hold all the answers. Her stomach muscles contracted. Just thinking about their meeting set her nerves on edge. She hoped Peter would be willing to talk, but she prepared herself for his customary resistance or mockery.

Finally, she was led into the infirmary where Peter Hay sat waiting for her. His hands were cuffed and connected to the table in front of him, his long legs splayed out and crossed at the ankles, and he sat slumped in the Formica chair as if he hadn't a care in the world. He looked up as she entered but didn't move. His eyes glinted, and a ghost of a smile turned up the very corners of his mouth. His presence was unsettling, his expression a stark reminder of the dangerous mind she was about to engage with.

"Hello, Doc. And no, I didn't lock up my mother. What do you think I am? A monster?" he asked, the mockery in his tone unmistakable.

"I'm not here to talk about your mother. I'm here to talk about how you feel now that you've heard she's alive. I'm guessing nobody here"—Simone paused and waved a hand to indicate their surroundings—"has thought to ask you how you feel."

She spoke in a condescending tone, barely hidden behind a thin veil of feigned empathy.

"Feelings?" Peter uncrossed his legs, adjusted his body in the chair, and leaned over the desk. His gaze pierced hers. "This is not a place for feelings, but if you want to know how I feel, I can answer you directly. The same way I felt when I thought she was dead: absolutely nothing. Our relationship was cold and distant. The great judge didn't care for children who didn't fit into her power plans. I didn't fit. I hated law from the start. I was messy! So why would she bother with me, and why should I care for her? The only time she remembered my presence was when it came time for our yearly *family* portrait."

The last words came out in his viper tone, dripping with sarcasm, and his lips contorted into a sneer.

"Since when does our good, morbid, necrophiliac Doctor work for the FBI?" he asked.

His question caught Simone off guard. Her eyes widened in surprise.

"I saw him on TV," Peter continued, putting his finger to his lips. "Shhhhhh, I won't tell his secrets, even if I think everybody here already knows them." He had lowered his voice. "But you know, he hasn't been back here in a long time. They used to be more careful."

Simone composed herself quickly.

"That's not the point, Peter. I'm not here to talk about Ed or your mother. I'm just trying to understand you, your personality. Do you remember our project for a book? It's on hold right now, but we need to continue. I thought recent events might have created an opportunity for me to understand you better." Simone pulled her voice recorder from her purse and put it on the table in front of him.

"You do know that *The Silence of the Lambs* has already been written, right, Doc? What you're trying to do here isn't exactly groundbreaking." He lowered his head, so his mouth was near the recorder.

"Yes, it is, and I can prove it." Simone nodded and continued in a firm tone of voice. "Clarice wasn't worried about Lecter's feelings. She needed his help. I don't need yours. All I want is to understand your motives."

"My motives for what, exactly? Killing women? You already know that... Childhood traumas..." he said in a mockingly dramatic voice, batting his long eyelashes. "For trying to kill my mother when I had the chance? Same roots, trauma. Different motivation." He shrugged nonchalantly.

Then his gaze locked onto Simone's, sharp and

unrelenting. He leaned forward slightly, as though daring her to flinch, waiting to see her reaction to his brazen confession that he had been responsible for his mother's accident.

Simone refused to respond to his attempt to intimidate her.

He's trying to cover up what he did—locking his mother away—with this new story.

"How did you plan your mother's death?"

"How I planned her death... That was super easy... I tampered with the brakes on her car... Nobody found the sabotage. I was a little bit disappointed; you know. She was a super judge, always putting criminals behind bars. Anyone could have gone after her, seeking revenge, but the experts who examined the car concluded she lost control and hit a truck That's it. Makes me think her peers didn't like her much and were just happy to be rid of her—or were a bunch of incompetents!" He shook his head.

"How about your father? He died with her in that car crash, didn't he?"

"Yes...but he was just collateral damage. I didn't know they'd be together that day."

"Why did you want your mom dead? Did you have another motive? If so, I'm not aware of it. You just said your motivation was different—different from what? The thing that drove you to kill your other victims?"

Peter clicked his tongue.

"Victims? I told you before—they weren't victims...they were just bored people begging God to take them into His arms."

He rolled his eyes upward, staring at the ceiling Then he looked back at her, his gaze indifferent, and continued in the plain tone of someone who didn't care about anything.

"My reason? Money of course. I needed to finance my ideas. She didn't agree. I would have never asked my father—I knew the answer would be no. So, when they both died, it worked out even better for my plans—their money got split between me and my sister."

"So, you decided to kill her. But when that plan failed, you locked her up in an institution and…what? Did you find another body to put inside a coffin? Nobody checked?"

Peter scoffed, his tone dripping with derision.

Are you nuts, Doc? I told you already—my mom was dead. It was her body inside a beautiful oak coffin I picked out myself, while I cried bucketloads of tears, of course. She was a little damaged from the accident, so there was no open coffin."

He swiped at his eye dramatically, brushing away an imaginary tear with exaggerated flair. The cuffs on his wrists clinked softly with the movement.

"Let's say I believe your story," Simone said, her tone measured. "You inherited some money, and then what? What did you do after that? What did you do with the money?"

She made a mental note to investigate Peter's inheritance, her instincts telling her there was more to uncover.

"It wasn't just some money—it was good money! I don't even remember what I did with my share." he said with a dismissive shrug. "And believe me, Doc, I'm not pretending. I killed my mother, accidentally my parents—she's been dead and rotting in hell for years." His voice dropped, cold and sharp, slicing through the room like a blade. "But now someone's mocking the world, bringing the old witch back from the dead like a damn nightmare."

He let out an artificial laugh.

"Maybe she'll even drop by for a visit." He leaned forward

and locked eyes with Simone. "Do you think she'll be proud of my accomplishments?"

"What would you do if she walked through that door?"

Simone pointed over her shoulder, and Peter stayed silent and didn´t move, just said,

"If there were even the slightest chance of that happening —and there isn't—I'd kill her again."

He is not lying, he believes his mother is dead.

His cold assassin's eyes were back. Their icy green depths spoke about how much he hated his mother.

"If you killed her the first time for money, and you got the money, what's the point in doing it again now? Why so much hate?" Simone asked, her voice steady, probing deeper into the abyss of Peter's mind.

His eyes narrowed, the cold glint intensifying.

"Why don't you go visit her in the hospital or in the cemetery and ask her? Maybe she'll enlighten you about all the formative events of my life. People say moms know their kids best..." he said, his voice calm and measured.

"Because I'm interested in your point of view, not your mother's." Simone pointed at him. "Do you want to know what I think about this whole story about your mom?"

She looked deep into his cold eyes, trying to read his thoughts. She didn't know what she would say next, but she needed to catch him off guard, had to unsettle him. Otherwise, this entire conversation would be a waste of time.

Peter raised an eyebrow. He seemed cool and calm, but the fidgeting of his hands indicated he wasn't as relaxed as he wanted to appear.

"Alright, Doc. Enlighten me. What do you think about my oh-so-wonderful mother and her impact on my life?"

"I think your mother abused you, not Carmen Luchese...

You loved that nanny. Your mother, on the other hand, would come to your room, touch you, and make you do things that disgusted you. That's why you hate her so much. You weren't interested in the money. You wanted to punish her for making you lick her pussy!"

Simone braced herself for the coming explosion, even as she experienced a pang of regret at using such vulgar language.

Peter's expression shifted from shock to anger. With lightning speed, he grabbed Simone's hand and twisted it. She heard a crack, and the pain shot straight from her wrist to her brain. She screamed, and the guards came running, but they were a little too late. Peter had already managed to overpower her, using his hands and the chain between his handcuffs to pin her neck against the table. Simone struggled to draw a full breath.

I'm not going to be his victim again.

Simone reached up and scratched at the hands wrapped around her throat, digging her nails in deep. Peter was too strong for her, but the shouts of the guards and the click of a gun nearby made him relax his grip. An instant later, he let her go.

Simone gasped for air, her throat burning. Her wrist had begun to throb, but her insides grew warm with the thrill of victory. She'd finally figured him out…knew what damage he'd suffered that drove him to behave the way he did.

The guards swooped in, pulling Peter away and securing him in restraints. One of the guards helped Simone to her feet, his face a mix of concern and anger.

"Don't ever think about coming here again! I will kill you!" Peter shouted from the door.

"Let's go!" One of the guards yanked on Peter's arm, dragging him out into the hallway.

Peter kicked and screamed obscenities, but the burly guards seemed more than a match for Peter's psychotic-fueled strength. Still, a bit of fear lingered, causing Simone's chest to ache. The reality of Peter's threat hung in the air, a stark reminder of the danger she faced in trying to provoke him.

Peter's obscenity-filled shouts faded as his escorts dragged him away down the corridor, and Simone sighed with relief.

"Are you okay, Doctor Bennet?" the guard who'd remained with her asked, his voice steady but tense.

Simone nodded, still catching her breath.

"Well, I think my wrist is broken, but I'll be okay. Thank you." She showed her arm to the guard.

I'll call a Doctor. Stay here, please," the guard said, touching her shoulder.

Simone's wrist throbbed with relentless pain, each pulse like a sharp reminder of her injury. She tried to examine it herself but quickly realized she was too hurt to assess the damage properly. After fifteen minutes of waiting, she straightened in the chair she'd slumped into as a doctor hurried into the room. He seemed well-trained in fractures and, after a thorough examination, determined that nothing was broken. However, he decided to immobilize her wrist for the next few days to ensure proper healing.

*****

Thirty minutes later, Simone left MacDougall and strode toward the parking lot. She glanced back at the complex of buildings.

I'm never going back to that place again. Carl and Ed are right; it is too risky!

Simone got into her car, her immobilized wrist throbbing with a dull ache. Gripping the steering wheel with her good hand, she drove away from MacDougall. As the prison receded in her rearview mirror, her breath and heartbeat gradually returned to normal. The encounter with Peter had been intense and dangerous, but it had given her crucial insights, too.

Simone paired her phone with the car and then dialed the number Ed had given her. She told the contact it was urgent and that she was leaving MacDougall. In less than five minutes, she was on the phone with Edward.

"Simmie, please tell me you're okay." The concern in Ed's voice came through loud and clear, but at least he didn't censure her.

"I'm fine. Please don't worry. Really. I've been to MacDougall, and I have news..." She drew a deep breath. "I think I know how you should approach your conversations with Olivia Hay."

CHAPTER FIFTY-EIGHT

You Must Find Her

Simone's week passed quickly, giving her very little time to process recent events or think about the pain in her wrist. Patients came and went, and one of them attempted suicide. Simone had learned enough about him to say with certainty that he didn't want to die. He desperately needed his family's support, and the attempt to end his life had been his way of crying out for their help. Simone had to provide him with support in the hospital, where she also took the opportunity to have the splint she'd been wearing removed.

Simone talked to Carl on the phone every night. She never told him about Peter's attack.

With each call a sense of normalcy slowly began to return. The heavy burden they had been carrying started to lift as news came in that Ophelia was cooperating with law enforcement. With the deal she struck with the FBI, Carl and his partners were cleared -at least that was the information Joseph received- and all eyes turned to Peter Hay, who now found himself under the glaring spotlight of suspicion. According to Ophelia's official statement, he had been involved in money laundering. Carl had no updates yet on Deena's statement.

Thursday evening was mild, the crisp air cool enough to be invigorating, so Simone decided to go for a run to shake off the stress that had accumulated over the week. She laced up her running shoes, feeling the anticipation of the open road ahead. She needed this—time to recalibrate her thoughts.

She hadn't had the time to exercise since before going to New York, and her body craved the rush of adrenaline she got when she ran, like an addict who needed a fix. She'd grown more and more anxious and irritable with each sedentary day that had passed. Running and meditating were her escapes, her way to disconnect from the pressures of reality. But for an entire week, she hadn't done either of those activities; her full schedule and her injured wrist hadn't allowed her.

The streets were quiet as she set off, her steady breaths syncing with the rhythmic beat of her footsteps. With each stride the worries of the week began to fall away, leaving only the simplicity of the run and the satisfaction of taking time for herself.

The cool air on her face grounded her, pulling her back into the present. She was determined to live in the moment, appreciating the trees, the houses, and the streetlamps along her path. In Simone's opinion, living in the here and now was the secret to happiness. It required a high degree of mastery over the mind, but that was where meditation came into play.

With each step, she let go of a little more of the past week's frustrations, and even the dull ache in her wrist seemed to fade, overshadowed by the crisp embrace of the morning air and the soft hum of nature around her. The run affected her physically, but it restored her sense of peace, as well. She passed a towering pine tree, glancing up and up to the lacy, swaying top branches.

So resilient and still green after a long winter—that's a true symbol of strength.

Unfortunately, life had other plans and was determined to pull her from the fragile sanctuary of her meditative calm. Her phone, which she'd stuffed into the pocket of her sweatshirt, buzzed softly. Normally, she would have left the stupid thing at home, but with a patient still in the hospital she couldn't afford to be unreachable. She stopped, taking a deep breath before fishing the phone out of her pocket. The screen displayed an unknown number. Simone's heart skipped a beat. Edward? She hadn't heard from him since she'd talked to him on Monday.

Taking another deep breath, she swiped to answer, hoping for good news but bracing herself for anything. The person on the other end had hung up, but suddenly, messages began to pop up on her screen.

Hello, Simmie, it's me, Ed. Just text me back. I think your phone is bugged, and WhatsApp messages might not be detectable.

Hello, Ed. How've you been? She responded quickly, texting as fast as she could.

A moment later, another message appeared.

This isn't the phone I got from the FBI, so write this number down somewhere. Get yourself another cellphone, but don't register it in your name. Just send me a message that says new bug. *I'll know it's you. Call me as soon as you have another phone. It's urgent, so please make it happen today.*

Simone waited, but no more messages appeared on the screen. Their conversation was over for now, and so was Simone's run. Her heart raced, not from exertion, but from the sudden surge of anxiety that gripped her. With a handful of words Ed had shattered the peaceful moment she had carved out for herself and had tossed her right back into the middle of her chaotic reality. She stood there, the phone still clutched in her hand, her mind spinning with the implications of Ed's messages.

*****

Simone rushed home as quickly as she could, her mind laser-focused on what needed to be done. On her way, she texted Patricia, asking for a discreet place to buy a phone. Patricia quickly responded.

Go to Walmart or Target and buy a burner phone.

A burner phone? What's that?

It's simple—a basic, prepaid phone. TracFone is one brand, but there are others. You buy minutes with the phone, and later you can get refill cards at Walmart or similar stores. Just grab several cards with a few hundred minutes each, so you don't have to keep going back.

Patricia added an image of a laughing emoji.

I don't want my name registered on it!

The reply came quick and confident.

You don't have to. That´ s why it is called a burner phone. You won't have to give up any personal information to get one, no ID, no proof of address. Just pick a phone, pay, and you're done.

Thanks a lot, Patricia.

You're welcome, Doc.

She drove with fierce determination, pressing hard on the gas pedal, her gaze barely skimming the streets as they blurred past, heading directly toward the nearest Walmart she could remember.

Simone pulled into the parking lot, locked her car, and hurried toward the supermarket, glancing around nervously to make sure no one was following her. Inside the nearly deserted store, she quickly oriented herself and headed straight for the electronics department. Simone spotted the phone she wanted, grabbed it and made her way to the cashier, still glancing over her shoulder and feeling foolish for her paranoia.

After paying, she rushed back to her car, her pace just shy of a sprint. She left the parking lot, squealing tires.

Some distance away, she pulled over to the side of the road and took a deep, steadying breath. With shaky hands, she unpacked the phone, inserted the SIM card, and silently prayed it had enough charge. To her relief, the battery was almost full. Without wasting another moment, she typed a simple message to Ed.

New bug. She hit send and scowled.

I feel like I work for the Mafia.

Ten minutes later, her phone rang.

"Hello, Simmie. Wow, that was a lot faster than I ever thought you could be. Is this a safe line?" he whispered, sounding as if he was talking to her from inside a closet or a cardboard box.

"It's a burner phone," she whispered back.

Edward chuckled, though he kept the volume low.

"*You* don't need to whisper," he said, amusement lacing his words. "I do because I'm talking to you from inside a broom closet."

Simone couldn't help but smile. She hadn't meant to mimic him. The image of Edward crouched in a tiny, dark closet, trying to maintain secrecy, added a touch of humor to the situation.

"Things are progressing slowly. Too slowly for my taste," Edward said.

She stopped smiling, reminded of the serious nature of Ed's situation.

"It's hard to bring a patient back to normalcy after they've basically been turned into a drug addict from being doped up for so many years," Edward said.

With the traffic going by her car, Simone could barely hear him, so she pressed the phone tight against her ear and focused on his words.

"Olivia has flashes from her past, but they seem to be from long ago, and her problem might be more than just the drugs; she might be suffering from early dementia. We're still trying to figure it out. I'm calling because I need to reach her daughter, but I can't let the FBI find out. If they can piece everything together on their own, my deal is off the table, and I won't be getting out of that hellhole. And now they've assigned me to take care of Olivia, it seems she trusts me, so I'm stuck. I can't move."

"I understand. How can I help you?" Simone asked.

"I tried calling Deena with this phone, but it looks like she's not answering unknown numbers. I sent a message, too, but there's no sign she's read it. Could you try calling her and ask her to call me on this number?"

"Yes, I'll do that now and call you after I talk to her."

Simone hung up and tried calling Deena, but the call went straight to voicemail. She sent a text message, but just like with Ed, there was no sign it had been received. Simone then called Edward back and explained what had happened.

"I know it's late," he said.

Simone instinctively checked the car's dashboard—*8:10 p.m.*

"But I really need you to drive to Deena Hay's house tonight. I'm not sure how long I'll have this phone. Once you're there, please explain to her that I need to talk to her. Send me a message from your burner phone, and I'll call her back."

Simone sensed the underlying urgency in Ed's words. Last time, it had taken Simone two hours to reach her house. She was closer now, but it would still take at least an hour and a half. She didn't hesitate—if it meant helping her friend, she would do anything.

"Don´t worry, I´m heading there now. Are you seriously inside the broom closet?" Simone teased him, trying to lighten the mood a little.

Ed laughed low again.

"No, at the hospital with Olivia. Thanks a lot, Simmie. I hate to put you in the middle of this, but you're the only person I can trust. Love you. Thanks again."

An instant later, the line went dead. Simone rolled her eyes.

Without a second thought, she retrieved Deena's address from her GPS and set up the system to provide her with directions.

Less than an hour and fifteen minutes. Not as bad as I thought!

She turned on some music to keep her company, pressed the gas, and headed toward her destination.

I'm going to turn into a race car driver if I keep this up.

As she headed down the highway, Simone glanced at her regular cellphone sticking out of her purse pocket. Should she call Carl? Returning her focus to the road, she dismissed the idea. Her husband was deeply involved in his problems. No sense in bothering him.

Which means I don't have to lie.

Telling him she was going to meet Deena would only ignite a conflict… one she wasn't ready to deal with tonight.

As she drove, her mind raced as she tried to piece together the best way to approach Deena.

Hey, I'm here to convince you to talk to the guy who was convicted of helping your brother commit his crimes…

The thought made her wince. That kind of bluntness wouldn't get her anywhere. She needed a plan, a strategy that could bridge the gap between Deena's guarded emotions and the sensitive situation at hand. And she only had an hour to figure it out.

At exactly 9:35 p.m., Simone parked in front of Deena's gate. The whole place was dark; not even a garden light glowed up near the house. She left the car at the entrance and, using her phone flashlight, tried to find the intercom. She buzzed it a dozen times, but no one answered.

Discouraged, Simone leaned back against the gate and nearly fell on her ass when the heavy iron began to swing inward. She scrambled to regain her balance and turned around.

The house, eerily quiet and dark, gave her a sense of unease. She hesitated for a moment, considering the implications of entering someone's property when the place seemed abandoned. Had she seen any dogs during her previous visit to the house?

Deena doesn't seem like the type of woman to have a pet.

Simone opened both sides of the double gate and returned to her car. It was a long walk, so she decided to drive up to the front door.

As the car approached, with no lights to illuminate the way, she saw the house—completely dark, with no sign of life. The only sound was the soft crunch of her tires on the gravel.

At the front entrance, she stopped, cut the engine, and left the car. The front door stood wide open. The house that once felt so imposing and secure now seemed like a stage set for something sinister.

She hesitated on the threshold, the eerie silence amplifying her every breath. The glow from her phone's flashlight barely pierced the darkness inside, revealing only shadows and vague shapes.

Stepping cautiously into the house, Simone called out.

"Deena? Are you there? It's Simone. I need to talk to you." Her voice echoed, but there was no response. Her pulse quickened as she moved deeper into the house, turning on the lights as she went. Her instincts screaming that something was terribly wrong. A singular thought crossed her mind.

Turn back and call Ed!

But his request and her concern for Deena pushed her forward.

Simone walked through the house, opening and closing doors, she called out for Deena but got no answer.

Everything was in immaculate order, nothing out of place. As she entered the library, Simone's gaze went to the perfectly aligned books and the neatly organized papers on the desk.

Either this woman has OCD, or she never sets foot in here.

After thoroughly scanning the first floor, she moved up to the second, opening and closing doors, but there was no sign of life.

Simone finally reached what appeared to be the main suite.

This room is as big as a small house!

She flipped on the lights, and her gaze was immediately drawn to a picture lying on the floor beside a safe with its door hanging wide open.

"I thought people only had safes like that in movies," Simone muttered under her breath as she stepped closer. She checked inside. *Empty*. Whoever had been here must have left in a hurry Why else would they leave the safe ajar?

Simone walked into the closet, the soft, plush carpet muting her steps. The air was thick with the scent of an unidentified perfume, a faint reminder of the person who normally frequented this space.

The closet, like the rest of the house, was eerily immaculate—everything meticulously in place, not a single item out of order. Simone ran her fingers along the hangers, each one holding a neatly pressed garment, perfectly aligned as if no one had touched them in days.

It was as if the house was holding its breath, waiting for something to break the silence. The pristine state of the closet made Simone pause. Maybe Deena was still around. The unsettling silence now felt like a prelude to an unexpected encounter. Maybe Deena had just been out shopping and was on her way back, completely unaware of Simone's presence—what if Deena showed up and caught Simone trespassing? After all, she hadn't received permission or an invitation to go traipsing around Deena's home.

Is my concern for her wellbeing a good enough excuse for being here? What now?

Suddenly, Simone recalled something from Carl's diary. Deena had mentioned wanting to quit law to pursue painting. Maybe she had a studio somewhere, and like all artists, had gotten lost in her creative process.

Simone walked over to the window, trying to peer outside. It was too dark to see much of anything, but in the distance, she noticed a gleam of water.

If there's a pool, maybe there's a place where she could have set up a studio, too.

Like a pool house. Her heart raced as she considered the possibility, hoping she was on the right track.

Simone descended the staircase with a sense of urgency, her footsteps echoing in the silence. She headed straight for the kitchen, recalling a back door she had noticed earlier. She scanned the walls for a switch to turn on the outside lights, but found none.

She opened the back door, and the night air greeted her, cool and still. She noticed a panel on the wall outside and hesitantly pressed a button. To her relief, lights flickered on, illuminating a breathtaking garden. In the center was an Olympic-size swimming pool, its surface shimmering under the newly lit lamps. Surrounding the pool was a U-shaped building that looked like it could house a gym or—if she was lucky—some trace of Deena.

"Deena, are you there?" Her voice echoed in the silence of the night.

As Simone hurried along the edge of the pool, she called out Deena's name. A sudden noise, faint but unmistakable, drifted on the breeze. Someone or something was hitting a wall, the rhythmic thud accompanied by muffled cries.

Her heart pounded, and her mind raced. Could Deena be locked in somewhere? Was she hurt? The thought sent a cold shiver down Simone's spine. She bypassed the building near the pool and headed along a short dirt path to another, older building a couple hundred yards down.

CHAPTER FIFTY-NINE

Dogs Barking Alone

As Simone approached the old building, the sounds grew clearer. She could now make out distinct voices—several people, it seemed—and somebody crying for help. Her pulse quickened as she reached what appeared to be a barn. A large iron gate-type door covered the entrance completely, and when she reached for the handle, she found it firmly closed with a massive padlock.

She gripped the cold metal, tugging with all her strength, but it was no use; the lock was secure. Panic surged within her, the desperate voices from inside fueling her anxiety. She glanced around frantically, searching for another way in, but there were no windows, and the imposing gate offered no easy solution. She knew she had to find a way to get inside, to discover what was happening behind that door, and to help whoever was trapped within.

Simone grabbed the padlock, shaking it in a futile attempt to open it, knowing deep down it was pointless.

"Calm down, I'm calling for help. I can't open this myself," she called out, trying to steady her nerves.

The muffled voices inside the barn quieted, and then she heard someone speaking, but the words were unclear.

Then a soft voice responded distinctly. "Understood."

Simone's first instinct was to grab her phone. With shaking hands, she dialed Edward, her voice trembling slightly as she frantically explained the situation. She relayed the details of what was happening, and as she spoke, she glanced around, scanning for any sign of movement or anything that could help her gain entry.

"Simmie, listen to me," he said, his tone measured and controlled. "It's going to take some time for me to get there, so I'm getting help. When they arrive, make sure they know you're there on my behalf, okay?"

Simone nodded, even though Edward couldn't see her. His words grounded her in the moment.

"Okay, Ed. I'll wait for them and make sure they know."

"Good," Edward replied. "Stay safe and keep your distance until they arrive. Don't try to do anything dangerous on your own."

Simone took a deep breath, feeling a bit more in control now."I won't. I'll be careful."

Simone turned back to the barn, her voice firm but gentle as she addressed the people inside.

"Help is coming, don't worry. We'll get you out. How did you end up in there?"

The same voice that had spoken earlier, a woman, responded,

"No English, just me, few. Hungry. Water."

Simone's heart sank. The situation might be more dire than she initially thought.

How many people are in there and how long had they been locked up without anything to eat or drink?

The urgency of the circumstance weighed heavily on her, but she had to remain calm until help arrived. "Understood, hold on." Simone reassured them. "We'll get you some food and help as soon as possible. Just stay calm; help is on the way."

"Okay." The woman sounded feeble, as if talking had drained all her strength.

Simone's heart raced as she hurried around the pool, the minutes feeling like hours. Finally, the sound of police sirens broke through the silence. She ran to the front of the house, eager to guide the officers in the right direction.

As the sheriff stepped out of his vehicle, Simone quickly introduced herself and explained the situation, making sure she mentioned that she was there on behalf of Edward Reynolds. The sheriff listened attentively before motioning to his deputies to grab the necessary equipment.

They moved swiftly, their actions efficient and coordinated, and then they followed Simone to the barn. One officer carried a pair of bolt cutters, the sharp glint of metal catching the fading light of the moon, while the others followed close behind, armed with water and blankets. Tension filled the air as they reached the locked doors. After a few attempts with the enormous bolt cutter, the padlock broke open. A couple of officers pulled the heavy doors open, revealing the scene inside.

A wave of nauseating smells hit Simone in the face. The stench of vomit, feces, urine, and body odor assaulted her senses, and she swallowed hard, trying not to gag. She had to fight her nausea and take deep breaths through her mouth to keep her composure.

"What the hell is this?" one of the officers said, his voice cutting through the tense silence and verbalizing Simone's exact thoughts.

As her vision adjusted to the darkness, her heart sank. A dozen young teenagers, half-naked, their eyes wide with fear and shock, huddled together in the center of the room. Their features looked Asian, and the realization struck Simone like a bolt of lightning.

These must be the pandas Edward has been investigating, remembering immediately the girls in the pictures.

The police officers approached and tried to communicate with the girls, speaking softly and offering them blankets and water, but the girls remained motionless, their heads low. Simone suspected they were too traumatized to respond, frozen in place. The sight filled her with sorrow.

How long have these girls been here?

The officers exchanged worried glances, as if unsure of how to proceed. One of them gently placed a blanket over the nearest girl, trying to coax her into trusting him, but she barely reacted. The others remained huddled together, their fragile bodies trembling.

Simone addressed them. "Who speaks English?" She spoke calmly, trying to convey comfort.

One of the smallest girls, visibly nervous, mustered the courage to step forward. She joined her thumb with her index, showing Simone the small gap between them, and said softly, "Just me, a little."

Simone crouched to the teenagers' level—they were all small in stature— trying to appear as non-threatening as possible and spoke slowly.

"Can you explain to your friends that they are safe now?" she asked gently, her voice soft but firm. "These men are police officers; they are going to help you. I'm going to help you. Nobody is going to hurt you."

The girl's wide eyes searched Simone's face as if looking for any sign of deceit. After a moment, she nodded slightly and turned to the others, speaking rapidly in their native language. As she spoke, the tension in the group seemed to ease a bit, the girls clutching their blankets tighter but no longer as stiff and frozen as before.

The girl turned to Simone.

"Need food," she said, holding up three fingers to emphasize her point. "Days. No food." She stared at Simone, her eyes pleading.

Simone's chest tightened at the girl's words. She nodded quickly, trying to offer reassurance. Simone's heart clenched at the girl's words. She nodded quickly, trying to offer reassurance.

"I understand. We'll get you food right away."

She promised her and then turned to the officers.

"Let's take them to the kitchen. I think we can find something in the refrigerator. They need to be fed before anything."

The sheriff hesitated, shaking his head.

"I don't know, ma'am. I think it's better to wait for the ambulances and take them to the hospital."

"I'm a Doctor," Simone replied. "Trust me, they need to recover their strength now. I can fix them something." Her tone didn't allow for any contradiction.

The sheriff finally nodded, his stern features softening as he seemed to finally grasp the gravity of the situation.

Simone turned to the little girl. Pointing to herself, she said, "I'm Simone."

The girl nodded and pointed to her chest. "Chun."

Simone repeated the name carefully. "Chun." Then she gestured toward the house and continued. "Chun, please ask the girls to follow me."

Simone pointed toward the house to emphasize her words.

"I believe we can find some food there." She gestured with her hands, mimicking the action of eating.

The girl nodded and relayed the message to the others.

*****

A few minutes later, the girls followed Simone, holding hands and walking in a line. When they reached the kitchen, Simone gave them more water. Hydration was more important than food, and the little bottles the officers had given them were long gone. After they figured out how the purified water dispenser worked, Chun helped fill the glasses Simone found inside the cabinets, while Simone opened the refrigerator. To her delight, she found eggs, milk, cheese, bread, and four apples.

I can make an omelet! That will do for now.

Chun, showing a sharp instinct for leadership even amidst her fear, found a bowl inside one of the cabinets and brought it to Simone. With small but skillful hands, she assisted in cracking the eggs. As they sizzled in the pan, she spoke softly to the other girls, urging them to help. They cautiously moved around the kitchen, their movements clumsy but determined, gathering plates and utensils.

Within minutes, each girl had a slice of bread, some apple wedges and a modest serving of what was supposed to be an omelet but ended up looking more like scrambled eggs, thanks to Simone's lack of skill at flipping them.

They clutched their plates tightly, eyes wide with anticipation, and ate hungrily, their heads bowed and their gazes fixed on the food. Watching them, Simone's stomach tightened with sorrow. Clearly, they hadn't eaten in days. She could see the desperation in their rapid, silent chewing, and in the way they glanced around nervously as if expecting the food to be snatched away.

The sound of ambulances arriving echoed through the air, a stark reminder that the girls needed to be taken to a hospital. Still, Simone held her ground, her focus unwavering as she let them finish their meal in peace. It wasn't until the last crumbs had been brushed away and the final bites savored that she finally turned to Chun. With quiet deliberation Simone reached out, her movements gentle as she took the young girl's hand in hers. She gave it a tender squeeze.

"We need to go to the hospital." Simone gave the girl a reassuring smile.

Chun's grip tightened, her eyes searching Simone's.

"Don't worry," Simone said, keeping her voice calm and low. "I'm coming with you. Let your friends know what's going to happen."

Chun nodded, her expression determined as she turned to relay the message to the other girls. Her calm tone and gestures seemed to soothe their anxieties.

However, once out front, when Simone motioned for them to get into the ambulances, the girls hesitated, clinging to one another, reluctant to split up and enter the separate cars. After another quiet but firm intervention from Chun, everyone got moving. Chun continued encouraging her companions, her soft words and excited nods gradually coaxing the girls to settle into the vehicles.

Simone approached Chun before she got into the ambulance.

"I'm going to follow you with my car." Simone pointed to her vehicle, letting the girl know she wouldn't be left alone.

Chun gave a small, brave smile, amazingly bright under the circumstances, and climbed into the last ambulance with two other girls.

As they departed, Simone kept her eyes on the last ambulance. The headlights illuminated the road ahead, but Simone's mind was clouded with unanswered questions. What had happened to those girls? How old were they? The image of their frightened, hollow faces haunted her thoughts.

CHAPTER SIXTY

Not My Problem

The hospital was bustling with activity as the girls were led through various tests and examinations, all of them huddled in one room since they refused to leave each other. They appeared even more fragile under the harsh fluorescent lights.

A Chinese American Doctor, Norman Wu, fluent in Mandarin, was brought in to communicate with the girls. However, despite his efforts, none of them would respond or submit to any of the procedures unless Chun was present. And Chun, in turn, would not move from Simone's side. She gripped Simone's hand and stuck to her like glue, as if Simone was the only bit of safety in a bewildering and terrifying situation.

The Doctor's gentle questions were met with silence, broken only when Chun whispered reassurances to the others, her presence providing a calm that no one could seem to duplicate.

The girls refused to respond to the Doctor's questions about their pasts, origins, or personal details and only answered basic inquiries about their current physical condition. They confirmed to the Doctor they had been left without food or water for three days. Who would abandon them like that? Who could be so cruel as to leave them to die inside that barn?

Food had been withheld often, Chun explained to the Doctor, as punishment when the girls refused to comply with orders. The Doctor asked what kind of orders, but Chun averted her gaze, pressed her lips tightly together, and didn't respond.

As it was late, past midnight, the hospital staff hurriedly prepared an improvised infirmary. They opened the doors between three adjoining rooms, rearranging the space to accommodate twelve beds. Chun carefully counted each bed. After she finished, she turned to Simone.

Simone met the girl's gaze and immediately understood. Chun was silently pleading for Simone not to leave. She turned to the Doctor.

"Can you fix up one more bed please? I'm not leaving the girls tonight." Simone spoke politely but firmly. She'd sleep on the floor if she had to, but she'd rather not...

The Doctor nodded.

"Of course. Ee'll fit another cot in here somewhere."

The Doctor motioned to the nurse nearby. The woman nodded and hurried down the hall to a nearby room. Minutes later, she had brought and prepared another hospital bed for Simone.

The girls had watched every movement with cautious eyes.

Before going to bed, the girls, following Chun's quiet command, formed a circle. In unison, they softly recited phrases, filling the room with their gentle, rhythmic murmurs. Simone watched in silence.

Are they praying?

Their faces reflected a look of serious solemnity that seemed far too old for such young girls. After a few minutes, they fell silent, broke the circle, and climbed into bed. Only

Simone and Chun remained standing.

Simone longed to take a shower and brush her teeth, but the girls needed her now more than she needed to take care of her personal hygiene. She settled under the thin hospital blanket and sighed.

"Simone?" Chun's faint, timid voice came from the next bed.

Lifting her head, Simone squinted in Chun's direction.

"Yes?"

"Thank you. Good night."

Simone's heart softened at the sweet gesture.

"Good night, sweetie. Nice dreams," she whispered back.

The moment Simone's head touched the pillow, she slept.

*****

Simone woke up to the sound of movement as a nurse entered the room, followed by two others pushing carts laden with food. The girls, who had been resting peacefully, began to stir, sitting up in their beds to receive breakfast, and Simone followed suit. She glanced down at her disheveled clothes and scowled. She could only imagine what a mess her hair must be. She'd need to return home soon. She'd told Patricia to cancel her first appointments that mornings, but Simone had patients scheduled for the remainder of the day. She checked her watch. This time of the morning, the drive back would take nearly two hours.

As she received a tray of breakfast, Simone resigned herself to eating before she left. The warm food was comforting after the long, emotionally exhausting night. As she took a few bites of scrambled eggs and spread butter on the soft bread, she mentally prepared herself for the conversation she needed to have with Chun. Would the girl understand Simone's need to see to her responsibilities to her patients?

As Simone finished her surprisingly tasty breakfast, Doctor Norman opened the door and peeked inside.

“Good morning, ladies.” He greeted them in English then repeated the words in Mandarin.

When no one responded, Simone glanced over at the girls. Their demeanors had changed. Whereas a moment ago, they’d seemed relaxed, lounging on their beds, eating their breakfasts, and talking to each other softly, they now appeared stiff. They seemed to recoil slightly at his presence; some hugged themselves tightly, while others quickly lowered their gazes. Simone’s stomach tightened as she observed their reactions. Clearly, men made the girls uneasy. They hadn’t reacted negatively to any of the female nurses.

As Doctor Wu approached Simone, he lifted a sheath of papers and waved them a bit.

“I have some results to share with you.”

He pulled up a chair and sat next to Simone’s bed.

“Most of the girls are dehydrated, all of them are suffering from malnutrition, and their blood and urine tests show an alarmingly high level of painkillers.” He spoke in a low voice, clearly hoping to keep what he said between Simone and himself. “Two of them have tested positive for HIV, one of them has chlamydia.” He scowled, his eyes narrowing until they were barely visible. “I need you here while I to try to talk to them. I want to learn more about their past so we can understand what they’ve been through and how best to help them.”

Simone closed her eyes as a wave of reluctance hit her full force. She opened her mouth to say no but then pressed her lips tightly together. Her first instinct was to distance herself from this situation as it was quickly becoming more complex and distressing than she had anticipated.

But as she glanced at Chun and the other girls, Simone

sighed. She couldn't just walk away. Turning back to the Doctor, she nodded slowly. Her stomach was a little sick, so she had to force a smile.

"Okay," she replied, "just give me a few minutes to contact my secretary, and then I'll be with you."

Simone had set her purse on a chair near the door the night before. She fished out her phone. The screen showed a low battery warning, so she dialed the number and left a quick voice message for Patricia.

"Cancel my whole schedule for today,"

she said then ended the call and dropped the phone back into her purse. Closing her eyes, she counted to three while she took a couple of slow, deep breaths, then she turned to the Doctor.

"Doctor Wu, please explain to them that I need to talk to them," she began, her voice steady. "Tell them I'm a psychiatrist, and I need some information so I can help them. Let it be clear that you are only going to be the translator. They seem to fear men."

She glanced at the girls. They gazed back at her with wary eyes, sitting with their legs still under the blankets. They seemed reluctant to leave the small comfort they had found. Simone could sense their unease, their hesitation, like a tangible weight in the room.

"I would like to speak with each of them individually, but I don't think it would be best to separate them right now. So, it would be better if we all sit in a circle on the floor. I'll talk to you, and you can translate. We'll wait for them to feel comfortable enough to answer," Simone said.

Doctor Wu nodded, and his glasses slipped down his nose. He pushed them back into place. He fixed his piercing gaze on Simone, and his expression seemed to indicate he understood this was a delicate situation.

He turned to the girls and began speaking softly in Mandarin, his tone gentle and reassuring. The girls' faces remained tense. A few of them exchanged uncertain glances, their fear still apparent but mixed with a flicker of curiosity.

Simone slowly lowered herself to the floor, crossing her legs and motioning for the girls to join her.

"Take your time," she added, her gaze steady on Chun, who was clearly the leader among them. "We're not in a hurry. We just want to help."

Chun hesitated, as if trying to process the words. Her English was poor, but after a moment, she finally nodded. She left her bed and whispered something to the others. One by one, they slowly began to move; they rose, walked to the center of the room, and formed a circle around Simone, their wide eyes fixed directly on her.

"I will talk for them; I know everything. Some of the girls don't even speak Mandarin. They come from villages where only dialects are spoken." Stepping into the role of leader, Chun explained these things to Norman, but her eyes were on Simone.

Simone nodded, took a deep breath in, and started to ask questions.

CHAPTER SIXTY-ONE

Commodities

Simone looked at Doctor Wu. The Doctor was patiently waiting for her questions to translate.

"Doctor Wu, I will talk normally, then you translate, okay? I will pretend I'm in my office, and these girls are my patients."

He nodded.

"Please call me Norman, Doctor Bennet."

"Okay. Same for me, just Simone is enough. Let's start?"

Norman nodded again.

"What are your names, and where are you from?" Simone asked the questions and Norman translated almost simultaneously.

Chun introduced her companions, pointing to each girl as she said their names. When she finished, she looked at Simone and said, "We come from China. Almost all the girls are from the countryside, small villages you've probably never heard of. I'm from Beijing."

"How did you end up in the U.S.?"

Chun lowered her head and took a deep breath. When she looked up at Simone again, the girl's eyes were filled with tears. "That's a long and not pretty story."

"I'm here to help all of you. I won't judge you for anything you tell me. The only reason I need to know these things is so I can figure out the best way to assist all of you." Simone reached for Chun's hand and held it gently. "Two of the girls have the HIV virus, and another has a sexually transmitted disease called chlamydia. If I can't understand the source of these infections, it's going to take me a lot longer to help you." Chun remained silent. Did she even know what these diseases were?

"Do you know what HIV is?" Simone asked, raising an eyebrow.

Gazing at a point somewhere above Simone's head and squeezing her hand tightly, the girl began to speak. Chun's words spilled out so rapidly, Doctor Norman had to gently ask her to slow down.

"I know," she said. "Unlike the others, I was kidnapped on my way home from school. I was in my last year, preparing to enter the university. I wanted to be a doctor." She gave a half smile before continuing her story.

"You see, girls don't usually have much value in China. The one-child policy made us disposable. Some of the girls here were sold by their parents. They were seen as burdens, and their mothers and fathers wanted a chance to have a son to secure their future. And some of the girls were simply taken from their homes. I'm the oldest here—I'm twenty now."

Unable to hide her shock, Simone stared at Chun with wide eyes; she looked no older than sixteen. Drawing a calming breath, Simone stayed silent. She didn't want to interrupt the girl's story.

"I was brought to the U.S. around four years ago. They didn't know my real age; usually, they want younger girls. The others here are between fourteen"—she pointed to a tiny girl—"and sixteen, but they were taken when they were much younger. For a long time, a new girl arrived and joined us every few months, but this past year, no one else has come." She shrugged and twisted her mouth.

Peter has been in jail for a year. If he's behind this—and I believe he is—that would explain why there hasn't been any new girls.

"We are sex slaves, Simone. Not me, at least, not anymore. They consider me too old for the job now, and since I can speak some English, they've put me in charge of relaying orders to the girls, taking care of them when they're injured, and trying to keep them calm. It's the only way I've found to survive."

Norman cleared his throat, but Simone saw the shock freeze on his face—his eyes widening with a raw, piercing pain every time he translated something cruel. Chun lowered her head again, and a thick tear fell from her face and dripped onto the floor. She wiped her cheeks with the back of her free hand, still holding onto Simone's, and continued.

"I don't know who they are, but they're men. They don't give us names. They keep us in an apartment—I don't even know where it's located. When they took us to that house... the one where you found us," she said, "it seemed like we drove for about an hour and a half. The apartment has no windows, and it's securely locked from the outside. The door is like a safe. We had no contact with the outside world, except when they came to prepare us for the customers."

"Prepare you for the customers? How did they do that?" Simone asked, although she thought she already knew the answer. She frowned but then quickly relaxed her features.

"They brought us videos—pornographic ones. They would separate the girls they wanted and show the videos, asking me to explain what the customers wanted from them."

The tears were streaming down Chun's face freely, and she didn't bother to hide them. Simone looked around; all except one of the girls were crying.

"I will make a quick stop." Said Norman, he stood up, went to the bathroom, and brought back paper towels. He distributed them among the girls but kept one for himself. Simone's throat grew tight. The poor Doctor had tears in his eyes, too. This wasn't easy for any of them. "We can proceed now."

"Chun, are you ready to continue?"

As usual, the girl looked to Simone as she spoke, then waited for Norman's translation before responding. She simply nodded and proceeded with her report.

"It was real torture because we had to watch what unknown men would do to us in just a few hours. The girls were always desperate, crying, and the new ones would have fits of rage—only to discover that they would be beaten mercilessly until they complied with the orders. They beat Mei." She turned and pointed to the girl whose eyes remained dry. "They beat her really badly last time, and she hasn't spoken or shown any kind of reaction since, and I'm afraid for her." Chun's voice grew thick.

"You're worried she may have lost her mind?" Simone asked softly.

"No!" Chun shook her head. "I'm afraid they might make her disappear like the others."

A thousand questions flooded Simone's mind, all tied to the missing girls, but before she could voice them, Chun continued.

"Whenever a girl was considered difficult, or the clients began complaining about their behavior, the men—the ones who kept us captive— would take them away."

"Can you explain what you mean by 'difficult'?" Simone asked gently.

Chun nodded.

"For example, one of them bit a man and nearly tore off his

ear. After that, she was taken from the apartment and never returned. I don't know what happened to her or to the others they took." She shook her head.

Tears streamed down Chun's face.

"How many girls disappeared?" Simone asked softly.

"After I was in the apartment, at least eight." Her voice was barely audible. "They were good girls, young...all of them had dreams. And they ended up being used, raped, and tortured by deranged people, and I believe they are dead now."

Simone gently touched Chun's face, the girl looked as if she was struggling to hold back an avalanche of tears.

Chun was stronger than she appeared.

Strong people usually endured a lot.

She took a few deep breaths, pulling herself together. She cleared her throat once more, straightened her back, and continued recounting the nightmare the girls had lived since they'd been kidnapped.

"Every night, there were clients. The girls never got a break—not even for a single day. Some days, the clients would come and go, an endless stream, a different face every hour. There were rooms set aside in the building just for this. Other times, we were taken to parties. I had to go along and struggle to interpret what the men wanted. I had to witness everything that unfolded."

Chun looked up at the ceiling, as if searching for a source of strength that would help her maintain control.

"By the end of the night, the girls were utterly drained, too tired to eat, and some of them in so much pain, they couldn't walk. I was tasked with giving them painkillers between clients—there was no food, just the drugs."

"That explains the painkillers in their urine," Simone murmured, glancing over at Norman.

The same realization showed in his eyes as they exchanged a look.

"What kind of painkillers did you give them? Do you remember?" Norman asked.

Chun nodded.

"For beginners, they used Tylenol. Girls who were more accustomed to the activities and worked longer hours would take Oxycontin, Methadone, or Butrans. When a girl was new to porn or behaving badly, they gave me syringes. I never knew what them was inside, but the girls always became calmer and seemed foggy. I believe it was some sort of illegal drugs."

Simone nodded.

Fentanyl? Or possibly even heroin?

"After I gave them painkillers, they were allowed to rest for ten to fifteen minutes before being forced to return to what they called 'work for your food.' Sometimes, this lasted for hours, and there were many different clients, multiples, or whatever deranged fantasies the men had in mind." She breathed deeply, her hands shaking. "Girls would go to the apartment, abused, bleeding from everywhere you can imagine. It was my responsibility to...fix them, I guess. When they were hurt, at least they'd be given a few days to recover before they were used again. But as soon as they were in reasonable condition, they were sent back to work. We were not seen as human beings but as merchandise."

Simone heard a soft cry and looked around at the girls sitting in a circle on the floor. Most of them were crying, two had their heads down, and one seemed lost in space. No doubt, they were reliving their individual stories through Chun's words. Their expressions were a mix of pain and despair, each tear a testament to the horrors they had endured. Chun's voice seemed to pull them deeper into their memories, dragging them back to the horrors they had experienced.

A human being could never truly forget the types of horrors these girls had endured, but maybe, with the right treatment and care, they could find a way to lead normal lives one day, for that it was important to know their trauma´s histories, painful as it could be.

Simone fought hard to keep her emotions in check. The girls didn't need to see her vulnerability right now; they needed strong people around them. People who could hold them up when they wanted to crumble.

Chun released Simone's hand and turned to the girls and, in the kindest, softest voice, told them to calm down. She reassured them that she believed they could trust Simone and Doctor Wu and told them they were safe now. It took several minutes, but gradually, the girls began to quiet down, their sobs subsiding into soft sniffles. Chun waited patiently, watching each of them, making sure they were regaining some semblance of control before she continued her account.

She is a true leader.

When Chun turned back to Simone, she offered Chun a tender smile. Chun reached out and took Simone's hand once more, gripping it tightly, as if drawing strength from the contact. Only then did she begin to speak again.

"Two years ago, they decided to force us into porn, so they took the prettiest girls to be filmed," Chun said, her voice trembling with anger and disgust. "They usually didn't use any protection in those films. I think that's where the HIV comes from. They made films focused on multiple partners. The girls taken for these were often strapped to some sort of medical table, and they were forced to endure six to ten men, each ejaculating inside them, over their bodies, and in their mouths, with no cleaning in between."

Her voice had grown quieter, falling to a whisper.

"When it was over, the girls were left covered in sperm, humiliated, and broken. They weren't even allowed to take a bath; they could only clean themselves once they returned to the apartment. I watched them scrub their skin raw with dish sponges, their faces twisted in pain. Like they were trying to wash away not just the filth, but the shame and agony etched deep into their souls." Chun scowled, her expression a mixture of fury and pain.

"How about unplanned pregnancy?"

"They used to give the girls contraceptives. I took them, too. But when they decided I was too old for the job, they stopped giving them to me. There was no consideration for our well-being, no care beyond keeping us just functional enough for their needs."

"No Doctors?"

"There was a guy I saw once or twice," Chun said, her voice filled with disdain. "But he didn't do much. He'd put some salve and bandages on their injuries if the girls were hurt badly enough during a sadomasochistic porn shoot, but that's about all. He never stitched up any of the bigger wounds, and he seemed cold. Like he didn't care, or he looked at us like animals. In my opinion, he was more of a butcher than a Doctor; he never left a prescription. Now that I think of it, I don't think he was a Doctor at all."

"You're safe now," Norman said softly, his voice trembling and hoarse. "I'm going to speak with the authorities, and you'll be placed somewhere secure. FBI victim specialists coordinate with local, state, and federal resources to offer shelter, food, clothing, and long-term psychological and even educational assistance. They even have job training. No more slavery—I promise all of you. I know it's hard to believe right now, but there are good people in this world, and your lives matter. You will have a chance to rebuild, to start fresh, or to return to your home country if that's what you choose."

After he spoke directly to Chun, he turned to Simone and translated what he said to the girl.

He's right—there are good people in this world. And he is one of them.

Simone offered him a reassuring smile filled with gratitude and quiet strength. He smiled back...a small gesture of hope shared between them.

Maybe I can help. If I offer to support these girls, I can come here—or wherever the FBI takes them—once a week...be there for them, make sure they know they're not alone.

The thought brought a surprising sense of peace that settled in her heart like a quiet promise. She wouldn't say anything just yet. Not when she hadn't slept well and was thinking so emotionally, but later, once she'd gotten some rest and could think clearly, she'd revisit the idea.

*****

Two hours later, Simone finally left the hospital. Concern for the girls weighed heavily on her heart. Her mind raced, searching for ways to help them—and others like them. A tightness had formed in her chest as she'd listened to their stories, each account of abuse pressing harder against her conscience.

Who is behind all of this? Is it Peter?

She had shown Chun a picture of him, but the girl hadn't recognized his face. When Simone asked about Deena and showed her picture, Chun had shaken her head—she had never heard the name or met the woman. She explained that they had been brought to the house three days before they'd been rescued, and she hadn't seen a single living soul there.

When she reached her car, Simone practically fell into the driver's seat. Her muscles ached, her head spun, and her heart broke for the girls. After fastening her seatbelt and leaving the parking lot, she connected her phone to the car's communication system and called Edward. He answered immediately, and Simone spoke fast as she reported everything she had heard and seen.

"It's exactly what I imagined when I found those pictures at Hay's house," Edward replied, his tone sharp. "I'd give a kidney to make that piece of trash talk. And no, you're not going back to that prison. Let the FBI handle it. They told me they're going to honor our agreement."

His tone had changed when he mentioned the deal he'd made; a note of satisfaction had crept into his voice.

"Can I ask what the agreement is?"

"I'm going to get out of that hellhole," he replied. "They're going to provide me with a new identity, and I'll work for them as a profiler. A clean start... Of course, I'll be far away from here."

"Good for you! I'm so happy for you, Ed. You deserve to get out of that shithole—you're no criminal."'

"Thanks, Simmie. It means a lot to me that you believe in me. I won't be able to stay in touch with you or even see my son. I'll have to start over completely. But at least it's a new life outside of a six-by-eight prison cell."

Simone was smiling to herself when a thought crossed her mind, and she shared it with Ed.

"Before we end this conversation, I need to tell you something. I think Deena might be Peter's partner in all of this. Don't you? Sometimes, when he talked about his crimes, he slipped and used words like 'we' and 'us.' I'm convinced he had a partner, and with everything that happened in Deena ´s house, I really believe she's deeply involved. What do you think?"

"I really don´t know," Ed said. "She came to see her mother the day we brought her in, but after that, she vanished. And now, everything points back to her house. The empty safe you found might mean she's already far away from here. The FBI is on her trail. Don´t worry, they'll catch her and maybe we will know the truth."

"I hope they do." Simone sighed. "But for now, I need to sign off. I've got to face my husband and explain my...night of adventures."

"Good luck, my dear. I need to go now, too. Someone just entered the broom closet."

Silence filled the car. Ed had hung up. Simone moaned softly, overwhelmed by all she'd learned. She wanted to talk to Carl and tell him everything. She tried his phone three times before someone answered.

"Good morning, Doctor Bennet. This is Lucy." The familiar voice of Carl's assistant, a brilliant young lawyer he enjoyed working with, came over the car speakers. "He's in front of the judge right now, but I'll let him know you called. Would you like to leave a message?"

"Good morning, Lucy. No, thanks, it's not urgent. Just let him know I've been trying to reach him."

Simone arrived at her office a short time later. She had a packed schedule ahead, thanks to Patricia having rescheduled most of Simone's patients. Even so, between her first appointment and the next, she managed to find a moment to call Norman. The good Doctor had kindly provided her with his personal phone number.

"Hello, Norman. How are the girls?" Simone asked.

"Hi, Simone. They're in good hands. Several people from Social Services were here about an hour ago. They agree with us that the girls might need to stay here for at least a day or two while they find a place for them. It's not easy since they need to stay together, at least for a while."

"I understand," she said softly. "If you need anything, please call me. And let me know when they're going to be moved—I'd like to be there for them."

"That would be great. They really trust you, and it'll make things easier for them," he replied.

"I'll be there, don't worry." Simone spoke in a firm voice to show she meant every word.

"I have to hang up now," Norman said. "I need to accompany them to an interview with the FBI. We managed to keep the agents away for a while, but it seems they're in a hurry. They need to catch the suspects, so the sooner they talk to them, the better. They have no patience with the idea of waiting until the girls are recovered. They want to hear their story, and they want to meet today. Chun said she's willing to talk, but only if I'm with her."

"Good. They're starting to form a bond with you, Norman," Simone said, relief causing her to smile.

"Not all of them, but it seems Chun trusts me," Norman replied. "I need to go now. Have a nice day, Simone."

"You too, Norman," Simone answered warmly.

*****

At almost eight p.m. that night, Carl finally returned Simone's call. She took a deep breath, preparing to recount the events of the previous night, but his strained voice and the weight of his words silenced her:

"Deena is dead, my love," he said, his voice tight with emotion.

He's crying.

"They found her body in a small motel room near Greenwich. The police determined she took her own life."

CHAPTER SIXTY-TWO

All that Matters

"Oh my God, that can't be true," Simone gasped as she recovered from the shock enough to speak. "How did you find out?"

"The authorities contacted her ex-husband, and he called me," Carl replied, his voice thick with grief. "She took a whole bottle of sleeping pills... She didn't leave a note, nothing. It's just not like Deena."

"I think I know the reason..." Simone said, and then before she lost her nerve, she hurried to explain everything that had happened the previous day—her trip to Deena's at Ed's request, discovering the girls', what they had said when she'd interviewed them, and finally, she voiced her suspicions about Deena. When she finished, she held her breath, bracing herself for a storm of anger.

"Deena was not involved. She was a good, decent woman; she would never take part in such crimes!"

His voice was firm but didn't contain a trace of the anger she'd expected.

He doesn't want to listen to reason right now. Just let him grieve.

"Honey, do you want me to come to the city? Or would you rather come home? We need to be together right now."

"I really don't know, love. I don't feel like having company right now; it's just too much for me," he replied, his voice heavy with sadness. "Deena was my wife and then my friend. She was such a lonely person… I never met any of her friends, if she even had any. She was always studying, always trying to improve herself, always had a book in her hands… Her ex-husband told me he couldn't think of a single friend she had besides me."

"When I met her, she seemed lonely to me, too, but not depressed," Simone said gently. "She was just bitter about everything her brother had done."

done."

"Honey, can you come to the funeral with me in the afternoon, tomorrow? It's being held at a cemetery near her home. Her ex-husband is in bad shape. He loved her, and she wanted a divorce after Peter's arrest because she didn't want to burden him with her troubles or saddle him with the stigma of being married to the sister of a notorious serial killer."

That's not what happened.

Simone had read about this in Carl's diary. When he met Deena, she told him she was bored with everything, including her current husband.

"Yes, I'll go with you. Just let me know when and where, and I'll meet you there."

"I keep wondering if my life will ever get back to normal," he said, his voice husky. "Ever since Lara, everything's been messy, one tragic event after another. It feels like karma for what I did to her."

His voice wavered, as if he struggled to hold back his emotions.

"There's no such thing as karma, and you didn't do anything to Lara—it was an accident." She reassured him softly. "I promise we'll find a way back to normality. Somehow, we'll figure it out. Now you take a shower and drink one or two beers; you deserve to relax."

"I just want a beer and some peace! I love you, Simone. You're the only good thing in my life right now. Thanks for being so patient. See you tomorrow. I'll let you know the time and place."

Simone was trying her best to be an adult and an understanding person, but the phrase 'I don't want company' wouldn't leave her mind.

I'm not just company, I'm his wife!

*****

Simone's schedule was a mess. She and Patricia had worked hard to fix it, but she needed to be with her husband. *He needs me*, she thought as she parked her car in the cemetery parking lot. Stepping out of the car, she spotted Carl walking toward her.

When he reached her side, Simone pulled him into a comforting hug. The crisp air carried the faint scent of damp earth and freshly cut grass, and the distant rustling of leaves was the only sound to break the silence. Carl stood in her arms for a while, as if drawing strength from her presence, before pulling away. He kissed her softly on the lips and took her hand, his grip firm but trembling. His face was wrinkled, and dark circles shadowed his tired eyes. They walked together, crossing the lot and entering through the large, iron gate.

The place where Deena would be buried was shadowy. The day was ending, and the fading light cast long shadows across the ground.

A closed white coffin rested over the grave. In the dim

light, it looked as if it was floating there, suspended between earth and sky. Only a few people were present, all of them unknown to Simone. A couple stood off to the side, speaking in hushed tones, and a tall, dark-skinned man with Arabic features wept quietly, his shoulders trembling as he sobbed.

"Do you know these people?" Simone whispered to Carl.

"Just Deena's ex-husband, Paul Cooper. The one who is crying."

The atmosphere was heavy with grief and silence, an unspoken sadness hanging in the air. Simone felt a deep pang of sorrow for Deena, a woman who seemed to have left this world with so few to mourn her passing, her final moments marked by loneliness.

Why would someone involved in a crime take her own life? Guilt? Regret? Shame? Fear of facing jailtime?

Was Carl right? Was Deena innocent of the crimes against the girls? A wave of doubt washed over her. If Deena was truly innocent, how could she explain her cold indifference toward her own mother, left forgotten in a clinic, drugged and abandoned, while the world believed she'd been the victim of a tragic accident?

The thought swirled as Simone glanced at the few somber faces gathered around the grave. Deena's lonely life, her apparent distance from others, and now this tragic end—it all seemed to paint a picture of a woman who had been more lost than malicious or evil. Simone's instincts told her there was much more to this story.

In her experience a suicide was rarely the act of a hardened criminal; instead, it was the final, desperate act of people who were sad, lost, or deeply ashamed.

The memorial was brief. A pastor offered a few comforting words, his voice echoing softly in the nearly empty cemetery. A cold wind blew against their faces, as if to remind them they were alive.

No one stepped forward to deliver a eulogy for Deena; the silence hung heavy in the air.

As the coffin disappeared into the grave, a swarm of reporters and photographers suddenly descended upon the scene, shattering the calm. Bursts of light from flashbulbs split the growing darkness, and reporters asked questions, shouting over each other in their effort to be heard.

The unexpected intrusion created a wave of chaos, startling everyone present. Carl instinctively moved closer to Simone, shielding her from the frenzy as he tried to lead her through the crowd of relentless journalists, each one eager to capture a glimpse of the burial of the mysterious woman whose death had raised so many questions.

Simone couldn't make out all their words, but two inquiries cut through the chaos loud and clear.

"Did she know it wasn't her mother in that hospital?"

"Do you know if Deena Hay would have been present for her mother's exhumation?"

Simone and Carl managed to push past the photographers, and they ducked into Carl's car. He gripped the steering wheel tightly, his face frozen in a scowl, his forehead wrinkled.

"We'll come back for your car later," he said in a tense voice. "Right now, we just need to get out of here. I don't understand any of this anymore."

As Carl gunned the engine and tore out of the parking lot, Simone nodded. Her heart was pounding, and her thoughts were racing. Had she heard them correctly? As they drove away from the cemetery, leaving the sparse gathering and the unanswered questions behind, she turned to Carl. He was focused on the road, his face a grim, determined mask.

"Did you hear what that man asked about Deena's mother's exhumation? Did you know anything about that?"

Carl shook his head, his brows furrowed and his eyes wide.

"Exhumed? What do you mean, exhumed? Isn't she in a hospital?" He turned to look to Simone.

Her stomach dropped.

"That's what I thought, too. But why would they be asking about an exhumation unless...unless there's something we don't know?"

"I'm going to call Joseph," Carl muttered, reaching for his phone.

Simone watched as he dialed the lawyer's number, her eyes fixed on his face. After advising his attorney about the reporters' questions, Carl fell silent. Simone tried to read the other side of the conversation based on her husband's changing expressions and occasional grunted yes or no. After a few moments, Carl ended the call.

"Joseph is going to try to find out what's going on," he said, his voice tense but steady. "He's on good terms with the FBI after we cooperated with them, and he'll dig into the information. If anyone can uncover the truth, it's him." He placed his hand gently on Simone's lap.

"Are you hungry, honey? How about an early dinner?" Simone suggested. "I didn't eat much today. We could find a nice restaurant nearby and wait for things to cool down before going back for my car."

"Great idea, woman," Carl replied with a faint smile, rubbing his stomach. "I don't think I've eaten anything since the news about Deena. My stomach is growling. Can you find us a place to eat?"

Simone grinned and held up her phone, showing the screen. "I'm already on this," she said with a playful wink. She typed in a few words then hit search.

She found a small Italian restaurant nearby—Carl's favorite type of food. Warmth spread through her as she remembered the first risotto they had shared when they met.

It was the beginning of our love story.

A moment she would always treasure.

The restaurant was cozy, with dim lights and beautiful silver candleholders casting gentle shadows on the tables. They were seated at a small table near the wall, surrounded by the comforting hum of quiet conversations and soft music. For a while, the world outside melted away.

They ordered quickly, eager to enjoy their meal and each other's company. For the next hour and a half, they talked, laughed, and savored the delicious food. Carl had chosen a bottle of red wine, and they raised their glasses in a toast to their love. Simone kept the conversation light, skillfully steering it away from the sadness of the day, not letting Carl dwell too much on the loss of his friend.

They both needed this moment, a break from the chaos, and a chance to find some peace. They had agreed to leave their phones in the car, shutting out the world and all its troubles for a little while. In this moment, their love and their time together were more important than any news—good or bad. Whatever was happening out there could wait. Right now, all that mattered was them.

*****

Carl and Simone were on their way back to the cemetery parking lot when Joseph called. Carl answered, holding the phone to his ear. Simone resisted the urge to suggest putting the call on speaker; she didn't want to intrude, but her curiosity grew with each passing second.

Joseph must have said something disturbing, because Carl's mouth tightened, and his jaw clenched so hard that a muscle in his cheek began to twitch.

Simone held her breath as a heavy weight seemed to tighten her chest.

When Carl finished the call, he turned to her, his eyes narrowed, his mouth moving silently as if he were trying to form words that wouldn't come.

"Carl, what is it? What did Joseph say?" she asked, her voice barely above a whisper.

CHAPTER SIXTY-THREE

You Won't Believe

"Let's just get to the parking lot, and then I'll tell you everything."

Carl drove the short distance in silence then pulled into the now-deserted parking lot next to her car.

"It's so creepy to be at the entrance of a cemetery at this hour," he whispered.

The gray stones of the gate, now closed and barely illuminated by the flickering streetlights, made the place look like something straight out of a scene in *The Addams Family* movie.

"Frankly," Simone muttered, "at this point, the only thing that scares me is what living people are capable of doing."

Carl didn´t answer. He put the car in park, unfastened his seatbelt, and turned to face her, taking both of her hands in his. His grip was firm as he looked deeply into her eyes.

"I don't even know where to start. It's just too much information!" Carl exclaimed, he took a deep breath, then slowly exhaled. "The world is totally crazy!"

He released one of her hands and ran his fingers through his hair in frustration then shifted, tucking one leg under his body and holding her hands again.

He's going to drive me crazy with all this suspense and theatrics.

"The FBI suspected something was off with the DNA results from the woman at the Autumn Clinic," Carl began, his voice tight. "Her DNA was nearly a one hundred percent match with Peter Hay's, which isn't normal. A parent's DNA typically only matches a little less than fifty percent."

Simone's eyes widened.

"So…what does that mean?"

"They ran another test on the woman at the clinic, comparing it with a sample they took from Deena during her visit—the one where she didn't recognize that woman as her mother. Something about the color of her eyes. The results didn't match at all. That woman…she's not Deena's mother," he added.

Simone shivered.

"Then who is she?

"They still don't know for sure," Carl continued, "so they got a quick judicial order and are going to exhume Olivia Hay's body, or whomever is in her grave—and that's what the reporter was asking about.

"They immediately suspected Edward," Carl continued, his tone of voice excited. "He had an agreement with the FBI to help them with something they call the 'Panda Girls' investigation, and in return, they'd offer him some kind of leniency or maybe even freedom. To keep tabs on him, they gave him a phone from a so-called 'friend'"—Carl made air quotes with his fingers—"he'd made at the hospital. The nurse was an undercover FBI agent in disguise, playing the part perfectly."

"So, they were onto him from the start?"

Carl shook his head.

"No, it started the moment Deena said that the woman at the clinic wasn't her mother," he explained. "That's when the FBI began to suspect something was off. But they're used to making deals with people like Edward, and they knew he might try to play them. So, they set up the whole operation to catch him if he was up to something. And Edward proved they are on the right track. He used that phone to make all sorts of calls, setting his plans in motion."

"The phone was a trap?" Simone rose her eyebrows.

"Yes," Carl said. "The phone was tapped, and Edward used it to call half the country, including you." He pointed to Simone.

Good thing I told him everything about that night.

"He called you to go to Deena's house," Carl continued, his voice tense with the weight of what he was saying. "He tried calling Deena a hundred times before that. Then he called his good friend officer Carlo to check an address, and after you called him, informing him about those people you found locked in the house, he reached out to him to help you get them out. And there's one more thing..."

Simone's heartbeat quickened, impatience with his way of recounting the events running through her veins.

"What?" she asked, already dreading the answer.

Carl hesitated for a moment. "He said something to his friend—a phrase that caught the FBI's attention. He said,

'When I get that woman, I will kill her.'"

Simone's eyes widened, and a cold shiver ran down her spine.

"They think he was talking about Deena?"

"That's their suspicion. They think he might have been planning something, and they're piecing it all together to see where this leads. They're trying to figure out just how deep his involvement goes and what he's capable of."

"How about the girls?" Simone asked in a tense voice. "Does he have any kind of involvement in that atrocity?"

Carl lowered his head, hesitating for a moment before looking back into Simone's eyes. He nodded.

"One of the girls was interviewed by the agents. She described a Doctor who would come to 'mend' them, and they suspect Edward is that Doctor."

Simone remembered that detail from her conversation with Chun. She recoiled, her hands moving instinctively to her head, trying to hold back the overwhelming flood of emotions.

"That's too much for me. I can't believe Ed is capable of that! He was always kind and gentle with his patients."

Carl leaned close to Simone and hugged her, caressing her hair. "I know, honey, I know," he whispered.

"Even if he's not directly involved," Simone said, pulling away from Carl and turning to face him. "He played me! I'm the one who was supposed to be helping him!" She jabbed a finger at her chest.

Even though her voice was sharp and loud, she harbored serious doubts about everything Carl had said.

I'm not going to jump to conclusions as I did before, I'm going to give Ed some credit.

Carl continued caressing her hair, trying to calm her.

"Honey, I don't think he's the type to be involved in human trafficking. Let´s wait for the FBI to finish their investigation. He must be desperate. He had information and saw a way out of that prison. I mean...if I were left to rot in jail, who knows if I wouldn't do the same thing? Let's not judge him just yet. If he calls you, just stay calm. Act like you don't know anything and like you're still trying to help him, okay?"

Simone nodded, her mind racing as she tried to convince

herself that there had to be some sort of explanation.

"I'm going to follow you home, honey," Carl said, still holding her hand. "We need to stay together."

Simone nodded, barely registering Carl's words. Every detail of their conversation replayed in her mind in an endless loop, but she couldn't believe Ed was behind all this.

She glanced in her rearview mirror, catching sight of Carl's headlights trailing closely behind.

Her chest tightened, as if a band of steel had wrapped around her. Fearing her heart might fail her, Simone took a couple of long, deep breaths. Ed had made mistakes—terrible ones. She could barely accept that he was a necrophile, but a criminal? Someone who used innocent girls, exploited their suffering? For what? Money?

Ed isn't the type of person who cares one bit about wealth.

With all the questions filling Simone's mind, the drive home passed quickly, her thoughts a constant, racing blur. Just before she reached the house, the trill of her cellphone broke the heavy silence. Simone dug her phone from her purse and without looking at the caller ID, she answered.

Norman, his voice calm yet urgent, sounded in her ear.

"Simone, could you come to the hospital tomorrow afternoon?" he asked. "We need your help with the girls' transfer to a house that Social Services have prepared for them."

Simone didn't hesitate.

"I'll be there," she replied firmly, her voice steady despite the storm raging inside her.

She hung up, feeling a small sense of purpose settle over her. Regardless of the chaos and doubt clouding her thoughts about Edward, she could still make a difference for those girls.

As she arrived home, with Carl's car right behind her, she opened the garage, and they pulled their vehicles inside to park. Carl leaked out, opened the door for Simone, and slipped his arm around her shoulder as they headed to the kitchen. "Love, I'm going to make us one of your herbal teas; we both need something soothing right now!" He unlocked the door then stepped back to allow her to enter the house before him.

"Do you want to take a bath first?" he asked.

He's wonderful. Even after losing his friend, he's still thinking about me first.

A warm sensation filled Simone's heart.

"Let me make our tea," she replied, smiling softly. "You need a bath more than I do, after everything you've been through these last twenty-four hours."

"There's no such thing as 'your grief is bigger than mine,' love." He whispered softly; his breath warm against her skin. "We're both hurting, just in different ways. But what matters most is that we're together, that we love each other. I love you so much."

"There's no such thing as 'your grief is bigger than mine,' love," he whispered softly, his breath warm against her skin. "We're both hurting, just in different ways. But what matters most is that we're together, that we love each other. I love you so much."

He pulled her closer, wrapped his arms around her, and his lips met hers in a deep, lingering kiss. His tongue entwining with hers, he moved his hands to the back of her neck. He kissed his way down the column of her throat, leaving a trail of warmth and liquid fire in his wake.

This man still turns me on, even in the middle of all this chaos!

His hand moved from her nape to her breasts so quickly that she barely had time to register the motion, only the rush of warmth spreading through her body. Just as she surrendered to the moment, the doorbell rang, breaking the spell.

They froze, the air between them charged and heavy with the abrupt interruption. Simone pulled back.

"Who could that be at this hour?" she asked. Her breathing was slightly erratic, her body still craving his touch.

Carl sighed.

"I'll check," he muttered, reluctantly stepping away from her and heading toward the front door.

"Carl, don't! Let me check the cameras first..." She followed him into the living room, but he was already swinging the door open.

A man in an FBI uniform stood on the doorstep, his expression unreadable.

"Carl Lourenzzo?" he asked.

"Yes," Carl replied, his voice weak.

Before he could say another word, the agent stepped aside to make way for another, and both men quickly grabbed Carl's arms. They twisted them behind his back and snapped a pair of handcuffs onto his wrists.

Simone gasped, her heart pounding as a third agent stepped forward, a piece of paper in his hand. His voice was loud and authoritative, cutting through the shock like a knife.

"You are under arrest for the murder of Deena Hay, human trafficking, and money laundering. You have the right to remain silent..."

The rest of his words became a blur in Simone's mind. Her breath caught in her throat, and she glanced frantically between Carl and the agents.

What's going on here?

She couldn't believe what she was hearing. Her mind told her it had to be a misunderstanding, while her heart insisted it was the truth.

Carl's expression remained steady.

"Honey, this is yet another mistake, but we'll face it together. I'm so sorry. Call Joseph for me, please."

CHAPTER SIXTY-FOUR

Where Shadows Breath and Truth Sleeps

A few moments after the agents led Carl out the front door, Edward entered the house. He moved quickly to Simone's side, gently helping her to sit on the couch. Without saying a word, he pulled her into his arms, his hand moving in soothing circles over her back.

A strange numbness wrapped around her, as she struggled to process what was happening. She had no tears left to cry, no energy to react.

What is going on?

She thought she had kept the question in her mind, but apparently, the words slipped out as a whisper. Edward pulled away slightly and looked directly into her eyes, concern etched across his face.

"I don't know how to explain it in a way that won't break your heart," he said softly.

"Just spill it, Ed," Simone said, her voice sharp. "I'm so tired of lies."

"Peter Hay had a partner, and he was involved in the panda girls' deaths," Edward began, his eyes locked on Simone's. "I was sure of it when I found the pictures of the Chinese girls at his home. The FBI is positive Peter had an accomplice, too. You told me he hinted at a second person when he was sharing his stories with you, remember?"

Simone nodded slowly, her mind racing back to those conversations with Peter. He had slipped up a few times when he'd said "we" instead of "me," and she'd thought the same thing back then that Ed and the FBI believed now. Someone else had been involved in Peter's crimes...

"The investigation focused on the Chinese man who visited him in jail," Edward said, "It seems he was only Peter's last lover before his conviction, so that lead turned out to be a dead end. The FBI couldn't find any proof that he was passing information outside the jail."

"When I went to the clinic, I was sure that woman was Peter's nanny," Edward said. "After I started reducing the dosage of the drugs they were giving her, she began to come out of her fog. She confirmed my suspicions and told me she knew Peter wasn't...normal, but she thought she knew how to handle him, and she genuinely loved the boy he used to be. Even after she was no longer his nanny, he would still come to her for advice."

Simone listened intently, her eyes widening as Edward spoke.

"She said Peter had confided in her about the abuses he had suffered at the hands of a previous nanny," Edward said. "He trusted her so much that, years later, he even told her when he killed the abusing nanny. She told me she was in shock, but she tried to understand him—she believed he had a reason for hating her and that child abusers must rot in hell."

Simone's stomach tightened as she listened. "A reason?" she repeated, her voice high. "She actually thought there could be a justification for murder?"

Edward nodded slowly.

"She was conflicted. On one hand, she saw Peter as the troubled boy she had cared for, someone who had been hurt and pushed to his limits, but also, she remembered what an adorable boy he was. She didn´t see him as a killer; she thought it was just a desperate act of revenge."

"My God, she didn't realize a monster was being born," Simone murmured, shaking her head in disbelief. "So much could have been avoided if she had just gone to the police."

Edward nodded.

"She believed she could handle him as she had when he was a boy, that she could somehow guide him back to being the child she had once cared for. She didn't see how far gone he was until it was too late."

"Too late?"

"He went to her after his mother's death," Edward said, his voice low. "He confessed to her, assuming she'd understand that he was behind it. But she didn't. She told him she would go to the police, that she couldn't protect him anymore."

A chill ran down her spine.

"And what happened next?"

Edward sighed.

"The last thing she remembered was telling him that she would turn him in. That's when everything went black. The next thing she knew, she was locked away in that fancy clinic...which is nothing more than a storage place for inconvenient people. The clinic is now in the custody of the FBI."

Simone shook her head.

"The worst part is that she still thinks he's a good boy. She believes that if he were truly a monster, he would have killed her outright. Instead, he used to visit her at the clinic."

"He locked her up and then visited her?" she asked.

Insane is a too gentle of a word to describe that lunatic.

"With flowers and gifts." Edward scowled. "When the FBI discovered payments from Carl's office to the clinic—sent by the same accountant who had worked for the Hay family—they started to connect the dots. Suddenly, Carl and Deena became prime suspects of locking Carmen or at least helping to keep her in the clinic."

"So that's why they took Carl... I thought they'd cleared him after they talked with the accountant," she said.

Edward shook his head.

"No, they already had the accountant. She hadn't disappeared; she had gone to the FBI on her own and was cutting a deal."

"The deal involved Carl?"

"It did. She told FBI she had been working under his orders. Carl was taken in for questioning without knowing the FBI had Ophelia and tons of evidence. While he was being questioned, his office and home were being bugged. They needed to see if there was any communication or evidence that could link him directly to the crimes. Ophelia didn't know the source of the money. Of course, she knew the names of the companies transferring it to the office, but nothing beyond that—she was just responsible for cleaning it."

"How about Deena?"

Edward sighed.

"Deena was invited to visit her mother at the hospital. We spread the story about Olivia Hay." Edward said. "The DNA tests? They were never actually done. We just put out the news to see how the people involved would start to move. You know, like putting a cat in a room full of rats."

"Not only the news. You told *me* it was done..."

He paused for a moment, his expression softening. "I had

to. I'm sorry about that, but let me continue..."

"Sure..."

"Deena didn't hesitate when she was contacted about her mother; she went to the hospital immediately," Edward continued. "When she saw the person who was supposed to be her mother, she told everyone right away that the woman was Peter's nanny. She knew it wasn't Olivia. She was the one who identified her mother at the morgue after the accident.

Simone listened carefully as Edward went on.

"To leave no room for doubt, she demanded a DNA test on the spot. She even gave samples herself, fully cooperating with the investigation. And then she went a step further —she suggested that her mother should be exhumed. As I told you, the test was never done, but we took the samples anyway and even entertained the idea of an exhumation.

"She was not involved," Simone said without thinking, but five seconds later, her psychiatrist's brain came up with another possibility. "Or she didn't know the full extent of everything that was going on."

Edward nodded and proceeded. "The FBI started monitoring all three of them—Carl, Deena, and Peter. We spread the news that we were trying to get an exhumation order for Olivia Hay's body, hoping it would shake things up and force someone's hand. And just like that, a new prisoner"—Ed made air quotes—"was admitted to MacDougall."

Simone nodded slowly, beginning to understand.

"And did it work?"

Edward sighed.

"It did. Deena continued to cooperate, waiting for her mother's exhumation. Peter made a phone call." Edward continued, his expression darkening. "The new prisoner, a muscular young man who quickly befriended Peter, got close enough to overhear him saying something about putting 'Plan Delivery' into motion. They couldn't trace who was on the other end since the call was so brief. But then something else happened."

Simone leaned in, her breath catching in her throat. "What?"

Edward inhaled deeply.

"The FBI had bugged Carl's phone, but he must have had another one, because they couldn't link the call to his number. However, they had also bugged his apartment, as I told you before, and at the same time Peter made his call, Carl received one. The FBI couldn't hear what the caller said. Carl simply responded, 'Understood.'"

Simone's eyes widened, and Edward continued.

"After that, Carl was heard making another call. He instructed whoever he phoned to begin with Plan Delivery, and then once that was completed, to 'get her.' The FBI reinforced their security both at the hospital and at Olivia Hay's gravesite, suspecting that 'get her' might refer to one of them. For lack of personnel, they had given up on continuing to monitor Deena's house. She had been nothing but cooperative, so they just kept her phone bugged.

"Until she didn't answer your phone calls anymore," Simone said, and then another thought occurred to her. "Or was that part of the plan?"

Edward shook his head.

"Unfortunately, no, or she should be alive. She really wasn't answering my phone calls. I made a mistake; I should have reported that to the FBI. They weren't expecting any contact with her until today when the exhumation was supposed to take place. But I needed to talk to her."

Simone's eyes narrowed.

"Your fake phone?" she asked, determined to get the full

story this time. She was done with half-truths.

"It was too easy to get," Edward said. "I knew it was bugged, but I needed to be the one to deliver the panda girls information. So, I pretended I didn't know it was compromised. That's why I had you get another phone and do everything to help me. I really needed to reach Deena, to ask her to search through the house. I had a lead about a secret place where Peter might have kept documents that the FBI hadn't found yet."

Simone's mind was racing.

"Where did this lead come from?"

"Carmen," Edward replied. "She's a good woman. Now that she understands how demented Peter has become. She told me about a hidden compartment under a floorboard that's opened by a small button you press on. Peter told her about it after he bought that house, just in case anything ever happened to him."

"Then I found the girls, and you forgot about the secret compartment?"

"I didn't," Edward replied, shaking his head. "I asked Carlo to check it for me."

"And what did he find there?" Simone's voice was barely a whisper but filled with the dread.

Edward filled his lungs with air.

He does that when he's figuring out how much he should tell me.

"Pictures...of Chinese girls," he said quietly. "More than a dozen, I guess around thirty. Some showed girls who were alive, and others—at least another dozen—depicted images of girls who were dead." He lowered his head.

Simone's eyes filled with tears.

"Oh no..."

"There were also notes written in Hanzi, characters that make up the Chinese language," Edward said, his voice heavy. "The FBI has already determined they are addresses in China. And there were pictures of your husband with some of the girls, like the one you found before, but in a more...intimate way, and pictures of Lara Parker...both alive and dead."

A cold shiver ran down Simone's spine, and her breath caught in her throat.

"But the most significant find," Edward continued, "The title to a property — a small building in New York City's Chinatown — was in the name of an unknown person. The FBI went there and found an accomplice inside, ready to set fire to everything. He identified himself as Liam Patterson, but that seems to be a fake name. He had no identification on him. The FBI is on it too, but so far, they haven't found any DNA samples in the criminal records that match his."

Simone brought her hand to her head—it felt like it was going to explode from the sheer amount of information she needed to process.

"Could it be the apartment Chun mentioned?" she asked, recalling the details of her earlier conversations.

"I think so," Edward nodded. "The FBI is waiting for Chun to recover so they can take her in for identification. But Liam Patterson has already confessed to everything—except his real identity. He claims he was acting under Peter's and Carl's orders.

"Partners in crime? All of Peter's crimes?" Simone's voice trembled.

Was I married to an assassin?

Edward shook his head. "The man only knew about the panda girls, which he referred to as teddy bears," Edward explained, his voice thick. "But he confirmed that both men —Peter and Carl—determined the fate of those girls. The delivery plan was made before Peter was convicted."

A cold wave of nausea hit Simone as Edward continued.

"And Carl... He ordered Deena's execution."

"Why?" she demanded, shaking her head in disbelief.

"'Plan Delivery' was the backup plan," Edward said, his face grim. "If the police got too close to their teddy bear operation, they would deliver the girls to Deena's house and let them die, make Deena disappear, and force her to write a letter taking the blame for everything. But she never wrote the letter. She never wrote *any* letter. When we got Carmen, I think Peter panicked, because during his visits with her, he used her as a confessor."

Simone's hands shook, and her heart pounded. "So, they wanted to use her as a scapegoat, and Carl was in on it all along?"

Edward nodded solemnly.

"Yes, Simone. It looks like Carl was deeper into this than anyone realized."

"Deena's death... Who was responsible?"

"They go by chess piece names—the King, the Queen, the Bishop and the Tower."

"And who's who?"

"Carl is the King, the Queen is obvious, Liam is the Bishop and there is a fourth guy, they called The Tower."

"So creative, and who is this guy?"

"Liam said that whenever they needed to send someone to their maker, they used the services of a professional. The only thing he had for the guy was a phone number. But the FBI hasn't gotten their claws on him yet. He's still out there." Edward continued, his tone grim. "Professional killers are hard to catch."

"Who took the girls to Deena's house?" Simone asked.

"Liam did. He oversaw everything—finding clients for the girls, sending them to the perverts, ensuring they obeyed, and managing the entire prostitution and porn operation."

Simone's heart sank.

"So, he wasn't just a hired hand; he was running the whole operation."

Edward nodded.

"Exactly. Liam was the linchpin, the one keeping everything running smoothly in exchange for twenty percent of the profits. And, according to him, there are eight more people involved in transporting the girls and in the porn film division, they call them The Paws, but they're still on the loose. The FBI is hunting them down, but they've managed to slip through law enforcement's nets so far."

"How about the pictures I found in Carl´s apartment? Did you learn anything about that?"

"I did, Liam confessed he had the password to open the door. Whenever Peter ordered him to...*disturb* you, he'd plant a picture or some piece of clothing there. Carl had nothing to do with that. It was just Peter being...angry or jealous of you."

"This is so unbelievable!"

He ran his fingers through his hair. "It really is. I'm sorry."

"My God, what a nightmare my life has become since that psycho crossed my path!" Simone exclaimed, putting her hands to her head in despair.

Edward looked at her and asked, "Which one?" Irony was clear in his voice.

Simone would have laughed if the situation wasn't so tragic.

"Good question," she replied bitterly. "Peter. He was behind everything. He approached me because I was Lara's half-sister, and he was curious about me."

But then, suddenly, a chilling thought struck her like lightning.

"Maybe Carl wanted a second chance with the dead woman's sister... Maybe he thought we had the same personality. How sick is all of this?"

She shook her head in disbelief before her voice dropped to a more urgent tone.

"And what about Lara's death? Was it really an accident?"

Edward shook his head slowly.

"That, I don't know. I think only Carl and maybe Peter knows the truth, and I firmly believe they'll never talk. They've always protected each other, no matter what."

"I have some evidence about that, but I didn't want to dig into it. I gave my husband a vote of confidence. I'll gather everything and give it to you. There's much more to this than we know — maybe if they're confronted with the facts, they'll confess."

"I don´t believe they will ever do."

"They've covered for each other all this time," she murmured, more to herself than to Edward. "It's like they've been playing this sick game, always one step ahead, always keeping each other's secrets. Do you think they have some sort of...relationship?"

Edward paused.

"Another question I can't answer, Simmie," he replied softly. "I had the same suspicion, but there's a lot about their relationship that we may never fully understand. Whether it was rooted in a deep, twisted loyalty or something more, it's clear they were bound together in a way that went beyond normal friendship or partnership. You know, sometimes people are drawn to each other because of their shared brokenness, their similar darkness." He compressed his lips.

"At least they are going to be reunited in jail…"

"I don't think so… It's better to keep criminals separated—otherwise, they might start coming up with ideas behind bars."

An agent entered the house, removed his cap. "Good evening, madam. I'm sorry to intrude, but we must go, Doctor Reynolds."

Edward nodded, acknowledging the agent.

"I know. Give me five more minutes."

The agent nodded and stepped out the front door.

Simone turned to Edward,

"Where are you going?"

Edward sighed, small wrinkles formed around his eyes and he forced a smile.

"I shouldn't even be here, but when I heard they were about to get Carl, I knew you would need support. I don't know exactly where they're taking me yet. I'll have a new identity, and I'll be working for the FBI as a profiler—maybe at Quantico, or perhaps on some mission where they need my expertise. We'll probably never see each other again."

Edward's eyes filled with tears, and he quickly turned his face away—but not before she could see. A sharp pain struck her chest, and tears stung as her eyes filled.

"Isn't that dangerous?" she asked.

"Dangerous is being locked inside a jail," Edward replied with a smile. "Another year in there, and I'd be transferred to some cuckoo house."

Simone reached out and took his hands, her tears streaming down her face. Without a word, they fell into each other's arms, crying together, their grief intertwining in the silence.

Simone looked at Edward, her arms still interlaced with

his.

"Thank you for being here for me, Ed," she whispered.

Edward's gaze softened as he looked at her.

"I will always find a way to protect you, Simmie. My love for you will never die. We're not meant to be together, but I promise you, I'll do everything I can to keep you safe. I love you, Simmie."

He pulled her into a tender embrace, holding her close as if trying to imprint this moment in his memory. They stood there for a while, finding solace in each other's presence, tears never ending.

Edward gently pulled away, giving her a peck on the cheek before rising to leave.

"One last question, Ed," Simone called after him.

He paused, turning back to her.

"Yes, just one more," he said, holding up his index finger with a small, knowing smile.

"Have you ever been a necrophiliac?" she asked, her voice a barely murmur.

Edward squeezed his eyes closed and faintly smiled.

"Find that answer inside yourself, Simmie," he said softly before turning and walking out the door. "Trust your professional instincts. You are great shrink."

Simone watched him go; her heart heavy with the weight of everything they had been through. As the door closed behind Edward, she stood in the middle of her living room, the emptiness of the space around her seeming to echo her uncertainty and pain.

She didn't know how she would cope with everything that had happened—all the shadows closing in around her, breathing in her ears as if mocking her beliefs, and the secrets that had long slept, now suddenly awakened.

How do I navigate the storm that's torn through my life? How am I supposed to mend my broken heart all over again?

EPILOGUE

2025

Woolsey Hall at Yale University was at full capacity, its 2,650 seats filled with selected guests, all formally dressed. Diamonds sparkled under the soft light on the first autumn day of the year.

Excitement buzzed through the air as the Woman of the Year prize ceremony was about to begin, honoring a woman who had made a significant difference in the lives of others.

The nominees, including Simone, were seated in the front rows, facing the grand, antique golden organ behind the stage. The hall itself, designed by the Beaux-Arts architectural firm Carrère and Hastings—the same firm that designed the New York Public Library—was a stunning backdrop for the prestigious event.

As the presenter of the award stepped onto the stage, a hush fell over the audience, all eyes fixed on him as he began.

"The Woman of the Year award honors women from across the country who have made extraordinary contributions to improving human lives in various fields. Tonight, we will celebrate the most remarkable among them." He held a golden card in his hand, waving it briefly as the audience applauded. "We would like to thank Yale University for allowing us to present this prestigious award in this beautiful auditorium." He turned to the university's rector, seated behind the pulpit.

The man acknowledged the gratitude with a nod and a smile. The presenter then opened the golden card and began to read.

"The woman who will receive this prize tonight has an

amazing curriculum," the presenter announced, his voice filled with admiration. "She is a renowned Doctor, a beloved professor, and an accomplished author. This woman has dedicated the last six years of her life to helping girls and women trapped in slavery, victims of human trafficking. Despite all the obstacles and hardships she faced —navigating a pandemic, fighting tirelessly, contracting COVID-19 and spending several days in the hospital—she never wavered. She even bent a few lock down rules to keep the foundation she created operational—because for her, standing still or staying at home was never an option. She had her foundation to care for."

He paused to take a sip of water from the crystal glass in front of him before continuing.

"The Panda Girls Foundation…"

As he said the name of Simone's foundation, a chill ran through her body. She couldn't hear the rest of the speech; her skin was covered in goosebumps. She couldn´t believe her ears.

"We invite Chun Lee, the director of the foundation, to deliver the prize to Doctor Simone Bennett, whom we also invite to the stage to receive her much-deserved award."

Simone stood, tears in her eyes as the audience erupted in applause. She carefully ascended the stairs, mindful not to step on her elegant black gown.

Chun, beautifully dressed in a *bois de rose* gown, stood waiting with the award in hand, a golden statue of a woman. Tears filled the younger woman's eyes, but she grinned at Simone.

Simone accepted the statue, and she and Chun embraced, crying, both knowing the immense effort it had taken to reach this moment. Chun whispered in Simone's ear.,

"A golden statue will never repay you for what you did for

us and for so many other girls."

Holding back more tears, Simone approached the presenter. They shook hands vigorously before the man turned and asked the audience for another round of applause.

When the noise subsided, Simone stepped forward to the podium, took the microphone, and began her brief speech.

"I would like to thank everyone who voted for me to receive this award." She lifted the statue for the audience to see. "But most importantly, I want to thank those who helped build and sustain the Panda Girls Foundation, which has helped hundreds of girls rescued from human trafficking and sexual slavery each year."

Simone paused to dry a tear before continuing. She turned to Chun, who stood at her left.

"Thank you, Chun, my right arm, a brilliant administrator, and a wonderful leader. I couldn't have done anything without you and your support."

Chun's tears were flowing freely.

"I also want to thank Doctor Norman Wu, a wonderful Doctor who freely dedicates his time to healing the girls at Panda. You became a great friend and an incomparable example of a human being. You've given everything you had—without expecting anything in return—to support this beautiful cause."

Breaking from her usual reserve, Simone blew a kiss to Norman, who sat between her daughter, Tammy, and her faithful secretary, Patricia, surrounded by six girls—all of them rescued from Deena's house that terrible night. They'd stayed with her and the Panda Girls house from the beginning.

Norman, after discreetly drying a tear beneath his glasses, formed a heart with his hands and mouthed, "I love you."

For a moment, their gazes locked, sharing a silent promise of eternal friendship and unwavering loyalty. Simone was the godmother to Norman and Chun's daughter, Mei—the couple felt like her own children.

Simone went on:

"There is another incredible person behind the Panda Foundation—one who truly surprised me. She became an active and devoted member, cooking for everyone, mending broken hearts with her warmth and kind words, and always finding the perfect joke to lighten even the darkest moments. Thank you, Elizabeth Reynolds. I believe you've found your true calling in life, and it is a beautiful one."

Beth, always the drama queen, was sobbing in her seat, one hand pressed against her heart.

Simone also thanked all the donors of the foundation, naming them one by one, especially her biggest donors, Benjamin Taylor-Miller and his wife Chivon. Some names—of those donors who preferred to remain anonymous—she respectfully kept to herself.

"To conclude my speech—which I know has been long—I want to make one final request." She gestured toward the audience, sweeping her index finger across the auditorium. "Please, if you ever come across someone or suspect that someone is in a dangerous situation, being used in any form, reach out to the authorities, or call us. The difference between a life of suffering and one of freedom can be just one phone call away."

When she finished, after shaking hands with a dozen dignitaries, she descended the stairs to a storm of applause, her gaze catching sight of a tall man in a dark suit, applauding her. But when she reached the bottom of the steps, the man was gone.

For the past six years, Simone had occasionally seen Edward at critical moments—when her missions to rescue kids were risky, or when an important event took place. He was always there, offering her silent protection, like a guardian angel. They hadn't exchanged a single word since the day Carl was arrested, but her heart warmed knowing Edward was still around, always watching over her, even during Carl´s trial.

Carl's trial had been difficult to watch, but unlike what she had done to Edward, Simone stayed through it all—listening to every piece of evidence against the man she thought she loved, only to realize he had never truly existed. He had been nothing more than an actor performing a role in a twisted play he'd created in his mind. The evidence was overwhelming, and he received a life sentence. Only then did Simone file for divorce—when there were no doubts left about who she had married.

Of all his crimes, they could never prove that Lara's death was deliberate. Carl claimed, to the end, it was an accident. As she approached her daughter, Patricia, and the girls, Simone felt free, loved, and at peace, her chest bursting with a wave of happiness.

Her life's calling had become clear—to help defenseless people recover from trauma and guide them toward a new life. Nothing was more fulfilling than that. While she still worked at her office a few days a week, helping patients in need of guidance, most of her time was devoted to the Panda Girls Foundation, teaching, and her two dogs, Tommy and Charlie.

Tommy was an old dog now, but he had a new brother who gave him energy and a great time. Charlie was rescued four years ago, and he had a tender heart and endless energy, even if he looked like a dried mango seed with his spiked fur.

As Simone stood among her loved ones, enveloped by love and gratitude, Simone knew she was exactly where she was meant to be. She was grateful for the hardships that had led her to this moment, to the discovery of a new and fulfilled life. She was finally happy and at peace.

Silently, she prayed:

Thank you, God, for making my path Your will and not mine.

THE END

If you are aware of human trafficking, child abuse, or child sexual exploitation, contact your nearest police station or call 911 in an emergency.

Human trafficking (U.S.): Call the National Human Trafficking Hotline at 1-888-373-7888 or text "BEFREE" (233733). You can also chat online.

Child abuse or exploitation (U.S.): Call or text the Childhelp National Child Abuse Hotline at 1-800-422-4453 (1-800-4-A-CHILD). Chat is also available. legalmomentum.org +3childhelphotline.org+3Childhelp+3

Missing children / child sexual exploitation: After notifying law enforcement, call the National Center for Missing & Exploited Children (NCMEC) at 1-800-THE-LOST (1-800-843-5678), or report online via the CyberTipline for child sexual exploitation.

One simple action can change a life.

ABOUT THE AUTHOR

A. Gavazzoni is a Brazillian Multi-Award-Winning Novelist of five published literary works within two novel series titled, 'Hidden Motives' and 'Where The Road Goes.'

Adriana has become a critically acclaimed popular steamy romance fiction writer of light erotic with cross-genres of steamy murder mystery suspense, historical romantic thrillers, coming-of-age, and women's gripping crime fiction. Adriana's break-out debut of "Behind The Door" book one of the "Hidden Motives" series firmly placed her on the literary map nationally and internationally. All her novels are available on Amazon Books, Amazon Kindle, and Kindles available within Kindle Unlimited. All her novels are featured on online literary book sites, Book Stores, and literary magazines.

Born and raised in Brazil, she is of full Italian lineage. By day she is a Brazillian lawyer, former professor of law, and also writes legal books. She speaks four languages: English, French, Portuguese, and Spanish. When she is not practicing law or writing her next novel, she enjoys many interests as a very active person and is an avid reader.

Adriana loves to dance, especially the (Tango), she enjoys cooking and enjoys good food and good wine. She believes in exercising along with living a healthy lifestyle. She enjoys traveling and visits New York often, but her "Happy Place" is always spending time with her big happy family and her pets as a passionate animal lover. Adriana continues to work and reside in Brazil.

Visit her websitefor updates and new releases at http://www.agavazzoni.com/

Printed in Dunstable, United Kingdom

78395462R10353